# NO ONE IS ALONE

Also by Rachel Vincent

*Every Single Lie*

# NO ONE IS ALONE

# RACHEL VINCENT

BLOOMSBURY

NEW YORK   LONDON   OXFORD   NEW DELHI   SYDNEY

BLOOMSBURY YA
Bloomsbury Publishing Inc., part of Bloomsbury Publishing Plc
1385 Broadway, New York, NY 10018

BLOOMSBURY and the Diana logo are trademarks of Bloomsbury Publishing Plc

First published in the United States of America in July 2022 by Bloomsbury YA

Bloomsbury books may be purchased for business or promotional use. For information on bulk purchases please contact Macmillan Corporate and Premium Sales Department at specialmarkets@macmillan.com

Library of Congress Cataloging-in-Publication Data
Names: Vincent, Rachel, author.
Title: No one is alone / by Rachel Vincent.
Description: New York : Bloomsbury Children's Books, 2022.
Summary: When Michaela's mom dies and she has to move in with her dad,
she discovers he's been married with kids all this time and she's the product of an affair.
Identifiers: LCCN 2021048151 (print) | LCCN 2021048152 (e-book)
ISBN 978-1-5476-0919-2 (hardcover)  •  ISBN 978-1-5476-0936-9 (e-book)
Subjects: CYAC: Grief—Fiction. | Stepfamilies—Fiction. | LCGFT: Novels.
Classification: LCC PZ7.V7448 No 2022 (print) | LCC PZ7.V7448 (e-book) |
DDC [Fic]—dc23
LC record available at https://lccn.loc.gov/2021048151

Book design by John Candell
Typeset by Westchester Publishing Services
Printed and bound in the U.S.A.
2 4 6 8 10 9 7 5 3 1

To find out more about our authors and books visit www.bloomsbury.com
and sign up for our newsletters.

For my father-in-law, who died following a long illness, while
I was plotting this book. Grammie has you to thank for
her irreverent sense of humor. You will be missed.

# NO ONE IS ALONE

# one

If I'd known what was about to happen, I would have said something more thoughtful to my mother than, "You have lipstick on your teeth."

If I could go back, I'd tell her I love her. I'd admit that I was lying when I said her red sweater hung weird on her, because I knew she'd give it to me. But most importantly, I'd beg her to take a late lunch. Or to eat in the hospital cafeteria, just this once. Or to look both ways when she crosses the street, which she'd been reminding me to do since I was nine and she let me cross the street by myself for the first time.

But I can't go back and change anything. I'm stuck with the memory of what I actually said, and with how she responded as she scrubbed lipstick from her teeth with the pad of her right index finger, staring into the rearview mirror of her car.

"You know I only do these things to test you, right?" She turned from the mirror, laughing with her bright blue eyes.

"You applied lipstick to your own teeth to test *me*?"

"Yes. To see whether, when faced with a moral dilemma, the daughter I've raised to be both kind and honest would rather spare my feelings or warn me that I'm about to embarrass myself."

"Rest assured, I'm always happy to tell you that you're about to embarrass yourself. Or me."

My mom laughed, and I laughed with her, mostly because I was in no hurry to get to first period Chemistry 2.

"Have a good day, and don't take candy from strangers," she said as she unplugged my phone from the car charger and handed it to me.

"Never trust a man who says 'trust me,'" I replied as I slid my phone into my back pocket.

"Don't put all your eggs in one basket. But also . . . don't forget to lay out some chicken for dinner when you get home."

"I won't," I said, because she was planning to make white chili, one of my favorites. Then I closed the car door, tugged my coat tight against the January cold, and jogged up the steps and into the school.

I didn't see my mother drive away. I didn't even say goodbye.

Five hours later, an office aide came to get me from class. On the way to the parking lot, my vice principal told me about the accident while she dug in her purse, looking for her keys. She opened her passenger's side door and threw empty fast-food wrappers and water bottles into the back seat so my feet would have room on the floorboard; then she rounded the front of the car while I got in.

It's weird, being in your vice principal's car. It's like visiting some parallel universe where teachers have lives outside their classrooms. I felt like I'd seen too much. Like I could never go back to being normal, now that I knew that Ms. Aaronson had Weight Watchers achievement flags on her key chain and an honest-to-God cassette deck in her car. After market. I think she had that thing installed on purpose to play the series of nineties grunge tapes on display in a clear plastic case on the dashboard.

I stared at them as we drove to the hospital, and I'm still thinking about them now, sitting in this hard plastic chair, molded to the shape of a generic human butt. Anything to keep from thinking about my mother on some cold operating table, her flesh splayed open while the surgeon tries to put her back together. To clamp arteries and repair organs.

I don't actually know what they're doing in there. No one has given me the specifics. But my mother's a nurse, and I've heard a lot of stories from her time in the ER, before she decided to specialize in neonatal.

I know what it looks like, beyond the swinging door. At least, I know enough to know that I don't want to see it.

Surgery is not fast. My mom said it feels rushed, especially in the ER, but that it can take hours.

This one is taking a lifetime.

I want Ms. Aaronson to go home, but she won't leave me here alone. She keeps asking if I want coffee or a snack, but all I really want is for this not to be happening. For it to be over. For the doctor to come out in a fresh surgical gown and tell me that everything's going to be fine. That I can go see my mother. That she'll be home in a couple of days and we should take it easy for a while. Watch movies and eat ice cream.

That's what we did when I got my tonsils out.

The door opens, and I look up. My eyes are ready to see that clean blue gown. That disposable cap they always wear on TV. Instead, I see . . . my dad.

Who called him?

*I* didn't call him. In fact, that never even occurred to me.

But when Ms. Aaronson stands to greet him, I understand. His name and phone number are in my file at school, which means the school knows almost as much about him as I do.

How to get ahold of him in an emergency.

My dad glances at me, and he looks worried. Sympathetic, in a complicated, polite way that would tell anyone watching that he and my mother aren't together. That his sympathy and worry are for me, not for her.

But there's no one watching.

Ms. Aaronson fills him in, speaking in a discreet whisper, and I catch a few phrases.

". . . on her lunch break."

". . . car came speeding around the corner . . ."

"Fortunately, she was less than fifty feet from the hospital already."

"No updates yet."

My dad thanks her with a pat on the arm, and you'd never know this is the first time they've ever met. In fact, today's the first time I've ever spoken to Ms. Aaronson, other than that time she stopped me in the hall to say that the hem of my shirt didn't quite reach the waist of my jeans, so I'd either have to cover up or go home and change.

I wore my friend Georgia's purple hoodie, but I only zipped it up when I caught a teacher looking.

Dad doesn't know about that, because a wardrobe violation doesn't count as an emergency.

Other things that don't count as a Dad-level emergency: chipping a tooth on the mouthpiece of my clarinet, locking myself out of the house after school, and getting my first period.

"Michaela," my dad says as he sinks into the chair next to mine. He's wearing slacks and a button-up shirt with a tie. "I'm so sorry. How are you holding up?"

"She likes the Greek place on the corner. That's probably where she was going." It doesn't occur to me for several more minutes that I haven't actually answered his question.

"Can I get you anything?" he asks. As if he's a waiter and I might be done with my plate. And really, that's what this feels like. I don't know how to be with him when there are no birthday or Christmas presents. When he isn't ordering us both the turkey special on the day after Thanksgiving or the red, white, and blue pancakes on July 3.

My dad is a pop-up parent. He appears on my birthday every year, and at least near most major holidays. He returns all my texts, and he calls when my mom tells him I'm sick. He pays child support every month and finances half my wardrobe and my extracurriculars. He sent flowers when my grandmother died. But most of the time, he lives his life and my mother and I live ours.

Don't get me wrong. I love him. I just don't know him well enough to know whether or not I should actually like him.

Yet here he is, on a moment's notice. He lives an hour away, so he must have come as soon as he got the call. I guess he should get credit for that much.

"If you're sure you don't need anything, I'm going to go see what I can find out." He stands again, and I nod. They'll tell him more than they told Ms. Aaronson, because he's family, kind of. And because he's a doctor. My dad's a family practitioner, not a surgeon, but professional courtesy is a real thing, so—

Before he can get more than a few steps away from me, the door opens again, and the doctor comes in. The real one. The surgeon.

He pulls the cap off his head and crumples it in one fist, and I know.

I can tell, from the defeat in that one gesture. From the fleeting look of failure in his eyes before he clears his throat and puts on his professional face, as his gaze slides from my father to me.

"No." I only hear part of it.

". . . damage was too extensive."

"We did everything we could . . ."

". . . so very sorry for . . ."

"No," I say again.

"Oh my God," Ms. Aaronson whispers as she sinks into the chair my father's just vacated. Her arm slides around my back and pulls me close, as if we actually know each other.

I stare at the floor. At the white tiles. And I blink.

<hr />

"Okay." My father sits next to me, and I look up, surprised. I don't know where Ms. Aaronson went. I don't remember her leaving. "I know this is really, really hard."

This is *hard*?

I feel like he should be better at this. But I guess general practitioners don't actually deal with death very much.

Neither do most high school juniors.

"But there are a couple of things we have to address immediately."

This doesn't feel real. Shouldn't I be crying?

*She didn't make it.*

The words echo in my head, but they carry no weight. I feel like I'm watching this happen on TV. Reading it in a book. I am not real right now. This room is just a set in a stage production. My dad is an actor playing a role. Waiting for me to say my lines.

"Can I go home?" My voice sounds too wispy. "Can we do this at home?" I'm not sure what *this* is yet, but I don't want to be here anymore.

"Of course, I can take you home. But you can't stay there by yourself. That's one of the things we need to figure out, honey."

Has he ever called me that before? I honestly can't remember.

"Obviously, you should come live with me." He gives me a shell-shocked smile, and I wonder what this moment means to him. He and my mother were a thing, way back when. They never married, but they made me, so there must have been something between them, other than a broken condom. He loved her, maybe.

She loved him, once. I know, because I asked. She can't stand the sight of him now, but that wasn't always the case. So maybe he loved her too.

How hard is it for him to suddenly lose someone he once loved, maybe?

"And really, I'm thrilled for the opportunity to have you with me full time, though I'm so, so sorry about the circumstances," he continues. Then he clears his throat. He stares at his hands while he picks at a hangnail.

I think he's forgotten his lines.

"But . . . ," I prompt.

"But . . . I haven't been entirely forthcoming with you about my . . . situation."

I don't know what that means. He lives in a tiny apartment? A one-bedroom house? He has a live-in significant other who hates teenagers? I've never been to his place—*he* always comes to visit *me*—and suddenly I understand why.

Somehow, I don't fit into his life. And right now, I really don't care.

"Dad, all I want to do is go home and crawl under the

covers." That's when the tears will come, I think. That's when this will feel real. Not here, in a cold hospital waiting room I've never been in before, but when I'm alone at home and Mom's not there. When her shift ends and she doesn't come home.

"Can you just go get it sorted out—make room for me on your couch, or whatever you need to do—then come get me? I kind of want to be alone in the meantime."

"You should *not* be alone right now." His chair creaks as he shifts, trying to get comfortable. But he can't. I know because I just tried the same thing, and the problem isn't the chair. It's this moment. We're stuck in it, even though the clock on the wall keeps ticking. The planet keeps spinning.

We're stuck in this moment where my mom has *just* died, but it doesn't *feel* like she died, and I don't understand how all the moments that came before have led to this.

I don't even know where I live anymore.

"You should be with family. And you have more of that than you know." He clears his throat again. "Michaela . . . I'm married."

"Oh."

There's more to this. I can feel it coming the way you can feel a train barreling toward you when the ground shakes under your feet.

"I've been married for twenty-one years."

*"Oh."*

I'm sixteen. Which means I was conceived roughly seventeen years ago. Four years into his marriage.

"You had an affair. With my *mother.*"

I stand, and suddenly I'm across the room, glaring at him. I take another step back, and my spine hits the wall, yet I want to keep going. I can't get far enough away from him.

"Your mother didn't want you to know, and you can't be mad at her for that." He's standing too, now. "She didn't want you to feel any less special than my—" His mouth snaps shut.

"Than your other kids." The train hits me then, and I feel myself splat against the wall, ruined bits of me dripping down the pale green paint.

If they couldn't put my mother back together, there isn't much they can do for me here either.

"You have other kids." The words fall at my feet in a jumble of nonsense syllables, along with every single word I've said or heard in the past hour. I'll have to sort them out later—reassemble them like a paleontologist piecing together mismatched sets of bones—because right now, I can't make any sense out of anything.

"Three," my father says. "Two sons and a daughter." He exhales slowly. "You have two brothers and a sister."

I've managed to draw that conclusion for myself, despite the fog I seem to be mired in.

"And we have plenty of room. So of course you'll come live with us." He doesn't sound sure about that. He sounds like a man who's writing checks out of someone else's account.

"So, they know about me?"

"My wife knows. Cynthia," he says. "She's always known. But she doesn't know about . . . this." He spreads his arms, indicating the entire hospital, evidently, and my teeth grind together at the thought that my mother is a "this."

That her death is a "this."

That I might also be a "this."

"I need . . . I need to make a call. I'm sorry. I'll be right back." He pushes open the door and disappears into the hall. Only that doesn't really make him disappear, because the door is glass, and I can see him pacing back and forth in the hallway, his phone pressed to his ear. His shoulders are slumped. He keeps pulling his fingers through dark hair I always thought of as just long enough to be cool, though now I realize that it's starting to gray.

I can't imagine what he's telling her. I can't imagine how she's taking the news.

What if she says I can't come live with them?

Based on the way he looks as he pivots and starts down the hall again, the conversation is not going well. And I can't really blame his wife for being mad. Knowing about me is one thing, but what wife wants her husband's illegitimate child coming to live with her?

"Illegitimate." I whisper the word, and it tastes sour on my tongue. What does it even mean? Not legitimate? But how can a *person* possibly be not legitimate? I mean, it's not like there's some kingdom I'm suddenly barred from inheriting, based on the circumstance of my birth. Right?

The entire concept sounds archaic and ridiculous. Yet I have no other word for it.

Why should I even *need* a word to describe my parents' relationship at the time I was born? Yesterday, I only needed to be me.

I know he said it was my mother's decision not to tell me, but that can't be the whole story. If my dad *really* wanted me in his life, he would have told his other kids about me. He would have brought me to his house.

*Secret.* That's what people mean by illegitimate. *Shameful.* My mom was my dad's dirty little secret, and by extension, so was I. Until now.

My phone buzzes in my pocket. It's Georgia, my best friend. I click to accept the call and hold my phone up.

"Oh my God, Michaela, I just heard about your mom." Her face takes up the whole screen, her brown eyes swimming in concern. "I'm so sorry."

"How did you hear?" I haven't told anyone. I haven't processed it enough to write it in a text yet.

"Katherine's an office aide in fifth period. She heard the attendance secretary tell the guidance counselor. And now everyone basically knows. I'm *so* sorry. It was an accident? Like, a wreck?"

"Yeah. I . . ." I glance over my phone to see my father still pacing. Still on his phone. He looks like he's being issued a death sentence. "Things are weird right now. Can I call you back?"

"Weird, how?" Georgia shifts her phone, and I recognize the tile behind her. She's in the school bathroom. The one next to the cafeteria.

"I . . . I have to go live with my dad."

"So you're *moving*?"

"Looks like it." And suddenly I realize that means I'll be leaving my friends. *All* of my friends.

Everything is happening too fast to process.

When I was a kid, I took ballet for, like, five minutes. The only thing I really remember is that they taught us how to "spot" during a pirouette—to find something for your eyes to connect with during each revolution, to stabilize you when the world is spinning around you.

The world is spinning around me now. It's spinning *out of control*, and I can't find my spot.

"Okay. We can deal with that. Where does your dad live?"

"Bradford." That's all I know. *How* can that be all I know?

"But that's not the weird part. Georgia, he has another family. A wife and three kids."

"Really? I thought your dad was some kind of confirmed bachelor, like, dedicated to playing the field."

"So did I." That's what I'd assumed, anyway, because my dad was an attractive, single doctor in his late forties. Or so I'd thought.

"But he got married and had three kids? Without telling you?"

"Not exactly. He says he's been married for twenty-one years. Turns out my mother was the other woman."

"And you didn't know? How could you not know? Have you never googled your dad?"

"Of course I have." Though the truth was that I hadn't

thought of it until Georgia told me she'd searched her mother's name and found out her mom was arrested for graffitiing the side of a building when she was our age.

I googled both my parents then, but I didn't manage to dig up anything interesting, except the fact that there were at least twenty different Oscar Bosches out there who were not my father.

On the website for his family practice, his bio describes Dr. Bosch as a "family man," but I've always assumed I was that family. Even though I'm a Rutherford, like my mom.

"I feel like *such* an idiot," I whisper. How did it never occur to me to wonder why I've never spent a single Thanksgiving day or Christmas morning with my own father? I just assumed my mother was hogging the holidays for herself, and that she wouldn't let Dad come. That *he* was absent because of how much *she* loved me.

"Your dad lied to you. You're not the idiot in this scenario," Georgia insists, leaning against the corner of the last toilet stall.

"Thanks." The door squeals open, and I look up as my father steps back into the waiting room. "I gotta go."

"Okay. Please let me know if there's anything I can do."

"I will." I end the call and slide my phone back into my pocket.

"We're all set," my dad says, and though he seems to be attempting an upbeat tone, he looks like someone just ran his soul through a meat grinder. "I'm going to take you home, for

now, and by the time we get to my house—your new home—
everything should be set up for you."

"How'd she take it?" I ask, side-stepping the arm my father
tries to wrap around me.

We're not there yet.

"Cynthia? Fine. Just fine. She's really great. You're going to
like her."

I won't, though.

As ungrateful as I feel, considering she's just said I can
come live in her house, even though she has every reason in the
world to resent my very existence, I don't even want to meet
this Cynthia.

I want to go home and lay out some chicken for dinner. Then
I want my mother to come home and cook it.

# two

"His name is Gabriel. Gabe," my father says as he flicks on his blinker and changes lanes. His SUV hurtles down the highway, rushing me toward my new life, before I've even come to terms with losing the old one.

My mother is gone.

It still doesn't feel real.

An hour ago, I stood in the middle of the living room, looking around, trying to make myself feel it. I know she's gone. My head knows, anyway. I heard what the doctor said, and I understood it.

But the rest of me hasn't caught up with my head.

My mother is dead, and that should have changed everything. Everything. The planet should stop spinning, shouldn't it? Curtains should swing shut. Lights should go out. Foundations should crumble. Kingdoms should fall.

Yet there my house stood, undamaged. Pictures still hung on the wall, perfectly straight, as if they hadn't felt a thing. As if they hadn't so much as swayed when the woman who'd hung them died.

Her coffee mug still sat in the kitchen sink. Her pajamas lay tossed across the foot of her unmade bed. She'd left the top off her moisturizer, because I'd come in this morning while she was prepping her face, frustrated because I couldn't find my left sneaker, and she'd stopped what she was doing to help me look.

How could she be gone, when she'd left the top off her moisturizer? The whole house had felt normal, like she would walk in any second and hang her stethoscope and keys on the hook by the garage door and ask me how my day was.

I wasn't able to shake that feeling while I stuffed clothes and makeup into my suitcase. While I wound up my laptop cord and slid it into my backpack.

Dad offered to stay there with me for the night. He said that would give me a chance to adjust to all of the change. To avoid rushing me out of my home. But it was also to give his other family a chance to get used to the idea of me moving in.

Thanks, but no thanks. I would have gladly stayed at home alone, but that house is Mom's space. *Our* space. It would be weird to see him touching her things. Drinking from her coffee mug. Sleeping in her bed, or even on her couch. That would feel almost . . . disrespectful.

At least at his house, I won't feel like Mom is supposed to walk through the door any second. At home, I would be waiting for it, even though I know it isn't going to happen. Even now, with the heated passenger seat of my dad's SUV warming my butt, I feel like my mother will text any moment to ask how I'm enjoying my long-overdue weekend with my father.

"He's seventeen. A good kid, and a great bass guitar player," my dad says as I scroll through condolences from basically everyone I know at school. "But a bit . . . unpredictable."

The news about my mother spread fast; Georgia was right about that. And I don't know how to respond. At first, I just kept replying with "Thank you" and "Thanks so much." But that started feeling stale around the time my phone started suggesting those words on its own, because I'd typed them so often.

"He even has a garage band."

But the truth is that even if I weren't distracted by the awkward stream of condolences, I wouldn't want to hear about my father's other kids. I mean, he has every right to love them. To be proud of them. I get that. But he's never told them about me. Not once.

". . . wrote the song themselves, and I really think it's something special."

I want to ask him what my favorite color is. What instrument I played in the middle school band, before I quit. What office I ran for—and lost—in the freshman class election. But I'm afraid he won't know any of the answers, and that will just make me mad.

"The little one is Cody. He's twelve. Seventh grade. He's really into video games, and he loves to do VR at the mall. His Christmas list was just a bunch of games I'd never heard of."

I have several new voice mails, and two are from the school, so I'm guessing those are condolences from the office staff. Or my teachers. But listening to them now, while he's talking, would be really rude. Right?

"And Emery is just a couple of months older than you," he continues, as soybean fields race by on either side of the highway.

"Wait, really?" I put my phone screen to sleep.

"Yeah." My dad acts like that's some kind of amazing coincidence, but all I can think is that Cynthia and my mom were pregnant at the same time. My father cheated on his *pregnant* wife. With my mother.

Cynthia must *hate* me.

"You two actually have a lot in common."

"Cynthia and me?"

"No, you and Emery. I've always thought you kind of look alike, which is no surprise, considering that you're sisters."

Sisters who each had no idea the other existed.

When I was little, I used to wish I had a sister. Someone to share clothes and secrets with. Someone to play games with. But I outgrew that fantasy long ago. And this was never how I pictured it, anyway.

"She's a really good student. Gabe couldn't care less about academics, but Emery's near the top of her class, and she's taking all the advanced courses. Just like you."

"Well then, how could we *not* get along?"

My father gives me a look. Possibly for the first time ever. He hasn't had much opportunity to be exasperated with me before, considering our holiday-and-birthday-based relationship.

"Michaela, I'm so sorry about all of this. I always intended to tell you about them. And them about you. I never meant to let it go this far. And this isn't how I wanted to introduce everyone."

An apology isn't going to fix this. But in my entire life, I've never yelled at my dad. "I know," I say, because I don't have the bandwidth to process my anger right now. It's all just . . . a lot.

He flicks his blinker on again and shifts into the exit lane.

I feel oddly anxious as we pull off the highway and onto the streets of Bradford, which looks so much like Oak Valley, my hometown, that they could both have been mass-produced by the same city planner. The street signs are blue here, instead of green, but I swear I've been in that café. And that flower shop. And that general store.

The high school, though . . .

Oak Valley goes up against West Bradford in everything from football to chess club, which means it's entirely possible that I've seen Gabriel and Emery at a game and had no idea that I was looking at my own brother and sister.

That thought feels *really* weird.

My father drives me through a quaint downtown, past several restaurants and a few residential neighborhoods before turning into one surrounded by brick walls. There's a set of broad iron gates and a place to type in a code, but the gates are standing open, so we drive right in.

"They close after dark," he explains. "The code is the last four digits of our home number. I'll write it down for you."

I nod, staring out the window as we pass house after two-story brick house. Rolling lawns and porch swings. Flower beds, brick mailboxes, and stone walkways. This is a much fancier neighborhood than mine, but I wouldn't call the occupants rich, exactly.

Though they're certainly not "hurtin' for anything," as my grandmother used to say.

I know which house we're headed for even before my father pulls to a stop at the curb, because there's a delivery van parked in the driveway, with the logo for a local furniture store painted on the side. The house is big. At least twice the size of the two-bedroom ranch-style where I live—where I *lived*—with my mom. Maybe bigger than that.

It's mid-January, so the lawn is brown, but the grass still looks thick and healthy, and I can picture what this yard will look like in the spring. Freeform flower beds line the front of the house, black mulch contrasting with a series of sculpted evergreen bushes, as well as a few wild-looking ones dotted with delicate little white petals.

I didn't know there were any flowers that bloomed in the middle of winter.

The garage is separate from the house but connected by a section of roof that extends across the driveway, forming a kind of broad tunnel. Allowing a peek into the backyard.

While I'm still staring out the window, my dad slams his door and rushes around the car into the driveway. There's a woman standing there, as if she's just come out of the house. She's busty but noticeably thin, despite the flowing blouse hanging loose over the waistband of her jeans. This can only be Cynthia.

My father stops a couple of feet from her. He looks like he wants to go closer but isn't sure if he should.

I'm not sure he should either. I'm kind of surprised that she's going to let him stay here, much less me.

"Cynthia has known about you from the beginning," he said as he drove me from the hospital to my house. "She was upset. Understandably. But we worked things out."

Still, I doubt she ever expected me to move in.

I get out of the car and pull my suitcase from the back seat. Thank goodness it rolls, because it's really heavy, even though I feel like I left most of my things behind. Like I left most of my *life* behind.

I pretend I can't hear my stepmother speaking to him in a fierce whisper.

"*. . . had to pay a two-hundred-dollar fee to get them delivered immediately, and even more to have the old one hauled off. . .*"

The front door of the house opens, and two men come out carrying a gorgeous sleigh headboard. It's big, and heavy, and . . . graceful. From a full-size bed, at least.

"*Emery's inside pouting . . .*"

In the driveway, they drape the headboard in a thick blue mover's blanket, then carry it into the delivery truck. A few seconds later, they emerge from that same truck carrying two long, narrow cardboard boxes.

"*. . . two hours' notice. How do you think they took it?*" My stepmother glances at me, and then her focus flicks back to my father, as if just seeing me is a shock to her system.

I know the feeling.

The movers carry the boxes into the house, and on the way, they pass a girl my age who's just stepped onto the porch. Her hair is long and dark like mine. For a second, she looks right at me, her arms crossed over her chest. Then she heads into the house without a word.

Emery. It has to be.

She doesn't want me here, and I totally understand that, because I don't want to be here. I didn't ask to come here. I don't want to know that my mom was the other woman any more than she wants to know that her father cheated on her mother.

At least she still *has* a mother.

I have no more choice about all this than she does, and I'm not going to feel guilty just for being alive.

But I do feel guilty about being *here*. Where I'm not wanted.

"Michaela!" My dad waves me forward, and I slowly push my suitcase up the slight incline of the driveway. The handle vibrates in my palm as the wheels slide over the rough concrete, and I drag my feet.

I don't belong here.

"I'm sorry," my dad whispers to my stepmother as I come to a stop at his side. Then he clears his throat and turns to me with a smile ten shades too bright. "This is Michaela. Michaela, this is my wife, Cynthia."

"So nice to meet you." She holds her hand out, and I shake it, because that's what you do. "I'm so, so sorry about your mother."

Her forehead is tense, her sympathetic expression too

heartfelt. She's trying really, really hard to tell herself that this is okay. To *make* it okay. I can see that. I can hear it in her voice.

"Thanks." That feels completely inadequate, but I don't know what else to say.

I'm sorry your husband cheated on you?

I'm sorry you're stuck with me?

"I know this is . . . difficult," she says, my hand still trapped in her soft, annoyingly supportive grip. "But I want you to know that you're welcome here. And if there's anything I can do to help with what you're going through, please let me know."

That's nice. She's *so* much nicer than I thought she'd be, even if her kindness feels a little bit forced. Even if the words—they're *exactly* the right words—feel a little bit stiff.

She's older than my mother, by several years. The lines at the corners of her eyes are more defined, and there's a permanent crease in the center of her forehead. She has a better sense of style, but the way she tugs at the hem of her blouse when she lets go of my hand says she isn't quite comfortable in it.

Maybe she dressed up for this, to carefully craft my first impression of her. Or maybe she always dresses up, because this is how she wants to be seen. Even if the clothes are a costume.

Or maybe I'm reading too much into this, because I *can't* like her. She's too short, despite the heeled boots, and she's too thin, despite the loose blouse.

She's kind, when my mother was funny. Insubstantial, when my mother was strong.

There isn't enough of her, in every sense.

But she's making a space for me in her home, when I know—I can *tell*—that looking at me reminds her of the worst period of her marriage. Maybe of her life.

Guilt settles into my feet like lead, miring me to this spot on the pavement, even though my backpack is heavy, and I'd like to put it down. This isn't my fault, but it isn't hers either. It isn't Emery's, or Gabriel's, or Cody's, but they all have to move over and make room for me in their lives, in their *home*, because seventeen years ago my dad did a horrible thing, and now we're all paying the price.

It takes two. I know. What I don't know is whether or not my mother knew he was married, and she isn't here to defend herself, so she gets a pass, for the moment. Because I can't be mad at her. I just can't.

"Michaela?" My dad is frowning at me. He looks worried. "Are you okay?"

"I'm fine."

I'm not fine, but what else am I supposed to say?

"Why don't you take her inside and . . . introduce her?" Cynthia says.

"Yeah." My father stands straighter. "Are you coming?"

"In just a minute."

She needs a moment. I totally get that.

My father takes her hand and squeezes it. Then he motions for me to come with him, but at first, my feet won't move. They still weigh too much. And anyway, being in that house will be too weird. I already feel like every breath I take is an imposition. Like I'm using air that belongs to someone else.

They don't really want me here, and I don't want to be where I'm not wanted. But I don't have any choice, so I follow him up the driveway, across the porch, and into the house.

The living room is too dark. Too formal. My living room at home has lots of windows, and the couch is cream-colored, the walls a light blue. But here, the couches are brown leather. The walls are a soft gray, but they don't do much to lighten the room, because the floor and the entertainment center are both darkly stained wood.

I hate this room. And it doesn't help that the only light is coming from a huge TV mounted to the wall in the middle of the entertainment center. On-screen, a video game character in bronze armor is swinging a sword at a monster with three heads, but both characters freeze as the front door clicks shut. A head appears over the back of the center couch, backlit by the television.

My father flips a switch, and a fixture overhead throws light into the room, illuminating a boy with Cynthia's sandy blond hair and my dad's goldish hazel eyes. Though I know who he is, and I know he's twelve years old, the thick sprinkling of freckles over his nose and cheeks make him look younger.

"Cody, this is Michaela," my father says. "Your mom told you she was coming, right?"

Cody nods. He's staring at me, but not in a hostile way. He looks honestly, openly curious.

"Hey," I say, shrugging the strap of my backpack higher onto my shoulder.

"Hey." He watches as my father—*our* father—leads me

through an arched doorway, opposite from the kitchen, and the moment we step into the hall, I hear the video game start up again, with the swashbuckling clang of a sword against armor.

"This is Cody's room." My dad pushes open the door to a cluttered bedroom decorated in video game posters. White bookshelves hold more collectable character figurines than novels, and there's a MacBook standing open on the matching desk.

I have one just like it. My dad gave it to me last Christmas. Though now it seems like he might have bought four of them.

"This is the guest bath." He points into a darkened room across the hall. "There's another half bath off the foyer, though, so you and Emery are the only ones who'll really be using this one. Cody and Gabe have a Jack-and-Jill.

"Gabe." My dad knocks once on the door next to Cody's room, then opens it without waiting for a reply.

"Hey!" A boy spins around in a desk chair and pulls off a bulky set of headphones. He stands, and I can see that he's tall like our father, but with a slimmer, younger build. He has his mother's brown eyes and our dad's thick, dark, wavy hair.

"Gabe, this is Michaela. Your . . . sister." My dad sounds like he's choking on the word.

I feel like I am too.

"Wow. So how weird is this?" Gabriel crosses his room—it's a guy room if I ever saw one, cluttered with dirty clothes and a couple of mildewy towels—and grabs my hand.

"Pretty weird," I admit as I shake his hand.

"I'm so sorry about your mom. Sorry we didn't get to meet before."

"Me too."

"But having you here is going to be *great*."

"It is?"

"Yeah! Two boys, two girls. We have enough for a polo team!"

"Polo?" Is he serious?

His eager smile says he may actually be.

"Or tennis doubles. Or *badminton* doubles. Or Ping-Pong doubles. Pretty much any kind of doubles."

Dad snorts. "Gabe is *not* an athlete."

"That is only true in the literal sense," my new brother insists. "I was awarded the 'Most Enthusiastic' trophy by my soccer coach when I was six."

I can totally see that. Gabriel's not bad, and he seems to be dealing well with the punch in the gut my arrival must be.

I look over his shoulder, and my gaze catches on a collection of three bass guitars, each mounted on a forked, padded guitar hanger on a navy accent wall, opposite his bed. One is a deep red, one's a solid black, and the third is electric blue, with black flame accents. That's it for decor; there's nothing else on his walls. But with two giant amplifiers on the floor and his desk cluttered with sheet music—some of it handwritten—I feel like I know who he is, even without posters or pictures.

"Nice to meet you," I say.

"You too! And give that polo team some thought!"

I nod, but I've already mentally moved on, because I can hear scratching noises and male voices coming from one of the rooms at the end of the hall.

"And this is your room," my father says, leading me past a

narrow door that can only be a linen closet. The door to my left is closed, but the one on the right . . . "You'll be sharing it with Emery."

Oh.

Oh, shit.

That's why she's been "pouting." I'm not just the product of her father's affair, come to rain on the parade her life has probably been for sixteen years. I'm also the stranger claiming half of her space and stealing her privacy.

No wonder she doesn't want me here.

# three

I stop just inside the doorway and press my back against the wall. There isn't much room to move around at the moment, because the deliverymen are still setting up one of the twin beds that obviously came in the boxes I saw them carry into the house.

That beautiful sleigh headboard wasn't a guest bed going into storage. It was Emery's.

"You got rid of her bed?" I whisper to my dad.

"That was all Cynthia," he says. "She didn't want you to have to sleep on the couch, like a guest. She was trying to make you feel at home."

"Yeah, well, Emery probably feels home*less*, now." Displaced, at the very least. And she obviously got no notice of the change.

"Cynthia moved pretty quickly," Dad admits. "But she meant well. I think she threw herself into this to show you that we want you here." So, basically, she overreacted. "She loves a project. And we *do* want you here, Michaela."

It's hard to believe that, considering that his kids *just* found out about me. They probably have no idea what they want out of all this. I don't either.

"We're almost done here," one of the deliverymen says to my father.

"Thank you. I appreciate you getting them here so fast."

The bed against the left wall is fully assembled, its brand-new mattress already in place, with a tag still stuck to one corner. But I don't know if it's okay to claim that one. I don't know if Emery cares which one she gets.

Does she get first pick, since this was her room? Is that fair?

Before I can think that through, Cynthia rushes into the room with two identical packages of bedding, one tucked under each arm in its plastic zipper bag.

"Thank you so much!" she says to the deliverymen as they lift the second mattress into place. Then she rips the sticker from the first bed and starts making it up without a glance in my direction.

Or at my dad.

"I hope you like the colors," she says as she stretches one corner of a fitted sheet over the mattress. "I didn't have much time to shop, and I didn't know what you might prefer." She says it all without looking up from her work, as if keeping her hands busy and her mouth moving will distract her from the living, breathing evidence of her husband's infidelity.

But surely she can't keep that up, if I'm going to live here.

"They're very pretty," I tell her as the deliverymen begin

gathering up the mattress wrappings, the extra screws, and the long boxes the bed frames came in.

And the colors *are* pretty. The comforters are white with a delicate gray floral print, which coordinates with the white panel bed frames and contrasts beautifully with the dusky pink walls. Cynthia has style. I have to give her that. But the disgusted huff coming from my left seems to disagree.

I turn to find Emery standing in the open doorway, her arms still crossed over her chest. "You could have at least let me pick out my own bedding," she snaps.

Her mother frowns. "You don't like the gray?"

Emery shrugs. "It's fine. Whatever." Then she turns to me, and I can feel her studying my face, cataloging the same similarities I'm noticing on hers. The same differences. This is *really* weird.

"Sorry about your mom," she says at last. Then she disappears into the hall before I can reply.

"I wish there was room for bigger beds. But I figured you'd both rather have floor space than rolling-over space. Right?" Cynthia says as she snaps the first comforter into the air, letting it fall neatly over the twin bed. "Cody! Bring the pillows!"

She moves on to the second bed, now that the deliverymen are gone, and when Cody arrives with a new plastic-wrapped pillow beneath each arm, I set my backpack on the floor and take one of them from him. They're new, and firm, and made of high-quality memory foam. They look really comfortable. But I like the one I left on my bed at home. In fact, I meant to bring it with me.

I stuff one pillow into the case Cynthia left at the foot of the freshly made bed, and when I look up, I find her doing the same with one of the pillows that evidently came from Emery's old bed. Apparently both of the new ones are for me.

"You really didn't have to go to all this trouble," I tell her.

"It was no trouble," Cynthia insists.

"Still . . . I feel bad about basically taking over Emery's room."

"You aren't taking it over. You're sharing it." My dad lays one hand on my shoulder. "And anyway, I think it looks really nice in here." As if that were the issue.

"There are more pillowcases in the linen closet," Cynthia says. "I'll bring you each one in a few minutes." She places Emery's pillow on the right-hand bed, then she begins gathering up all the plastic the bedding came in, and she leaves the room.

"Thank you, hon!" my father calls after her. He sits on the edge of my new bed and pats the spot next to him. I sit, and this feels strange. But the truth is that nothing has felt entirely normal for hours now. "Don't worry about Emery—"

"Dad, she obviously hates me."

"No." He shakes his head. "No, she just needs some time. I'll talk to her."

"Time and a heart-to-heart aren't going to give her back her full-size bed or the other half of her room."

"But she's getting a sister out of the deal," he says. "And so are you."

I roll my eyes, and he exhales slowly.

"Okay. I know it's not that simple."

"Maybe you were right. Maybe we should have stayed at my house tonight." To give his family a chance to adjust to this in theory, before I actually crashed into their lives. To give *me* a chance to adjust.

"It's a little late for that now." Another sigh, and the box spring groans when he stands. "Either way, this space is half yours, and I don't want you to feel bad about that. You've lost enough."

"I—"

"Here you go." Cynthia marches through the doorway again, evidently unaware that she's interrupted anything. "I found a matched set of pink ones. They're a shade darker than the walls, but I think they'll do just fine." She hands me one pillowcase and starts stuffing Emery's extra pillow into the other.

"They're great. Thanks."

"Thank you, hon." My dad backs toward the door. "I'm going to have a little chat with Em, then I'll go pick up some dinner."

Cynthia nods as he disappears into the hall. Then her eyes widen briefly when she realizes she's alone with me.

"Thanks again for all of this," I say, because it's clear that she needs an easy out. Permission to exit the room.

"Really, it's no problem. Let me know if I can get you anything else." Then she flees gracefully into the hall.

I start to unpack my clothes, but then I realize there's only one dresser, and we haven't discussed allocation of the drawers. So I venture into the hall, and again I notice the closed door across the way. It's too wide to be another linen closet, and if there were another bathroom, my dad wouldn't have said Emery and I would be sharing the one down the hall. Which means this door is another room. A guest room, or maybe a home office.

Irritation flares like lit coals deep in my chest. If there's another room, why the hell are they making me share with a half sister who clearly resents my intrusion?

I feel a little less bad about taking up space in Cynthia's life now, if this is some kind of exercise or craft room that she's unwilling to give up, for her daughter's sake, if not for mine.

I head down the hall into the living room, on my way to the kitchen. Cody's gone and the TV is dark, but the light is still on, and the room looks slightly less dungeon-like now.

". . . but she *just* lost her mother." My dad's voice is coming from the back porch. I step away from the window when I realize I can see him sitting on the porch swing next to Emery. "Don't you think you can find just a little bit of sympathy? Is it going to kill you to give up half of your room, when she's lost so much more?"

"Don't do that," Emery snaps. "Don't put this on me. I *do* feel bad for her. I'm not heartless. But it isn't my fault her mother died. It isn't my fault you *cheated* on *Mom!*"

"Em—"

"But I'm the only one being forced to make any sacrifice for *your* mistake."

"You're not the only one this affects," my dad insists, while an uncomfortable anxiety begins to claw its way up my throat. She's right. This was his fault, but she and I are the ones being shoved together. Being forced to give up privacy and share space with a stranger.

"Bullshit!"

"Watch your mouth!"

"Seriously? You cheated on your wife and brought home your love child, but I'm in trouble for *cussing*?" Emery demands, and she's saying what I've been thinking.

She reminds me a little bit of Georgia. Which means that Emery Bosch is the kind of girl you'd rather have as a friend than as an enemy.

"I've made mistakes, but I'm still your father," Dad says.

"Yeah, and you're hers too. That's the problem."

My dad exhales, long and slow. "Your mother has known about this from the beginning, and she chose to forgive me. I can't force you and your brothers to make the same decision, and I understand that it's going to take some time, either way. But I *am* going to ask you not to make this any more difficult for your mom, who's doing the absolute best she can. Or for Michaela, who bears no responsibility for this at all. And who lost her mother not six hours ago, Em. I promise you that whatever you're feeling right now pales in comparison to that."

"I get that. And I feel really bad for her. But I . . ." She glances down at her lap. At her hands, I think, though I can't see them from where I'm standing. "Dad, this is *so* messed up."

"I know. But here's the bottom line: you've led a very privileged life. You've had everything you ever needed, and much, much more. And kids share their rooms all the time. This is normal—"

"It isn't normal to share a room with a *stranger.*"

"—and it isn't going to kill you. And it's our only choice, so I don't want to hear another word about it. You *will* make it work." Dad stands, and the swing creaks as it shifts backward. "I'm going to pick up some dinner, and we're going to eat as a family, and you're going to resist any selfish urges you may have to make this worse. I've already told Michaela what a wonderful person you are."

He didn't, actually.

"Don't make a liar out of me."

"Fine."

I scramble back from the window and into the kitchen as my dad's steps cross the porch, and I pull open the refrigerator door as he comes into the house. "Hey," he says when he sees me. "Finding your way around?"

"I was just looking for something to drink."

"It's all up for grabs. Except for the alcohol. The liquor cabinet is locked."

I roll my eyes at him. "I don't drink."

"Glad to hear it. I'll be back in twenty minutes with dinner."

"Okay."

He looks like he wants to say something else. But then he just grabs his keys from the counter and heads out the side door. He isn't actually running, but he's certainly running away.

Cynthia comes in from a hallway across the kitchen. I'm guessing it leads to the main suite, and probably the laundry room, since the tour my dad gave me didn't include either of those. "Hi," she says, and I close the fridge when I realize I'm standing with the door open.

"Hey. Dad said I could . . ." I gesture at the fridge.

"Of course. Help yourself. And if there's anything you want that we don't have, just add it to the list." She gestures at the pantry door, which is painted with chalkboard paint inside a white frame.

So far, the list includes Doritos, tampons, tomatoes, and world peace. Punctuated by a smiley face with curly pink hair.

Cynthia opens the fridge and pulls out a bottle of white wine, which she uncorks and pours into a glass from the dish drainer. She takes a long sip, then sets the glass down and uses kitchen shears to open a cardboard box sitting on the counter.

"I know I said it before," she says as she begins pulling pack-ages of gauze bandages and antibiotic cream from the box, stacking them neatly on the counter. "But I'm really sorry about your mother. But I know she's in a better place now."

Better than at home, with me? Better than in the kitchen, cooking the chicken I never got a chance to lay out? That is *not* possible.

"And at least she didn't suffer. I mean, that's what Oscar said. That she went pretty quickly, and that she probably didn't feel a thing. That's a blessing, if you think about it."

"A blessing." My mother's death was a *blessing*, because she *probably* didn't suffer? She's in a better place now?

Is Cynthia serious? Next, will she tell me that time heals all wounds, and my mother would want me to move on and enjoy my life?

My chest seizes up, and my throat starts to burn. My jaw aches, which is when I realize I've been clenching it. I back out of the kitchen without getting anything to drink.

*Now* this feels real. Now that I'm staring at someone else's mother, standing there alive and well, exhausting her repertoire of trite platitudes when she never even *met* my mom. *Now* my mother feels gone. But I'm not sad. Not yet.

I'm *pissed*. I'm suddenly *so* goddamn angry.

Cynthia glances at me, then at the fridge. "Seriously, you're welcome to anything you find in the fridge or the pantry, except for my wine. I want you to feel at home here, Michaela."

"Really?" My voice sounds tight. But she doesn't know me well enough to recognize the sound of my rage. Because she's not my mother.

"Of course. This is your home now."

"Thanks. Really, thank you." I spin and practically race toward my room—Emery still hasn't come in from the porch—and dig in my suitcase until I find the three framed pictures I brought with me. One is of my mother and me at Disneyland, from last summer. The other two are just of her. I took them both, using actual film, back when I thought I might grow up to be a photographer.

I carry all three photos back to the living room, where I place them on various end tables. I have to move a few pictures of my half-siblings to make space, but when I'm done it doesn't just look like I live here—it looks like my mother lives here too.

I turn to the kitchen, expecting Cynthia to be watching me. Instead, she's staring at the picture of my mother that I took in the park last year, when the lily garden first began to bloom. My mother looks *beautiful*. Stunning. Healthy, and vibrant, and more like me than I ever noticed.

Cynthia picks up her glass and gulps from it. Then she pours another. She holds it so tightly I'm afraid she's going to snap the stem. Then she turns around and walks straight back to her room without a word.

For just an instant, I feel wildly, blissfully satisfied. Then I feel guilty.

I sink into an armchair, and those tears I couldn't seem to summon earlier suddenly come so hard and fast they leave me choking.

# four

An alarm goes off at 5:45 in the morning. I sit straight up in bed, staring into the dark for several seconds before I realize what I'm hearing. Before I figure out where I am.

The bed feels wrong. The mattress is firmer than it should be, and the comforter is too soft. The streetlight shining through the window is too bright, and the shadows are all in the wrong place.

Then I remember.

New house. New room. New sister, who's hardly said a word directly to me, and who seems perfectly willing to sleep through her alarm.

"Hey," I say into the dark, but she doesn't move. The alarm keeps beeping. It's the *worst* sound. "Hey. Emery."

She keeps sleeping, so I throw the covers back, climb out of bed, and cross the room, intending to tap her phone myself and turn off the alarm. But before I've taken three steps, she rolls over and slaps the phone lying on her nightstand.

The alarm stops, and I go back to bed.

Nine minutes later, it starts beeping again, and I realize she only hit the snooze button.

"Emery!" I snap.

She grumbles something that entirely lacks syllables and slaps her phone again. I put my new pillow over my head, because I know what's coming. And sure enough, the alarm goes off again at 6:03 a.m. This time, finally, Emery gets up.

I watch from under my pillow as she turns on her lamp, lifts her phone from the charger, and heads across the hall into the bathroom. When I hear water running, I get up and turn off her lamp.

I'm not going to school today. My dad said I wouldn't have to go until after the funeral. That I should have some time to process. And that's the first thing I've agreed with him on since . . . maybe ever.

I try to go back to sleep, but the whole house is awake now, alive with unfamiliar sounds. Cody is pounding on a door down the hall, demanding a turn in the bathroom he shares with Gabriel, but Gabriel can't hear him, because he's playing music loud enough to be heard over the shower. The high-pitched whine of a blender echoes from the kitchen, and a second later, I hear the sizzle of grease.

I smell bacon. My stomach rumbles.

Emery comes back from the bathroom and turns on the overhead light. I peek from beneath my pillow again as she closes the door, and I see that her hair is done—flat-ironed into a brunette waterfall—and her makeup is perfectly applied. She pulls her T-shirt over her head and drops it on the floor. A second later, her pajama shorts land next to it, and she turns her back to me to dig in her dresser for a bra and some clothes.

My new sister is not modest.

She dresses, grabs her backpack, and leaves the room without turning off the light.

With a groan, I get up to flip the switch and close the door, but as I climb back into bed, I can still hear morning sounds that are obviously normal in the Bosch household. Footsteps. Cody shouting over the last strip of bacon. Emery slamming kitchen drawers as she searches for the metal smoothie straw her mother swears was in the utensil drawer yesterday. My father thanking Cynthia for her patience and promising to be home as early as he can.

Only Gabriel is quiet, and I assume that's because he's listening to music in his headphones now.

Finally, a door opens, then closes, and silence descends. They're all gone. I throw my extra pillow across the room and go back to sleep.

---

A strange, warbling shout wakes me up. My eyes fly open, and I throw my arm over my face to block the light. It's too bright. I've slept late.

Like, weekend late.

I sit up, my heart pounding. What the hell was that sound?

"I'm coming!" Cynthia shouts, and I groan as I pull the blinds back and look out the window centered over my headboard. Her car is still in the driveway, even though my phone says it's nearly 10:00 a.m.

I pull on the leggings I left on the floor last night and grab my phone, then I venture out of my room for the first time in twelve hours. I really have to pee.

That warbling voice cries out again, and this time it forms a groaning word. "Cynthia."

"Coming!"

My stepmother comes around the corner from the living room, and she's moving so quickly that by the time she notices me, it's too late for her to stop, so I lurch out of her way. My shoulder hits the wall, and she stumbles to the other side of the hallway, one hand clutching the front of her shirt in surprise.

"Michaela! I'm sorry!" Her other hand flattens against the wall, and she exhales in a huff. "I thought you were still sleeping."

"I was. I—"

"Cynthia!" The voice is louder this time. Stronger. But it's still a groan.

"Sorry. Just a minute." Then Cynthia disappears into the room across from mine, which is standing open for the first time since I got here.

I peek through the doorway, and as I've already figured out, that room is not a home gym or an office. It's not a craft room. It looks like . . . a hospital room.

There's a bed in the middle of the floor, but it's narrow and high, and it has metal side rails. The headboard end has been raised, and there's a woman leaning against it, propped up by several pillows.

She's old. *Really* old.

Cynthia rounds the bed to stand on the far side, where she picks up a pill bottle from a collection arranged neatly on a side table. She squints at several handwritten lines in a notebook lying open next to the pill bottles. "It isn't quite time," she says.

The woman on the bed groans, clutching the left side rail with white fingers. Her skin is stretched taut over swollen knuckles, her veins standing out through pale, thin flesh.

"Okay, it's only ten minutes early." Cynthia opens the bottle and pours two pills into her palm. She gives them to the woman, who pops them both into her mouth. Cynthia hands her a big, plastic, hospital-style cup, and the woman takes a long swig from the corrugated straw. She swallows the pills, then sighs as she leans back against the pillows.

Her eyes open. They focus on me.

"Emery." She waves me forward with one swollen, shaking hand.

I turn to Cynthia, unsure what to do. What to say.

"Oh, Mom, this is Michaela. Oscar's *other* daughter."

The woman's gaze narrows on me, her brows dipping low. "His other daughter?"

Cynthia shakes her head at me, silently giving me permission to go on with my day. And I do have to pee. But this woman reminds me of my grandmother, who died last year.

"Hi." I step into the room, my right hand outstretched. "I'm Michaela. It's nice to meet you . . . ?"

"This is my mother, Aundria Turner," Cynthia says as I take the old woman's hand. "The kids call her Grammie."

Grammie's hand is *so* soft. Her skin is shiny. Her eyes are blue and a little milky, but alert. A poofy white cloud grows from her scalp, above thunderclap eyebrows.

"It's nice to meet you, Grammie." I let go of her hand and retreat into the hallway, then I dart into the bathroom.

Ten minutes later, I head into the kitchen with freshly brushed teeth and a growling stomach.

Though I can still smell the morning's bacon, there's no sign of whatever breakfast Cynthia made for her kids, except for the blender standing in the sink, with the last of Emery's smoothie drying in the bottom. So I pull open the freezer drawer and seize a box of chocolate chip waffles. I've just dropped two into the toaster and I'm shoving the box back into the freezer when Cynthia walks into the kitchen.

She opens a cabinet and pulls a plate down for me, then adds a butter knife and a fork from the drawer to the right of the dishwasher. There's a butter dish on the counter, and she lifts the lid from it and pushes it toward me.

"Thanks."

The toaster pops, and I use the fork to lift the waffles out onto my plate. By the time I've buttered them, Cynthia has set a bottle of maple syrup on the counter. I pour some on my waffles. Then I see the price tag on the nice glass bottle, and I pour a little more.

I take a seat at the breakfast bar, and I'm halfway through my first waffle before Cynthia speaks.

"My mother is in home hospice," she says. When I can only frown at her—I have no idea what hospice is—she sighs. "That means her medical care is focused on keeping her comfortable. Treating her pain." Another sigh, this one heavier. "It's cancer. I took a leave of absence from my job to take care of her, until she's back on her feet. So . . . that's what I do now."

"What did you do before?" I ask around my mouthful.

"I was a realtor. I still have my license, and I hope to go back to it someday, but at the moment, that's a bit of a bittersweet wish."

I don't know what that means, but it sounds very sad.

She shrugs, and the gesture feels . . . hopeless. "I'm sorry that means you can't have your own room."

Tears flood my eyes, and I don't know what to say. I don't know why I'm crying. I drop my fork onto the plate and slide off the barstool. Then I run back to my room and slam the door.

I collapse facedown on the bed, crying into my new pillow.

---

I stream stupid comedies on my laptop all day long, huddled under the covers in my new bed. Trying not to think about anything. Not my mom. Not Grammie, shouting for Cynthia all day long. Not the new sister who left her pajamas lying on the floor.

Not anything.

Cynthia knocks on the door, offering to make me a sandwich. I tell her no thanks. I'm not hungry, but mostly, I just don't know how to be here. This isn't my room. This isn't my house. But my real room and my real house aren't mine anymore either. I can't stay there by myself. Not at sixteen, with no way to pay the rent.

I have nowhere to go. I belong nowhere.

At 3:24, I hear music above the laugh track of the sitcom I'm watching. I take out my AirPods and realize I'm hearing chords played on a bass guitar.

School is out. My brothers and sister are home.

I close my laptop and throw back the covers. I can't hang out here anymore, because Emery will come in soon, obliterating my refuge. And to be fair, she has as much right to this room as I do. Maybe more. But I'm not going to let her run me out. Or see me hiding.

On my way down the hall, I glance into Cody's room, which is empty, then into Gabriel's room. Gabe is standing in the middle of the floor with his back to me. He's bobbing his head to music I can't hear—clearly wearing AirPods—and playing along with chords of his own, on his bass guitar. The solid black one.

Grammie is asleep, propped up in her bed, and the guest bathroom is dark, its door open. There's no sign of Emery, but when I step into the living room, I find Cody on the right side of the big leather couch, holding a PlayStation remote. The console is still booting up, lighting the living room with a soft blue glow.

"Wanna play?" he asks, and before I can answer, he leans forward and grabs a second remote from the charging station on the coffee table. The remote glows white as he turns it on.

"Play what?" I sit and take the remote, because I have nothing else to do. And because there's a plate of pizza rolls on the table, next to a twenty-ounce Dr Pepper dripping condensation onto a cork coaster.

Cody grins and selects a game from the menu on the giant screen. It's the one he was playing the other day. I don't catch the name of it, but the icon has both dragons and swords, and wispy blue and green swirls of . . . magic. I think.

"You'll have to show me how," I say as the game loads with an instrumental fanfare. "And share those." I nod at the pizza rolls.

"Help yourself. But you gotta get your own drink. There's a beverage fridge under the counter, at the edge of the breakfast bar."

"Seriously?" They have a refrigerator just for drinks?

"Yeah. If you don't see what you want, add it to the list on the pantry door."

"Anything?"

He shrugs as I head into the kitchen. "Yeah."

The beverage fridge turns out to be a mini-fridge disguised by a regular cabinet door. I kneel and pull it open. It's full of twenty-ounce bottles of soda, sparkling water, and giant cans of flavored iced tea.

I grab a soda and open it as I head back to the living room, where the game has loaded. "There's a place my mom and I used to go on special occasions, for hibachi. They have these bright-colored sodas in glass bottles, with little marbles at the top."

"Ramune." Cody doesn't even look up as he clicks his way through the menu, setting up our game. "I like the mango."

"I like green apple. And lychee," I tell him. "You think they'd get those, if I put them on the list?"

Cody turns from the TV screen. "Your mom just died. They'll buy you whatever you want." He plucks the other remote from the coffee table and hands it to me. "Could you tell them you like the mango ones, too?"

I snag a pizza roll. "Sure."

Cody shows me how to create a character—she's a bustier, wild-haired version of me, with long dark hair and huge blue eyes—and how to swing my sword half a dozen different ways. Then we embark upon a dragon-slaying adventure, ignoring Cynthia's reminders to her son that he should be starting some homework.

The sun goes down, and my dad comes home. I can feel him watching us for a few minutes before he retreats to his room to change out of his white coat and button-up shirt.

Cynthia starts dinner, and though the scents of tomato and garlic make my mouth water, I can't look up from my game to see what variety of Italian food she's attempting, because if I do, I'll get eaten on-screen.

Cody and I end our campaign when his mom calls him to set out the plates. Presumably, at some point I'll be assigned some chores, once the grace period for grieving expires. But I'm not in any hurry for that. I'm fine with feeling like a guest here, for now.

As he stands, Cody drops his phone in my lap. It's unlocked. "Give me your number," he says.

That feels weird. If he were my real brother, he'd already have my number. My dad sent me all the "family numbers," but I guess he didn't send them mine, so I enter my information into Cody's contacts, then hand his phone to him in the kitchen, where he's just set a decorative canister full of silverware on the table.

My mom and I always filled our plates from pots and pans left on the stove, so it feels kind of weird, and oddly formal, to see Cynthia set a big bowl of spaghetti on the table, on a trivet. Emery follows with a plate of garlic bread—I'm not sure when she got home—and Gabe is right behind her with a bowl of salad. My dad sets a glass of ice water at his place and another in front of the plate I assume belongs to Cynthia.

The whole thing has the feel of chaotic choreography, and I can only stand back and watch, relieved to see that a place has been set for me.

Cody sinks into one of the chairs and nods at the empty one across from it, motioning for me to set my soda down in front of the unclaimed plate. I do, and as Cynthia comes in with a bottle of Italian dressing, Gabe sits next to me and across from Emery. Then, suddenly, food is being passed. Silverware clatters against serving dishes, and Cody overpowers his salad with dressing.

Emery picks the tomatoes from her salad, and Gabe does the same with his cucumbers. They're all obviously accustomed to this routine, and they should be comfortable in it, but no one's talking.

Last night, my dad brought home pizza, and I ate a slice on a napkin in my room. Alone, by choice. I expected to hear the Bosches talking over their dinner, like big families do on TV, but they were pretty quiet, which seemed to make sense, on the night their dad brought home his love child. But I thought they'd all basically be over it by now, so it takes me by surprise that no one seems to know what to say tonight.

Is that because I'm here? Am I the problem?

Finally, my dad gives it a shot. "This is good," he says, lifting a fork wound up with pasta toward his mouth. "New sauce?"

"No," Cynthia says. "But thanks."

For another couple of minutes, everyone chews in silence. Until I can't stand it.

"What about Grammie?"

They all turn to look at me, and I wonder if I've messed that up.

"Aundria, I mean." My face feels suddenly warm. "I guess I shouldn't call her Grammie. She's not my grandmother."

"No, that's fine, of course," Cynthia says. "But she's pretty much bedridden, so she eats in her room."

"Alone?" I frown.

"She likes it that way," Emery snaps. "She's not exactly a people person."

Having been properly chastised, I retreat into silence, stuffing my mouth with another bite of spaghetti. The sauce *is* pretty good. For canned.

My phone beeps as I'm stabbing a bite of lettuce, and I pull it from my pocket. The screen lights up with a side-eye meme. I laugh out loud.

Across the table, Cody chuckles at the meme he's sent me.

Emery glares at him, evidently personally affronted by his attempt to make me feel welcome. Or maybe he usually sends her memes during dinner.

Something tells me that her alarm is going to go off for a solid hour tomorrow morning.

# five

There's a life insurance policy." My father bites off the last syllable as the waiter stops beside our table with a tray. He sets a bowl of corn chips between us, then gives us each a glass of ice water and a smaller bowl of salsa.

"Queso?" he asks.

"That would be great," my dad says. "And spicy relish, please, when you get a chance."

"Yes, sir." The waiter tucks the empty tray beneath his arm. "I'll be right back to take your order."

My father plucks a chip from the bowl as the waiter leaves. "There's, um, a life insurance policy," he says again. "And she left a will." He's taken the day off from work so we can get everything organized for the rest of my life. For the end of my mother's.

"How do you know?" I put a handful of chips on my plate and salt them.

"She gave me a copy of both of them, years ago." He pats

the folio on the empty chair beside him. "Do you want to read them?"

I stare at the folio, my chip forgotten. He brought my mother's will? To a Mexican restaurant?

I shake my head. I can't quite bring the menu into focus; I'm definitely not up to my mother's last will and testament. Or her insurance policy. "Just give me the highlights."

"Okay." He crunches into the chip and closes his menu. I've never been here, but this is his favorite restaurant, and he obviously knows what he wants. "I read through everything again last night." After our super-awkward spaghetti dinner. "As far as I know, she hasn't updated her will since your grandmother died, so everything that would have gone to Nonna will go to you. Everything she owned is yours, actually."

Because other than a few cousins I haven't seen since I was a kid, there's no one else. My mother's brother died in a motorcycle accident the year I was born. Her dad died long before that. It was just me and my mom, for most of my life.

"You can keep whatever you want, of course. Though we won't have room to store everything at home. If you want to keep any of the furniture, we can get a storage unit until you're old enough for a place of your own. Smaller things can be boxed up and put in the garage. Though that space is limited."

The words on my menu blur together. A picture of a taco platter melds into an image of a fajita chicken salad in a deep-fried corn bowl.

"So, we're just going to box up her whole life? *My* whole life?"

"No." He exhales slowly. "I'm sorry, Michaela. I absolutely

will make sure that you can keep *everything*, if you want. Like
I said. But space is a practical matter." And it's not like he's
going to ask Cynthia to put one of her brown leather couches in
storage so I can sit on cream-colored cushions I actually like.

Though, to be fair, I'm not sure I really want to see my
mom's things shoved into Cynthia's house either. Square peg,
round hole and all.

There has to be a reason my mom never forced her way into
my dad's life. I'm not going to do that to her now, posthumously.

"I know," I say at last. "It's fine."

He eats another chip, extending the pause before he continues. "The house is a rental, and we have less than a week to get
everything out before February's rent would be due. When I
spoke to the landlord yesterday, he offered us an extra month
without charge, to be kind. But I'd rather just get this over with.
Assuming you feel the same way." Dad pauses again, and I can
feel him watching me, but I don't look up. "Or, you can take
your time. That's fine too."

"No. Let's just do it." Dragging this out won't make it any
easier. "What, exactly, will we be doing?"

"You just mark what you want to keep, what you want to
store, and what you're willing to part with. The movers will
take care of the rest."

"What happens to the stuff I don't want?"

"It'll be donated or sold. If you have a preference, let me
know. Cynthia has some experience with estate sales. She had
to get rid of an entire house full of stuff when her mother moved
in with us, so—"

"Donate it." I don't want Cynthia's hands all over my mom's things. And I *really* don't want her to go through everything and decide she wants to keep any of it.

The waiter comes back with a dish of queso and a bowl of pickled carrots, peppers, and onions—my dad's spicy relish. He opens his notepad and takes a pen from his apron.

"I'll have the beef fajitas with black beans." My father sets his menu on the edge of the table.

"Good choice." The waiter turns to me, and I realize I have no idea what I want.

"Um . . . tacos."

"Beef, chicken, or fish?" the waiter asks.

"Chicken." I close my menu and try to hand it to him.

"Shredded or fajita?"

"Shredded."

"Corn shell, or flour?"

"Corn." I don't mean to snap at him, but I'm seconds away from just grabbing the leftovers from the next table, which hasn't been cleared yet.

"And for your sides?"

"Double rice," my dad says before I can start yelling. I don't know *why* I'm so mad, but suddenly I feel like a can of soda that got dropped on the floor and will spew the moment the tab is popped. "She'll have double rice. That's all. Thanks."

The waiter nods, takes our menus, and disappears into the kitchen.

"You don't like beans, right?"

"Yeah." Finally, I look at my dad. "That's right. Thanks." I dip a chip into the queso, then eat it. "Is that all?" I ask as I pick up another. "I just take everything I want to keep, and I label everything else?"

"At the house? Yes. But we have an appointment at the funeral home this afternoon too."

"To pick out a coffin and flowers?" The only funeral I've ever been to was my grandmother's, but I wasn't there for any of the preparations. My mom took care of everything.

"The funeral director will have a list of choices that need to be made. You can be as involved as you want."

"We never talked about this. I don't . . . I don't know what she'd want." I know that she preferred New York–style cheese-cake over French. That she took her coffee with sweetener from the blue packet, a little bit of cream, and one pump of sugar-free vanilla coffee syrup. I know that she liked fuzzy socks over slip-pers, musicals over plays, and those little cubed pepperonis on frozen pizza, rather than the round slices. But I have no idea what kind of coffin she would want. Or—

"I don't even know if she wanted to be buried. We didn't talk about this at all." Maybe she would rather be cremated.

"That's okay. It's normal." My dad reaches for my hand across the table, and I tuck it into my lap. "She was only thirty-eight years old," he continues, unfazed by my rejection. "She had no reason to believe she'd die anytime soon. Neither of you did." He exhales slowly. "She hadn't bought a plot yet, but her will specified a funeral and a burial. And a cemetery. And her life insurance policy will cover all of that, so really, it's just a mat-ter of picking out what you want for her."

"How much is it? Her life insurance."

"One hundred thousand." My dad holds my gaze, though I hadn't been sure he'd tell me at all. Some adults think kids can't understand money. "There'll be quite a bit left, and it'll go in a savings account for your college tuition, because those were her wishes, according both to her will and to a discussion she and I had years ago. You'll get a survivor benefit from Social Security, too, until you turn eighteen. I suggest you put most of that in savings as well."

I nod. I'm assuming a survivor benefit is exactly what it sounds like.

The waiter appears again and sets a bright yellow plate in front of me. "It's hot," he says.

I stare at three hard-shell tacos, stuffed with shredded chicken and cheddar cheese. There's a selection of toppings on the side of the plate, next to my double helping of rice.

I'm not hungry.

As the waiter leaves, my dad piles beef and onions onto a warm tortilla. "There's also your mom's bank accounts. I don't know what's in them, but there were numbers listed in her will for both a checking and a savings account. Once the bills are paid, whatever's left will be yours. Though you won't have access to it until there's a death certificate on file."

"There won't be much in the bank." There's a reason we live—*lived*—in a rental house. "I didn't even know she had life insurance."

"She needed to be sure that you'd be okay if something happened to her. To be prepared for the worst-case scenario."

That's what I'm living in now. The worst-case scenario.

I spoon tomatoes and lettuce onto the first taco, then dribble some queso on top. "She told you that? About the insurance?"

"Many times. You were all she ever thought about, Michaela. You, and what was best for you, and whether she was doing right by you. And whether you'd be okay without her, if you had to be. That's why I have a copy of her will and of her life insurance policy. She did everything right, honey. Everything she could."

Yet she never told me the truth about my dad. About his other family. Did she believe that knowing about the Bosches would be bad for me?

By the time I've finished half of one taco, my father has devoured two fajitas and most of his beans. "You can take that to go, if you want," he says.

I nod and put the taco down, while he gestures to ask the waiter for the check.

"We'll have to close out all the accounts too. Utilities. Credit cards. Cell phone. But I can handle all that, once we have a death certificate."

"What about my phone?" I nod to thank the waiter for the leftover container he offers me. "It's on my mom's account."

"Oh." My dad frowns. "I'll call and see if I can get your service switched over to my account. Your mom and I have the same provider."

"Will I lose my number?"

"I don't think so." He hands his card to the waiter, along with the check.

Everything's changing. Somehow, I thought that living with my dad's family instead of my mom would be the bulk of the change. And I guess it is. But the little changes keep adding up. Falling like snowflakes, tiny and inconsequential on their own. But they keep piling up on the roof of my life, threatening to cave in on me. To bury me.

Just in case, on the hour-long drive back to Oak Valley, to my house, I text all my friends to tell them that I may soon have a new number.

———⊙≋⊙———

Georgia's car is parked in front of the house when we pull into the driveway. She gets out when she sees us, and when she hugs me, I burst into tears. It's only been two days since I saw her, but everything's changed.

Everything.

"You okay?" She sobs into my hair, still hugging me, while my dad goes to unlock the door. He has his own key, in case of an emergency.

"No," I admit. Georgia smells like fruit-scented shampoo and aloe-scented hand sanitizer. I never thought of them as comforting scents before, but they are. Especially considering that everything Emery wears smells floral and artificial. "What are you doing here?"

"Like I'm going to let you pack up all your mom's stuff by yourself." My dad, evidently, doesn't count.

I hoped she'd show up, of course. That's why I told her we were coming. "What about school?"

She shrugs as she finally lets me go. "There's nothing going on today that I can't make up." Georgia links her arm through mine as we walk up the driveway. I open the door and let her into the living room, where my dad is standing in the middle of the floor, staring around as if he has no idea where he is.

I know the feeling. I grew up here, but right now, I feel like I've never even seen this room.

It's cold.

We turned off the heat before we left two days ago, so that's part of it, but I have a feeling that even once the heat kicks in, it's still going to feel cold in here without my mom.

"Dad, you remember Georgia?" He's met my best friend at least half a dozen times, mostly on my birthdays, so he has no reason not to remember her. But then, he's spent the past sixteen years forgetting to tell me I'm not an only child, so who knows what he remembers?

"Of course. It's nice of you to come."

"Yeah. You too." Georgia heads into the kitchen. "Coffee?" She's constantly over-caffeinated and more than familiar with our single-cup system.

"Hot chocolate," I call out. I hate coffee.

My dad sets his folio on an end table and pulls out a thick pack of sticky notes in assorted shades. "What's your favorite color?"

"Blue." I feel like he should know that.

"Okay. Blue for everything you want to store at the house. Red for everything going into long-term storage. Green for everything you want to donate or sell—"

"Donate."

"—and you can pack up everything you want to keep with you in a suitcase. Or two. But no more than two, I think. That's about all that'll fit in your room. Not counting your clothes, of course. You can take all of those."

Cynthia has ordered two chests of drawers to replace Emery's dresser, so we'll each have our own space.

From the kitchen comes the sound of one pressurized stream of water, followed shortly by another. Georgia returns to the living room with two mugs: coffee for herself, and hot chocolate for me.

"Did you want anything, Mr. Bosch?" She sets my mug on a coaster so I can pick it up without burning myself.

"No, thank you, Georgia."

I'm not really listening while he explains the system of sticky notes to her, because I'm thinking through the next step.

I can take all of it, if I want. Cody's right. My mom just died; my dad will give me anything I want. He'll store every bit of this for me, if I ask him to, and in a couple of years, I can get a house of my own—maybe I can rent *this* house again—and set everything up just like my mom had it.

That probably wouldn't be healthy, though, psychologically. And it would eat through savings my mother intended for me to spend on college.

"We don't have to do this all today." My dad's statement breaks through my thoughts, and I look up to find him watching me, arms crossed over an Oklahoma City Thunder shirt. It's his weekend uniform, even though today is a Wednesday.

"But you said we should just—"

"I know what I said. But if you need more time, we'll take more time. We can come back again tomorrow. I can take another day off."

"She could stay here tonight." Georgia turns to me, cradling her steaming mug. "I could stay with you."

"I'm not going to leave you two here alone," my dad insists, even though we're sixteen. Old enough to babysit someone else's kids overnight, if we want. Old enough to drive. To work. To plan a funeral.

"You could stay with us," Georgia tells him.

"I have to go home tonight."

"He has a family, remember?" I pick up the red stack of sticky notes, and on the edge of my vision, I see my father's frame tense.

Georgia clears her throat and pretends to study the books lined up on the bottom shelf of the entertainment center.

"But we can come back tomorrow, if we need to," my dad says at last.

"How much time do we have today?"

He glances at his watch. "It's just after noon. We have to be at the funeral home at four thirty. So, four hours."

"Let's get moving, then."

I show my dad where my mom kept all the bills and financial stuff, and he sets up at the kitchen table, where he starts calling all of the utilities to schedule shutoffs. A couple of them won't help him until there's a death certificate, but most just want the account number and her Social Security number.

He's also canceling her one credit card, her automatically refilled prescriptions—for migraines and allergies—and auto-billed services like Netflix, cable, and internet.

As mad as I am at him for lying to me for my entire life, I'm grateful that he's here to turn off all the bits of my mom's life that she left running. I could probably hunt down all the account numbers and passwords myself—my mom was pretty organized—but I'm definitely not up to explaining to a dozen different "account specialists" that my mother died suddenly and I have no further need for her cell number. Her gym membership. Her jigsaw puzzle of the month subscription.

Georgia and I take the sticky notes and get to work. We start in my mom's room, where she sets up a cardboard box and an open suitcase on the bed. We put all the pictures and makeup and toiletries in the suitcase, because I'm keeping them. To that, we add a couple of my mom's favorite books and DVDs, the clothes that someday I think I'll be able to wear without crying, and the shoes I can shove my feet into. I keep her stethoscope, and her framed nursing license, and her laptop. Her favorite mug, every keepsake she bought on vacation, and the pillow she slept on. And that fills up the first suitcase.

My eyes water as I zip it closed.

Georgia packs up my personal belongings, while I slap sticky notes on everything I see, sorting them into "keep," "store," and "give away" categories.

At first, I'm sniffing back tears as I pull sticky notes from the stack, but after about half an hour, I feel numb. I decide to put my mom's bedroom furniture and mine into storage, along with her favorite chair in the living room. I tell Georgia to put a green sticky note on the rest of the furniture so it will be donated.

I pack all the clothes I can't or won't wear and label that box for donation. I slap a red "into storage" sticky note on the cabinets that hold our dishes and plates. Georgia suggests I keep the coffee maker, toaster, and microwave for my college dorm, so I do, but I tell her she can green-note everything else in the kitchen.

The entire process is beyond bizarre. I know that if I let myself feel this moment, I won't be able to let go of anything.

Anything.

Not the sifter my mother only used at Thanksgiving. Not the denim jacket she wore in middle school, that she let me use for a Halloween costume when I was twelve. Not the twenty pairs of fuzzy socks she wore all winter long, which have long since lost the little nonstick pads on the bottom.

So I dial out completely and take Georgia's advice every time she offers it.

"You look good in that sweater." So I keep it.

"You know damn well you're never going to make homemade waffles." So I donate the waffle iron.

"Remember when we made cocoa bombs with your mom last year?" So the half-dome silicone chocolate molds go into my "keep in storage" box, even though I'm probably never going to use them again.

The funeral home is a blur of inconsequential choices.

My mother isn't here to care whether she's buried in oak or mahogany, silk or satin, so I don't care either. And I can't stand to think about my mom actually lying in that coffin. So I don't. I just point to things when the funeral director shows me options. When he lists my choices, I almost always pick the last one, because I've already forgotten the first few.

Near the end, I zone out, and my dad takes over, and by then he's fully qualified. He remembers my mom's favorite flowers—calla lilies—and he knows that she wouldn't care what music they play softly during the viewing.

The hard part is her headstone. I don't know what it should say, but it's the last impression people will have of her. It's the first and only impression people who never met her will have. Those words feel important. They feel like my very last opportunity to say something to her. About her.

But there's only room for a few words.

I don't want to mess it up, but the funeral director is staring at me from across a small round table that's probably supposed to feel solemnly intimate, but really just forces me to sit too close to a man I've never met before, while he inserts himself into the memory of my dead mother.

My dad sits next to me, and when he sees me struggling, he starts to reach for my hand. Then he stops, probably so that I can't pull away from him in front of this stranger. "There's no need to stress over the epitaph. It's supposed to honor her, but it isn't expected to truly capture who she was. There isn't enough space for that."

"If I may make a suggestion," the funeral director says, and the bolts I shoot at him with my eyes have no effect. He lifts one hand to frame the words in the air as he says them. "Beloved wife and mother."

"Wife?" I spit, anger suddenly burning so hot within me that my face feels like a bonfire. "She wasn't anyone's wife."

"Micky—"

"Don't call me that. You don't get to call me that." My mother used to call me Micky when I was upset, but my father doesn't have that right.

"Michaela . . ."

I turn to the funeral director, and for the first time I notice that according to his name tag, he's actually an "Advanced Planning Specialist." Whatever that means. "He never married her."

There's a lot more to that. There's a torrent of words—facts, ready to be hurled like accusations—weighing down my tongue, but I don't need to say them, because my dad already looks like I've just punched him. As if he's the victim here.

"Oh. Well, 'beloved mother,' then," the man across the table says, going out of his way not to make eye contact with my father. Because heaven forbid the funeral home's advanced planning specialist be made uncomfortable by my father's infidelity.

"Sure. 'Beloved mother.'" It's true, at least. Completely inadequate, but one hundred percent true.

## six

Before we've even pulled out of the funeral home's parking lot, I begin to regret my decision. My mom deserves more than two words on her headstone. Two words to be her memorial forever. I deserve a better opportunity to tell the world what she meant to me. But my dad's right. There isn't much room on that stone marker.

"How did you meet her?" I ask minutes later, staring out the windshield as the hood of my dad's car devours miles of highway. I think kids whose parents are together already know things like that. I think they sit around on Saturday mornings eating pancakes and bacon, listening to stories about their parents' pre-kid romance. "At the hospital?"

I ignore the silenced buzzing from my phone.

Georgia wants to know how it went at the funeral home, and I don't know what to tell her. Half an hour ago, I posted an uncaptioned picture of a coffin on Insta—the first thing I've said online since my mom died. Now my other friends are sending more condolences I don't know how to accept gracefully.

"That would make sense, wouldn't it?" my dad says. "But no. I met your mom at an all-night diner around the corner from the hospital. I was about to start a late shift, and I stopped in for a to-go cup. There was no Starbucks around here back then. Coffee came black, or with cream and sugar, and you couldn't order it from your phone."

"Mom was at the diner?" I don't care about his prehistoric caffeine woes.

"Yeah. She was with a couple of other nurses who'd just come off a shift. I didn't recognize her. Later, I realized that was because she was brand new; she'd graduated nursing school less than a month before. But I could see from her ID badge that we both worked at the hospital. And that her name was Jessica." He goes quiet for a second. "Her friends called her Jess."

So did I, when I was mad, but I didn't want to push her far enough to get in trouble.

"How old was she?"

"Twenty-two," he says. "I'd just turned thirty-one."

"And, what? She was young and hot, so you hit on her? Even though you were married?"

"No. I just said hi, as I was paying for my coffee." He exhales slowly. "Believe it or not, I didn't go out *intending* to cheat on my wife."

"You *accidentally* had sex with someone you weren't married to. I can totally see how that might happen."

I expect him to snap at me, like he snapped at Emery. To remind me that he's still my father and insist that he deserves some measure of respect. But he doesn't say any of that. He just lets me openly skewer the relationship that produced me. Then he continues.

"But then I saw her at the diner again, later that same week. That time, she was having dinner alone. I watched her. I couldn't help it. When the bill came, she realized she'd left her wallet at work, so I paid for her meal on my way out. And I left my phone number on the check." My dad shrugs. "She called me ten minutes later, to thank me."

"Did she know you were married?"

"I don't think so." My dad's Adam's apple bobs, but the only thing he could possibly be swallowing is guilt. "I wore my ring in the diner, those first couple of times, but I don't think she noticed me or my ring. And I took it off for our first date." He stares out the windshield, but I can tell he's not seeing the highway. "I can't speak for your mother, Michaela. I can't tell you why she stayed with me, once she found out I was married. But I can say that I don't think she would ever have given me the time of day in the first place, if she'd known. I lied. *I* started this. That's on me."

He exhales, as if he's just made some kind of soul-cleansing confession. As if the pain of that should wipe his moral slate clean. But it's a lot more complicated than that. He can't take it back. And even if he could, that wouldn't bring my mother back or fix my life.

It would *unmake* me.

I can't decide how I should feel about my father's infidelity. Cheating on your wife is a really shitty thing to do. But if he hadn't, I wouldn't be here.

"When did Mom find out about your family?"

"About a month in. I told her. All our coworkers knew I was married, of course, so I knew that secret wouldn't keep. I had to ask her not to tell anyone about us. And I had to tell her why."

"Why didn't she dump you right then?" That's exactly what the mother I knew—the woman who raised me—would have done. But she wasn't that woman yet, obviously.

Are my dad's lies the reason she became that woman?

"Because I told her I was going to leave my wife. And that was true, at the time."

"You were going to leave Cynthia? Because honestly, that sounds like something a man cheating on his wife would say to his girlfriend, just to keep her on the hook."

He turns away from the road to look at me again, and there's something complicated peeking out at me from behind his eyes. Something nostalgic and almost proud, but at the same time . . . guilty. And amused. It's like he doesn't know how he should feel about my commentary on his life.

I don't either.

"You sound so much like your mother. She said something very similar, at first. But eventually she believed me."

"Well, I don't."

"I know. And I guess the truth doesn't really matter at this point. Water under the bridge and all. But the fact is that marriages face obstacles every day, for a million different reasons, and Cynthia and I were going through a rough patch at that time. We were really solid for the first five years or so. It felt like us against the world while I was in med school. We thrived on the challenge. On sleepless nights and rushed meals. Night shifts and marathon study sessions. She helped me cram. We were in it together. Then I graduated and got a job at the hospital, and she got pregnant with Gabe. The stressors of her pregnancy mimicked my time in med school, only this time, *I* was there for *her*."

He shrugs, and the steering wheel shifts a little, with the motion. "But then things settled down, and there was no challenge tying us together. 'Us against the world' became 'us against diaper rash,' and . . ." He shrugs.

"What you're saying is that you got *bored?*"

"Not exactly. At least, I didn't think of it that way, at the time. Having a baby is never boring. But then I met your mother, and she was funny and exciting. Being with her was exhilarating."

I rolled my eyes at him in the rearview mirror. "You mean your *secret* was exhilarating."

That thought left a sour taste in my mouth. He was a thrill-seeker, and my mom was the thrill. Or sneaking around was the thrill. Either way, that's not exactly the start of a timeless romance.

"That was part of it, I think. But that wasn't *all* of it. You know how compelling she could be. She had this way of making everything feel like an adventure. She found joy in the smallest, craziest, *dumbest* things. She made everything fun. I fell for her, Michaela. I fell hard. I would have left Cynthia right from the beginning, if not for Gabe."

But how could I believe anything he said, when he'd been lying to me for sixteen years?

"Then Cynthia got pregnant again, and when I told your mother, she ended it. She said that thinking about that baby—Emery, of course—put things into perspective for her. She said that we'd been selfish, and she couldn't justify that anymore. She couldn't keep pretending that we were the only ones being affected by what we were doing."

"What about how *I* was affected?"

"She didn't know about you yet. She didn't find out she was pregnant until shortly after she ended things with me, and *I* didn't find out for several months after that. I think the wound was still too raw. She just didn't want to see or speak to me."

"When did she tell you?"

"She didn't, really. We'd been avoiding each other, which wasn't too hard, since we worked in different departments. And I'd decided to go into private practice, so I was busy putting plans into place. But then one day I ran into her in the parking garage, and I could see that she was pregnant. And I'm proficient at basic math, so . . ." He shrugs.

"How far along was she?"

"Around six months. Emery was born about a month after I found out about you, and you were born nine weeks after that."

"And suddenly you had two families."

"Yes." He flicks on the blinker, then slides into the far-right lane. Our exit is coming up, and already I can feel the timer winding down on this moment of truth. He won't talk to me like this in his house. Where his wife and kids could hear. This is a Highway Conversation, and it has an expiration date.

"Did Cynthia know?"

"I told her, a couple of days after I found out your mother was pregnant. Before that, I'd thought I could put Jessica behind me. I thought I could put that whole broken period of our marriage behind me. I'd decided there was no real reason to tell Cynthia, because knowing would only hurt her, especially while she was pregnant."

"Seriously?"

"It was a selfish thought. I know that now. But at the time, that's what I told myself. Then I found out about you, and I knew I wanted to be a part of your life. That was never in any doubt."

He turns to look at me for long enough to make me nervous about oncoming traffic, and in the end, I meet his gaze because I'm worried that if I don't, he'll get us both killed.

"Michaela." His gaze pleads with me, though his tone remains steady. "I never even considered walking away from you. I want you to know that. I was always going to be your father."

Yeah. My part-time father, who lied to me about his family. About *my* family.

"So, I told Cynthia." He turns back to the road, squinting into the setting sun. "I thought she was going to kick me out, but she said that would be letting me off too easy. Leaving her to raise two small children on her own. So instead, I moved into my study."

"What study?"

"I had an office in our previous house. We didn't buy our current home until Cynthia got pregnant with Cody, and we knew we'd need more room."

These are things I'd already know, if I'd ever *really* known my own father.

Instead, I only got pieces of him. Slices of information that, in retrospect, seem designed to tell me as much as he could about who he was, without really telling me *anything* about his life. Like a game of misdirection.

When I asked, once, where in Bradford he lived, I got a story about how, despite the high tax rates, the high percentage of school bonds passed make it possible for anyone to live there and send their kids to some of the best schools in the state. Which now seems odd, considering that he wasn't sending *me* to those schools. When I asked if he decorated like a bachelor, he told me about his old, beat-up leather recliner, which is, in fact, in his living room. He just didn't mention he wasn't the only one around to sit in it. And when I asked if he put up a real Christmas tree every year, he offered to buy my mom and me a new artificial one, because my allergies seemed to be getting worse. He was really good at steering the conversation back to me.

I just wish I'd realized that was what he was doing at the time.

"I slept on my office couch for nearly a year," he continues. "Emery doesn't remember any of that, though, and I doubt Gabe does either. But eventually, Cynthia and I worked things out."

"And she was okay with you seeing me?"

My father sighs. "She's never been anything but supportive of that. She knows that none of this is your fault, Michaela. And she's never resented the time I spent being your father."

"But you guys never told your kids about me."

He takes another deep breath as we turn into his neighborhood, and the gate looms ahead. "We discussed that, when you were all very little. But your mother didn't want you to know, so Cynthia and I decided not to tell Gabe and Emery either. At least, not until Jess changed her mind." He meets my gaze in the mirror. "There was no sense in them hearing about a sister they couldn't meet."

"What about Cynthia? Did she ever want to meet me? Did you show her my pictures? Or did you just . . . hide me away?"

Another sigh. "It's complicated, Micky."

"Don't—"

"Sorry. But it *is* complicated. Or, it was. She wanted me to be involved in your life. She believed that you deserved as much of my time as I could give you. She still believes that. But you . . ." He frowns as he punches our passcode into the keypad. "But she . . ."

"I get it, Dad."

"I don't think you do. It isn't you she objects to."

"It's what I represent. What I remind her of." Her husband's infidelity.

"Yeah."

"And that hasn't changed, has it? How could it?"

The gate slides open. "Things are different now."

"For me. But not for her. I still represent something horrible to her, and now she has to see me every day. And I'm sure that when she looks at me, she's really seeing Mom." And now she sees my mom's picture all over her own living room. And she has to wonder . . .

"Were there other women?"

"No." My father doesn't hesitate, and part of me wonders if that's because we're rounding the corner now, and his house is within sight. If he's trying to wrap up this conversation before it can follow him into his home. "No, Michaela, this wasn't about cheating. I wasn't out looking for someone to jump into bed with. I met your mother, and I couldn't get her out of my head. I fell in love with her, and if I hadn't already been married, I'd probably still be with her."

"Do you think you were supposed to be?"

"Do I think I was supposed to be what?" he asks as he turns into the driveway, and he's only half listening now. The garage door is open. The light is on, and Cynthia's car is inside.

I'm already losing him.

"Do you think you were supposed to be with my mom, instead of Cynthia? Do you think something went wrong, cosmically, and you just . . . met the wrong woman first? That your destiny was, like, screwed up by the butterfly effect, or something?"

The words sound dumb, even as I say them, but it wouldn't *suck* to believe that my mother was more than just a long-term fling. That my conception wasn't a mistake.

My dad turns to look at me as he shifts into park. I can see him trying to refocus. To split his attention between me and the life waiting for him inside that house. "I don't believe there's any such thing as destiny, Michaela," he finally says. "Life presents us with opportunities, and we make choices. Some of those choices are poorly thought out. Most of those choices have to be made before we know what life is going to offer us tomorrow, or next week, or next year." He twists the key to turn off the engine, then pulls it from the car. "If I'd met your mother first, I probably would have married her. And I would have loved her, and I like to think we would have been very happy. And I think that would have been the right choice. But I met Cynthia first, and I loved her, and I married her. Which is why I should never have pursued Jessica, no matter how well we connected. Cheating on my wife was a mistake. And I have to live with the consequences."

My eyes fill with tears, and my father sucks in a sudden, regretful breath. "No, Michaela, *you* aren't a consequence."

"Yes, I am, and you have to live with me." That's never been clearer.

He takes my hand, and this time he won't let me pull away. "That's not what I meant. I don't think of you as a consequence. I think of you as my daughter. The consequences are the rift in my marriage. The way Emery looks at me now. The way everyone will look at me, when and if this becomes public knowledge in my practice. In the community. And that has nothing to do with you. You understand that, don't you?"

I nod, because that's what I'm supposed to do. Because that's the only way he's going to let this conversation end and let me out of his car.

He's wrong, though, and I can't tell whether or not he knows it.

I am his consequence. He has to live with me—literally, now. I'm the reason his staff will whisper behind his back and reassess their opinions of their boss. The reason the other parents at school will gossip. The reason the neighbors are probably already talking.

But I'm not the only mistake he made.

"How did Cynthia get pregnant? With Emery," I add when he looks confused.

"What do you mean, how?" This isn't a birds-and-bees kind of moment, and he knows that, but he hasn't yet figured out what I'm actually asking.

"If you were going to leave your wife for my mom—if your relationship with Cynthia was already over—how could she possibly have gotten pregnant?" I blink at him from the passenger's seat, and a gleeful bolt of satisfaction fires through me when I see comprehension surface in his gaze. "I mean, if you were really about to divorce Cynthia, why were you still sleeping with her?"

For a moment, he can only stare at me. I stare back, silently daring him to admit the truth.

"It's complicated, Michaela."

"By 'complicated,' do you mean 'something inconvenient for me to explain'?"

"Michaela . . ."

"It's okay. I get it. You were going to leave your wife for my mother, but you weren't serious enough about that to actually stop sleeping with her. Or start using protection. *That's* how much my mom meant to you."

"Honey—"

"No." I get out of the car and open the back door, then jerk one of my suitcases onto the driveway. "You were right before," I say as he emerges from the driver's seat. "You made a mistake, and now you have to live with the consequences." I slam the back door and start marching toward the house. "And I am *perfectly* willing to be those consequences."

## seven

Michaela!" my dad calls after me from the driveway, but I keep walking. There are two more suitcases in the car, but my dramatic exit would be ruined if I go back for them, so I decide they can wait.

Cody is in the living room playing his dragon-hunting game, illuminated only by light from the TV screen. There's an algebra book on the coffee table next to a plate littered with crumbs and smears of pizza sauce, but I doubt he's even opened it.

"Hi, Michaela," Cynthia says from the kitchen. She's wearing an apron and holding a chopping knife. "Dinner will be ready in about half an hour." She looks like she wants to say something more but isn't sure what that should be. *Did you have fun planning your mother's funeral?* doesn't exactly roll off the tongue.

"What are you making?" The whole house smells amazing, and despite the day I've had, I'm starving.

"Pineapple chicken curry, with whole grain rice."

I *love* curry, but I've never had it homemade. My mom and I always ordered takeout. *Please, please, please don't let her ruin curry for me.*

"Cody!" Cynthia snaps as I roll my suitcase over the travertine tiles that stretch from the foyer and down the hall. "For the last time, turn that off and start your homework!"

Cody mumbles something beneath his breath, and the PlayStation beeps as it shuts down.

Gabe's door is open, but his room is empty.

I peek into Grammie's room as my suitcase *thunks* softly over the tiles. She's asleep in bed, while the news plays on a television mounted on the opposite wall.

My bedroom door is closed. My hand hovers over the knob.

"Seriously. It's not that bad, Em." Gabe's voice comes from inside. I pull my hand back and listen.

"Bullshit. Mara was supposed to stay the night this weekend, but that's not going to happen anymore. I can't ever have a sleepover again, apparently. I mean, my bed is the size of a yoga mat. Two people won't fit."

"You could sleep in the living room, on the camping mattress. Or, you could *actually* go camping. Put up a tent in the backyard. I'll build a fire for you, and you can roast marshmallows."

"You're not allowed to build fires anymore. It took you three months to grow back your arm hair last time."

"But I looked *great* with bald arms." He sounds almost nostalgic. "I looked like a male stripper."

"*Gabe*," Emery groans.

"Fine. Better have your sleepover in the living room, then."

"There's no privacy in the living room. Not that there's any in here, anymore. She's *always here*."

"She's not here now," he points out, and the irony of me standing right outside the door makes my face burn.

"You know what I mean. I have no space of my own anymore. How am I supposed to have any sort of a social life, with her curled up in some kind of depressive episode across the room?"

"She's allowed to be sad. And if you're expecting your entire social life to play out in your bedroom, I think we've uncovered the real root of your—"

"Gabe! I'm serious!"

"I know. But she lives here now, Em. This is her home too. As it should be."

"That's easy to say when you still have your own space. But you'd be just as frustrated as I am if they'd given her Cody's room and shoved him in with you."

"Not true," he insists. "I would teach Cody to play bass in the middle of the night, in a blanket fort constructed across our twin beds. Ooh, and I'd dress him like my mini-me. Then I'd grow a goatee, just so I could draw a little baby goatee on his chin in Sharpie."

"You are *so* full of shit. *I'm* the one all this is falling on. I've lost my room. My privacy. My bed. My ability to have anyone over . . ."

Anger flares deep and white-hot in my chest as Emery describes the havoc I've unleashed upon her life. Yet fresh tears stand in my eyes. I can't tell if I'm hurt or pissed off, and I can't decide which one I should be.

"She's lost all that too," Gabriel points out.

"But that isn't my fault! And she's going to be at school next week," Emery moans. "Everyone's going to know that our dad is a lying . . . *adulterer*! And that our mom just let him get away with it, like a doormat!" Her pitch rises with every word, until I'm afraid she's going to start whistling like a teakettle. Or maybe that I will.

The pressure building inside me is vicious.

"I mean, how are we supposed to introduce her? 'This is my dad's secret love child?' Is that even a thing anymore?" I hear footsteps, and I realize she's pacing while she rants. "Hey, come meet the human result of my dad's affair?"

I reach for the doorknob again, ready to burst into the room and confront her. But my hand won't turn the knob. I'm frozen there, listening to all the ways I've ruined her life, through no fault of my own, and then I realize that she's right. I *am* everything she's calling me. I probably *have* ruined her life.

The fact that none of that is my fault doesn't make it any less true.

Blinking away tears, I spin, leaving my suitcase by the door while I head down the hall to the living room. Cody is still on the couch, and now the lights are on. His algebra book lies open on the coffee table, and there's a notebook on his lap. He's on problem number three.

"Hey." He looks up when I come in, then frowns. "What's wrong?"

"Nothing." Everything. "Need some help?" I sink onto the couch, wiping my eyes with both hands.

"Nah. It's easy. I just don't want to do it."

"I hear ya." The kid never seems to do any homework, but he gets perfect scores on most of his tests, according to his mother, which gives him a B average in most classes. I can't tell if that makes him the smartest kid in the world, or the dumbest.

Cynthia pulls a chopping knife from the block to the right of the stove and sets it next to a cutting board on the island. "Hey, Michaela, how do you feel about setting the table?"

I feel like she wouldn't be asking me that if I were her kid. She's treating me like a guest—like a family friend—and I can't tell whether that's because I'm not hers or because today, I picked out the dress my mother will wear for all of eternity.

"Sure."

By now, I know where the plates and silverware are, and I know I'm supposed to refill the napkin caddy from a bulk package of white paper napkins in the pantry. And I know that everyone grabs their own drink on the way to the table, which means I don't have to mess with glasses.

"Thanks." Cynthia sets a bowl of salad on the table as I set out the last plate. This is my third dinner here, and each one has come with a different salad. Tonight's appears to have apples, almonds, and raisins on a bed of dark green kale. "It's Gabe's night to set the table, but I'm not sure where he's gone."

I don't tell her that he's in my room, listening to Emery's complaints about no longer being her father's only daughter.

"No problem." Setting the table is a weird chore. I always assumed it was something people only did on television, like making the bed. But maybe my mom just ran a more casual household. Or maybe, with only two of us there, it just seemed more logical for us to each fill a plate from the food on the stove.

I don't think Cynthia does anything casually. My first night here, my dad brought home pizza, and instead of eating it out of the boxes, Cynthia made Cody set the table. They ate the most casual of fast foods on actual plates, with a side salad of mixed greens, tomatoes, red onions, and olives. Which meant there were dishes to be done.

On pizza night.

"Cody, will you text your brother and sister and ask them to come to dinner?" Cynthia drizzles a homemade dressing over the salad and puts a set of tongs in the bowl.

"There's no need to text them," my father grumbles as he steps into the kitchen from outside. "We're all in the same house."

"Yes, but I don't want to—"

"Emery!" my dad bellows. "Gabriel! Come eat!"

"—hear a bunch of shouting," Cynthia finishes, shooting him an exasperated look. "I have a headache."

"Sorry." My dad opens the door again and leans out, and when he straightens up, he's holding my last two suitcases. "Michaela," he says as he sets them on the tile, next to the built-in cubbies where you're supposed to put your shoes and hang your coat when you come in.

There are five cubbies. Grammie and I don't get one.

"Thank you," I say as I pick up the first suitcase. It's an old one, without wheels, and it's heavy, because of how much of my life it contains.

"Micky, I . . ." My dad drops his voice into a whisper as Cody heads through the kitchen into the dining room with a bottle of Dr Pepper in one hand. "I don't want to leave our conversation like that. I'd like a, um, follow-up."

"Sure. Whatever."

I grab my other suitcase and haul them both through the kitchen, banging one against the counter, then into the living room. Emery passes me without a word, and Gabriel is right behind her. He sees my bags and, without asking, he takes the largest one from me and leads the way to my room, where the one with wheels is still standing outside the door.

Which is when I realize he knows I was there. And that I heard Emery.

"Don't judge her based on one temper tantrum," he says as he sets my suitcase at the end of my bed. "She was just venting, and she didn't know you could hear her."

"I know."

Gabe sinks onto my mattress. Evidently he has more to say. "It isn't just about you, anyway. It's more about Dad. And Mom, too, a little. And the timing sucks. Em just broke up with her boyfriend, and now—"

"Now she's lost her bed, and her room, and her privacy." I lift the lightest suitcase onto the mattress next to him and unzip it.

"Yeah, but that's not your fault."

"No. It isn't." I flip the suitcase open and grab a stack of shirts. My chest of drawers isn't here yet, but Cynthia made Emery clear out one drawer for me, and I'm damn well going to use it.

"She knows that. She's just having a hard time, and she doesn't know how else to deal."

"You seem to be handling all this just fine," I point out.

"She would be too, if—"

"If I would just dress up as her mini-me?" Let her give me winged eyeliner, with a Sharpie?

"No. *God*, no. Do *not* drive in her lane," Gabe says. "She's a road hog."

"So, there's nothing I can do, then?"

"Other than wait for her to come around? Probably not. But hey!" Gabe stands and runs one hand through his long, rock-star hair. "I suspect there are women all over the world who *wish* their sisters would stop talking to them."

"So, I'm living the dream?"

"A dream, anyway."

"That's certainly one way to look at it," I say as I follow him out the door. "Thanks."

"Yeah," he says. "You're my sister too." But instead of heading toward the dining room, he goes across the hall.

"Aren't you gonna eat?" I ask as I walk backward in the opposite direction.

He nods. "I just want to check on Grammie first." He knocks on her door, and when there's no answer, he eases the door open and steps inside.

He's the only member of the family, other than Cynthia, who's even gone in that room since I got here.

---

Emery's alarm goes off at 5:45 again, and she hits the snooze button for a full half hour. But when she gets up, she heads into the bathroom without turning on the overhead light to blind me. I decide to call that progress.

An hour later, all three of the Bosch kids have left for school. I get up and open the freezer, where I find four different kinds of frozen waffles—chocolate chip, blueberry, gluten-free, and homestyle whole grain. Evidently that's what happens around here, when you're not super specific with the grocery requests you write on the pantry door chalkboard.

I toast three of the chocolate chip waffles and bury the gluten-free box beneath a giant bag of pizza rolls, just so I won't have to look at them.

While I'm eating, a hospice aide comes to give Grammie a sponge bath. I'm not sure what else the aide is doing in there, but I know Grammie doesn't like it. And she has a *very* advanced understanding of how profanity works, for an old woman.

I almost feel sorry for Cynthia, who spends half an hour trying to calm her mother down in soft, soothing tones.

The hospice lady leaves, and Cynthia goes for a run. Grammie is napping, so I practically have the house to myself. And I have nothing at all to do. No good way to distract myself from thoughts of my mother's funeral tomorrow.

So I snoop through Emery's half of the closet.

Georgia only has one brother, but my friend Katherine is the middle of three girls, and she and her sisters are always borrowing one another's clothes and makeup.

I wonder if Emery and I will ever be close enough to share

clothes, like real sisters. Or whether that would even be possible. We have similar facial features, but she's noticeably bustier than I am, and her hips are wide enough to give her a dramatically waspish waist. Like her mother's.

My mom gave me great legs and narrow hips, as well as advice on how best to show them off. Which is why I doubt any of Emery's clothes would look good on me anyway. Or vice versa. So I close the closet and study the framed photos arranged on her desk. They're all of her with her friends at various school functions. In the stands at a school football game. Dressed up at some formal dance. Handing out Halloween candy in an Alice in Wonderland costume.

Gabe said she just went through a breakup, but there are no shots of her with a guy. I wonder if there used to be.

The most noteworthy thing about her pictures is that she went through the cost and effort of printing and framing them. I've only ever done that with family photos, but Emery doesn't have any pictures on display of her parents or her brothers.

Bored, I head into the kitchen to grab a glass of water, then sink into an overstuffed leather armchair in the living room. I set my glass on a coaster and pull my phone from my pocket. I have seventeen missed messages—probably more condolences—and I'm about to scroll through them when Cynthia comes in through the back door, with her own phone pressed to her ear, beneath strands of hair that have escaped her ponytail.

She's wearing a purple hoodie over gray Lululemon leggings, her cheeks flushed from the cold and from exercise. She looks healthy and invigorated. She looks alive.

She doesn't see me, and that's fine. I don't want to answer any more polite questions and well-meaning attempts to make me feel at home. Not with my mother staring out at me in the dimly lit living room, from her photo on the end table.

"Well, what else am I supposed to do?" Cynthia says as she pulls a bottle of Vitamin Water from the beverage fridge. She sounds a little winded from her run. "It isn't the poor girl's fault that her father couldn't keep it in his pants and her mother had no respect for the sanctity of marriage."

Stunned, I stare at her from the unlit living room. She twists open her bottle, her phone pinned between her ear and her shoulder, and she still hasn't noticed me. She would *never* say something like that if she knew I was listening.

That's how I know she means it.

"And the funeral is tomorrow. How am I supposed to hold my head up high at my husband's dead lover's—"

I spring up out of the armchair as if the cushion has just ejected me. I don't realize I'm crying until snot drips from my nose and I have to sniff it back up.

Cynthia spins around, squinting into the dim room, and I can tell the second she spots me.

"You're *not*. You are *not* supposed to go to your husband's dead lover's funeral!" I shout at her. "I don't want you there. I don't want *any* of you there!"

My father may be a cheater, and my mother may have been a home-wrecker, but my stepmother is an unconscionable *bitch*.

Cynthia stares at me, horrified. She's still holding the

phone, though it isn't pressed to her ear anymore. Her water stands forgotten on the counter. "Michaela, I—"

I slide my feet into a pair of sneakers someone left by the front door, and I storm out of the house, clutching my phone. As I walk down the street, I schedule an Uber to pick me up. My mom's checking is still attached to my Uber account. God *please* let there be enough money in there to get me—

Where am I going?

There's only one place I want to be.

I stand on the corner, shivering in the short-sleeved tee and pajama pants I slept in, staring down the street in the direction of my dad's house. I'm afraid that Cynthia will come out any moment and try to stop me from leaving. Or that she's called my dad and his car will come barreling around the opposite corner, from the neighborhood entrance.

But none of that happens. The Uber arrives, and I get in. The driver twists in her seat to frown at me. "You okay?" she asks, and that's when I realize I'm still crying.

"No, but I'm a big tipper." I wipe my face on the bottom of my shirt. "Drive. Please."

She shrugs as she pulls away from the curb, and we don't say a word to each other during the hour-long drive. She listens to K-pop, occasionally glancing at me in the rearview mirror, and I text Georgia.

My stepmother is a bitch. I'm coming home

Thirteen minutes later, I get her reply.

I have mock trial after school, but I'll be there as soon as
I'm done impeaching witnesses

My response:

Please bring pizza

———⊶⊷———

The Uber can't park in my driveway, because it's taken up by a
moving truck.

Shit.

I thank the driver and get out of the car. The front door of
my house is standing open. As I march up the driveway, my
borrowed shoes sliding strangely around my bare feet, a man
comes out of my house carrying a cardboard box sealed with
packing tape. "Main bedroom" is written on one side.

He's carrying my mom's things. He's boxed them up, and
now he's loading them on a truck, ready to haul them off. And I
gave that the okay. I labeled her things and decided which ones
it was okay to get rid of, and now I regret that like I've never
regretted anything in my life.

I'm not ready to see her things tossed out. I'm not ready to
see her buried, surrounded by members of my family who
weren't members of *her* family. By people she never even met.

I stare around the living room in shock. The couch is gone,
and the armchair is gone, and the coffee table is on its side,
padded and all taped up, leaning against the entertainment

center, which has been stripped of all books, movies, and knick-knacks. Though their outlines remain in the dust.

There are two more movers in the kitchen. They all have dark hair, and they're wearing matching polo shirts with the name of their moving company printed in an arc over their hearts. They've taken apart the kitchen table. Its dismembered legs lie scattered across the floor, while they wrap and pack dishes at the small, tiled peninsula.

My mom and I lived in an apartment when I was a baby, but I don't remember that. This is the only home I've ever known. This is *everything* I've ever known. And now, strange men are carrying pieces of my life away in neatly labeled cardboard boxes.

"Stop!" I shout.

The mover coming back in from the truck freezes on his way through the front door, one foot still on the porch. The men in the kitchen turn to look at me through the arched doorway. They didn't even know I was here.

"Ma'am?" The first mover steps into the living room. "Brian" is embroidered on the left side of his shirt. "Can I help you?"

"Yeah. This is my house, and I need you all to just . . . stop!"

He grabs a clipboard from an end table wrapped in padding and reads something from it. "We were contracted by Mr. Oscar—"

"Bosch. Yeah. That's my dad. I'm sorry, but you're going to have to come back next week, or whatever. I'm not . . ." Fresh tears blur the room. "I'm not ready for this yet."

One of the other men speaks up from the kitchen. "We're

only here because there was a cancellation." According to his shirt, his name is Trent. "If we can't finish up today, it'll be at least two more weeks before—"

"That's fine." I cross my arms and run my hands over my exposed skin, which is now covered in chill bumps. It's freezing in here, with the door open. "I'm sorry, but you have to go."

"Seriously?" Brian says.

"Yeah. Sorry."

The other two men come out of the kitchen. One is carrying two bulky packing tape dispensers, while the other pushes a dolly with nylon straps wrapped around the handles.

"Also, I'm, um, going to need the key." I will *not* be able to sleep here knowing that three strange men have a key to my house.

Brian digs the key from his pocket and drops it on the end table on his way out the door.

"Thanks. And again, I'm sorry. I'm just . . . not ready." As I close and lock the front door, I hear the heavy metallic squeal of the ramp being shoved back into its spot beneath the moving van, then the loud scrolling *clang* as the door is rolled down like a garage door and secured in place.

I watch out the window as the moving van pulls out of my driveway and heads down the street, carrying half of everything I own with it. Then I turn to survey the remains of my living room.

And I burst into tears.

# eight

Georgia shows up at twenty minutes after four, with a pizza.
I let her in, and I must look like a total wreck, because she
takes one look at me and wraps me in a one-armed hug, miraculously not dropping the box.

"Come on. Let's eat, and you can tell me what happened."
She heads into the kitchen, but stops halfway there when she
notices, through the archway, that my table is now in pieces.
"Okay, then we'll—" She turns, clearly ready to set the pizza on
the coffee table, and realizes that it isn't where it should be.

"Hang on." I lower the coffee table onto all four legs and
push it into the middle of the room, stepping over scraps of
packing tape wadded into crinkly balls and loose bits of shredded brown paper that were evidently used as packing material.

Georgia sets the pizza on the coffee table, and we sit on the
floor and eat right out of the box, though it won't sit evenly on
the table, because the edges are all padded and taped up for
moving.

"So?" she says around a bite of pepperoni and cheese. Yes, we're pretty basic pizza eaters. You really can't beat a classic. "What did the step-bitch do?"

"She called my mom a home-wrecking whore."

"Oh shit. Really? What did your dad say?"

"He wasn't there. She was talking to a friend on the phone, and she didn't know I was there either. And she didn't say 'whore' in so many words. Exactly."

"So, what did she say? Exactly."

I drop my crust into the box and grab a second slice. "She said my mother had no respect for the 'sanctity of marriage.'"

"Objection, your honor." Georgia gestures with the uneaten half of her slice. "Misleading the jury."

"And the jury would be . . . ?"

"Me." She shrugs. "And you misled me into believing that your stepmother actually called your mom a home-wrecking whore."

"Well, that's what she meant. And my mom's body isn't even cold yet."

"I admit, it was a bitchy thing to say. And the timing is . . . unfortunate. But Cynthia does seem to be the victim in all of this—"

"I kinda think *I'm* the victim."

"—and it sounds like she thought she was ranting to a friend, in private. Which we've both been known to do."

I drop my slice into the box. I'm not hungry anymore. "She insulted my dead mother. My very *recently* dead mother. And while I like Georgia Pearson, mock trial defense attorney extraordinaire, what I really need right now is Georgia, my best friend, who's willing to call my mean stepmother a bitch and just . . . be on my side."

"Done." Georgia flips the pizza lid closed and slams her hand down on top of it. "*Screw* that bitch!"

"Screw her!" I shout. "My mom may not have been perfect, but at least she didn't serve bougie salads with goat cheese and weird grains."

"Yeah!" Georgia stands with the pizza and heads into the kitchen, where she slides the box into the fridge. "She served *iceberg* and *bacon bits*, like a *normal* mom!" She pulls open the upper cabinet, where the glasses are supposed to be, and when she finds it empty, she just shrugs and sticks her head into the sink so she can drink from the faucet. "What kind of weird grains are we talking about, anyway?"

"Something called . . . farro?"

Georgia leans against the archway, looking into the living room. "Was it good?"

I shrug. "I mean, yeah, it was pretty good, but that's not the point."

"Not the point!" my best friend echoes. "Her salads are weird, and she's a bitch!"

"Yeah. Hey, I think there's still some ice cream in the freezer. You wanna grab a couple of spoons and see if the TV in my mom's room is still hooked up?"

"I *do* want that. Unfortunately, I have a paper due at midnight, and I haven't actually started it yet."

"The *Animal Farm* essay?" I ask, and she nods. Ironically,

I started that one last week, but it's never going to be due, because I don't go to school there anymore. I don't go to school anywhere anymore, though technically I'm registered at West Bradford High School now.

"You wanna come over and hang out while I work? It'll be boring, but at least you won't be alone."

"No. Thanks, though." I want to be here. This might be the last night I get to spend in my real home.

"You sure?" She rests her forearms on my shoulders and laces her fingers behind my neck, then leans with her forehead pressed to mine. "I don't want to leave you here all alone."

"I'll be fine. I'm just gonna watch TV and miss my mom, surrounded by what's left of her stuff."

"Your dad knows where you are?"

"Yeah." I got a storm of texts from him before Georgia got here with the pizza. Cynthia told him that I ran out of the house in my pajamas, and the movers called to tell him that I'd kicked them out. He wanted to come pick me up, but I told him that I needed one more night at home. And if he wasn't sure why, he should talk to his wife.

In the end, I called him, and we compromised on me staying home with all the doors and windows locked, and him keeping his entire family away from the funeral tomorrow so I can say goodbye to my mother in peace. He didn't sound happy when he hung up the phone. But I'm beyond caring how *he* feels right now.

"Okay." Georgia lets me go and plants a kiss on my forehead.

"Do your grief thing. And text if you need anything. I'll totally sneak out after my mom goes to sleep and write my paper here."

"I'll be fine. But thanks."

She leaves me the pizza, and I wonder, as I walk through the kitchen, if the real reason Georgia left is that the movers have already packed up the coffee machine.

The fridge sounds weird. Actually, it sounds silent. I pull open the door, and when the light doesn't come on, I realize that at some point while they were packing, the movers unplugged it. Which explains why there's nothing left in it but my pizza and an open box of baking soda. I pull the fridge away from the wall—thank goodness it's on wheels—and plug it back in. And suddenly I *really* miss the fully stocked beverage fridge at my dad's house.

I drink from the faucet, then head into my mom's room. The movers must have just started in here, because her stuff seems mostly untouched. The bed is still made and everything.

Well, it's not made, exactly—my mom only made her bed when she changed the bedding—but the sheets and blankets are still tossed back, just like she left them when she woke up on Monday morning. The day she died. So I take off my borrowed sneakers and crawl into her bed.

The pillows still smell like her. But there's something . . .

I reach toward my feet, beneath the covers, and grab the fuzzy lump that my toes have found. It's one of her fluffy socks. The kind with the no-skid patches on the soles. I stare at that sock, wadded up in my hand, knowing that she probably couldn't figure out, the other morning, where she'd lost it. Knowing that if she hadn't been hit by a car on her lunch break, she probably would have gotten into bed that night and found the sock with her toes, just like I have, and she'd lie here and laugh at herself.

That's what I should do.

Instead, I cry.

My phone beeps with a text from my dad, and I ignore it as I blink through my tears and grab the remote to the TV still standing on my mom's dresser. It's old, and the screen's kind of small, but it's still plugged in, and it still works. Unfortunately, the cable's already been turned off—my dad works *fast*—so I have to get out of bed to put in a DVD. I pick one of my mom's favorites.

*Steel Magnolias.* It's adapted from a play, and though my mom loved the theater, she never got to see this one onstage, because she was just a kid when it came out. But she loved the movie.

It's the daughter who dies in this one, not the mom, but I bawl all the way through it, because I know what's coming. And because I need to cry.

After the movie, I grab the pizza box and set it in the middle of my mom's bed. I really wish the movers hadn't thrown out my ice cream. There's still a box of popcorn in the kitchen, but the microwave is gone, so I'm stuck with cold pizza.

My mom only owned a few movies. Like most people, we pretty much streamed anything we wanted to watch, but she had DVDs of childhood favorites, as well as a few that we liked to watch together. Mostly musicals. My mom had a great voice. She used to tell me that she had trouble, back in college, choosing between nursing and a vocal performance major.

*Into the Woods* was her favorite musical. She saw it twice in local theater productions, and she streamed the Broadway version about a billion times. And, of course, she was thrilled when the movie came out when I was a kid. So she bought it on Blu-ray.

As I slide the disk into the player, I'm thinking of all the times we watched this one in the living room, sharing a big bowl of popcorn or a pint of ice cream. Singing at the top of our lungs, with food in our mouths. We knew every word.

Tonight, I don't sing. Tonight, I cry, and eat pizza, and miss my mom while I watch her favorite musical.

Tonight, I say goodbye.

———❦———

I have nothing to wear to my mother's funeral. I thought I'd be getting ready at my dad's house, so I took my dress and heels there the other day, but now I have two hours to get ready, and my closet is empty. So I wear one of my mom's dresses.

The only dark one she owned is her "little black dress," and it's probably not entirely appropriate for a funeral. She hardly ever wore it, because she didn't date much—she always said there'd be time for men when her daughter was grown—but those things never go out of style, right?

Georgia shows up on my doorstep wearing a sad smile and holding a big bundle of thick black material over one arm.

"What's that?" I say as I let her in.

She shrugs. "You said your dress was too short. So I brought a fix." She holds up the bundle, and I realize it's a long, black wool coat. It's nice. It has thick, pointed lapels, four large buttons, and a matching wool sash at the waist. "It's my mom's."

"She said I could borrow it?"

"I didn't ask. But it's not like she'd say no."

Because my mom died. I can have whatever I want, at least until she's buried.

"Thanks." I try the coat on, and it's a perfect fit. It hides my inappropriately short hem and makes me look . . . dressy and mature. "Seriously, thanks," I say, meeting Georgia's gaze in the bathroom mirror.

She shrugs again. "You only bury your mother once, right?"

"God, I hope so."

---

Everyone I've ever known is at the funeral. Well, everyone except my new family. People keep coming up to me to tell me that my mom took great care of their babies in the hospital. That she saved lives. That she made a difference.

All her coworkers are here. Her bosses. They're hard to recognize, without scrubs and name tags, and I may be imagining it, but they seem as uncomfortable in their dress clothes as I am. There are so many of them here that I worry there's no one left to work in the NICU.

My teachers are here. My friends. My principal and the vice principal, Ms. Aaronson, who drove me to the hospital.

Ms. Aaronson asks me how I'm doing. She asks where my dad is. When I tell her that I told him not to come, she asks me again if I'm okay.

"She just doesn't like him much right now," Georgia tells her. Ms. Aaronson nods, as if she understands.

Several people get up to talk about my mom. They stand at the front of the room, next to the big picture the funeral home had printed, beside all the flowers we ordered and a bunch that people sent. They tell sweet, funny stories about my mom at work, saving lives. My mom at girls' night out, painting ceramics and ordering a different cocktail—never more than one—every week.

She liked to have fun, but she was responsible. She was a mom.

I don't get up and speak. The funeral director asked if I wanted to, when we were planning this, and I told him I wasn't sure. When the time comes, he looks at me from the front of the room, where he stands unobtrusively next to the door. I shake my head.

I can't. I don't know what to say. There are a million words milling around in my head right now, but they won't form an orderly line. They refuse to make sense.

I can still feel my mom. But I can't explain her to a roomful of mostly strangers.

So we adjourn and a limo takes Georgia and me to the cemetery.

---

I lay a single white calla lily on my mother's casket, centered perfectly, just before they lower it into the ground. There are tears in my eyes, but they won't fall. I can feel people watching me, and I'm pissed that they're what I'm thinking about as I *truly* lose my mother.

———∞∞∞———

"The funeral was nice," Georgia says as we change out of our dresses in my mom's room. She's brought a garment bag for hers, but I just hang mine back in my mom's closet, for the movers to pack up. The sticky note on the door says, "Donate everything inside."

"The funeral was *awful*." I jerk my T-shirt over my head, and it leaves my hair standing up all over the place.

"I know." Georgia shrugs. "But you're supposed to say that it was nice." She pulls her jeans up and zips them. "So, now what?"

I exhale as I sink onto the edge of the bed. "I can't really hang out here anymore. There's no food, and they're cutting the power off this afternoon. And I have to start school on Monday." Which means I have the rest of today and all weekend to put up with Emery before we go our separate ways at school.

At *her* school.

"So, I guess I'm going back."

"You can stay with me tonight."

Actually, I can't. I've already asked my dad, and he said that if I wasn't back by 4:00 p.m., he'd call out the National Guard.

I don't know him well enough to assess the reality of that threat.

"Thanks, but—"

"Come on, Mick." Georgia gives me her best pout, and I realize I really like her lipstick. But it won't work on me. I'm too pale.

I probably should have worn makeup to the funeral. I left mine at my dad's house, but I could have used some of my mom's. Why am I just now thinking of that?

"It's Friday. We could see if Izzy and Katherine wanna come over, and—"

"Thanks, Georgia. Really. But I wouldn't be very good company today." And I don't really feel like socializing on the night of my mother's funeral.

She must understand that, because she lets it go. "Okay. I guess this is goodbye, then."

"I'll only be an hour away," I tell her.

"Only a text away," she corrects me, holding up her phone. I know she's right, but it won't be the same, not seeing Georgia on a daily basis.

"Yeah."

"Love you." She pulls me in for a hug that somehow holds me together, even as it tears me apart.

Then she leaves, and it turns out I was right. Goodbye still feels like goodbye, even with her only a text away.

---

I'm alone in my house. The power is off and half of the furniture is either disassembled, packed up, or both. I realize this may be the last time I ever stand here, in the only home I can remember. Then I realize that no longer really matters.

My mom doesn't live here anymore. I don't either.

I shove my keys into the pocket of an old coat I found in the closet and take my mom's set from the hook by the front door. Her keychain is the bobbly eyed cat I gave her several years ago. One of the cat's pupils is stuck and no longer bobbles, so it's kind of creepy, but I'm keeping it.

I step out the front door, but before I can lock it, I realize I've forgotten something, so I race back inside and grab the dress I wore to the funeral. I can't donate that one. Not anymore.

With it draped over my arm, the hanger tapping against my hip with every move I make, I lock the front door. At the end of the driveway, I turn and look back at the house, one last time.

*Goodbye, old life.*

Then I click the key fob and unlock my mom's car. I'm not putting the car in storage. It's a five-year-old black Honda Accord. Nothing special. Nothing fancy.

But it's mine.

# nine

I can hear my dad and Cynthia talking before I open the door, but they go silent as I step into the foyer.

Cynthia appears from around the corner as I take off the shoes I borrowed. "You're back!" She sounds truly relieved. Then her expression . . . deflates. "Michaela, I'm so sorry. I—"

"Let's just move on, okay?" I say as my father appears in the living room behind her.

"Sure. Of course. I just . . . I feel like I should apologize. I'm, um, I'm going through some things right now, with my mother's illness, and . . ."

"And your husband's illegitimate daughter moving in?"

Cynthia flinches. "Yeah. I'm still trying to figure out how to deal with everything, and I'm sure that's true for you too. But my problems shouldn't add to yours."

I'm not sure how to respond. She's right, but it seems rude to say that out loud, when she's trying to apologize.

"I think it's going to take a while for us all to get used to the change in our family dynamic," my dad says. "Until then, we just need to cut each other a little slack."

"Sure. I can totally cut Cynthia some slack for insulting my dead mother before she was even buried. No problem." I leave them both staring after me.

I glance into Cody's room on my way down the hall. He's sitting at his desk with a textbook open. I'm sure he's supposed to be reading, but he's actually playing a game on his phone.

Gabe's room is empty. Mine is not.

"Hey," I say as I shrug out of my mom's old coat.

Emery doesn't reply. She definitely heard me, but she's wearing AirPods while she scrolls through something on her phone, so she can pretend she didn't.

I hang the coat on my half of our closet rod, then turn to dig some clean clothes out of my drawer in our dresser, and I discover that the matching chests of drawers were delivered while I was gone.

"Yours is on the left," Emery says. In case I couldn't guess that mine was on the side of the room that also holds my bed.

"Thanks." *Kill 'em with kindness.* That was one of the clichés my mother often threw at me with a grin. I could never tell whether or not she was being ironic about that one, but I'm gonna kill Emery with kindness.

If that doesn't work, I may just kill her.

Someone has already put clothes in a couple of my drawers, establishing one for pants, one for tops, and one for underwear and socks. My money is on Cynthia. I change out of my pajamas, which feels like a weird thing to do at four in the afternoon, but that's pretty much the state of my life right now.

Emery goes back to ignoring me while I change. I pull my hair back into a sloppy ponytail, and I can hear cooking sounds coming from the kitchen. But I also hear music, coming from the backyard. The song ends abruptly and is replaced by voices. I hear someone demonstrating a chord, and I realize Gabriel isn't just out there blasting Spotify on a speaker.

I head through the living room and out the back door, then across the lawn in my bare feet—cold, dead grass pokes at the soles—until I'm standing in the open doorway of the outbuilding. Which I now realize is actually a garage.

It's a *second* garage, parked at the end of the section of driveway that runs through the porte cochere, as my dad calls the roof that connects the house to the larger, main garage.

This second garage is evidently home to Gabriel's band. He has an *actual* garage band.

The rolling bay door is closed, but the people-sized door is open, and no one has noticed me standing there yet, because they're all looking at a guy holding an electric guitar.

"—and I think the chorus would have more impact, if we—"

I step inside, because it's *really* cold out, and my foot sends an empty soda can clattering across the floor. Everyone spins to look at me, and all I can do is wave.

"Hey!" Gabe sets his bass on a guitar stand and motions for me to come inside. "Guys, this is Michaela." He hesitates for a second, and I wish I hadn't come out here. That I hadn't forced him to introduce me to his friends. "My surprise sister," he finishes with an awkward-sounding laugh.

"Your *surprise* sister?" The drummer stands and rests his sticks on the top of his drum set.

Gabe shrugs. "I remember asking for another brother for Christmas, when I was, like, eight. I think Santa must have some kind of shipping delay." He grins at me. "And I guess they ran out of boys."

"You know Santa is your dad, right?" the guitar player says.

Gabe frowns. "That makes the whole 'come sit on my lap' thing sound kinda creepy."

"It's creepy no matter how you look at it." The drummer rounds his drum set and offers me his hand. "I'm John Thomas Mitchell."

"Hey." I shake John Thomas's hand.

"And this is Josh Kang," Gabe says. "He plays lead guitar and sings, most of the time."

"Nice to meet you," I say. "Sorry for intruding. I just heard music, and . . ." I shrug.

"That's awesome, actually," Josh says. "Music is supposed to pull people in." He grins at Gabe, over my head. "I'd call that a win."

"We need to get through this at least one more time before we lose our drummer to tacos and a movie with his girlfriend," Gabe says. "But you're welcome to hang out and listen, as long as you promise to play the part of the adoring crowd."

"Happy to." I like all three of them. Gabe, for introducing me as if I were an actual human being with feelings. John Thomas and Josh, for playing music and not minding an audience.

"Here." Josh grabs an empty bucket and turns it over for me to sit on.

I sit, wishing I were farther from the door, but unwilling to move and risk kicking over another can. Or tripping over a power cord. Or otherwise drawing attention to myself and away from their rehearsal.

John Thomas counts them off, and the music starts again, and they're not bad, for a three-member high school garage band. The song is an original, I think, and Gabe sings harmony on a mic taped to a broken stand.

Halfway through the song, I start humming along, and by the end, I'm singing the chorus beneath my breath. It's pretty catchy.

The guys finish practicing, and I follow them out of the garage and down the driveway. Both John Thomas and Josh live in this neighborhood, it turns out, which is why neither of them drove. They both head in opposite directions, once they get to the road.

"See you Monday!" Josh calls as he disappears around the corner. And for a second, I think he's talking to me. Then I realize he's talking to Gabe, who just reminded him about bringing his extra amp next time.

As we head back toward the house, I notice something strange about the garage at the back of the property, now that I can see it framed through the arched porte cochere. "Hey, why is that garage taller than the other one?"

Gabriel squints into the dark, toward where a set of exterior fixtures light up the garage from either side of the tall bay door. "I think the previous owners had a camper, or a big trailer, or something. That's why it's out of the way, back there. They didn't use it very often. We do, though. Last summer, I jumped off the roof onto our trampoline."

"We have a trampoline?"

"Not anymore. That *may* be related to the roof-jumping incident. Because of how I bounced off the trampoline onto the ground and broke my right leg in three places."

"Seriously?"

"Yeah." He bends to pull up the leg of his jeans, showing off a long scar on his shin. "Got a leg full of metal to show for it. Makes airport security a real adventure."

"Why would you jump off the roof?"

"John Thomas dared me to."

"So?"

Gabe's nose crinkles, his lips half pursed in a frown. "Do you not understand how dares work?"

"Evidently not," I say, and he laughs. "Well, it's nice of your parents to let your band practice back there."

He snorts. "I'm pretty sure they're happy to have us so far away from the house."

———— ∞ ————

"Hey! Emmy!"

I swallow a groan as I stop in the middle of the hallway. I was on my way to the kitchen for a snack, planning to take a bowl of popcorn back to my room and enjoy having a Saturday afternoon to myself while I watched a movie on my laptop.

A blond girl named Mara picked Emery up right after lunch so they could practice for whatever extracurricular activity my half sister does after school. I saw her through the window, but she didn't come in. I don't think Emery has told her about me yet.

Gabriel plays bass guitar and occasionally sings. Cody lives on his PS5. But Emery has done a good job of hiding most aspects of her life from me. I suspect that's because she hasn't yet figured out what to tell her friends about me. Or maybe she just doesn't want me in her life.

"Em!" the voice calls again, and I turn slowly toward the bedroom across the hall from mine. Cynthia's mother is wide awake and sitting up in bed, waving me forward with one wrinkled, age-spotted hand.

"Hi, Mrs. Turner," I say as I hover in her doorway. We haven't spoken since Cynthia first introduced us, and though I've been calling her Grammie in my head, I don't want to presume. Even if she does think I'm Emery.

"Mrs. Turner!" She huffs and gestures at me more frantically. "Emmy, grab that big brown photo album from the bottom shelf for me, will you?"

Unsure, I glance at the shelf across the room. The album is leather-bound and padded—the old-fashioned kind, where the photos actually have to be glued or taped to paper pages. It looks old.

When I don't move from my spot in the doorway, she laughs. "Don't be scared, girl! I'm not dead yet!"

I stare at her for a moment. Then I exhale. "You're not dying. Cynthia said you'd be back on your feet soon."

"Cynthia's full of shit." She frowns at me, squinting. Then she grabs a pair of thick glasses from the hospital-style rolling table next to her bed and puts them on. And she squints some more. "You're not Emery." Her gaze roams me. "It's that hair. You and my granddaughter have the same hair."

"Really?" I run one hand over my head, tucking my long, dark hair over one shoulder. "I hadn't really thought about that. Though my dad thinks we have the same eyes."

"Can't see your eyes from here. Come closer, child."

I cross the room, and she seizes my hand with a disarming speed and strength. Then she pulls me even closer. "Yup. Bright blue, and big as saucers. No one would ever mistake the two of you for strangers."

That's probably what Emery's so upset about. It's not like she can tell people I'm an exchange student, or some orphan they took in. We may not be built alike, but evidently our faces proclaim our shared DNA to the world.

"The album's on the bottom shelf, child." She lets me go, but she's still staring, as if she's trying to remember something. "Oscar's other daughter?"

"Yeah." I cross the room and squat to pull the album from the shelf.

"I remember that. Cynthia told me, years ago. I never caught your name, though. Back then."

"Michaela," I remind her. "Rutherford."

"And your mother?"

"Died. Almost a week ago."

"I'm so sorry, child. That really is the shit end of the stick, isn't it?"

"Um . . . yeah."

"She must have been young. What happened?"

Dad says that Grammie is "of an age" where, like her hip joints and her eyes, her verbal filter no longer works well. He's not wrong.

"Some idiot was texting behind the wheel and hit her on the crosswalk." This is the first time I've said that out loud. It *hurts*.

Grammie makes an angry noise deep in her throat. "Did he get what's coming?"

"He pled guilty to negligent homicide." According to what I heard my dad saying to Cynthia last night, that's a misdemeanor. He hasn't been sentenced yet, but the most he can get is a fine and up to a year in county jail. Ninety days is more likely.

My mother is *gone*, and in a few months, that asshole can move on with his life, like nothing ever happened. But I'm trying not to think about that. Things are hard enough right now, without dwelling on things I can't change.

"And now you live here. Whether you like it or not." Grammie sighs. "Looks like we have something in common."

I'm not sure how to reply to that, so I hold up the album. It's surprisingly heavy. "Just set it here." She pats her lap, but I'm worried that it'll be too much weight on the fragile lumps formed by her legs beneath the covers.

"Mrs. Turner—"

"Call me Grammie." She grabs the album and drops it onto her lap, then opens it to the first page.

I lean in for a better look at the old black-and-white photo, and the next thing I know, we're halfway through the album. I've heard stories about and seen pictures of her parents, as well as her brother and sister. And several cousins. I know where she grew up and how each of her family members died.

She's the last of her siblings.

"That was my Larry, on the day we married." Grammie taps one short, yellowed fingernail on a photo of a handsome young man in a suit. Next to him is a younger version of Grammie, wearing a wedding dress. She's laughing, her head thrown back, clutching his hand as they come down the front steps of a church. On either side of them, people in dress clothes throw handfuls of rice, which the old camera caught as tiny little smudges. "There are more photos, of course. There's an entire wedding album down there." She waves one hand at the shelf across the room. "But this one has always been my favorite. And about a year after that day, came this one." Grammie turns the page again, and there's only one picture centered in the next one. It's of an adorable baby girl in a dress, sitting up with an actual rattle clutched in one fist.

The photo is in color, but it's reddish with age, so I can't tell the true shade of her dress. But even toothless, the girl's smile is recognizable. "That's Cynthia?"

Grammie nods. "She wasn't such a bitch back then."

I laugh. I can't help it. But then . . . "She's doing the best she can." I know that, even if I don't want to be here. Even if I'd much rather have my own mother back. Even if she and I have every reason to resent each other. "She quit her job to take care of you."

"I know that, child. And lord knows that's more than my other two ungrateful progeny would ever do. But a woman confined to her bed has limited sources of entertainment, and my daughter has a thick skin, so . . ." Grammie shrugs.

"Limited sources of entertainment?" I point at the huge television mounted on the wall opposite her bed. "Isn't that thing hooked up to cable? You guys get, like, eight hundred channels. Including premium movies." Even though no one ever seems to watch the actual TVs in this house.

"And yet there's nothing on worth watching, unless you want to remodel your backyard by hand, fall in love with a teenage vampire, or learn to speak Spanish from a soap opera. Though I have to admit, there is a certain appeal to the thought of being able to cuss in multiple languages."

I laugh. "You sound like every kid who was in my eighth-grade French class." I grab the remote from her rolling tray table and turn on the TV. "But I refuse to believe there's nothing worth watching, across *eight hundred* channels." I pull up the scrolling guide. "What do you want to see?"

She lists a bunch of movies I've never heard of, and finally I understand.

"Did any of those come out after 1980?"

"I highly doubt it."

"Okay, so you want classic movies. Streaming is going to be your best bet, and the Bosches subscribe to all of the streaming services. Seriously. Apparently cost is no issue. And the pass-words are all the same."

I log her into Netflix. "You can set up your own user profile, and it'll keep track of what kind of stuff you like to watch. Or, you can drive Cynthia nuts by using hers, and it'll start sug-gesting all of your favorite shows and movies to her."

"Let's do that."

I select Cynthia's profile and type "classic movies" into the search bar. "There are only a few here, but the Classic Movie channel has its own streaming service. You just have to log in using information from your cable account. My mom set my grandmother up through the app a few years ago, and she loved it. I don't have that log-in info, so you'll have to watch Netflix for now, but Cynthia will be able to get you into the Classic Movie account. And if she doesn't know how, you'll have fun watching her try to figure it out."

Grammie grins at me. "That's perfect. Thank you, Em—I mean Michaela."

I hand her the remote, and as she selects a movie called *Cool Hand Luke*, I look up to find Cynthia standing in the door-way, watching. There are tears in her eyes.

———— ∞ ————

"That was very kind of you." Cynthia pulls a glass down from the cabinet and runs water in it from the kitchen sink. She looks sad, but not unhappy. Not really. "Her actual grandchil-dren don't go in there very much. I think they're not really sure how to deal with her . . . decline."

But I didn't know Grammie before she got sick, so I haven't seen any decline.

"I have to warn you, though. She won't always recognize you. Not even as Emery. She has good days and bad days, and the bad days can be hard."

"Cancer can make you forget people?"

"I suspect it could, if it were in the brain. But my mother is in the early stages of dementia. Unrelated to her cancer. The bad days are difficult for my kids—especially Cody—so they've kind of pulled away from her."

I guess I can understand that. But also, they still have a mom *and* a grandmother. And they seem to be totally taking them both for granted.

## ten

Emery's alarm goes off at 5:45 a.m., as usual, and this time, I get up. She'll snooze for the next twenty minutes, but we share a bathroom, and I already understand that on school days, I'm only going to get my fair share of hot water and mirror time if I'm the first one out of bed.

Emery starts pounding on the door at 6:04. My teeth are brushed, but I only have shadow on one eye. I open the door.

"I need to shower," she snaps, taking in my wet hair and half made-up face.

"We're going to have to work out a schedule." I go back to my eye makeup.

"Get. Out."

"One second." I apply two coats of mascara, then grab my brush, hair dryer, and flat iron on my way into the hall. She slams the door behind me.

I take my things into the powder bath between the kitchen

and the living room, and too late, I realize I forgot my heat pro-
tectant. But Emery has definitely locked the door, and she definitely will *not* get out of the shower to let me in.

I plug in the flat iron and let it warm up while I blow-dry my
hair, hoping I don't wind up with heat-damaged ends on my first
day of school, and when I turn off the dryer, I can hear my dad
talking from the kitchen.

"—told her that if she wants to be the first one in the shower,
she needs to get up earlier. We are *not* putting in another bathroom. Three and a half baths should be plenty for seven
people."

"The girls will figure it out," Cynthia replies, accompanied
by the sound of liquid being poured.

"Hopefully without any future six a.m. text rants," my dad
mumbles.

"We do have something to discuss, though," she says as I
begin to section off my hair.

"What?" The dread in my father's voice feels almost tangible.
He sounds tired.

"The car."

"What c—"

"You know what car."

I groan as I pull the flat iron through my hair, careful not to
bump my ear.

Cynthia sighs. "We didn't let Gabe have a car until he was
seventeen, and I feel like that was a solid decision. He had a full
year of driving under his belt by then, and—"

"Gabe set his own hair on fire when he was twelve and jumped off the garage roof last year. You really think Michaela is a bigger risk behind the wheel?"

"I think we've established a house rule, and if we go back on that for one daughter, we'll have to for the other, or else we'll be hypocrites. And if we give Emery a car, this will be a *five-car* household. Which seems more than a bit ridiculous. And wasteful."

"So you want me to tell her she can't keep her mother's car?"

Just when I was starting to truly tolerate my stepmother . . .

"We can put it in storage. She can drive it next year. It just isn't fair for her to have one, when Emery doesn't."

I set the flat iron on the counter. It lands heavier than I intended, then it slides into the sink, but I'm already in motion. I march through the living room and glare at them from across the island. "I'm keeping the car."

Cynthia pointedly looks at my father, silently telling him that he should take this one.

"Michaela, we just think you're a little young—"

"Well, the state of Oklahoma disagrees. That's why they issued me a license."

"But they didn't issue you a car," Cynthia points out, in a tone so patient and rational and . . . *infuriating.* "And you don't have any way to pay for gas, and maintenance, and your registration and inspection, and—"

I turn to my dad. "Didn't you say something about survivor benefits?"

He nods, and Cynthia glares at him. "From Social Security. Until you turn eighteen."

"And isn't that intended to help make up for things my mother isn't here to provide for me anymore?"

"Well, yes . . . ," he admits.

"Then I'll use that. And if it isn't enough, I'll get a job. Does Gabe have a job? Does he pay for his car, and gas, and maintenance?"

My dad glances at Cynthia, and her frown swells until she looks like the angry emoji.

"No," my dad admits. "We pay for his car."

"It's used, and it doesn't cost much," Cynthia adds in a failed bid to convince me that her children aren't hopelessly spoiled.

"Mine's used too, and my mom paid it off last year, so there's no payment."

"The survivor benefit should more than cover gas and maintenance, but I want what's left to go into savings," my dad says.

"Oscar! That isn't fair to Emery. She's older than Michaela, and she doesn't have a car—"

"And I don't have a mom." I shrug. "Sometimes life isn't fair. I'm keeping my car."

As I march back toward the powder bath, I hear my dad sigh. "I'll call this afternoon and have it put on our insurance plan."

———— ✺ ————

I don't get to drive my car to school, even after my victory in the Battle of the Teenage Driver, because it isn't insured yet, and because I don't have a parking pass. So, while Gabriel drops Cody at the middle school, then takes himself and Emery to school, I ride with my dad. He has to come in and finish my registration, anyway.

Gabe will take me home, but I'll have some time to kill after last period, because he and Emery each have some kind of extracurricular function after school.

Though there are seniors in several of my classes, Gabe is not one of them.

Emery and I turn out to have one class together: US History, right before lunch, during which she ignores me entirely. She doesn't mention me to any of her friends, that I can tell—not even the blond girl who picked her up Saturday—and I can't help thinking that that's only going to make it more awkward for her, when they eventually figure out that she and I live in the same house. But it's not my job to teach her about concepts like forethought. So I read the chapter in my textbook, mostly ignore the teacher's rambling lecture, which veers into foods from the seventies that you can't get anymore—who on *earth* is Baron Von Redberry?—and smile at the classmates who make eye contact.

After school, I roam the halls, learning the lay of the land. West Bradford has a wealthy tax base, according to my dad, and that's evident in the facilities. There's a pool, two gymnasiums, and separate buildings both for the JROTC unit and the dance team. Seriously.

I have no idea what Gabe and Emery's extracurricular activities are, but I peek into the woodshop, the band room, the gym, and the choir room before I finally find Gabriel at orchestra rehearsal. My brother, it turns out, also plays the upright bass.

As I wander through the arts wing, my gaze catches on a poster tacked to a huge corkboard. It's an announcement for auditions for the school musical. They're doing *Into the Woods*.

I feel like someone's just punched me in the chest. This feels like fate.

I check the date on the poster. It's today. It's *right now*.

They're auditioning for my mother's favorite musical on my first day at this school. Three days after her funeral. One week after she died.

I've never sung in front of anyone, other than Georgia and my mom. And I don't really care about the musical itself, though obviously I'll go to see it. What I care about is that I didn't get to write anything good on my mother's headstone, and I couldn't make myself say anything at her funeral. I just didn't have the words.

But *these* words are already written, and I know them by heart. All of them. No matter which song I choose. Though, truly, there's only one that really makes sense.

"You wanna audition?"

Startled, I spin around to find the most gorgeous boy I've ever seen watching me from the middle of the hallway. There's a folder tucked under his arm, and I can't help noticing that his sleeve is tight around his bicep. But it's his eyes, really, that hold my attention. Golden brown, and rimmed in thick, dark lashes.

He nods at the poster. "It's still going on, if you're interested."

I'm not. Not interested in getting a part, anyway. But my audition doesn't have to be about impressing a judge. I can get up there and sing a song from her favorite musical as a tribute to my mom.

"You don't have to sign up or anything." The boy runs his free hand through a mass of dark, loose curls. "Ms. Bond will let anyone audition. You just walk onstage and sing any song from the musical: movie or stage."

"Really?" Evidently I'm seriously considering this.

Even if no one else knows why I'm really singing, my mom will know, right? If she's still out there, in any form, watching, she'll know I'm singing for her.

"Yeah." His gaze roams my face, and I fight an urge to run one hand through my hair. To primp. "Are you new here?"

"It's my first day."

He smiles, and dimples appear in his cheeks. Honest-to-God dimples. "Good timing. Come on. I'll show you where the theater is."

He's just assuming I even know a song from *Into the Woods*. Which is a good bet, considering that he caught me staring at the poster.

He turns, and I follow him around the corner into a lobby, toward two sets of double doors, both of which are closed.

This is a good idea. I know all the songs—the soundtrack versions, with minimal dialogue interruptions—and this is the *definition* of a fortuitous opportunity. One I may never get again.

And, honestly, I'd probably follow this particular boy into the chess club or onto the soccer field, even though I'm completely unqualified for either of those.

I'm feeling good about this. Until I follow him past the double doors and through a smaller entrance around the corner, into a large, oddly shaped room where old set pieces line the walls. The room is crowded with huge crates, and random pieces of furniture, and frame-mounted doors that lead nowhere.

Running through the center of the room is an open walkway painted with black-and-yellow stripes. The boy leads me down that path—I feel like Dorothy on the way to Oz—and suddenly I find myself backstage.

This space is cavernous. The floor is plain concrete, but the walls are painted pitch black, and there's a catwalk high overhead. There are kids standing around everywhere, staring at sheet music, humming familiar tunes under their breath. A girl in the back is softly singing scales, sitting on a bench in front of an old, upright piano.

Onstage, a girl I've never seen before is singing "I Know Things Now," Little Red Riding Hood's solo. Her voice is soft but on pitch, and suddenly, as I watch her stare out at an audience I can't see, my heart starts to pound, and I realize this is a huge mistake.

I can sing to my mom at home, in the shower. Or in front of the mirror. I don't have to be onstage. I don't need to be in front of people who can laugh at me. I don't have to embarrass myself to pay tribute to my mother.

The girl onstage finishes her song, and there's light applause from out front. The audience is small, thank goodness. Or maybe it's large, but most people didn't clap.

My throat feels thick.

A voice over a microphone thanks Kylie for her audition, and the girl smiles, then walks offstage. Right past me. Then that voice shouts, "Next!"

There are people everywhere, but no one makes a move. They all seem to be watching the boy I followed into this colossal mistake, as if waiting for him to step into the spotlight. As if he somehow has dibs on the next audition. And I realize they all know him. Backstage, this boy is *someone*.

He gives me a little nudge, and suddenly I'm walking. I'm onstage, in front of a row of panels intended to bounce sound out at the theater. I'm standing in a literal spotlight, and even though the audience is right in front of me, I can't really see them. And *now* I realize the problem with the song I planned to sing.

"Name?" the voice asks over the microphone, and when I squint, I can make out a folding table in front of the stage, and three forms sitting behind it.

"Um . . . Michaela Rutherford," I say.

"Use the mic." The woman in the middle—Ms. Bond, presumably—gestures at the microphone on a stand in front of me, and I step up to it. "And tell us what you're going to sing."

"My name is Michaela Rutherford, and I was going to sing 'No One Is Alone.' But it's a duet, and I've just realized I don't have a partner. So I'll just—"

Footsteps echo from my right, and when I turn, I see the boy who brought me here walking across the stage, holding a microphone. "I'll sing with her."

"Thank you, Ben," Ms. Bond says. She turns to a man sitting on her left, who has a laptop connected to a large speaker. "Mr. Lacey, is the music ready?"

He nods. Then the first notes ring out, as Ben hands me his microphone and unclips the one from the stand for himself.

My heart is racing, but there's no more time to be nervous.

I start singing, and I didn't get a chance to warm up, so that first high note is a stretch. And it comes early. It's a weak note, and my face is burning. I can feel people watching me, even if I can't see them.

Ben comes in with his first line, and his voice is a smooth, beautiful, robust baritone. No wonder everyone here knows him. He's incredible.

My next lines play off of his, and he smiles. I keep singing.

Then I hear the *words* I'm singing. Passages about parents making mistakes and people sharing the experience of solitude, which seem to have an all-new meaning for me now.

I hear my mother singing the words. I feel her next to me on the couch. Curled up on her bed. Sitting in the driver's seat of the car. I hear her, and I remember.

And I sing.

Ben's harmony weaves through the words. He seems to feel the music, and he's easy to sing with. He shares the spotlight, instead of stealing it.

I relax, and the notes come easily. The song evens out, and I . . . enjoy it.

Our final, harmonic note rings out across the stage, soft but heartfelt, and the music fades. Applause rises from the audience, and it's much louder than the clapping for Kylie.

Startled by this reminder that, as the song says, I am not alone, I forget to dedicate my performance. Instead, I hand Ben my microphone and run from the stage, down the steps into the auditorium.

"Thank— Well, she's already gone," Ms. Bond says, and people laugh. My face is *flaming*.

I'm standing in the far-right aisle, trying to catch my breath. Behind me, a familiar voice speaks, and I turn to see Josh Kang, the singer and guitarist in Gabe's band, standing onstage in the spotlight. Another boy walks in from the wings, holding a microphone.

I turn again, intending to make my way to the last row and watch from the shadows, but I stop when I see Emery standing at the back of the theater. Glaring at me.

Josh and the other boy say their names, and as the intro to "Agony" begins—as my sister projects absolute, soul-shredding rage at me from across the theater—I realize that Emery's extracurricular activity was an audition for *Into the Woods*. And that just as with her bed, her room, her family, and—evidently—her entire existence, I've now intruded on another aspect of her life.

I've taken something else that belonged to her.

—∞—

Emery doesn't speak to me on the way home. She doesn't speak to Gabe either, even when he realizes something is wrong and asks what happened. She just stares out the passenger's side window. I take my cue from her and stare out my own back seat window.

Gabe declares that the advantage to his sisters both playing the silent game is that we can't complain about his music. So I wind up sitting through a ten-minute survey course in French rap artists.

I didn't get to see Emery's audition; I guess she went on before I got to the auditorium. And I have to admit, I'm curious. My dad told me about Gabe's band, but he didn't mention anything about Emery and musical theater. I have no idea whether or not she's any good. Or what role she auditioned for.

At dinner, Emery eats in silence as she picks red onion from her butternut squash, cranberry, and quinoa salad. There's nothing green in it, so I'm not sure how that's a salad, but whatever.

"How was school?" my dad asks. Cynthia has already heard all about how I betrayed Emery by trying to steal her part in the school musical—turns out, she also auditioned for Cinderella—but my father has no idea he's just marched right into a conversational minefield.

His gaze flicks from face to face.

"I got a D on my history quiz," Gabriel says. "But it's okay, because according to Mr. Larimore, those who don't learn from history are doomed to repeat it." He shrugs. "So I'll just learn it all when the reboot kicks in."

Cynthia's sigh seems extra heavy.

Emery ignores Dad's question, and I shrug it off.

Cody launches into a story about some poor middle school kid who spilled oil on his crotch during a science experiment and had to field questions all day long about whether or not he'd peed in his pants. Because unlike water, the oil wouldn't just dry.

When Cody finally digs into his salmon filet, my dad turns to me. "Michaela? How was your first day?"

"Fine," I say.

"That's it? Did you like the teachers? Make any friends? Did your schedule work out, or should I call and—"

"It was fine, Dad."

Emery hasn't mentioned the audition, so I'm certainly not going to bring it up.

"Did you get your parking pass?" my father asks, and I look up to see that Emery's glare has grown *fists*. She's punching me with her eyes right now, and I think she may be seconds away from lunging across the table to literally choke me.

Instead, she turns to her mother, her fork clutched so tightly it's cutting into her fingers. Her grip is all wrong. You can't eat with the fork held like that. All you can do is stab.

"She gets to keep that car?"

"Well, honey . . ." Cynthia shoots a helpless look at my dad. Cody's focus volleys around the table.

"Yes." My dad punctuates his statement with a big bite of fish so he can't be expected to elaborate.

*Coward.*

"Am *I* getting a car?"

"Not yet, honey. We still think you're too young, and too inexperienced a driver—"

"I'm older than she is!" Emery gestures with her fork, and several grains of quinoa fly across the table.

My dad sighs. "Yes, but Michaela has extenuating circumstances."

"*Bullshit!*" Emery roars. Then she blinks and deliberately sets her fork down. I can practically see her pressing the reset button; she knows exactly how to play her parents. "Sorry. But let's look at this logically, okay? Yes, Michaela's mother died, and that's objectively awful. I could not be more sorry. But that doesn't miraculously make her a better driver than I am. Or older than I am. There is no logical connection between her loss and getting to have a car, despite the rules you've both laid out for this entire household."

I have to admit, I'm impressed. She reminds me of Georgia as she makes her case. But I don't care about her logic.

"I'm keeping the car. It's mine. I inherited it from my *dead mother*. And if *it* goes, *I* go."

Everyone stares at me.

"Mom?" Emery demands.

Cynthia sighs. "Em—"

"So you're going to pick her over me? Over your *own* daughter?" Emery throws her napkin on the table and storms out of the room.

"Jesus Christ," my dad groans as he stands.

"Just leave her alone." Cynthia refills her water glass from a pitcher next to the garlic braids. "She'll calm down."

My dad sets his napkin next to his plate and leaves the table, headed for his bedroom. Gabriel watches him go. "More for the rest of us," he declares, scooping Dad's uneaten quinoa onto his own plate.

Cody, eyes wide, shovels another bite of salmon into his mouth and gives me a hesitant smile.

Beneath the table, I slide my hand into my pocket and curl my fingers around my car keys. Just to make sure they're still there.

## eleven

So, Cinderella, will we be seeing you at the festival tonight?"

I spin away from my locker, my heart pounding. I know that voice, but I can't make myself truly believe it until I see Ben, the boy I sang a duet with yesterday, standing behind me in the hallway. First period doesn't start for ten more minutes. I can't remember where my first class is, or where I parked my car.

I have no idea how he found me. Or why. But so far, my second day of school is already *infinitely* better than the first was.

"The festival is callbacks, of course," he says. "And they're at three fifteen, not actually tonight. But I'm sticking with the metaphor. The theme works."

"The theme?" I turn back to my locker and grab my English text.

"You, as Cinderella. Showing up out of nowhere at the festival."

"You mean the audition?"

"That's what I said. The festival." He leans closer, grinning, and whispers, "I'm really into this metaphor." Then he steps back, still smiling, as if he can't hear my pulse racing. "Seriously, after you ran out of the theater, I checked the steps to see if you'd left behind a golden slipper. It was *quite* the dramatic exit. In character from start to finish." His brows rise. "Impressive."

"You think I did that on purpose?" That I fled the stage, like Cinderella fleeing the festival from the musical, as part of my audition.

Okay, now his metaphor makes sense.

"Well, you did appear out of nowhere—"

"*You* dragged me into that audition."

"—and you left without telling anyone who you are."

"I literally said my full name, right there onstage."

He grins. "Michaela Rutherford. Do you know how hard it was to track down your locker number? Fortunately, Tate, one of our ASMs, is an office aide."

"ASM?" I ask as a herd of basketball players migrates from one end of the hall to the other, in matching purple-and-silver letter jackets.

"Assistant stage manager. You probably saw Tate backstage, holding a clipboard."

"You got my locker number from one of the stage managers on a production I had no intention of auditioning for eighteen hours ago?"

"*Assistant* stage manager. And yes. But she drew the line at giving me your phone number, so if you're feeling generous . . ."

He holds out his own phone. I'm supposed to take it and add my number to his contacts.

Instead, I close my locker and turn to fully face him. "What's the deal with callbacks?"

"You're reading for Cinderella, which means you're going to get another chance to disappear on me. And if you're not going to give me your number"—he pockets his phone—"then I hope you actually leave a slipper behind this time so I'll have some way to track you down again."

I laugh. "I think the metaphor is played out."

"Yeah." His grin widens, flashing those dimples at me. "But it was cute while it lasted, right?"

West Bradford is twice the size of my old school, and I don't know a single person here, except for Gabriel and Emery. I have no idea where Gabe is, and Emery wouldn't throw me a rope if a portal to hell opened up beneath my feet, so yes, having a gorgeous boy track me down like the prince searching for Cinderella? Beyond adorable. But I'm not going to tell him that. Nor am I going to tell him how nice it is not to be standing here alone, in a packed hallway full of strange faces.

"So, wait, I got a callback? Like, a second audition?"

Ben rolls those golden-brown eyes at me. "Right. Like you didn't know." Then he frowns. His gaze narrows on me. "You *didn't* know. Why didn't you check the call sheet?"

"The call sheet?"

"On the bulletin board, outside the theater. Ms. Bond posted callbacks at seven this morning."

"Why would anyone come to school at seven in the morning?" That's a full hour before class starts.

"To check the call sheet. There were half a dozen of us there before she pulled into the parking lot."

Well, that explains why Emery's friend Mara picked her up before I'd even finished putting on my makeup.

"Wow. You guys really take this seriously." I turn in the direction that I hope leads to my first-period class, and to my surprise, he falls into step beside me.

"Theater's kind of a big deal here." Ben shrugs. "I mean, it's not football, but our football team kind of sucks. Our theater department, though . . ."

"They always take first place at the state championship?"

"Yeah. We do," he says, steering into the skid of my joke. "State musical theater champs, five years running." He throws one fist in the air. "Go Dawgs!"

My new school mascot is the bulldog. Or, in local vernacular, the Dawgs.

"Seriously, though, West Bradford has the best theater department in the state. We've won awards. So, a callback is a very big deal, especially for a show like *Into the Woods*, where there's no chorus. Only featured roles."

"Because fewer kids will be onstage?"

"And because they'll all have lines." Ben stops and pulls his phone from his pocket to glance at the time. "Where are you headed?"

"English."

"Oh, good. I have Spanish, and it's in the same hall.

Anyway . . ." He starts walking again, and I try to pay attention to what he's saying, instead of staring at the curl falling over his forehead. "The cast will be twenty people or so, depending on how many roles Ms. Bond doubles up."

"Doubles up?"

"Yeah. Sometimes the same actress who plays Cinderella's mother also plays the Giant's Wife, because they're smaller roles, and those characters never appear onstage at the same time. Anyway, we only need around twenty cast members, but *eighty-four* people auditioned yesterday. Forty got callbacks. And you're one of them."

I'm one of them. I sang well enough to be called back to read lines. For Cinderella—one of the lead roles.

"So, if you haven't already grabbed a side, we should—"

"A side?"

"A printout of your lines, for the callback." He tilts his head to the right, and that doubles his cute quotient. "I have no idea why they're called that. You don't have to memorize them or anything, but you should at least know what they are so you can decide how to play the role."

How to play the—

Suddenly this all hits me, and my pulse feels like bass pounding through the speakers at a dance club. I don't *really* want to be in the musical.

Do I?

"Okay, wait." I stop walking, and Ben stops beside me. "I appreciate the heads-up, but I'm not doing callbacks. I wasn't even really auditioning. I just wanted to sing the song."

For a second, he looks thoroughly confused. Then he grins. "Okay, Cinderella. Just come to the festival for one more night. If you don't like what you see, you don't have to dance."

Dance, in this resurrected metaphor, obviously means "read lines."

"But if you do decide to join us, you'll be dancing with me. Cinderella's sides are from act two, scene two, where the Baker finds her alone at her mother's grave. And I'm reading for the Baker, so . . ."

"So, we'll be doing a scene together?"

"You and me, and everyone else who got a callback for Cinderella and the Baker. Here." He swings his backpack from his shoulder and digs inside it, then pulls out a sheet of paper. "I already have it memorized, so take mine. Just read through it before you decide not to show up. Picture yourself in the role, playing Cinderella, with me as the Baker. Because I *will* be the Baker."

"You seem pretty sure of that."

He shrugs. "This is my year. Ask anyone." He hands me the sheet of paper, and I take it. Then Ben backs away from me, down the hall, grinning as he swings his backpack onto his shoulder. "See you at the festival . . ."

---

I have trouble concentrating in English, but that's mostly because I'm paying absolutely no attention. By the time the bell rings, I've read through the "sides" at least twenty times.

Cinderella only has a few lines, and they were easy to memorize, considering that I've seen the play at least a dozen times.

But I'm not going to audition. I can't be in a musical. I can't stand onstage and sing and dance in front of hundreds of people.

Which is why I have no idea how I wind up in the lobby outside the theater, at 11:35 a.m., when I'm supposed to be standing in line in the cafeteria for a soy-based cheeseburger and a whole wheat bun. I guess I just need to see it for myself.

Sure enough, there's my name on a list of callbacks pinned to the corkboard. Just like Ben said. What he didn't mention, probably because he had no idea I would care, is that Emery is one of the other actresses called back for the role of Cinderella.

Ben also didn't say that I've been called back not just for the role of Cinderella, but for the Baker's Wife and for Little Red Riding Hood as well. That's three of the four female lead roles.

"Why am I the only person who's been called to read for three roles?" I mumble.

"It's because she doesn't know you."

Startled, I spin around to find Josh Kang standing on my right. The theater door swings shut behind him with a soft thud.

"I'm sorry, what?"

He glances at the call sheet. "Ms. Bond probably called you for three roles because you're new, and she doesn't know yet where you'll fit best," he says. "But she knows from your audition that your voice could carry any of the female lead roles."

"Except the Witch." But when I glance at the sheet again, I realize that no one got a callback for the role of the Witch.

"Oh, I think you could play the Witch," Josh says, and I realize he's holding a couple of pages with lines printed on them. Sides, for his own callbacks. "But the Witch has already been cast."

I study the sheet again. "Where does it say that?"

"It doesn't. But Kat Torrez is the Witch."

"How do you know?"

"I know because she's Kat Torrez. And because I saw her audition." He shrugs. "She does community theater in Tulsa, and she's basically West Bradford theater royalty."

"Okaaayy."

"You'll understand when you meet her."

I have my doubts. But then, I'm new to theater. I'm not even sure I want to *be* in theater.

I glance at the call sheet again and see that Josh is reading for both the Narrator and for Cinderella's Prince. "I heard you sing yesterday," I tell him. "I thought you'd be up for the Baker."

"Um, no. Ben McGrath will be the Baker. And Jon Escobedo will be Jack. Technically, they're both being considered for both roles, but Ben will be the Baker. I'd bet my brand-new amp on it."

"So, the results are basically already presumed?"

"No, but there are only so many possibilities for the principal roles, and most of us have been doing theater here for years, so we're familiar with each other's ranges and abilities. But the freshmen are always wild cards. As are you."

I'm a wild card. I have no idea whether or not I should be happy about that.

"Did you come for your sides? They're on a table right inside." He turns to point at the theater doors.

"I . . ." Really, I'm not sure why I'm here. Or whether or not I'm coming to the callback. But I guess I should be prepared, just in case. "Thanks."

"No problem. See you this afternoon."

"Yeah." Maybe.

Josh heads down the hall, and I go into the theater. The massive space is empty, but the stage lights are on. There's a table to the left of the entrance, under the gallery and behind all of the floor seats, and on it are several very small stacks of paper. Evidently I'm one of the last to pick up her sides.

I find the lines for the Baker's Wife and Little Red Riding Hood, and instead of heading to the cafeteria, I grab a soda and a bag of chips. I eat in my car while I read through the lines.

I'm not going to audition.

But . . . the applause *did* feel good. For just a moment, as the last notes of the music faded, the applause felt . . . warm. Pleasant and approving.

I've felt out of place and alone in the week since my mom died, but in that moment, before I freaked out and fled from the stage, I felt like I belonged. Like I'd done something right.

But I forgot to dedicate the song to her.

What if I actually *do* get a part? I could dedicate my entire performance to her.

Or I could freak out onstage again and humiliate both myself and the rest of the cast. Why take the chance? I'm not going to audition.

I'm really, really not.

———oⱭⱭo———

At ten minutes after three, I find myself around the corner from the auditorium, leaning with my back against the wall where the audition poster still hangs. People pass me, headed for the theater. Some of the faces are familiar, but I can't put names to them. I don't know whether or not they're my competition. Whether they would root for me or against me.

"Have you decided?" Ben says, and I look up to see him leaning against the wall across the hall. His arms are crossed over his chest, and he's holding nothing—no backpack, no sides, no phone.

"I . . ."

"It's not as scary as it seems." He shrugs. "You made it through the hard part already."

"I'm not *scared*," I insist. But of course I'm scared.

"Well then, what do you have to lose?"

Nothing. The answer is absolutely nothing. I've already lost everything I ever had, and Emery isn't going to like me even if I don't audition, so really, what's stopping me?

"I'm not going to read for Red Riding Hood. Three is too many."

He shrugs. "So just don't go up on stage when they call for that one."

I push off from the wall, and Ben gives me a big, dimple-framed smile. He rounds the corner with me, and we're the last ones to step into the theater.

"This way," he whispers, because Ms. Bond is already onstage about to speak. I follow him down the left-hand aisle, toward two seats in the second row, which are inexplicably empty. He plucks his bag from one and his jacket from the other, and I realize he's saved them for us. I sink into the aisle seat, pretending I don't feel the stares aimed my way.

Ben is an entrenched member of the theater department, and I am a stranger in a strange land. But his people could be my people too. Instant friends—if I don't blow the callback.

"Okay, everybody find a seat!" Ms. Bond projects from the stage without a microphone. She doesn't need one. She's in her midforties, dressed comfortably in jeans and an oversized black tee that reads, "Stage Right," with an arrow pointing to the left, and "Stage Left," with an arrow pointing to the right. Her long, silvering hair is pulled back into a loose ponytail. Her earrings appear to be red rectangles, dangling nearly to her chin.

Behind her, a semicircle of stackable classroom chairs has been set up across the brightly lit stage.

Ms. Bond holds up a spiral-bound notebook. On the cover, "Into the Woods" is printed above a familiar silhouette of a tree. "As you already know, after three years of lobbying from my theater arts, drama, makeup lab, and stagecraft students, as well as cast members of previous years' productions, I have finally decided that our program is strong enough to tackle *Into the Woods*."

Cheers and applause erupt from the students around me.

"This is a nine-week production, which means opening night is not quite two months from now: on March 25. And this production is a *beast*," Ms. Bond says, to even more applause. "The music is challenging and interesting. The set design will be . . . fun." She glances offstage, and someone laughs from the wings. "And as you might have guessed, that's already underway. There's no chorus in *Into the Woods*, so if you get a part, you will be speaking and singing. The only exceptions are the Giant and Milky White, the cow, both of whom will be speaking—or mooing—from offstage. We don't have a choreographer this year, because there's very little dancing in *Into the Woods*—"

Someone cheers from the rows behind me.

"—which cuts a full week from our typical rehearsal schedule. But the cast will be working with Mr. Rayburn, West Bradford's choir teacher, who is also the musical director for the production, on your vibrato, sustained notes, and projection. And . . . there will be some kissing."

Several more people cheer.

I pick at a hangnail until it starts to bleed. Cinderella doesn't kiss anyone onstage, but what if I get cast as the Baker's Wife?

"Okay. Let's get started! As you can see, I am standing on what's called the apron." Ms. Bond gestures to the floor beneath her feet—the curved center section, right at the front. "And behind me, arcing from stage left"—she gestures to the right—"to stage right"—she gestures to the left—"are twelve chairs.

When I announce the part you've been called to read for, please come up onstage and take a seat. It does not matter where you sit—"

A hand goes up from the row in front of me. "Can we sit on the floor?"

"Shut up, Link!" Someone shouts from my right.

"No, Lincoln, you may not sit on the floor," Ms. Bond amends. "It does not matter which chair you choose, but you must sit in one of the chairs." The raised hand drops, and Link and his friends laugh. "And you must stop wasting my time with inane questions. Are we clear?"

Heads bob all across the auditorium.

My palms begin to sweat.

"Once you are on the stage, I will call people forward in various pairings and ask you to read lines together. My goal is to see if you can act, and to assess your chemistry with the other people up for a variety of other roles."

Several people hoot and cheer, and Ms. Bond rolls her eyes.

"Okay, let's have everyone who received a callback for the Wolf and Little Red Riding Hood."

It's a small group, made even smaller by my absence, though no one comments on that. Two girls and two boys make their way onstage, and I watch, fascinated, as Ms. Bond takes a seat on the floor, cross-legged, with her back to the audience—the "house"—and pairs the potential cast members.

It doesn't take long. My favorite pairing is Link as the Wolf and a girl named Lexie as Little Red Riding Hood.

Ms. Bond releases the Wolves and Reds, and she calls up everyone reading for the Baker, the Baker's Wife, and Cinderella's Prince.

Ben and I stand. Josh Kang is right behind us, and when I turn, he gives me a reassuring smile. I climb the stairs and realize that Lexie is still onstage, waiting to read for the Baker's Wife. She's my competition.

Ms. Bond pairs Lexie with Josh as Cinderella's Prince. Then she pairs Lexie with Ben, as husband and wife. Then she calls Josh and me to read the scene where Cinderella's Prince finds the Baker's Wife alone in the woods. It's the scene that reveals the Prince as a playboy and shows that the Baker's Wife isn't entirely satisfied with her life either.

It's the cheating scene.

I can't help thinking about my parents, and I don't want to do this scene. That comes across in my performance, and I hope I haven't cost Josh his role.

I take my seat with my face flaming, and Ms. Bond doesn't call me up for any other pairings.

When she dismisses Cinderella's Prince and the Baker's Wife, I stand, ready to escape not just the stage, but the entire theater as well. I'm not cut out for this. Today, the spotlight feels like the blistering desert sun, blinding me. Scorching me. My tongue is so thick and dry it seems to take up my entire mouth.

But before I can make it down the stairs, she calls Cinderella and Little Red Riding Hood to join the Bakers already on the stage. Reluctantly, I take my seat again, and Ben smiles from the chair next to mine. "Just look at me," he whispers. "This is my year, but it can be your year too. *Our* year."

His dimples flash at me. He seems to see straight through to my soul.

I don't get a chance to see who else has joined us onstage, because Ms. Bond calls Ben and me first. I stand, clutching my sides, but I don't need the pages. I can be Cinderella at her mother's grave—I understand far too well how she would feel.

I can talk to the man who wants to comfort her and warn her of impending danger. I'm starting to understand that part too.

Ben and I play our parts, and it's like they were written for us. He kneels when he discovers that I'm a princess, and the awe on his face is astonishing. His sudden stunned shyness hints at a respectful attraction. At the connection that will allow Cinderella and the Baker to wind up together, after her prince has cheated on her twice. After his wife has died.

At the end of the short scene, Ben, as the Baker, insists that I come with him and be safe. He gives me his hand, and I let him lead me offstage, and in the wings—in this brief moment, in the dark—he squeezes my hand.

"That was great," he whispers, and I'm still smiling as we walk back to our seats.

Until I see that Emery is the other girl called up to play Cinderella, and as I've come to expect, she is glaring at me with enough fire to incinerate planet Earth.

Ms. Bond calls Emery with Jon, the other guy reading as the Baker. Then she calls me with Jon, but she doesn't call Emery with Ben.

Even though I didn't come up to read as Red earlier, Ms. Bond asks me to take that part with Emery as Cinderella, in the scene where she's comforting Red over the loss of her mother and grandmother. And, in the grand tradition of art imitating life, it's a *total* disaster. Emery's Cinderella seems almost comically incapable of empathy for Red, and I'm so tense, standing onstage with her, that I bumble my lines, even with them right in front of me.

But finally, I am done. Ben and I take our seats, while Emery reads as one of the stepsisters. I watch the rest of the callbacks, relieved to be sitting in the shadows once again.

"Thank you all for your hard work this afternoon!" Ms. Bond calls, when all the pairings are finished. "Mr. Rayburn and I are going to put our heads together over the next couple of hours and decide on the casting that makes the most sense for this particular production of this particular musical. I want you all to know that everyone who took the stage today is very talented and could without a doubt carry any of the roles you read for. That's why you got a callback. But casting isn't just about talent, or about any particular performance. It's also about onstage chemistry. It isn't enough to sing Red's part well, and to memorize her lines. Our Red Riding Hood has to have chemistry with her Wolf. They have to work well onstage together, to make the audience *believe* he wants to *devour* her. To make them *believe* she's as fascinated by him as she is scared of him—that those two awakenings go hand in hand. So what I'm saying is that if you don't get the part you want, it isn't because you aren't good enough. It's because I thought you would be stronger in a different role, with a different grouping of actors. Understood?"

Heads nod all around me, but there is no cheering. The fun part is over, at least for the moment.

"Okay, that's it!" Ms. Bond tucks her notebook beneath her arm. "The cast list will be posted tonight at nine p.m., out there on the call board, as well as online. If you want a link as soon as it's posted, text 4653 to the number written at the bottom of each of the sides, to sign up for the theater department's Remind group text system."

With that, auditions are over.

# twelve

I hang around after callbacks, chatting with Ben, intending to offer Emery a ride home. I know she's mad, but we still live in the same house. But she won't look at me. Not even to glare. She just marches out of the theater with Mara, her blond friend from our history class, who read for both stepsister parts.

At home, Emery ignores me from the moment I walk through the door. She doesn't mention callbacks, so I don't either, and while it's clear that my dad has no idea they even happened, Cynthia is so on edge at dinner that I suspect her daughter gave her an earful the second she got home.

Gabriel talks about his band's new song, and Cody launches into an argument that video games are actually good for a "growing boy's" attention span. Emery glares at her dinner.

I glance at my phone beneath the table, checking the time. Seven forty-five. Still an hour and a quarter to go.

My nerves are out of control. I feel like I'm going to throw up.

I almost hope I don't get a role; at least then, this would be over. Emery might even stop hating me. And when the nerves fade, I may actually be able to eat.

But if my name is on the cast list, Emery might turn our bedroom—or this entire house—into a permanent war zone.

———❀———

"Oooh, that one." Grammie points at the screen, but I can't tell what her finger is aimed at. *"12 Angry Men."*

"Oh! Okay." I use the controller to select the icon. "We read the play in school last year, but I've never seen the movie."

I'm excused from the paper due in English, because I wasn't here to read the series of poems being analyzed, and I've already done the chemistry vocab sheet and a handful of the problems from my Algebra II class, so I have time to watch it with her. I pull my usual chair up next to her bed and set my Ramune soda on her rolling tray table.

The movie is pretty good, for an old film, but there isn't a woman in the entire thing. The same was true of the play, but I'm not sure I understand why. Were women not allowed on juries back then?

"Stepsister!" Emery cries from down the hall. "I'm a stepsister!"

Grammie pauses the movie, and my heart begins to pound so hard I can actually hear it. The results have been posted. I got into the movie and completely forgot to check the time, but Emery signed up for the text alerts.

She's crying now, and Cynthia is comforting her in a low-pitched, calm voice, as if Emery just found out she has six weeks to live. Her tears feel totally over the top. She got a part. She's going to be in the musical.

"What's going on?" Grammie asks as I pull my phone from my pocket.

"They posted the results of the audition. For the school musical," I add, when she looks confused. I open my browser and reload the screen, and there's the list.

It doesn't take me long to find my name. It's the fifth one down.

### Cinderella: Michaela Rutherford

My hand flies to my mouth to cover my smile. I feel guilty about being happy.

But there's more, and now I understand why Emery is so upset. It isn't just that she didn't get a principal role. It isn't just that I did. In addition to her role as Lucinda, Cinderella's stepsister, Emery has been cast as my understudy.

*Shit.*

I would have been disappointed, in the end, not to get a role, but I would have gotten over it, because I didn't have my heart set on being in the musical. But Emery evidently did. And if she was their second choice as Cinderella, she's *really* going to see this as me stealing her part now.

That was not my intent.

"Emery?" Grammie says as I stand. But she's looking at me, and she seems confused.

"No, I'm sorry. I'm Michaela. I have to go, but you enjoy the movie, okay?" I press Play on the remote, then hand it back to her.

"Hey! It's a good role!" Cynthia is practically pleading with her daughter now, from the archway leading to the living room, and they turn when I step into the hall.

"I guess you saw," Emery snaps. "You got the role, and I'm your understudy."

*The* role. As if I aimed for that one on purpose, just to keep her from being Cinderella.

"When I sang yesterday, I didn't even know you were auditioning. And today, I read for three different roles." I'm talking to Cynthia now, because she looks like maybe she believes Emery. That I intentionally took something from her daughter. "It's not like I got to pick my own part. Ms. Bond put people in the roles she wanted them for. I didn't mean for . . . I mean, this wasn't, like, premeditated. I didn't even know about the audition until after school yesterday. I just . . ." I shrug. "I just saw the poster, and the next thing I know, I'm onstage." I have no idea what to do with my hands. I can't remember how normal people stand. "I just wanted to sing."

"I've been practicing for *weeks*, and she just waltzes onstage and steals my role. As if it were nothing!" Emery throws her arms into the air. "And now she has my part, opposite Ben, and I'm her *stepsister*! What is it they say about art imitating life?"

I consider pointing out that she and I are half sisters, not stepsisters, but this doesn't seem to be the time.

"Ben's in the musical?" Cynthia says. But she doesn't really sound surprised.

"He's the Baker!" Emery groans, tears standing in her eyes.

He is?

I lift my phone again, and sure enough, there's his name, right below mine. I hadn't even noticed.

It *is* his year. And that means we'll reprise our duet, and I can't help being excited about that. He has a beautiful voice, and if he hadn't suggested I audition—if he hadn't sung with me—I probably never would have had the nerve to belt out even one note.

"Well, honey, maybe that's a blessing," Cynthia says.

"It's not. It's a humiliation. All my friends know I wanted that part. Ms. Bond knew. I told her Cinderella was my dream role, and . . ." She trails off, glaring at me again.

"I'm sorry, Emery. Really. I wasn't trying to take anything from you. I didn't know you were auditioning, and I wasn't even trying to get a part, at first. I just wanted to sing the song, because it's one of my mom's favorites."

She rolls her eyes, as if I've played the "dead mother" card one too many times. As if I only use it to get away with ruining her life. But then she frowns. Her gaze narrows on me. "So quit."

"What?" I'm frowning now.

"If you don't want the part, quit. The role will default to me as your understudy, and they'll cast a new stepsister."

"I . . ." I could do that.

But I don't want to.

Cynthia stares at me, waiting for my answer. Emery looks almost hopeful, and I get the sudden impression that if I agree, she will smile. She will race down the hall and pull me into a hug and declare to the world that I am her best friend. We can be real sisters and share our room in peace.

If I just give up this thing I earned, fair and square. This thing I now know that I want. This chance to be a part of something, and make friends of my own, and dedicate my performance in my mother's favorite musical to her.

This chance to hear applause and know that it is meant for me.

So, in what is perhaps the most selfish moment of my life, I say, "No."

Cynthia presses her lips together, but she doesn't argue.

"Why not?" Emery demands. "You said you didn't even want the role."

"I didn't. But now I do."

"Now that you know I want it, too? See?" She turns to her mother, fists clenched. Eyes blazing with fury. "She's doing this out of *spite*."

"No, this has nothing to do with you," I insist. "I—"

"What's going on?" My dad appears in the doorway behind them, and Cody finally sticks his head out of his room, where Cynthia has banished him until his homework is finished.

"They posted the cast list, and Michaela got my part," Emery snaps.

"Michaela auditioned for the musical?" He turns to me, surprised.

"Yes, she just randomly walked onstage and got the role I wanted. She just admitted she doesn't even want to be in the musical, but she won't give up the part, even though she doesn't want it, and as her understudy, I'd go on in her place, because she's a stone-cold—"

"I do want the part," I tell them, and suddenly the hallway feels too crowded. And it is *not* a friendly crowd. "I didn't want it when I stepped onstage, but then I sang, and it felt good. And there was applause, and that felt good too. So I do want the part. And I *earned* it."

My dad turns to Emery. "Well, it sounds like that clears things up. She's not trying to be mean. She actually wants the role."

"You always take her side!" Emery spins and marches past me into our room.

"There are no sides!" my father shouts after her. "I'm not in charge of the goddamn casting!"

"Oscar!" Cynthia snaps. Then she follows Emery into the bedroom, where we can hear her assuring my half sister that her weeks of hard work have paid off, and that one role will look just as good on her college applications as any other role. The important thing is that she'll be *in* the musical.

"What really happened?" my dad asks as he follows me through the living room and into the kitchen.

"Exactly what I *said* happened." I grab a Dr Pepper from the beverage fridge and twist it open. "I saw the poster for the audition, so I got up onstage and sang. It was supposed to be a tribute to my mom. *Into the Woods* is—was—one of her favorite musicals, and we've watched it a million times. So I sang for her. And it felt good." I sip from the bottle, coughing when the bubbles go up my nose. "And I got the part." I rub my nose, trying to ease the burn. "I didn't do it to be mean. I didn't even know Emery was auditioning. I'm not trying to ruin her life, Dad."

"I know." He sighs and sinks onto one of the barstools behind the breakfast bar. "She'll see that too, eventually."

But I have my doubts. I'm perfectly capable of seeing this from her perspective, and I admit, it doesn't look good. She probably *does* think I'm out to get her.

"Don't worry." He pats my back as he stands to head into his room. "She'll calm down."

I take my drink outside and sink into one of the chairs clustered around an outdoor fireplace. It isn't lit, but that's fine. Out here, it's cold but quiet, so I pull up the cast list on my phone again. And I decide it's okay to feel happy about my role.

Alone, in the cold, where no one else can see.

I glance over the list of names, and I don't expect them to mean anything, because I didn't really make any friends today, except for Ben, maybe. But I also recognize the name of the girl cast as Rapunzel, because she sits next to me in chemistry. And . . .

Josh Kang is Cinderella's Prince! That's two people I know among the cast. Two people I *kind of* know. And a girl whose name I recognize. I feel like that's a pretty good start, considering I've only been at West Bradford for two days.

Maybe, despite Emery's resentment, the musical will be awesome.

Maybe living here won't suck.

I text Georgia an exclamation-point-riddled message telling her my good news, and then I lean forward and stare at the fireplace, trying to figure out how to light it. And whether or not we have marshmallows.

"Congratulations."

I jump, startled half out of my own body for a moment, until I realize that Gabriel is sitting across the patio in another chair. In the dark.

"On the role," he adds, when I can only stare at him.

"Thanks. What are you doing out here, all alone?"

"Not a thing." But he's holding something, and as I watch, he lifts it toward his mouth and inhales. It isn't a cigarette. There's no glowing tip. He's vaping.

"How'd you know about the part? I guess you heard Emery yelling . . . ?" I add with a glance behind me, at the house.

"No, Josh sent me a screenshot of the cast list. He's one of the princes."

"Yeah, I saw."

"So, Em's upset?"

"'Upset' seems like an understatement. Your mom's trying to calm her down."

"Yeah." He inhales again. "That's sort of a recurring theme around here." It's weird to hear him like this. Usually, Gabriel is more . . . spirited. Relentlessly sanguine, actually. "She's got her work cut out for her this time, though."

"Let me guess. Emery wants to be on Broadway."

"No." He shrugs. "Well, maybe. But I think this is more personal for her than truly aspirational."

"Because *I* got the role she wanted? You think she wouldn't be this upset if it had gone to someone else?"

He thinks about that for a second, the vape pen bouncing in his grip. "I don't think this is about you. Not entirely. Josh said you auditioned with Ben McGrath?"

"Yeah. So?"

Gabriel leans forward in his chair, and light falls over him from the dining room window. His eyes look glazed. I don't think he's smoking nicotine. "Did I tell you that Em and her boyfriend just broke up? Like, two weeks ago?"

Oh my God. "Don't say it."

But he says it anyway. "She and Ben McGrath spent all of Christmas break practicing for that audition, with him as the Baker and her as Cinderella. And now he's singing that duet with you, in the play she wanted to star in."

I get it now. "I drove in her lane."

Gabriel snorts. "You parked your car—another sore point— across both lanes and basically set up a roadblock. Like, with flares, and traffic barriers, and those strips of metal that puncture tires."

"Okay, but I didn't mean to do any of that."

"I know."

"So, what's the upside?"

"The upside?"

"Yeah. You're supposed to tell me that everything may seem like it sucks right now, but it'll be okay, because history will repeat itself, or airport security will be an adventure, or something. What's the perspective that makes all this okay?"

Gabe gives me a look I can't quite interpret, with his face half shrouded by shadows. Then he takes a long hit. "I don't know," he finally says. "I guess sometimes things just suck."

# thirteen

Hey," Ben says, and I swallow my surprise as he slides into the space behind me in the fish stick line. His eyes are *so* bright. "You have to sit with us so I can make introductions."

"Yeah. Okay." Do I sound too eager?

Today has not gone as I'd hoped. An instant cluster of theater friends failed to materialize during my morning classes, mostly because there aren't many theater kids *in* my morning classes. Though the girl who was cast as Rapunzel did smile at me in chemistry.

I spent the period before lunch in AP History, where Emery and her friend Mara ignored me for fifty straight minutes. *I am not her problem. I'm not *actually* a roadblock. But she's not ready to see that.

When we've paid for our lunches, Ben leads me to a round table in one corner, where there are two empty chairs. I think they've been saved for us. "Guys, this is Michaela Rutherford, who snagged the part of Cinderella on her second day at West Bradford."

"Yeah. I have a question about that," I say as I set my tray down. "Why is this place called West Bradford, if there's no East Bradford?"

"There used to be a Bradford High, and a West Bradford High," the girl to my left says. She's the girl from chemistry. Bella something. "But due to 'fiscal concerns,' they consolidated the schools into one campus, back when my mom was a kid. And since this was the newest one"—she throws one arm out to gesture at the entire school—"everyone now goes to West Bradford."

There don't seem to be many fiscal concerns here. Which explains her air quotes, I guess.

"That's why there are two main buildings," Ben adds. "The math, science, and history classes are all in the original one, and English, foreign languages, art, and music are in the new building, with the big gym and the theater connecting them."

The little gym sticks off the edge of the complex like a broken thumb.

"That would have been helpful to know on Monday," I say as I tear open a ketchup packet.

"Looks like you found your way around pretty well," the girl across the table says. She has dark hair and eyes, and pale brown skin. "You made it to the audition just in time."

"Well, that was thanks to Ben. I'm hoping he's about to introduce you all . . ."

"Oh!" Ben picks up a fish stick and gestures with it. "This is Lexie Zahir, who's playing the Baker's Wife." He points to the girl across the table, who does a mock bow, as if she's already taking a curtain call.

I remember her from callbacks. I liked her for Little Red Riding Hood until I saw her read for the Baker's Wife.

"And on your left is Bella Moretti, our Rapunzel."

"Hey," Bella says. "You're in my chemistry class."

"Of course." In fact, I sit right next to her.

Ben points to the guy on his right, seated between himself and Lexie. "This is Cole Houser."

"Are you in the musical?" I ask him as I dip a fry in my ketchup. He doesn't look familiar.

"Behind the scenes." He rubs the back of his hand across his nose to scratch an itch. "I'm A-1."

"As in . . . steak sauce?"

He laughs. "Audio one. I'm in charge of sound engineering."

"So, the music?"

"No, microphones and stuff like that."

Lexie snatches a fry from his tray. "In a couple of months, Cole will be at work under your shirt, with a strip of skin tape."

I glance from her to him. "Wait, what?"

"It's called mic tape," Cole clarifies. "The battery pack for your microphone goes under your shirt. In the back. And the mic goes here." He touches the center of his own hairline, at the top of his forehead. "The wire runs under your wig." He shrugs. "My job includes miking the cast. The pit orchestra will be playing the music live."

"Just like a real production!" Somehow, that makes me even more nervous.

Cole laughs again. "Yes. And if I do say so myself, we put on a pretty good show. We got an upgrade to our sound system last year, and we got new lights last fall, so—"

The boy to Bella's left clears his throat. "Sorry," he says when I turn, and I realize he's the only one who hasn't been introduced yet. Though I already know who he is, from the auditions. "But if you don't interrupt Cole, he'll go on about decibels, and frequencies, and echo quality all day long. I'm Jon Escobedo." He actually extends his hand for me to shake, over Bella's lunch tray. "I'm playing Jack."

I shake his hand. "So, this whole table is cast members?"

"And Cole," Ben says.

"And Cole," I repeat as Cole rolls his eyes.

"Yeah, but this is just a fraction of the cast." Lexie stabs a hunk of iceberg and a cube of tomato with her plastic fork. "Half of the theater kids are in second lunch, and at that table over there by the window, you have the Narrator, the Wolf, the Giant, and both stepsisters."

I follow her gaze to find Emery glaring at me from across the cafeteria, surrounded by friends, including Mara, who was cast as the other stepsister, and Link, who got the part as the Wolf.

"So," Bella says around the food she's chewing, holding one hand over her mouth. Then she swallows the bite. "Where did you come from?"

It takes me a second to realize she's not asking about my previous school.

"Yeah," Jon says, from her left. "You just appeared onstage out of nowhere, in a poof of smoke and a fanfare from a string quartet."

Lexie laughs. "Maybe she should be playing the Witch instead of Cinderella."

She clearly means that as a compliment.

"I don't remember any fanfare or smoke." I frown as I glance around the table. "Actually, I hardly even remember singing. I wouldn't have been there at all, if it weren't for Ben."

Ben shrugs. "I found her in the hall, staring at the poster, and I just sort of . . . pointed her in the right direction."

"He physically led me through the door and nudged me onto the stage. And he had no idea whether or not I could sing." I turn to him suddenly. "What if I'd totally sucked? You volunteered to sing with me before you had *any clue!*"

Another shrug, and this time he's smiling, dimples echoing his grin. "I had a feeling about you. And I wasn't wrong, was I?"

That seems to be the general consensus. And suddenly the cafeteria feels as warm and welcoming as the spotlight did. Though, as I chew my last fish stick, I swear I can feel a cold glare, centered right on the back of my head.

---

I'm a decent student, but I have trouble concentrating all afternoon, because all I can think about is rehearsal. The first one is this afternoon, the very day after the cast list was posted.

What if my audition was a fluke? What if I only sang well

because I was singing for my mother, and without that emotional mandate, I suddenly can't carry a tune?

What if I humiliate myself and lose every friend I've made today?

The official text reminder gave a classroom number, and when I find it, I see that someone has arranged the tables into the shape of a horseshoe. There are paper nameplates in front of every chair, but rather than the students' names, they're the names of the characters.

"Come in!" Ms. Bond calls, when I hesitate in the doorway. There are only two students in the room so far, standing next to a table where the scripts are stacked. I don't know either of them.

I've never formally met Ms. Bond either, but I saw plenty of her yesterday onstage.

"Michaela, right?" she says, and I nod. "Grab a book and find your seat. You're a little early, but everyone should be here soon."

I'm early because I wasn't sure how long it would take me to find the classroom, and I didn't want to show up late. But now I'm afraid that I look too eager.

The other two students take scripts—they're evidently called "books"—then they find their chairs. The girl turns out to be Sage, playing Cinderella's Stepmother, and the boy is Rapunzel's Prince. He's the guy who sang with Josh at the first-round audition.

I take a book and settle into my seat, in the middle of the

left-hand side of the squarish horseshoe. Between empty chairs assigned to Little Red Riding Hood and Cinderella's Prince.

This feels weird. I feel like everyone is staring at me, even if there's only two people, so far.

I open the script and begin to read through it. Other cast members start to filter in, and Ms. Bond tells them to take a book and find their seats. She walks around the inside of the horseshoe, setting pencils next to every nameplate.

"We're going to take notes," she explains. "But you should write your names on your books in ink."

I turn to pull a pen from the backpack leaning against the front leg of my chair, and I nearly collide with Josh Kang as he takes the seat on my right.

"Hey, Cinderella!" He smiles and sets his book on the table. "Do you have a pen?"

I don't have any classes with Josh, so I haven't seen him since my disastrous read for the Baker's Wife. I'm *so* glad that didn't cost him the part.

"Yeah. Just a sec." I find the pen stuck beneath my history text at the bottom of my backpack and hand it to him. "So, have you done this before?"

"Written my name?" He grins as he prints it at the top of his script. "A few times. I could also manage my phone number, if you—"

"Michaela!"

I spin around as Ben walks into the room, with Lexie Zahir and Cole Houser on his heels. "Hey."

"Hey." Ben grins at me as all three pick up books. "Glad to

see you found the room. Though I was prepared to head up a search party, if necessary."

"Fortunately, Cinderella made it to the festival on her own," I tell him with a smile.

He grins back. "That's *my* metaphor."

Josh sets my pen between us on the table and opens his book.

"Mr. Houser, the crew is meeting in the auditorium today, with stage management and with Mr. Lacey," Ms. Bond says from the whiteboard, where she seems to be listing a series of deadlines. Evidently we have three weeks to memorize our lines and be "off book." "Your books are set up in there."

Cole makes a show of dropping his script back on the stack. "Consider my course corrected!" Then he backs out of the doorway with more drama than I would have expected from someone who works behind the scenes. And bumps right into Emery.

"Oh, sorry, Em!" Cole says as he spins around, his face flaming. "Didn't see you there."

"Yeah, well, I'm invisible, in case you haven't heard." She glances at me over his shoulder. Then she frowns as she turns back to him. "I thought you were going to audition this year. You'd have been a great Jack."

"I'm totally not offended by that!" Jon Escobedo shouts from his chair across from me, behind the "Jack" nameplate.

"No offense!" Emery shouts back at him, and I realize that she knows most of the cast. My new friends are her old friends.

When they figure out she hates me, will they hate me too?

Cole runs one hand through the explosion of tight curls

spiraling from his scalp. "I was going to." He's speaking softly now, and I strain to hear him as I pretend to study my lines. "But . . ."

I look up to see him shrugging.

"Maybe next year," he finishes.

Emery's frown deepens. "You're a senior. There is no next year."

Cole lifts one brow at her. "They said the same thing in 1999 and in 2012, yet here we are."

Emery rolls her eyes.

"I meant next year, in college."

"Yeah. Sure," she says. But she obviously doesn't believe that. If he's scared to walk onstage in high school, that'll only get worse in college.

That might have been me, if Ben hadn't practically shoved me into the spotlight. It might *still* be me on opening night, if my nerves get the better of me.

"Welcome to week one of rehearsal!" Ms. Bond calls. "Everyone take a seat!"

Emery gives Cole a sympathetic pat on the shoulder, then comes into the classroom with Mara at her side. They grab scripts and settle into chairs across the room from me. Emery sits behind the "Lucinda" nameplate. Mara takes the chair next to her, behind the card labeled "Florinda." The other stepsister.

"We're going to start out today with a table read." Ms. Bond frowns. "Lincoln. Find your chair. Here's a hint: it's the only one left."

Link pushes off against the wall where he's leaning at the back of the room, and finally he sinks into the Wolf's chair, at the apex of the horseshoe. "Question: The Wolf is only in a couple of scenes. When I've said my lines, can I go?"

Storm clouds roll over Ms. Bond's eyes. "No, you may not. Today, everyone stays for the entire reading, in order to familiarize yourself with the script. Tomorrow, at your first music rehearsal, you will get copies of our production schedule, both in hard copy and via email, and it will tell you which groups I expect to call on any given day. We will rehearse four days a week, most weeks. You are expected to be here when your role is called—for the principal roles, that's most rehearsals—and when the schedule says 'company,' you will *all* be here.

"I do not want to waste your time. If you are not called, you do not have to be here. But the theater is a family, and those of you who would like to hang out when you aren't called may always help with sets and costumes backstage. Everyone will be expected to contribute a minimum of ten hours to that endeavor, over the next six weeks. Our ASMs will be monitoring the sign-ups. In case you're not sure who those are, both the cast and crew are listed in the back of your book. As is the official Remind text account. Please, if you have a phone, sign up for that. It's the easiest way to keep up with changes to the schedule."

I flip to the back of my script and glance at the crew list. It's *huge.*

What on earth is a "flyman"?

"I expect you to bring your book to every rehearsal, and

starting tomorrow, you will also bring pencils and highlighters so you can take notes on the pages. I hope to be off book by the end of week three, but off book does not mean unprepared. You'll still need your scripts. And before I forget, you will all take very good care of these books. Should you lose or damage yours, the replacement cost will be five dollars or an extra hour of set construction. Understood?"

We all nod. My hand tightens around my pen. I'm starting to get nervous.

"Okay. Before we start the table read, we're going to go around the room and introduce ourselves, in case any of you don't know your fellow cast members."

I can feel several gazes settle on me.

"Just tell us all your name, what part you're playing—for the people seated down the row from you, who can't see your nameplate—and tell us whether or not you've done any theater before. We're going to be spending a lot of time together, so let's get to know one another!" Ms. Bond sits on the table at the front of the room, tucks her legs beneath her, and points at the first cast member on my side of the room.

"Hey. I'm Aaron, and I'll be your Narrator for this year's spring musical. You should note that I have no musical numbers, and for that, you're all welcome."

Everyone laughs.

"And your previous stage experience?"

"Yeah. Last year I was Hook, in the fall production of *Peter Pan*, and last semester, I played Oberon in *A Midsummer Night's Dream*."

Aaron is evidently overqualified for the role of Narrator, but cannot carry a tune. Everyone seems to know and like him.

My nerves multiply and my palms begin to sweat.

It turns out that most of this year's cast members had roles in *Peter Pan* or *A Midsummer Night's Dream*, or last year's spring musical, *The Addams Family*. Ben played both Peter Pan and Gomez Addams. Lexie played Wednesday Addams and Hermia.

And the infamous Kat Torrez, who has purple contacts and a head full of amazing, purple-streaked, waist-length curls, has had a lead role in every high school production for the past three and a half years, as well as four community productions in Tulsa.

This year's Steward, Cinderella's Father, and Mysterious Man are all freshmen. One had a small part in *A Midsummer Night's Dream* last semester, and the others are both new to the stage.

As am I.

Ms. Bond calls on us in a crisscross pattern, instead of going straight down one side of the horseshoe and back up the other, which puts Emery ahead of me.

"Hey, I'm Emery Bosch, playing Lucinda."

"Woo!" Link shouts, and she flashes him a dazzling smile.

"I was Tiger Lily in *Peter Pan*, and I was last year's Grandma Addams, in *The Addams Family*." She's smiling, but she looks tense. Then she aims that tense smile at me, because it's my turn, and I can practically see what she's thinking.

Am I going to tell people that we're sisters? She clearly

hasn't told anyone yet, except maybe Mara, and I'm assuming that's because she doesn't know how to . . . explain me.

"Michaela?" Ms. Bond says.

All eyes turn my way, and I can feel Josh's gaze on me, from my right. He knows who I am, but he hasn't said anything.

"Hey. I'm Michaela Rutherford. I'm new. This is actually my third day."

"So, you auditioned for the musical on your first day of school?" Link doesn't seem to believe me.

"I didn't really intend to. I just kind of wound up onstage." I glance at Ben and find him grinning.

Link whistles, evidently impressed.

"And have you been in another production?" Ms. Bond asks.

"No. I'd literally never even stepped onstage before Monday. But I love musicals," I assure her, suddenly worried that I've disqualified myself.

"That much is clear. We're glad to have you." She turns to Mara.

"Hey, I'm Mara Avery, playing Florinda," she says. "I was one of the Ancestors in *The Addams Family*, and one of the natives in *Peter Pan*. So, I'm happy to have a character with a name this year."

Everybody laughs.

I can feel Josh staring at me. He must wonder why neither Emery nor I mentioned the fact that we're related.

He's up next, and in his introduction, I learn that he played Lucas, Wednesday Addams's love interest, in *The Addams*

*Family.* Though he evidently has no interest in stage productions that don't involve music.

He does not divulge the Rutherford/Bosch family secret.

We make it through the table read without incident—and with many laughs—but it's nearly 6:00 p.m. when we finally finish. "Okay, you'll get copies of the production schedule tomorrow, but it's already up on the board, right now!" Ms. Bond says as everyone stands and begins to stretch, shoving scripts into their backpacks. "Music rehearsals start next week, with Mr. Rayburn, for the full company. Monday through Thursday." She points at the whiteboard. "And we'll start blocking onstage the week after that. One week after *that*"—she taps the board—"I want us all off book. And between now and next Monday, I want you all to watch *Into the Woods*, at least once. The stage version, not the movie. I'll be showing it here, at one p.m. on Saturday, but you're welcome to watch on your own instead. You can stream the Broadway version for free on YouTube. Legally.

"Have fun with it!" she adds as we start filing toward the door. "Have a viewing party with your friends! But while you're watching, make note of the differences between the professional production and our licensed version, and be prepared to discuss!"

Half the cast has already wandered out the door, but they can still hear her. In fact, I think people can hear her down in Dallas.

"Hey!" Ben finds me in the hall. "Do you need a ride?" A set of keys dangle from his right index finger.

"Oh, thanks, but I actually drove."

"Well, then, I'll walk you to your car."

I can feel Emery glaring at us as we pass her and Mara in the hall, but I can't tell whether she's angrier about the fact that I drove or the fact that Ben is walking me to my car. And when I turn to see if she needs a ride—we *are* going to the same place—I see her disappear around the corner in the opposite direction.

"So," Ben says as we step into the parking lot. The sun has gone down. The wind is cold, and there are only a few dozen cars in the lot now, lit by the orangish glow of a series of security lights. "You wanna get together and watch the Broadway version?"

I've seen it at least half a dozen times, with my mom. I already know the differences between that version and the one we just read through. But—

"Yeah. That sounds great."

"Saturday night?" Ben says. "My house?"

I feel warm, deep inside. "Perfect."

As Ben heads for his car, I get into mine and pull my phone from my pocket. I've already opened my mom's text thread, ready to tell her about the cute boy at my new school who seems to like me, before I remember that she's gone. That if she weren't, I never would have met Ben McGrath. The realization that I will never again confide in my mother—or keep a secret from her—brings scalding tears to my eyes.

I take a deep breath and reach for a tissue from the console.

## fourteen

It's leftover night!" Cynthia calls as I come through the front
door. She knows it's me because everyone else comes in
through the side door, under the portico, but I park out front,
because there's no room for my car in the garage. "I made a
command decision, since I didn't know how late you and Emery
would be. Is she with you?"

"She's right behind me." Mara's car pulled into the driveway
before I could even get out of mine.

"So, how was the first rehearsal?" my dad asks as I cross the
living room.

"It was good," I say. He looks like he'd like to hear more, but
I'm still not used to seeing Dad on a daily basis, and I have no
urge to confide in him about boys or stage fright. And it doesn't
seem fair that the parent I actually want to talk to will never
be here again.

I lean over the couch to scruff Cody's hair, and he ducks
away from my hand without looking up from his video game.

He's in the middle of a very tense battle with a silver dragon, and he appears to be armed only with a sword.

I'm more partial to magic staffs.

The microwave beeps, and as I slide onto a stool at the breakfast bar, my dad opens it and takes out a steaming bowl of spaghetti. "There's enough of this for two," he says as he sets it on the counter.

"There are also two mini meatloaves, a salmon filet, and two slices of pizza," Cynthia says as she sets a container of leftover green beans in the microwave.

"I call the pizza!" Cody shouts from the living room.

"Damn it!" Gabriel swears, and I turn to see him crossing the living room from the hall. "That's fine." He grins, and I'm glad to see him looking like himself again. "It's old anyway."

Cody snorts as he shuts down the PlayStation. "Old pizza is still better than fresh meatloaf."

He's not wrong.

The side door opens, and Emery steps into the kitchen carrying her backpack. She glances at the chaotic assortment of dishes being warmed up. "Leftover night? Is there any pizza?"

"Cody called it," her mother says.

"Damn it!" Emery snaps, and her little brother laughs.

Emery and Gabe claim the spaghetti, and Cynthia and my dad get the meatloaf. Which leaves me with a two-day-old salmon filet and green beans, as well as a leftover slice of garlic bread. This is my very first Bosch family dinner without some weird kind of salad.

We sit at the round table with our mismatched meals, and

before my dad can ask any of his "real" kids how their day went, Emery starts talking.

"So, Ms. Bond wants us all to watch the Broadway version of *Into the Woods* by Monday, and several of us want to get together on Saturday and make a night of it. Pizza. Popcorn." She shrugs.

Cynthia and my dad exchange a look. It's a hopeful look, but kind of fragile, as if they're worried that one wrong move on their part will shatter her good mood into a thousand pieces. And honestly, that's a valid concern.

"That sounds like fun," Cynthia says at last. Her smile feels cautious. "So, everyone's getting along then? In the cast? No . . . conflict?"

At first, I think she's talking about Emery and me. But she hasn't even glanced at me. This feels more like it's about Emery and someone else. Ben, maybe?

"Yeah. It's fine. So, can I host it here? We have the best setup."

"You want to have a viewing party for your theater friends here, on Saturday night?" My dad sounds like he's just trying to make sure he has the facts straight, but then he aims a pointed glance at me.

And *now* it's about me.

Emery rolls her eyes. "Of course, Michaela can come. She'll be here anyway, right?"

"I think that's a great idea!" Cynthia looks at my dad again, and it's like they're trying to hold an entire silent conversation. As if we can't see that they think this is some kind of wonderful opportunity for Emery and me to become friends. "And I'm happy to bake cookies, or brownies, or anything you guys would like for dessert. I could do mini-cheesecakes. Or mousse cups. Or petit fours!"

"Well . . ." Emery hesitates with a bite of coiled noodles halfway to her mouth.

"Oh, let her bake," Gabriel says. "She gets bored here, by herself all day."

"I'm not bored," Cynthia insists, while my dad chews his meatloaf.

She's not by herself during the day either. It's like they don't even remember Grammie exists.

"I just want to help," she adds.

Emery rolls her eyes. "You want to be the center of attention. You want all my friends to say, 'Mrs. Bosch, these tiny little tarts are so beautiful!' But this isn't the Cynthia Bosch Bakery Exhibit."

"Emery!" my father snaps. "Don't be mean to your mother!"

"Why do you have to be such a bitch?" Gabe demands, and I stare at him, shocked.

"Gabriel!" Cynthia cries. "Don't call your sister names."

"I was defending *you*!"

"I don't need to be defended."

"He's right," Emery says, though she doesn't look particularly contrite. This seems to be a strategic regrouping, rather than an admission of defeat. "I'm sorry. You can make something if you promise to keep it simple."

Cynthia nods.

I gape at Emery. I can't imagine being mad at my mom for wanting to bake something for my friends.

"I'm serious, though. Don't turn it into a *project*. You get stressed out when you're working on a project, and when you get stressed out, you snap at everyone. And we're just going to eat the brownies, or whatever. It's not like they'll be on display in a museum."

"Of course. I won't make a fuss." Cynthia cuts a bite of her meatloaf, staring at her plate.

Emery sighs. "Mom. I'm sorry. I didn't mean . . ."

My half sister tries to walk back remarks that obviously hurt her mom's feelings, and watching their interaction, awkward as it is, makes me miss my mother in a wholly new and painful way.

It feels weird to miss arguing with my mom, but right now, I'd give anything for a dinner spent debating my curfew or trying to snatch her phone while she scrolls through the social media feeds of some loser I've just told her I have a date with.

A date. Shit.

Ben isn't a loser, obviously. And I'm not sure our Saturday night plans count as a date. But—

"Michaela?"

I look up and realize that isn't the first time Cynthia has called my name. "What?"

"Emery asked if there's anyone you want to invite for the viewing party."

"That's not exactly what I said," Emery corrects. "But yeah, you can invite a couple of people. Bella, Lexie, and I aren't really friends anymore, but anyone else is welcome."

Anymore? So, they *were* friends? Did Emery sit at my table in the cafeteria last semester? Either way, Bella and Lexie aren't the problem.

Would it be worse to ask if I can invite her ex-boyfriend to the party, or to admit that I'm going to be watching the musical at his house?

"I'll . . . um . . . I'll let you know." I shove a bite of salmon into my mouth, and Cody starts talking about the career day presentation they watched at school, and how video game testing is an *actual job.* And the conversation moves on without me.

Thank God.

---

I help Cody clear the table, and then I head into the hallway with my backpack, intending to dig into some homework. But Emery is standing in our bedroom doorway, staring into the room. She seems to be looking at my bed.

"What's wrong?" I follow her into the room, and she sits on the edge of her unmade bed.

"If I throw a watch party, I'm going to have to figure out what to tell people about you."

"You're just now realizing that?"

"No." She scowls at me. "I've been trying to figure out how to explain . . . *you*"—she gestures at my face—"without making my family look . . . bad."

"We are who we are," I say. Then I realize she wasn't actually including me in the category of "my family."

I sit on my bed, facing her from across the room. "Okay, look. I get that you have your own perspective on this. But I'd just like to point out that I exist as a real, live person, above and beyond my role as your dirty little secret."

Emery sighs. "I know. I'm sorry I've been such a bitch. I *do* understand that you didn't ask for this—" She raises her arms to indicate our shared room. Likely our shared existence. "—any more than I did. I just . . ." She shrugs and scoots back on her bed until her spine is against the wall, her knees tucked up to her chest.

I shouldn't ask. I don't really care, and asking will only piss one of us off. Still . . . "You just what?"

"I just . . ." She leans forward and folds her legs, crisscross. "It seems like you play the 'dead mother' card whenever you want something. Usually something that isn't fair to *me*."

I speak through clenched teeth. "My mom isn't some card I'm playing to inconvenience you, Emery."

"I know. But come on. You get to have a car because your mother died. And you auditioned for the part I wanted in the musical because your mother died."

"Neither of those have anything to do with you. I didn't know you were auditioning, and even if I had— I mean, a role in the musical isn't a piece of stale pizza you can just call dibs on. *Ms. Bond* gave me the callback, and she didn't know I was only there to sing for my mom. She just decided I might be right for the part."

"But if you weren't there, she'd have given it to me."

"Maybe. Or maybe if I weren't here, someone else would have gotten a callback. The cast dynamic would be entirely different, and Lexie could be playing Cinderella, and you'd be *her* understudy. But we'll never know, because I *am* here. And I'm not going anywhere, because I have nowhere else to go. And you're right—I'm no happier about that than you are."

"I—"

"And if I were *truly* playing the 'dead mom' card, I'd have used it to get you moved into that tall garage out back so I could have this room to myself."

"Oh my God! Would you really—?"

"No. I'd never take the practice space away from Gabriel's band."

I can see fury raging behind the pink splotches in her cheeks. Then she realizes I'm kidding. And she actually laughs. "Okay, I guess I had that coming. Though, if there were a bathroom out there, I'd move in voluntarily." She exhales slowly. "I guess you heard about me and Ben?"

"Gabe said he's your ex."

"Yeah. I . . ." Another sigh. "It's weird for me in the musical, now. I *love* the theater. And I think I'm pretty good at it, and I thought—*everyone* thought—that Ben and I were going to be the Baker and Cinderella. We were going to get to sing together onstage. Then we broke up, and he got his role, but I didn't get mine, and I think part of that is chemistry."

"Between you and Ben?"

"Yeah. Or whatever the opposite of chemistry is. Ms. Bond

was never gonna cast exes in lead roles opposite each other. She thinks it'll bring too much conflict to the cast."

I shrug. "She may have a point."

"Yeah. So, when Ben and I broke up, she basically had to choose whether to give him a lead role or to give me one, and I really, really wanted to show that I'm as good as he is. That he didn't 'carry' me last semester. That the West Bradford theater department doesn't *belong* to Ben McGrath. But then you showed up, and—"

"So we're back to this being my fault?"

"No. But you were convenient for the cast. You're good, and that gave Ms. Bond a strong pairing with Ben's Baker. But there's really no one better than Ben in the program, so if she'd cast me as Cinderella, she would've had to cast an inferior Baker opposite me, to avoid the conflict."

"So you're admitting this isn't my fault?" Her back-and-forth is giving me whiplash.

"Yes. But I still think that if you weren't here, Ms. Bond would have been forced to let Ben and me prove we can keep our private shit offstage."

I haul my backpack onto my bed and scoot back across the mattress until my position mirrors hers. "I'm sorry that me being here means you lost so much." I'm not sorry for *being* here. But I can give her that much.

"I don't blame you for any of this."

I'm not sure I believe her. But she *is* trying.

"The family stuff is Dad's fault," she adds.

"Yeah." I pretend I don't hear the way she bit off the end of her sentence, as if there's more she wants to say. As if this could possibly be *only* Dad's fault. As if it doesn't take two.

Emery crawls off her bed and softly closes the door. "I want to ask him why he did it. Why he cheated." She sinks onto her bed again, and I can tell from the way she's looking at me that she thinks I may know something. "Has he said anything to you? About that?"

There's no good way for me to answer; she's not going to want to hear what I know. But I'm going to try, because this is the longest conversation we've ever had that didn't end in shouting or tears.

"I asked him the other day. Why he cheated." I pull my chemistry text from my bag so I don't have to look at her while I speak. "He said he and your mom were going through a rough time. And he took full responsibility."

"How?"

"How, what?"

"How did he take responsibility? What does that really *mean*?"

"I don't know." But that's a very good question.

"He just, what? Said he's sorry?" Emery sounds incredulous. "That he'll never do it again?"

"Yeah, basically."

She fumes. *Audibly.* I think that in her own head, she may be breathing flames. "When we were kids, they used to tell us that taking responsibility meant taking some kind of action. That it wasn't enough to just say you're sorry. We were expected to *demonstrate* that."

"How?"

"Gabe stole a pack of guitar picks from the store when he was twelve. Dad found out and made him go return them in person and apologize to the store manager. Gabe was humiliated. But I doubt he ever stole anything again."

I suspect Emery has a couple of similar stories of her own, but she doesn't volunteer them, and I don't ask her to.

"But it's not like Dad can just take his infidelity to the store and return it." She brushes her palms together, as if she's dusting them off. "No harm, no foul."

"I guess not."

"It's not like he can ever make this up to my mom. No 'demonstration of regret' will undo this. He's getting away with it. And *she's* the one who's paying the price for his mistakes."

"Because I'm here?"

"I . . . well, yeah." She flinches when she realizes what she's said. "I know that's not your fault, but yeah—Mom's now stuck raising her husband's love child."

This conversation makes me feel like I'm rolling around on hot gravel, naked. Exposed and endlessly uncomfortable. Bruised and burned with every move I make. "Well, fortunately for everyone involved, I'm basically raised. And if it makes you feel any better, he slept on his office couch for a year after he cheated."

"He did?"

"Yeah. I guess he had an office, in your last house?"

She nods. "He had one here, until Grammie moved in. But so what? Did him sleeping on the couch undo all the cheating?

No." She answers her own question, because she isn't really asking me. "Some things can't be fixed. Sometimes there are no amends to be made. My dad just . . . got away with it."

"You think he got away with it? He almost lost his marriage. He almost lost you and Gabe."

"But he didn't. She just forgave him, because if she hadn't, she'd have been stuck raising two kids on her own, and she didn't get a say in his decision to cheat. The only say she got was whether or not to be a single mother."

"She told you that?" I can't imagine Cynthia saying something like that.

"Not in so many words."

"It must be weird, hearing your mother explain why she decided not to leave your dad."

"Yeah." Emery doesn't ask me how weird it was to find out that my dad has a secret "real" family. "He's just . . . I mean, he's still my dad, but it doesn't feel the same anymore. All my memories are kind of . . . tainted."

"Tainted, how?"

"I mean, like, I can't think about the princess birthday party they threw me the year I turned four without wondering if he went out that night, after I went to bed, and cheated on my mom. When he stepped out to take a phone call in the middle of Gabe's freshman concert, was he really on the line with a patient, or was he talking to some other woman? Was he late to Cody's fifth-grade graduation for the same reason? I don't know how my mom can ever trust him again, knowing that he lied to her for so long. That he cheated.

"I don't know how *any* of us are supposed to trust him."

I have no answer for her. For the first time, I can truly see this from her perspective, and Gabriel's right; it isn't me she's mad at. And this isn't a problem we share. Yes, our father basically lied to me too, though technically he never said I *wasn't* his secret love child. But finding that out didn't destroy my trust in him the way it has for Emery because I don't have the same kind of relationship with him that she evidently had. I didn't see him on a daily basis or think of his word as unimpeachable. I didn't know much about him at all, and when I found out that he had a "real" family, after I got over the initial shock, I felt more like I'd just cleaned my glasses and could finally see everything clearly, than like my entire world had been upended.

It made sense that my father had another family, because surely he had to be *somewhere* during all those days and nights when he wasn't with me.

And it's not that finding out didn't hurt. But it wasn't the huge shock for me that it was for Emery.

Still . . .

"Yeah, he got away with leaving my mom alone with a kid too. And she didn't have a choice in that." Not unless she was willing to ask him to leave his "real" family. Which she was not. But Emery isn't ready to hear that the fate of her mother's marriage was less in Cynthia's control than she even knew.

She nods. "If I'd cheated on a test at school, I don't think people would just look the other way. I don't think they'd make me say I'm sorry, then just let me keep the A."

The "A" in this scenario is obviously my dad's wife and kids. And house. And reputation. And she's right. He got to keep *everything*.

"I don't think they'd trust me to take any more tests at all!"

I roll my eyes. "I think that's where your analogy breaks down. Cheating does not get you out of future tests."

"You know what I mean."

"Yeah." It isn't fair that he got away with it. And she can't trust our father now. She can't trust her memories of her own childhood anymore.

But she can, evidently, trust me.

Emery stares at me from across the room, and for the first time since I met her, there's no resentment in her gaze. It doesn't ripple between us, like heat rising from a blacktop parking lot in the middle of an Oklahoma summer.

The air is clear. Mostly.

"Okay, so Saturday? Watch party? Pizza and whatever overblown, fancy mini-desserts my mom comes up with?"

I nod, because I can't tell her about Ben now. Not when she's finally starting to not entirely resent my very existence.

# fifteen

Hey! Wanna kill some zombies?" Cody asks as I drop my car keys into the bowl on the breakfast bar.

"What happened to the dragons? Kill them all already?"

"Several times over. And the new *DeathBite* game just came in, so . . ." He picks up a remote and holds it out to me.

"I'd love to, but I *really* have to memorize a couple more scenes from the musical. We only have three weeks to be off book." And as of today, one of those weeks is basically over already.

"After dinner?" He looks so hopeful that I hate to disappoint him.

"Sorry, but I'm going over to Lexie's after dinner, to—"

"To run lines with her and Bella. I know."

"Yeah. Sorry."

It turns out that Lexie lives two streets over, in my new neighborhood. Across the cul-de-sac from Josh. They both used to ride the bus to school with Gabe and Emery.

"S'okay." Cody goes back to his game.

"I promise we'll play on Sunday, okay?"

"Sure."

I dig my script out of my bag on my way down the hall, then knock on Grammie's doorframe. "Hey!" She's watching a black-and-white movie—*Casablanca*, maybe?—but she smiles when she sees me.

"Emery! Come in!"

My smile falters, but I come in anyway. "I have to study my lines, but I can do that in here, if you want some company."

"What lines?"

"For the play. Remember?"

She doesn't remember. I can tell she's confused from the narrow set of her eyes. From the tense line of her jaw. Today, she hasn't just forgotten my name—she truly thinks I'm Emery.

"It's a musical. We're doing *Into the Woods*, and I'm playing Cinderella." I sit in the chair next to her bed. "And Cinderella has a *lot* of lines."

I study my script while she watches her movie, and after a few minutes, I hear her snoring softly. Grammie is asleep, sitting up, with her head fallen forward so that her chin is practically resting on her collarbone. I stand and grab an extra pillow from the armchair by the window and gently work it behind her head. Then I take the bed's remote and lower the head end of her mattress until she looks more comfortable. She snorts, but she doesn't wake up.

"You're good at that," Gabriel says, and I look up to see him standing in the doorway.

"Thanks." I grab my book and ease the door shut as I leave the room.

"You've had practice?"

"No. My grandmother died in her sleep. Suddenly. We didn't even get to say goodbye."

"Jesus. And then your mom."

"Yeah." We're plodding down the hall slowly. At our backs, Grammie is still snoring. Up ahead, a zombie snarls from the living room television. "But those were more than a year apart."

"Still . . ."

"Yeah. You should spend some time with your grandmother," I tell him. "While you still have her."

"I know." He shoves his hands into his pockets and shuffles his feet as we walk. "But she's asleep every time I go in there, and the last time she wasn't, she called me Oscar."

"Well, you *do* look like Dad."

Cody curses, and I glance at the screen as we step into the living room. His character is on the ground, flailing while a zombie rips out his throat with its teeth.

"How's it going?" I ask Cody.

"I've died three times in the past ten minutes. But I know what I'm doing wrong now."

"Playing video games?" Gabe quips, and Cody rolls his eyes.

"Dinner's in five," Cynthia calls from the kitchen. "Whose turn is it to set the table?"

It's Cody's, but I feel bad about not playing *DeathBite* with him, so I say it's mine. Gabe offers to help. When Cynthia leaves the kitchen to check on her mother, I lean close to Gabe as I set out plates, and he follows me with napkins. "I need some advice," I whisper.

"Oh, good." He grins at me, brows arched. "I *totally* feel qualified to run other peoples' lives. What's this about?"

"Your sister."

"You mean *our* sister?"

"That's the one." I exhale. Then I spit it out—quietly. "What's the best way to tell her that I can't come to her *Into the Woods* watch party tomorrow night because I'm going to be watching at Ben's house? With Ben."

"Alone?"

"I think so." I don't look at him. I'm really using this as a practice revelation, more than I am looking for advice, but I'm not ready to see whatever judgment is swimming in his eyes.

"You're hanging out with her ex? Alone?"

I exhale again as I set the last plate into place. "Yeah, but it's not like that. At least, I don't think it's like that. The musical is a school assignment, so we're basically doing homework together."

"On a Saturday night."

"Yeah. But he invited me before I knew about Emery's party, and I can't exactly ask her if I can bring him, so . . ."

"Well, shit."

"Yeah. I've managed to go two days without invoking her wrath or accidentally taking over part of her life, and it's been nice, not worrying that she's going to kill me in my sleep. But I'm running out of time to tell her about Ben, and while I'm sure it'll be better coming from me than if she finds out on her own, I'm not sure how to do that without kicking off World War Three, here in the Bosch household."

Gabriel whistles as he returns the extra napkins to the cabinet. "Okay. So, here's what you do." He leans in close again. "Start writing your last will and testament. And keep in mind that I'm *super* fond of that Bluetooth speaker on your nightstand. The one shaped like an old-timey radio. Does it double as a phone charger, by any chance?"

"So, she's going to kill me?"

He nods solemnly. "Like, slasher movie carnage. But it'll be fine, because my mom's sister is a defense attorney. She'll probably go for justifiable homicide."

Maybe Lexie and Bella will have better advice for me.

———— ∽∞∽ ————

"You and Emery Bosch are *sisters*?" Lexie's hand goes still, her ice cream scoop half buried in the carton. "You're kidding."

"Oh my God, I can totally see it!" Bella gasps, staring at me from her seat across the island, at the breakfast bar in a house that looks very similar to mine on the inside. "You two have the same hair. And eyes."

"So I've heard."

Lexie drops a ball of ice cream into the first bowl. "And you auditioned in a duet with her ex?"

"To be fair, I had no idea who he was at that point."

Bella's brows arch nearly into her hairline. "And now you're going to 'watch *Into the Woods*' with him."

"No need for the air quotes. We're *actually* going to watch the musical."

"Is that okay?" Bella takes the bowl Lexie offers her. "To go after your sister's ex?"

"I'm not going after him. *He* invited *me*. And she's my half sister. Who doesn't even like me."

"I mean, would you go after your sister's boyfriend?" Bella asks Lexie.

"Alison is five." Lexie hands me the second bowl, and my spoon clinks against the edge. "Her boyfriend literally ate a worm on a dare yesterday. So . . . no."

"Your five-year-old sister has a boyfriend?" I ask as I scoop the first spoonful.

"She has three of them." Lexie shrugs. "She's five."

Her parents took her sister to dinner and the latest *Pirate Princess* movie, but Lexie stayed home to run lines with us. Technically, we're doing schoolwork, but it's Friday night, at the end of my first full week in a new school. It feels *good* not to be sitting alone in my room, with AirPods and Netflix.

"I meant, if she were our age." Bella takes her bowl into the living room, and I follow, while Lexie puts the carton back into the freezer. "I'm just trying to wrap my mind around the morality of this, and I don't have any sisters."

"So, flip the script," Lexie says around a huge bite of peanut butter swirl. She sits on the arm of the couch, then spins around so that her feet rest on the seat cushion. "Would you go out with your brother's ex-girlfriend?"

"Violet? In a heartbeat. She's gorgeous." Bella digs a min-
iature peanut butter cup from her bowl with her spoon. "But
that's not the same—I don't think my brother would care. Girls
are much more likely to be territorial in that respect. Especially a sister, I would think."

"I met her less than two weeks ago. We're not really sisters,"
I insist.

"And especially considering that Em and Ben *just* broke up,"
Lexie adds.

"Were they together long?"

"Not terribly," Bella says. "Less than a year. But this year,
Ben was the new 'it' boy in theater, after Josiah Brandt
graduated—he went to William & Mary on a partial scholarship—
and Emery's so smart and pretty. Last semester, they were
basically West Bradford theater's power couple, and everyone
thought they were going to star in *Into the Woods* together.
When they broke up . . ." She shrugs. "It was like when my parents divorced and split everything down the middle. He kept
the couch, and she kept all the dishes."

"What did Emery keep?"

"Mara, and Aaron, and Link."

Mara is her best friend and fellow fairy-tale stepsister, Link
pretends to howl at the moon every time Emery walks into the
room, and Aaron, the Narrator . . . I think he's just jealous of
Ben's voice.

"And Ben? What did he get?"

"He got us. And Jon," Lexie says.

"What about Cole Houser?" The student audio tech had sat with Ben at lunch, but he seemed friendly with Emery at rehearsal.

Bella frowns. "You know how sometimes they ask the kid which parent he wants to live with, and the kid can't pick, so he gets shuttled back and forth, in split custody?"

"Shuffled," Lexie corrects with her mouth full.

Bella rolls her eyes. "Fine. *Shuffled* back and forth."

"You're saying Ben and Emery got split custody of Cole?"

"Yeah. And just like any kid of divorce, he thinks it was his fault, and he gets anxious when they're in the same room together."

"Does that have anything to do with why he didn't audition?"

"No." Lexie presses one hand to her forehead, breathing through an obvious brain freeze. Then she sets her nearly empty bowl on the coffee table. "Cole has crippling stage fright. He was never gonna audition. He only said he would because Emery told him he should, and he has a *devastating* crush on her."

"She has no idea," Bella adds.

"And she never will, because—"

"Because he's as scared to ask her out as he is to step onstage," I finish.

Bella nods. "Exactly."

"And even if he did ask her out, she'd say no, because she and Ben *just* broke up," Lexie adds.

"What about Kat? Where does she fall on the Emery/Ben divide?"

"Nowhere. Kat's above it all. She's a theater kid, but she takes her craft super seriously and she's too busy with community theater and voice lessons to hang out much."

I set my empty bowl down and grab my script. "So, you think I shouldn't watch the musical with Ben?"

Bella shrugs again as she digs a highlighter from the bag at her feet. "That depends on which is stronger—your crush on Ben or your loyalty to your sister."

"The truth is that I hardly know either of them."

"Then maybe you should avoid being alone with Ben until you're sure of what you want," Lexie says.

Bella nods. "And what you're willing to do to get it."

It's solid advice. And it's exactly the advice Georgia gave me via text yesterday. But—

"I can't invite Ben to Emery's watch party."

"And you can't invite us either, because Ben got us in the divorce." Bella grins at me. "But you can invite us to *his* watch party."

"He isn't having a watch party."

"He will be, if you bring us!"

"That's brilliant." I grab my phone and tap out a text to Ben.

Hey, so Em's having a watch party, and Lexie & Bella aren't invited. Is it cool if I bring them tomorrow night?

His reply comes a few seconds later, and it's so amenable that I'm almost disappointed. Did I imagine tomorrow night as more than he intended for it to be?

I paste on a smile as I pick up my script. "It's officially a watch party. I can drive you, Lexie, if Bella will meet us there."

"Perfect!" Bella shrugs. "I'll bring Lexie home and stay the night. My mom won't care."

Lexie seems unfazed by Bella inviting herself to a sleepover, and suddenly I miss Georgia and the kind of easy friendship we're now forced to approximate through texting and FaceTime.

Bella turns to me, and I realize we're not going to do much script reading tonight after all. "So, you really didn't know you had a half sister and two half brothers? How is that possible?"

I sigh as I settle in to tell a story I suspect I'm going to be repeating a lot over the next few days. Unless Emery's version beats mine to market.

---

"Hey," I say from the bathroom doorway. I've already showered, and I still brush my teeth and do my makeup in the powder bath so I can understand Emery's suspicious glance at me in the mirror as she spits toothpaste into the sink.

"Hey." She runs water into her cupped palm, then uses it to rinse her mouth. "What's up?"

The first week of rehearsal is over. Our truce has held for three days, and part of me wonders if it could be permanent. If we could be real sisters—maybe even friends—if I tell Ben that I'm not into him. If I choose her over him.

But that isn't fair. Ben's interest in me—and mine in him— has nothing to do with Emery. He doesn't even know she's my sister, and I didn't know he was her ex when I sang with him onstage.

Also, why should I have to run a list of potential dates by Emery before I accept an invitation? Why should she get to decide who I hang out with?

This is my life, right? And if I've learned anything from losing my mother this suddenly, it's that life can end at any time. You have to make the most of it.

I feel like that's a cliché she would appreciate.

"Michaela." Emery sets her toothbrush on the charger and grabs her moisturizer. "What do you want?"

"I, um, I can't make it to your watch party tonight, because I already said yes to another one."

"Oh. Okay." She shrugs at me in the mirror as she spreads cream onto her face with both hands. "Actually, that works for me. I haven't quite figured out what to tell people about . . . this." She waves one hand around, gesturing at the entire house. "About our half-sibling situation. About Dad."

I'm not sure what to say, so I keep my mouth shut.

"I know I have to tell them something, but if you're not here, then I guess I'm kind of free to tell the story . . . my way."

"*Your* way?"

She frowns as she screws the lid back on the moisturizer. "I mean . . . That's not what I meant. It's just . . . it'd be weird to have to tell them what Dad did in front of you. To have you there while I explain all this. That would feel like the teacher standing over your shoulder while you take a test."

"I'm the teacher in this scenario?"

"Kinda. Because I'd be worried about getting it right. That you're, like, mentally correcting my answers as I make them."

And suddenly I'm considering turning Ben down just so I can be here tonight, to set the record straight when she throws me and my mom under the home-wrecker bus. Because it sounds like that's what she's planning.

"So, have you . . . Have you told anyone?" She's staring at me in the mirror now, a bottle of foundation in her left hand. "About Dad?"

"When anyone asks why I transferred to West Bradford, I tell them that my mom died, and I had to come live with my dad. But I hadn't told anyone who my dad was until last night."

Emery spins around to face me. "Who did you tell?"

"Lexie and Bella. We were at Lexie's, memorizing lines, and—"

"*Nooo*," she groans as she turns to face the mirror again, both hands gripping the edge of the counter.

"This was going to come out eventually, Emery."

"I know."

"I couldn't just keep pretending I disappear from the face of the planet when I leave school in the afternoon."

"I *know*!"

"And anyway, Lexie already knew I lived in this neighborhood. She just didn't know which house."

"Well, if Bella Moretti knows, everyone knows." Emery makes angry swipes at her face with a foundation-covered sponge. "I was just hoping to kind of . . . shape the narrative. I guess we'll just have to make the best of it." Her motions become smoother, and her pores disappear. "So, Lexie's having a watch party? That's where you're going?"

"I'm watching with Lexie and Bella. But not at Lexie's . . ."

Emery's hand goes still again. She meets my gaze in the mirror, and her entire body tenses. I think she knows the answer to her question before she even asks it. Probably based solely on the fact that I keep not telling her where I'm actually going. "Whose party is it, Michaela?"

I exhale. "Ben's."

She spins to face me again, her fist clenched around the sponge. Tiny rivulets of foundation ooze between her fingers, as if her face has melted off from the fire of her own rage. "Tell me you're not going out with him. You said you didn't even know him at the audition, and I believed you, and—"

"No, you didn't! You said I was intentionally trying to ruin your life."

"Okay, yes, I overreacted. I was upset. But now you're going out with him behind my back, without even telling me, and—"

"I *am* telling you. And we're not going out. We're watching a school-assigned movie. With Lexie and Bella. And maybe Cole and Jon. I don't know who all will be there."

"Cole will be here. He didn't say anything about Ben having a party."

I can only shrug. Everything I've said is true, and if it doesn't *entirely* represent a thorough explanation of how the whole thing happened, that's only because I'm trying to keep the peace in this house, without telling an actual lie. Or giving up my right to have a life of my own, which Emery has no say in.

If my mom hadn't died and I'd met Ben at an Oak Valley vs. West Bradford football game, I'd be perfectly within my rights to hang out with him. To *go* out with him, even. Why should my living here change that?

"Look, I'd already told Ben I'd watch the musical at his house before I knew about your party, and I didn't tell you because I knew you'd twist this into more manufactured evidence that I'm trying to ruin your life. Which is the same reason I didn't just invite Ben over here instead."

She drops her sponge into the sink and holds her hand out as if she's bleeding. Foundation drips onto the rug. "Ben McGrath is *not* invited to my watch party."

"That's why I'm going over there!"

"Okay. I can't stop you from doing that, but—"

"No, you can't."

"But you're not going out with him?" she continues as she rinses her hand.

"It's not a date." I'm, like, eighty-five percent sure that's true. Sixty percent, minimum.

She picks up a small blush compact and clicks it open. "And you're not *going* to go out with him?"

"Emery, it's none of your business who I go out with!"

"It is, though! He's my ex, and you're my sister, and that's just *wrong*!"

"You have literally never called me your sister before. You

don't get to play the sister card whenever it's convenient to you—"

"Damn it!" She slams the compact down on the counter, and the compressed powder disk shatters into clumps and granules of Orgasmic Flush. The compact slides off the counter and hits the rug, where sparkly, pale pink dust rains down into the loose, fluffy pile as if someone has given Tinker Bell a good shake, right over our heads. Only this moment doesn't feel magical. It feels like I've just taken an ax to the front door of our home and tried to bring the whole thing down around us.

"If you don't give a shit about me, then stay away from Ben for your own good," Emery growls through clenched teeth. "I'm telling you, Ben McGrath is the *biggest*—"

"What on earth is going on in here?" Cynthia demands, and we both spin toward the hall as she steps into the doorway.

"They're fighting again." Cody appears behind her, holding a half-eaten blueberry muffin. He glances at Emery's Orgasmic Flush–splattered foot. "Also, we may need a new rug."

# sixteen

I thought my new home was big, but the McGrath residence puts it to shame. I almost feel embarrassed to park my car in the driveway. It's overdue for a wash.

"Holy crap," I whisper, staring up at the house through my grimy windshield.

"Yeaaah." Lexie laughs from my passenger seat. "I thought about telling you, but I really wanted to see *this*." She makes a circular gesture aimed at the shocked look on my face.

Bella pulls up behind us, and I feel better. She's missing two hubcaps—the scuffs on the sides of her tire say she lost them when she hit a curb—and there's a dent in her front bumper. When I get out of my car, I see that her doors are scratched around the handles from what can only be her own fingernails.

She gets out, and she looks amazing—was I supposed to dress up for this?—and she clearly doesn't care about either the state of her car or how huge Ben's house is. So, I decide I don't care about those either.

But I do miss Georgia. It's Saturday night, and twenty minutes ago, she posted a pic of herself in the arcade, with Sara and Izzy. They're playing air hockey. Georgia's T-shirt reads, "Don't make me use my mock trial voice."

I gave her that shirt for her birthday last year.

It's weird to be here and to know that life didn't just stop at Oak Valley when I left.

"Hey!" Bella loops her arm through mine and half drags me up the driveway, which is made of bricks laid out in a herringbone pattern. I can't remember ever seeing a driveway that wasn't concrete.

This neighborhood is a step up from mine. Which I wouldn't have thought possible. We're in Bradford, Oklahoma, not Hollywood.

Lexie catches up with us on the front porch, and the door opens before we can ring the bell. It's Jon Escobedo, not Ben. Evidently this really *is* a party now.

"Hey, come on in. We're just getting the projector set up."

"Projector?" I ask as I step over the threshold into a marble-floored, two-story foyer.

Jon grins. "Never been here, have you?"

I haven't been anywhere in Bradford except school and Lexie's house, so . . . "No."

"Hey, guys, come on in!" A woman in a short, tight, sparkly dress clacks her way across the foyer in black stilettos. "Mr. McGrath and I are going out, so we won't be in your way. Help yourself to anything you like from the kitchen, but stay out of the bar."

Not the liquor cabinet. Not the shelf at the top of my mom's closet, where she kept an emergency bottle of vodka. The bar.

There's an actual bar. In the den. I can see it from here.

Mrs. McGrath—who else can she be, with Ben's dark curls and golden brown eyes?—heads down a wide hallway without waiting for a reply.

"Jesus," I whisper as I stare down two steps into a sunken, round den with an honest-to-God domed ceiling. "What do Ben's parents do for a living? Mine gold?"

"They're both lawyers," Bella says.

"I think three of his grandparents were lawyers too," Lexie adds, and I assume she's kidding until she continues. "His grandpa helped keep some famous hedge fund manager out of jail in the nineties, and the family law firm has been going strong ever since."

I follow Jon down two steps, where I roam slowly around the room, running my fingers across dustless, heavy, dark wood furnishings. Studying family photographs that were obviously professionally framed.

There's an ornate occasional table across from the massive fireplace. I think it's mahogany. It has thick, curved legs and clawed feet, and on top is a carefully arranged collection of silver-framed photos, each of the same two boys. One of the boys is clearly a young Ben. The other has lighter hair that waves without truly curling.

"Ben's brother, Jeremy," Jon says from over my right shoulder. "He's a senior at Princeton, and he just got into Harvard Law."

"Holy shit, seriously?"

"Yeah." Lexie huffs from her seat on the top step, as if she doesn't really want to come into the room. "You'd never know, huh?"

"No. Ben's so *normal*."

"Yeah." Bella gives me a solemn nod. "His dad *hates* that."

I study the pictures. Ben and Jeremy both played baseball and soccer for years. There's a shot of them as small children, staring at the chessboard set up between them as if the fate of the world depends upon the outcome of their game. One picture shows them both in Boy Scout uniforms. In another, they're seated next to each other in a fancy restaurant booth, each holding a piece of sushi with a set of chopsticks. Ben looks like he's around four years old in that one.

There's Jeremy in a suit, giving a speech behind a podium. Here's Ben accepting an award. If a more perfect child than the McGrath boys ever existed, he or she must be mounted behind glass somewhere in a museum.

"Hey, do you guys want to grab something to eat before we hit Play?" Ben asks, and I look up to see him standing in the broad, arched doorway, next to Lexie. He grins when he sees the backpack hanging from my shoulder. "Or were you planning to take notes?"

I don't need to take notes, but I thought I should come prepared, just in case. I shrug as I let my backpack slip from my shoulder so I can set it on the floor. "I wasn't sure whether this would be more of a group assignment or a true watch party," I say as I step into the foyer.

"This is a real watch party." Ben leans in to whisper the rest, and I catch my breath. "Thanks to you."

He stands up again, and my gaze catches his, and suddenly I feel like the sun is shining directly on me, even though we're inside.

His attention feels like a spotlight.

Bella giggles, and I turn to see that everyone's staring at us. "Should we just go home?" she asks with a grin.

"No!" I practically squeal.

Ben laughs. "Cinderella is shy. Nobody let her out of your sight, or we'll wind up staring at an empty shoe."

"Okay, we're leaving!" Mrs. McGrath calls, and I exhale, relieved as everyone follows her voice and the spotlight dims.

I trail Bella into a massive white-on-white kitchen, where I practically have to squint against the glare of light reflecting off several perfectly polished stainless steel appliances. I can't tell that they've ever been used, and they certainly didn't produce the feast laid out on the massive granite island.

I was expecting pizza, or some open bags of chips and a bowl. Instead, Ben's parents have supplied his impromptu watch party with a platter of tiny three-bite sliders, a dozen plastic shot glasses full of shoestring fries standing on end in pools of ketchup, a tray of mini-tacos, and a platter of grilled fruit kabobs.

"We'll be back by midnight." Mrs. McGrath drapes a long red wool coat over her arm. "You're all welcome to hang out until then."

Except for me. I have to be home at eleven.

"There are plates on the counter and drinks in the fridge," she adds.

"But stay out of the bar." The man who enters the kitchen is tall, like Ben, but in every other respect he looks much more like Jeremy, based on what I've seen in the photos.

"I've already told them." Mrs. McGrath brushes off her husband's shoulder, then runs her hand down his arm in a gesture that makes it clear that she just wanted to touch him. There was no lint to be removed.

"You guys are watching something for school, right?" Mr. McGrath grins, and I can see his son in the expression. "Clever excuse for a party. Is this the debate team critique? Last year's championship exhibition was really—"

"It's *Into the Woods*," his wife tells him, her eyes slightly narrowed. "The Broadway version."

Mr. McGrath's jaw tightens. Ben stares at the tile between his shoes.

"These are the theater kids, hon. Ben's not doing debate this year."

"Yes, yes, that's right." But Ben's dad hasn't actually forgotten that. He's just an asshole, in a very expensive suit. "Are they going to dress you up in tights again?" He turns to the rest of us with a broad grin, as if we're in on some private joke. "There's no experience on earth like watching your son prance around onstage in a skin-tight green leotard."

"I was playing Peter Pan," Ben says through clenched teeth. "That's the lead."

"All I know is that you and the little fairy were both wearing tights."

"That was me!" Bella pastes on a broad smile. "I was Tinker Bell."

"And you were brilliant," Mrs. McGrath says. "Daniel, let's go. We're going to be late."

"Of course. You kids enjoy your . . . show." Mr. McGrath turns toward the door, and his gaze falls on me. "Emery, it's nice to see you a—" His eyes narrow. He turns to his wife. "That's not Emery."

"This is Michaela," Ben says. "Em's sister."

I glance at him—I didn't know for sure that he'd heard—then I turn back to his dad. "Nice to meet you, Mr. McGrath."

"Yes. You too." Then he turns to take his wife's arm, and as he escorts her out the door, I hear him whisper, ". . . enough like Em to be her alibi . . ."

"I've got the projector all set up," Ben says. "You guys go find seats, and we'll be right there." He's talking to everyone else, but he's looking at me.

They've already filled their plates, so in seconds, the kitchen is empty. And Ben's still staring at me. "Sorry about my dad."

"Someone should remind him that baseball pants are just as tight as . . . well, tights."

"Not quite, but that's a good point." He shrugs. "He's not a fan of the theater."

"He's an asshole."

Ben nods. "Yeah. That too. But he's a damn good lawyer."

"I'll keep that in mind, in case I have to murder my sister."

He doesn't laugh. But he does step closer. "Why didn't you tell me?"

"About Emery?"

"About who you are."

"Why didn't I tell you that my dad cheated on his pregnant wife with my mom? That isn't typically how I introduce myself. Why didn't you tell me your dad thinks you aren't a real man because you sing onstage?"

His brows rise. "Point taken." He exhales slowly. "I wouldn't have asked you out if I'd known you were Em's sister."

"You didn't ask me out."

"Yes, I did. But then you asked if you could bring Lexie and Bella on our date."

"And you threw in Jon because . . . ?"

"To even out the numbers. Since it's a party now. I invited Cole and Link, too, but they're going to . . . well, to your house, I guess."

"Yeah. They were already there when I left." I take the empty plate he hands me. "Who told you? About me and Emery?" I expect him to say Lexie or Bella.

Instead, he says, "Josh Kang. Yesterday. But he didn't just come out and say it. He thought I already knew." Ben takes three sliders and a mini taco. "Why didn't I already know?"

"Because Emery isn't taking the whole thing very well, and I was trying to give her a chance to tell her friends before it was all over school. But she just kept not telling them, and then I told Bella and Lexie, and . . ." I shrug.

"Well, once Bella knows, everyone knows."

I laugh.

"What?"

"That's what Emery said." I take a slider, a taco, and two little glasses of fries. Then I add a fruit kabob, because my mom would tell me to eat something healthy, if she were here. "So, what happened with you and Emery?"

His hand hovers over a second taco. "She didn't tell you?"

I shake my head. "But she *really* didn't want me to come over here."

"What!" Ben fakes shock as he pulls open the refrigerator. "Emery Bosch, trying to control someone else's life? I don't believe you."

"So, that's not some special treatment she saves just for me?"

"Hardly. When we were together—" He bites off the rest of it as he sets two Cokes on the counter.

"When you were together . . . ," I prompt.

"Nothing. Never mind. I'm not going to stand here and talk bad about your sister."

"Well, she's not exactly out there singing your praises. And you don't have to bad-mouth her. You could just tell me the truth."

Ben twists open the lid on one of the sodas and takes a long drink. "Did you really just meet her?"

I nod. "Two weeks ago, on Monday."

"Okay. Look, she has issues. She has to be in control of everything. In charge of everything. And nothing is ever her fault."

"Oh my God, it's like you live in our house!"

"You could not *pay* me to live in that house. When we were together, she had to know where I was every second of the day. If I was late, I got interrogated. If I forgot something, you'd think I canceled Christmas. And the drama! Every mistake I made was *obviously* an attempt to ruin her life. Everything I said wrong was a sword driven right through her heart."

I laugh. "She *does* belong in the theater."

"You have no idea. But you will. She has this way of remembering things . . . wrong. To her own advantage."

"Yes, she does."

"And I *swear*, she makes things up. I think she really believes half of them."

"She lies?"

"Kind of. She'll take a kernel of truth and sort of . . . cook it. Until it blows up to five times its normal size. Like popcorn." He makes an exploding gesture with his hand. "Just wait. One day she'll, like, let you borrow her lipstick or something, and the next day she'll *swear* you stole it a month ago."

I roll my eyes as I pick up my plate in one hand, my Coke in the other. "I'm so glad I got out of the house tonight."

"Me too. Come on." He leads me into the den, but it's empty. There's no projector. No Lexie, Bella, or Cole.

"Where is everyone?"

"In the theater."

"*Of course* you have a theater."

"We're just stopping here for refreshments."

I glance at the food on my plate. "In that case, I'm confused about what I'm holding."

Ben sets his plate on the bar, then ducks out of sight and comes up with a bottle. "Want some?"

"Don't your parents watch the bottles?" They both told us to stay away from the bar.

Ben actually snorts. "He'll assume she drank it. She'll assume he drank it." He carefully pours some of the clear liquid into his soda bottle, then screws the lid back on and gently turns the bottle over, once. "So?" He holds the liquor bottle up, offering it to me.

"No, thanks. I drove. And I have a curfew." And I've never had a drink in my life.

"Eleven?"

"Yeah." I guess Emery has the same curfew.

Ben's theater is a windowless room on the first floor. The walls are painted a dark, glossy gray, with a huge white screen on one wall. There's a projector mounted from the ceiling, and I'm not sure how it works, but it's currently projecting the paused title frame from the Broadway production of *Into the Woods* onto the screen.

There's staggered leather seating for six, with cupholders.

The seats recline. I think they may be heated.

Jon and Bella are sitting in the second row. Ben and I join Lexie up front, and this feels like that scene in *Annie*, where Daddy Warbucks rents out an entire movie theater just for his poor, underprivileged orphan. Or maybe it's to impress Miss Farrell.

I'm not sure whether I'm Little Orphan Annie or Grace Farrell in this scene, but I'm duly impressed.

Ben is nice, and beautiful, and talented, and he has his own movie theater. How could Emery *possibly* have screwed this up?

I finish my snacks half an hour into the production, and Ben takes my plate, stacks his on top, and sets them both on a side table. When he sits down again, he reclines his chair, which is attached to mine on one side, and Lexie's on the other.

I recline mine too.

It's weird to watch this in Ben's house. In his theater. Every time I've seen it before, I've been with my mom. Usually on our living room couch, shouting out the lyrics.

No one here sings. At first, I assume that's because we're eating. But Ben is genuinely watching this, and I don't think he's seen it before. Of course, he's also halfway through his spiked Coke, so I can't really tell how much of his somber attention is because he's impressed by Bernadette Peters and how much is because he's literally consuming a depressant.

At intermission, he pauses the projector and jumps up to flip on the lights. I get up to go to the bathroom, and when I turn, I see Bella and Jon making out in the row behind us.

"Oh my God, get a room," Lexie says as she stands.

"Do *not* get a room," Ben counters. "Stay out of the rooms."

"Bathroom?" I grab the dirty plates on my way out of the theater. "Is that one off-limits?"

"That one's fine," he says. "On the left, just past the kitchen."

Lexie follows me, and I whisper as we head down the hall, "Are Bella and Jon together?"

"No. Not as of this afternoon, anyway. But Bella does

whatever she wants. With whomever she wants." Lexie shrugs. "It's part of her charm."

"And Jon?"

She arches both brows at me. "Would *you* turn down Bella Moretti?" Before I can answer, she gestures at the powder bath next to the kitchen. "You take that one. I'll use Ben's."

I duck into the kitchen first and set the plates in the sink. When I'm done in the bathroom, I head back into the kitchen for another soda. Ben finds me staring at the closed fridge as I try to decide if it's rude to just . . . open someone else's refrigerator.

"Go ahead." He snags another slider from a tray kept warm by a little candle burning beneath it. "Take whatever you want."

I pull open the fridge and grab another Coke.

"You okay?" he asks, studying me as if the answers to the ACT might be hidden behind my eyes.

"Yeah. It's just weird to be watching this without my mom."

"Jesus. I heard about that, but I wasn't sure if it was . . ."

"True?"

"Well, you never know about rumors."

"She was hit by a car. Not quite two weeks ago."

"I'm so sorry." Ben frowns, concern echoing in the dip of his brows. "Are you sure you wanna do the play? I mean, won't that just make you think about her every day?"

"I hope so. I'm not trying to forget her. I'm . . . I'm kind of dedicating my performance to my mom. As a tribute. Since I didn't get to say goodbye."

"Wow. That's amazing." He frowns. "That sounded stupid.

I mean, that's the single best reason I've ever heard of for doing a high school musical."

"Well, Emery disagrees with you."

"You've just described the entire ten and a half months we were together. Seriously. Our entire relationship, in that one sentence."

I laugh. "I've only known her for a couple of weeks, but you and I seem to have that in common."

"I think we have a *lot* in common." He turns to lean against the giant refrigerator next to me, his arms crossed over his chest. "But seriously, you've obviously seen the Broadway version before, so if you wanna bow out, I—"

"No. There's no point in going home. Emery's playing it in the living room."

His grin heats up. "I wasn't suggesting you go home. I was saying we could do something else, while they finish the musical. Do you play pool? There's a game room . . ."

I laugh. "*Of course* there's a game room."

He shrugs. "My parents live by the 'work hard, play hard' philosophy."

"What about you?"

He leans down and whispers into my ear. "I pretty much just play hard."

"*Shocker.*"

He leans in for a kiss. I close my eyes as his lips touch mine. His hands find my waist and he tilts his head, deepening our connection. Sparks fall like a meteor shower behind my eyelids.

And just like that, Ben McGrath takes center stage.

# seventeen

Get out! Get out! I don't need you!"

I sit straight up in bed, startled awake by the shouting. The light is off, but the room is brightly lit, because Emery opened the curtains when she got up. If I ask, she'll say something about daylight being good for mental health, but the truth is that she's hoping the sunlight will wake me up before I *choose* to be awake. Because I stayed up until two in the morning texting Ben.

She did the same thing last Sunday, the day after our dueling Broadway watch parties, when she saw a good morning message from him on my lock screen. She hasn't been openly angry about Ben and me, but she's elevated passive aggression to a whole new level.

According to my phone, it's just after 9:00 a.m., but the joke's on Emery, because it wasn't daylight that woke me. It was Grammie.

I'd hoped to sleep for another hour, because it's a Saturday, and I don't have to be anywhere. But I'm awake now, so I change out of my pajamas and cross the hall into the bathroom as quickly as I can so Grammie won't see me.

As much as I like her, I do *not* want to get drawn into another argument between her and the home hospice aides who come to bathe her.

"Mrs. Turner, you have an open wound, and I really need to clean it!" Today, it's Rita, and the poor woman sounds exasperated.

Teeth brushed and face washed, I pad down the hall, barefoot, to find Cody already on the couch, eating dry cereal like popcorn. "Zombies?" he asks, the very second he sees me.

"Yeah. Just a sec."

Even though it's a weekend, there's no sign of breakfast in the kitchen. Cynthia is removing all the silverware from its drawer and stacking it neatly on the counter. I give her a questioning look as I pull open the freezer drawer and take out a box of toaster pastries. The kind with creamy filling.

"The utensil sorter is filthy," she explains as she sets the last serving spoon on its stack on the granite countertop. Then she pulls the storage tray out of the drawer and submerges it into a sink full of soapy water. Her movements as she scrubs are short and harsh, her posture tense. The more Grammie shouts, the harder Cynthia scrubs.

I take my toasted pastry and a glass of chocolate milk into the living room, where I drop onto the couch next to Cody. "Let's do this," I say with my mouth full.

We hack at animated zombies, and every time I die, I take

a big bite of my breakfast while the game respawns my character.

During the reloads—I'm *seriously* bad at this—I can hear the hospice worker speaking softly, calmly to Grammie, trying to convince her to cooperate for her sponge bath. For the cleaning of her wound. Cynthia says it's a bedsore. Rita can't make Grammie cooperate. According to my dad, she has the right to refuse care, but it's hard on everyone when she does.

When she starts shouting again, Cody turns up the volume. Cynthia replaces the silverware sorter and starts pulling food—then *drawers*—from the refrigerator. She's armed with rubber gloves and a bottle of spray cleaner, and I *swear* when my dad comes in from the bedroom, he takes one look at her and thinks about fleeing.

Like, going for a run, or heading into the office, even though his practice is closed on the weekends. I can see it in his face.

Instead, he takes a deep breath, grabs a loaf of bread and a stick of butter Cynthia's just removed from the fridge, and starts making toast in a skillet.

The next time my character dies, I scarf the last bite of my breakfast and take my dishes into the kitchen. "You wanna play?" I ask as I load my plate into the dishwasher. My dad looks up, and I nod into the living room, where Cody's launched a mini-mission on his own.

Dad glances at the TV, and I can see his interest die. Zombies aren't his thing. Neither are video games. In the three weeks I've been here, I haven't seen my dad sit next to Cody on the couch even once. Somehow, it turns out, he's a pop-up parent in his own home.

"Um, let me know if he switches over to chess. Or Stratego. Or . . . hopscotch. Anything but *that*." He waves one hand at the screen. Then he plucks his toast from the skillet with his bare fingers and executes a retreat to the main suite.

Cynthia pulls the vegetable drawer from the fridge and wedges it into the long, farm-style sink.

Cody glances into the kitchen as I reclaim my seat on the center couch cushion and grab the second controller. "You and I have something in common," he whispers.

"Something other than a deep-seated *need* to slay zombies from the back of an armored truck and scavenge for post-apocalyptic supplies?"

He doesn't smile. "You're the baby that nearly broke their marriage, and I'm the one they had to try to fix it." On-screen, he stabs a zombie through the eye with a crowbar. "Neither of us should exist."

I blink at him, my controller practically dangling from my grip. *Damn.* Dad thinks Emery is the smart one, but I think he's selling Cody short.

"That's *not* true. There is no 'should' or 'shouldn't' exist. We're here, so we exist, no matter how we came to be here, and I happen to think you and I are *killin'* it." I point at the screen with my controller. "Get it? *Killing* it?"

Cody rolls his eyes, without turning away from the TV.

I look into the kitchen to see if Cynthia has heard any of what he's saying, but she's put on headphones.

Half an hour later, Rita comes into the living room, carrying a bag of supplies. Cynthia takes off her headphones and gives her a fragile, hopeful look. "I've done what I can, for now," Rita says. "Someone will be here tomorrow to try again. We really need to get that bandage changed."

Cynthia exhales and thanks Rita, then goes back to her deep clean of the kitchen as Rita leaves.

"Hey. You up for a good deed and a different game?" I ask Cody as I pause the zombie slaughter.

He gives me a questioning look.

"Shut that down," I say as I open the game closet and scan the contents. Box after box of board games, checkers, chess, and an entire collection of dust-covered toddler games.

Cody hesitates, but then, at my back, I hear the sound of the PlayStation shutting down.

My gaze lands on a case of dominoes, and I grab them. "Come with me." I don't tell him where we're going, because I don't want to give him a chance to say no, but he catches on when I head for the hall.

"*Michaela*," he whispers, lurching forward to grab my hand. To stop me. "She doesn't know who I am most of the time."

"I know. Sometimes she thinks I'm Emery. But that's not her fault."

"But it's *weird*. It's creepy."

"Weird, yes. Creepy? No. She's just confused. She's scared, and lonely, and they may have the cancer under control, but dementia can't be cured. So . . ."

Cody gives me a strange look. "They don't have the cancer

under control." He's still whispering. "She's dying, Michaela. That's why she's here. That's what hospice is for."

"What?" I glance over his shoulder, but Cynthia's not in the kitchen anymore. "Your mom said—"

"She lied. Or she just can't make herself say it. But Grammie is dying."

Yet he's twelve, and he can say it. Of course, Grammie isn't his mother.

Cynthia is losing her mom.

I thought it was horrible, losing my mother suddenly. Losing Grandma Louise the same way. But maybe it's worse to have to watch it happen. To watch and know there's nothing you can do.

"Okay. Well, that makes it even more important that you spend time with her. While you still can."

"Maybe for a few minutes . . ." He looks profoundly uncomfortable.

"Cody. This isn't about you. It's about her. She's alone in there most of the time. And she's more scared than I even realized, if she knows she's dying."

"I think she does. Most of the time," he amends.

"Okay. Come on." Still clutching the dominoes, I head down the hall to Grammie's room. I can hear Cody's steps at my back. I peek through the open door and see that Grammie is sitting up in bed, scowling at the TV. "Hey!" I call as I push the door open. "Want some company?"

"Emery?" She smiles and waves me forward.

"No, it's Michaela. Emery's . . . not here." She left before I even got up.

Grammie's smile falters, but then she regroups. I see recognition in her eyes. "Of course. Come in!"

"And I brought someone special." I step into the room, revealing Cody behind me in the doorway.

"Cody!" Grammie's joy makes me smile, but there's an echo of something painful beneath that. She looks so happy because this is a rare and special treat. I haven't seen him visit her even once in the three weeks I've been here. And it isn't because he's a bad grandson. It's because he doesn't know how to handle death. Or dementia. And I can't really blame him for that.

Cody smiles. He's obviously relieved. "Hey, Grammie." He doesn't seem to know what to say next, but that's fine.

"So, I was thinking about that game you said you used to play with your kids, when they were younger. I figure if Cynthia can learn it at six, Cody and I can manage it at twelve and sixteen. What was it called?"

I hold up the dominoes to jog her memory.

"Chickenfoot!" she cries. "But that's a double-twelve set, and we only need them through double-nine. Here, let's lay them out!" She pulls the rolling tray table into place over her bed and starts handing us the cup, tissue box, and half-eaten candy bar to clear it.

Cody helps her clean off the tray, and I pull two chairs up next to her bed, while Grammie lays out the dominoes we'll need, then begins turning them facedown so we can "draw."

She shows us how to form a "double chickenfoot," and "chickentoes." We play a practice round. Then she gets serious, and in the next round, she shows us how to block each other's moves.

Two hours later, I hear music coming from the backyard, so I stand and excuse myself. "No!" Grammie cries. "We can't play with only two people." She turns to Cody. "Gabriel, tell her to stay."

Cody blinks, surprised. But he recovers quickly. "Why don't we play checkers, instead?"

"Want me to bring you the board?" I ask.

He picks up the iPad on her dresser. "Got one right here."

As I leave, he's showing Grammie how to play board games on the iPad, and explaining that when he's not here to play against her, she can play against the computer. Which he calls the AI, which leads to an explanation of artificial intelligence in gaming.

I smile on my way down the hall.

In the kitchen, I grab a soda, and I can hear Cynthia moving things around in her room, where her stress-cleaning has evidently continued in the main closet. Which means my dad has already left for his Saturday afternoon tee time. I head out the back door, toward the garage. Gabe's band is practicing, and I don't recognize the song. I think they've written a new one, and I really like it. It's haunting and slow, and it makes me feel . . . wistful. Probably because of the minor key.

I stop in the doorway, and I wish I'd brought a jacket. The first week of February is still cold.

Josh is singing. The notes flow like honey: smooth, and slow, and sweet. He's playing guitar too—Gabe is on his bass—but the vocals are the real star here. That, and the words. It's a song about hidden beauty. Beauty where you don't expect to find it. About that moment of joy when a flower bud opens. When a baby smiles. When daylight breaks through the clouds, even if you know that rain is coming.

The drums are a slow, steady backbone for artful lyrics. I wonder who wrote them?

Then the chorus kicks in, and the song speeds up a little. But mostly it . . . intensifies. The passion behind each note grows, and Josh's voice hits an intense, longing tone.

He sees me, and he smiles in the middle of the note.

Gabe turns to see what he's looking at, then waves me inside, tossing his head at my bucket. And it is *my* bucket now, because I always sit on it while I listen.

I step over wires and an old flat tire, rounding a child's bicycle missing its rear wheel, and I sit on my bucket. And I listen. When the final note rings out, I start clapping. "That was beautiful!"

"It's still missing something," Josh says. "I think it needs some harmony."

"In the bridge?" Gabe asks. "I can mess around with it."

"Yeah. Let's go through it again, and—"

I stand, glancing at my phone.

"You're welcome to stay," Josh says.

"You're even more welcome to bring out some drinks!" John Thomas calls from his drum stool.

"Well, as flattered as I am that you see me as a worthy roadie, Ben's going to be here any minute. We're going to watch a movie."

"Here?" Gabe asks. "Isn't this supposed to be a Ben McGrath free zone?"

I shrug. "Cody said Emery's staying the night with Mara, so . . ." This may be my only chance to hang out with him here, where I'm at least marginally more comfortable than in the museum where Ben lives.

Gabe blinks. I know him well enough by now to know that means he's decided to keep his opinion to himself. He seems to be of the "don't date your sister's ex" mindset, but since he's also a charter member of the "judge not, lest ye be judged" club, he hasn't come straight out and said anything. And I can live with that.

"Anyway, that was great, you guys. See you later." I turn and start to head across the lawn, but Josh's voice calls me back.

"It's her! Michaela!"

"What?" I spin to find him staring at me, his eyes wide with some kind of epiphany.

"You're what we need. What the *song* needs. Not just harmony. *Female* harmony." He turns to Gabe. "Her. It's a duet. I mean, I just now realized it, but that's what's missing. This should be a duet. With Michaela."

He seems totally sure of that, and I have to admit, I'm curious. We've just spent week two of *Into the Woods* rehearsal working on the music in the choir room, with Mr. Rayburn. Josh and I know each other's voices.

"Sure. Why not?" John Thomas says.

Gabe looks intrigued. "A *girl*, singing with a boy band?" His eyes widen. "Guys, what if they take away our man cards?"

I laugh, and Josh turns to me again. "What do you think? Will you give it a shot?"

"I don't have time to learn the song right now. Can you ask me again later?" I glance at my phone again as I hear the growl of an engine from out front. "Ben's here. This is not a no!" I call over my shoulder as I jog across the grass, toward the driveway. "It's a definite maybe!"

I head down the driveway to where Ben has just parked in front of the house. "Hey!" I'm a little breathless, and I hope my cheeks are flushed. I hope I look excited to see him. Because I am.

"Hey." Ben closes his door and pulls me close for a kiss. A real one. Our first kiss was one week ago today, and since then, there have only been little baby kisses stolen in the hall at school, when no one is watching. "Has the wicked stepsister vacated the castle?" he whispers.

"She's my half sister. And she's not wicked."

"Would that be a yes?"

"Yes. Everyone else is here, except my dad, who's playing golf. Emery's staying the night at Mara's."

"A stepsister sleepover." He shudders dramatically. "Every prince in the land will sleep uneasy tonight."

"Ha, ha. So, what are we watching?"

"Well, it's a week before Valentine's Day, which means it's lady's choice."

"I am positively *drunk* with power . . ."

Ben links his arm through mine as we walk back up the driveway. "Let me know if you'd rather be drunk with actual alcohol, because I can make that happen."

I glance uneasily at the house, where my stepmother has pulled everything out of her bedroom closet, determined to reorganize the whole thing before my dad takes her out to dinner tonight.

"Well, not here, of course," Ben amends. "But it's Saturday. We could go out. We could do anything." He leans in to nibble my ear, and warmth drips down my throat to land in the molten pit my stomach has become. I want everything he's offering. I want that, and more. And yet . . .

"Let's just stay here." It's early days, in whatever this is between us, and my life is a roller coaster at the moment. Highs and lows like whiplash. "Is that okay?"

"It's perfect." Ben settles onto the couch while I grab drinks from the kitchen. When I join him in the living room, I'm surprised to see that he's already turned on the PlayStation and opened one of the streaming apps. It's an unpleasant reminder that he dated Emery for ten and a half months. He probably knows his way around this house better than I do.

Maybe we *should* have gone to his house.

We curl up on the couch, and I pick one of the trending romances, and for the first half of the movie, we have the living room to ourselves. Cody must have heard us and decided to hang in his room. Gabe and his bandmates are still in the garage. And, in his quest to become a walking doctor cliché, my dad will evidently golf all day long.

But just as the heroine discovers that she actually loves the man she's been pretending to hate, Cynthia emerges from the main suite like a bear from hibernation, desperate for sustenance. She stops in the middle of the kitchen when she realizes, squinting into the living room, which is only lit by the glow of the screen, that I am not watching a movie alone.

"Ben?" She sounds thoroughly confused. It's *possible* I forgot to tell her he was coming over.

It's equally possible she didn't know Ben and I are a thing now. I didn't tell her, and Emery only seems to confide in her mother when it will somehow benefit her.

Ben pauses the movie and leans forward on the couch so he can see her around me. "Hi, Mrs. Bosch. How are you?"

"I'm fine. I just . . . didn't expect to see you here." And she doesn't sound happy about that.

"Should I go?"

Cynthia stands a little taller, and I can practically see her inner hostess warring with Mama Bear, who obviously wants to kick her daughter's ex out of the house. "No, of course not. Any guest of Michaela's . . ." She blinks, as if she's not sure what she's even saying. As if she had no intention of ever welcoming Ben McGrath into her home again. "Can I get you guys anything to eat or drink?"

I think we've broken her. I think smoke is about to come pouring out of her ears. Her face is about to swing open on little hidden hinges, revealing a robot completely overwhelmed by the task of feigning conflicting human emotions.

I know how she feels. I don't want to hurt Emery. But it isn't fair—to either Ben or to me—that she should get to decide who I go out with.

"We're fine," I tell her. "Thanks."

Cynthia pours herself a small glass of white wine and goes back to her closet.

I have no idea how the movie ends—I assume the girl gets the guy; it *is* a romance—because Ben and I aren't really watching by then.

The back door flies open as the credits roll, and I jump off the couch, mortified to have been caught making out with my new boyfriend. Praying Emery hasn't come home. But it's just Gabe.

"Hey." He lifts one eyebrow at me, and then his gaze slides toward Ben. For once, he doesn't seem to know what to say.

"Hey." Ben reaches for the controller and stops the movie.

John Thomas and Josh come in behind Gabe, and I feel like my face is on fire. But Ben is completely unruffled. "Band practice?" he guesses.

"Yeah." Josh glances at me on his way into the kitchen, and I have an overwhelming urge to stare at my feet.

"What's the name of the band again?" Ben asks as he tugs on my hand. I sink onto the couch next to him, and he puts an arm around me.

Josh accepts a water from Gabe. "The Nuclear Option."

"Did we actually vote on that?" John Thomas asks as Gabriel hands him a soda. "I liked 'Broken Compass.'"

"We definitely voted."

"Yeah, but we all three voted for a different name," Gabe says.

Josh's gaze falls on me, and I feel uncomfortable in a way I can't quite describe. "Given any more thought to the duet?"

"What duet?" Ben asks.

"Gabe's band has a new song, and they want me to try it out with them. To see if a female voice is what's missing."

"Cool. Can I hear it?"

"Yeah," Josh says. "We're playing at Sage Andersen's party next week. You can hear the whole set list then."

Sage is the junior playing Cinderella's Stepmother. She's also a cheerleader in the running for valedictorian, padding her college applications with every extracurricular she can find.

"Wanna go?" Ben asks me.

"I haven't been invited."

"Yes you have. Sage invited the entire cast."

"And the football team. And the cheerleaders, and everyone she knows from last year's debate team, and every Girl Scout from her third-grade troop." John Thomas shrugs. "Her parents have a huge house, and they spend their anniversary on a different Caribbean island every year."

My mom and I used to watch *Island Life* and dream about moving to St. Maarten, like all those people on the show who sold everything and relocated to the Caribbean. But if we sold everything we owned, she'd joked, we'd only be able to afford a few grains of sand.

"So?" Ben says. "Sage's party, next Saturday?"

"Sounds like fun." No one in Oak Valley throws parties like

that. I've never been to one. I've only seen stuff like that on TV, and the truth is that it didn't look real then.

I'll believe this party when I see it.

"Great." Ben stands. "Walk me to my car?"

"You're leaving?"

"It's a little uncomfortable for me here," he whispers. "But you can come with me. My parents aren't home . . ."

Gabe, Josh, and John Thomas are in the kitchen, digging through the fridge, but I think they can hear us. I feel like they're *listening*.

"Next time," I say. "But I'll walk you out."

Ben pouts, and I laugh.

We kiss, leaning against his car, until my dad pulls into the driveway. He parks without pulling into the garage. "Michaela?" he calls as he gets out. He pushes a button on his key fob, and his trunk pops open. "And . . . Ben."

"*Super* uncomfortable," Ben whispers. Then he raises his voice. "Hi, Dr. Bosch."

"Hi." My dad hauls his golf clubs from his trunk, and for a second, I'm afraid he's going to pull out a driver and hold it like a baseball bat.

"I was just leaving," Ben says. He gives me one more kiss on the cheek, then gets into his car and drives away.

"Ben McGrath?" my dad says as he slams his trunk. "Seriously?"

I fall into step with him. "For a week now. I'm surprised you haven't heard."

"My kids never tell me anything," he growls.

"Or—alternate theory—you don't listen."

I jog down the driveway, toward the back garage, where I can hear music playing again, and I leave my father staring after me.

"Okay," I say from the doorway. "I'm ready. Teach me this duet."

# eighteen

Music rehearsals were one thing, but blocking onstage is . . . harder. Remembering where to be, what to say, who to look at. How to evoke emotion with every gesture.

This is not my strongest suit.

"Cinderella!" Ms. Bond stands on the apron, her silvery hair twisted into a messy bun. Today, her theater-themed T-shirt reads, "I'm not yelling; I'm projecting." And boy, is that accurate. "I need you stage left of Baker's Wife. You've just fled the king's festival after discovering that the prince may be hot, but he's a total snore."

"Not offended at all," Josh quips from offstage, where he's painting tree leaves.

I move to Lexie's other side. We're not off book yet, so we're all holding scripts as we work our way through the scene. Except for Ben and Kat. They've already memorized their lines, and their scripts, pencils, and highlighters are lying at the front of the stage so they can take notes if they need to.

I'm worried that it makes the rest of us—namely me—look bad, that the two actors with the most lines are already off book.

Mostly the principal roles have been called today, but half of the rest of the cast is backstage, painting set pieces with the crew members. Several more are in the girls' dressing room, an oddly shaped space that leaks the rapid *sht-sht-sht* sound of the sewing machine every time someone opens the door.

Emery is here somewhere, but I can't tell where, with the lights shining in my face. Despite the fact that we share a room, she's hardly spoken to me in a week and a half. Since Ben's watch party.

"Guys, we're halfway through week three! There are only two more rehearsals until we're off book!" Ms. Bond calls as we reposition ourselves to start the scene over. "You should all be nearly there by now!"

"My lines are memorized!" Link calls from somewhere backstage.

"You only have, like, four lines!" Bella shouts at him. She's wearing an old, paint-splattered men's button-up shirt to shield her clothes as she paints stones on Rapunzel's tower. The very one she'll be standing in onstage.

Link also has an entire song to himself, but that doesn't really count. No one has trouble memorizing music; it's the spoken lines that give people problems.

"Okay, let's start where Baker's Wife enters from upstage, pulling Milky White. Cinderella, Prince, and Steward, be ready in the wings."

I stand just offstage with Josh and a sophomore named

Chris, who's playing the Steward. Lexie walks onstage, pulling an imaginary white cow, and Josh elbows me. "You're on," he whispers.

I rush onstage—the script says I *dash*—clutching my book. I'm supposed to be breathless from fleeing the festival, so I'm gasping, clutching my chest.

Sure, I can sing, but I'm not a great actress.

Emery laughs from somewhere backstage, and I can feel my face burn. This isn't supposed to be a funny part.

We go through the scene—it's *rough*—and finally the music starts, for "A Very Nice Prince," my duet with Lexie. But Ms. Bond stops us before I actually get to sing.

I stifle a groan. My face is *on fire*. She's going to take the part from me. I know she is.

"Michaela, please lay your script at the front of the stage."

"What? Why? We're not supposed to go off book until next week." I can feel everyone staring at me. Even the faceless forms sitting out front, in the "house." "I still have two rehearsals—five days—left to—"

"You haven't glanced at it once all afternoon. You already know your lines, so there's no point in carrying the book around."

Okay, yes, my lines are technically memorized. Ben and I have been running them all week, over FaceTime, but . . .

"It's a book, not a security blanket!" someone shouts from backstage. That wasn't Emery, but I think it might have been Mara. Who is definitely, certainly, without a doubt in league with my wicked half sister.

"She's not wrong." Ms. Bond tugs on the hem of her T-shirt with one hand, her massive three-ring binder tucked under her opposite arm. Her glasses are perched on her head, where she can just flip them down when she needs to glance at the script. "You don't need it," she insists. "You're just using it as a crutch—"

"Because I'm not sure I know *every* word."

She steps forward, and the weight of her attention is practically giving me hives. I feel like a convicted prisoner staring at the executioner. "You need to trust yourself."

Okay, so she's not exactly chopping my head off. But I'm intensely uncomfortable with being singled out.

I guess I should suck less.

"You're ahead of half the cast anyway," Ms. Bond continues. "So if you forget a word here or there, no one's going to laugh."

"I might laugh," Link admits. He's wearing a set of wolf ears, so none of us can forget who he's playing. Ever. "But I'll be laughing *with* you."

"Just put the script down and let yourself sink into the role. Trust yourself to know the words so you can start learning the *part* instead. So you can be Cinderella, instead of Michaela Rutherford *playing* Cinderella. Okay?"

I can still feel everyone staring at me, and it does *not* feel good. But I guess I should get used to that. There will be several times that many eyes on me in less than six weeks. Assuming I survive rehearsals.

I walk toward the front of the stage and set my book right at the edge, next to Ben's. I take my highlighter and pencil from my pocket and lay them on top of the book. I feel like an imposter as I return to the wings. I'm worried that people will think I'm some kind of diva, walking around without my book, five days before I have to have my lines memorized.

But also, I already miss the security of having the words there, in case I need to glance at them.

"Show-off," Josh whispers from the shadows.

"That wasn't— I didn't mean to—" He's tapped into my worst fear.

"I'm just kidding!" he whispers as Lexie takes her place again. "Seriously, Mick!" He's started calling me that in the garage, when I hang out with the band. When I sing with them. "If I spent more time memorizing lines and less time writing lyrics, I'd be as prepared as you are."

I wish I were in the garage at home right now. I wish I were singing with Gabe, and Josh, and John Thomas, instead of waiting in the wings, half terrified.

Josh elbows me again, and I dash onstage, breathing hard, but not gasping this time. I guess I should tone that down. At first, I feel naked without my script. Without the safety net—pacifier?—beneath me. But then I realize that since I'm not holding the book, I'm free to actually act. To move my hands. To gesture. To be Cinderella.

It's still not as great as singing, but it's enough to get me through the spoken lines. And this time, when the music starts, Ms. Bond doesn't stop us.

Since I'm not holding my script, I can take off my slippers—today, that role is being played by my yellow Vans—and rub my feet, which are ostensibly sore from fleeing the prince. Giving the Baker's Wife a chance to notice that they're the exact pair of golden slippers she's been looking for.

At the end of the scene, I run offstage with my shoes.

"Okay, that was better! Let's take ten!" Ms. Bond calls. "And remember to keep the walkways clear. It's *very* important that nothing is left on the yellow-and-black-striped walkway, because during the production, both cast and crew will be rushing down that path, and someone could easily trip and break an actual leg if costumes and set pieces are left on the walkway."

A dozen voices mumble in assent, and suddenly Ben is at my side, in the wings. "That was great." He pulls me close, and I find my lips pressed against his, right there in front of half of the cast and crew. And now the warmth burning inside me isn't limited to my face, and it isn't imposter syndrome or stage fright.

I feel like Ben just made a public declaration about me. Everyone knows we're together now. He's not trying to hide this. To hide me. I hate that I feel validated by that, but I do. And I don't want to think that has anything to do with my dad trying to hide my mother for the entire length of their relationship. As if she wasn't good enough to be seen with.

But it probably does.

When he finally lets me go, I can practically feel someone staring at me. Not the approving, amused gazes of the masses adoring their acknowledged theater It boy. What I feel is the cold bite of steel at my back.

Emery is glaring at me, from somewhere in the shadows. Openly hating me from the wings. I can feel it.

And yet, when I find the eyes watching me, they're not my half sister's baby blues, but instead a piercing set of purple contact lenses.

Kat Torrez is watching me.

No, she's watching Ben.

"Little did our hero and heroine know . . . ," Aaron Pagett says in his Narrator voice as he walks by, ". . . but they were not alone, making out in the private back seat of Ben's BMW. They were, in fact, in *full view* of the entire cast and crew. Under a microscope, some might say . . ."

Suddenly embarrassed, I hide my face in Ben's shoulder. He wraps his arms around me as he laughs.

Kat steps forward to smack the back of Aaron's head, then hauls him down the walkway by a fistful of his right sleeve. "What did we say about your role as Narrator?"

He gives her an exaggerated stage pout. "Stick to the lines in the script and stop narrating people's actual lives."

"That's right. And what did we say about *consequences*?"

I smile as she pulls him through the door into the brightly lit storage area where all the old set pieces and prop furniture are haphazardly stacked against the walls. Aaron *has* been narrating a lot lately. After school, he provided a completely unnecessary voice-over as Bella and Jon tried to pry her bag of Fritos from a glitchy vending machine in the lobby. So no one's taking him too seriously.

The only person who might is Emery, and she's . . . well, she seems to have disappeared entirely.

---

When I step out of the bathroom stall, I find Emery standing in front of the row of sinks along one wall. Her back is to the mirror, and her arms are crossed over her shirt. She's not checking her hair or reapplying lip gloss. She's waiting for me.

We're alone, and I have a horrible suspicion that she locked the door or something.

Do high school bathrooms even lock?

"Hey," I say as I run water from the faucet next to her, as if this is totally normal. As if I don't feel like I'm being accosted. She turns to stare at me in the mirror but says nothing. Lucinda hasn't been called for rehearsal today, but as my understudy, Emery has to be there anytime Cinderella's part is called.

But I don't need an understudy to pee.

"What's up?" I lather my hands, pointedly not glaring at her in the mirror.

"I know you're not going to believe me—"

"I won't, if you say things that aren't true."

"—but Ben's only with you to get to me."

*Ouch.* That's a new low.

"He didn't even know we're related until after he asked me out," I remind her reflection.

"That doesn't mean he wasn't trying to rub you in my face. You kinda look like me. You can sing. He found you staring wistfully at a poster for the musical, and he took you up onstage not two weeks after we broke up, because he knew I'd be watching. Because he wanted me to see him onstage with some other girl, singing the song we were going to audition with. *Together.* He thinks he's replacing me with my—"

"Your what? Your real-life understudy?"

She shrugs, anger roiling behind her eyes. Bulging in the clench of her jaw. "You *are* playing my part. And I don't mean Cinderella."

I turn off the faucet and grab a paper towel from the dispenser. "Do you not think it's *possible*, even just a little bit, that Ben likes me for me, and not as part of some overblown plot to piss off his ex-girlfriend? Can't you just *consider* the possibility that I don't live my life in reaction to something you said or did—or someone you dated—before I even knew you?"

"If you knew him like I do, you would—"

"How am I supposed to get to know him at all, with you dripping poison in my ear all the time? Why can't you just let me have this? I lost my mom, and my house, and my hometown, and my friends, and my school. I don't even feel welcome in my own bedroom anymore. Why can't you just let me have the *one thing* that makes me feel better? The one thing that's easy and fun? Don't I deserve to be happy just a little bit?"

"Of course." To her credit, she looks conflicted. "Believe it or not, Michaela, I am not trying to stand in the way of your happiness. But can't you find something that makes you happy that doesn't also make me miserable?"

"Oh my God!" I throw my arms in the air. I can't help it. "You're not the victim here, Emery!"

"And you're not the star." Her fists are clenched.

"I have to be back onstage in ninety seconds." I take a deep breath. "Was there anything else?"

There are little white marks in her palms, from where her fingernails dug into them. "He's not what you think he is."

"Okay." I reach past her to throw away the towel, but when I head for the door, she steps into my path.

"I know he makes you feel special. Pretty. Talented. *Loved.* He's really good at that. It's, like, his evil superpower. But none of it is real."

"So, Ben is secretly evil, and because I have no value all on my own, he's dating me just to make you jealous. Have I got all that straight?"

"That's not what I'm—" She looks more frustrated, now, than mad. "Not to make me jealous. To hurt me."

"Got it. I promise that when this blows up in my face, I won't say you didn't warn me." I reach around her for the door handle, but she scoots to the left, blocking me again.

"Will you just *listen*?" Emery reaches for me, and I back away from her. "I'm trying to help you."

"Like you tried to help me by insisting I give up my part for you? *How* could I not have seen it before? You're right; I *would* be much happier if I gave you my boyfriend, and my part in the musical, and my half of our bedroom. Wow, Emery, how can *I* become a selfless saint like you? Always thinking of others. Is that . . . ?" I squint at the air six inches above her head. "Is that a halo?"

"Michaela. I'm telling you the truth. Ben McGrath is a liar and an asshole, and—"

"I can't. Oh my God, I can't do this." Talking to her is exhausting and pointless, like trying to run a marathon in heels. "Emery, I think you and I should call a truce. I think we should try to truly get along, for the sake of the rest of our family, and I think the only way that's going to work is if we agree not to talk about Ben McGrath. Okay? Not about your past relationship with him or my present one. Sound fair?"

She exhales. Her shoulders slump. "You're not going to listen, are you?"

"I *have* listened. But you're right. I don't believe you, because everything you've said about him sounds bitter and vindictive, and everything he's said about you sounds one hundred percent on-brand for Emery Bosch. So . . ." I shrug.

Her perfectly powdered brows dip, forming lines like a set of reverse parentheses above her nose. "What did he say about me?"

"Nothing." *Shit.* "I'm due on set. Will you please move?"

"Not until you tell me what he—"

"Fine! He said you were controlling. And melodramatic. And that you twist the facts."

"*He* called *me* a liar?"

"No, he said you twist the facts. And I've personally seen you do that to me. So why wouldn't I believe that you'd do that to him?"

"Oh my God."

"Will you please move?"

"You're totally under his spell."

"Emery!" I cry. And when she still doesn't move, I grab her arm and haul her out of the way.

As I march down the yellow-and-black walkway, through the storage room into the dark backstage area, I turn to glance back at the bathroom, and I find Mara and Emery huddled together, watching me. Tears stand in Emery's eyes, and I can't tell whether she's pissed off or hurt. Or both.

But I am sure that I have *not* managed to call a truce.

# nineteen

Zombies?" Cody asks from the couch as I cross the living room behind him.

I pull my phone from my pocket to glance at the time. I have a little bit to spare, so I drop onto the couch next to him. "What are you doing here tonight, anyway? Didn't your mom say something about a middle school dance? Like, for Valentine's Day?"

He huffs. "They don't have actual dances until high school around here. It's a 'social.' Game Night."

"On Valentine's Day weekend?"

He shrugs as he signs into his PlayStation account. "The timing is an unfortunate coincidence."

"I highly doubt that. What kind of games are we talking about?"

"They set up a bunch of board games at small tables. Chess. Checkers. Battleship. Stuff like that. You just grab a spot when one opens up. There's a Karaoke Korner—two Ks. Seriously.

A trivia tournament. Giant bowling. Giant Jenga. Giant Connect Four. They're really big on giant games."

"Sounds like it."

"There's a scavenger hunt, too, so girls usually try to bring weird things in their purses. And they always close with a massive game of red rover." Another shrug. "That one's always a hit, even though everyone claims to be too old for it."

"That sounds like fun!" I grab a remote from the charger on the coffee table. "So why the hell are you hanging out on the couch, on a Friday night, with your sister?"

Cody shrugs again. Then he hits the start button. "Radioactive bloater, on your left."

I shoot the green, glowing zombie in the head. He explodes, and my character dies of uranium exposure, or something like that. Because I forgot to put on my protective gear. "Seriously. Why aren't you hanging out with friends tonight?" I ask as I open the quick menu and my character pulls on a bright yellow chemical warfare suit.

"They all have dates."

"To game night?"

He nods as he drives a golf club through the head of a half-rotten "lurcher."

I guess the timing of game night wasn't a coincidence after all. "Did you ask anyone?"

He kills two zombies with one bullet, and an achievement pops up on the screen. "Yes!" Cody shouts. "But no, to the date question."

"Is there anyone you *wanted* to ask?"

"She would have said no."

"How do you know?"

Cody shrugs again.

"Seriously. You never know until you ask."

"I know."

"How can you possibly—"

"Michaela." Cody pauses the game and turns to me, his eyes shining with a muted pain that breaks my heart. "Look at me." He gestures to his face. To a cluster of acne on his forehead, and a matching patch on his chin.

"Anyone worth your attention won't care about that," I tell him.

Cody rolls his eyes and unpauses. "Yeah. That's why you're with Ben."

"As a matter of fact, I'm with him because he's nice, and he's talented, and he's funny."

"Right. It has nothing to do with the fact that he looks like a model in a face soap ad."

I sigh as I shoot a zombie lumbering toward me. Cody has a point. I didn't know that Ben was talented or funny when I followed him backstage three weeks ago. I followed him because he was beautiful. Denying that would make me a liar and a hypocrite.

"I'm twelve, not stupid," Cody says. "I know why you're with Ben instead of Josh."

"Josh Kang?"

Cody nods.

"Okay, that's out of left field. But you're wrong. Josh is a great guy, and—"

"And he's just as talented as Ben. Maybe more talented; Josh writes his own songs."

How did this become about Josh?

"Yes, he does. And they're good."

"But do you think he's cute?" Cody pauses the game again, and I realize this *isn't* about Josh. It's about the small patches of acne on Josh's cheeks, back near his ears. It's about how Cody thinks that if I'm not with Josh, it must be because of his skin, and he's drawn some kind of heartbreaking conclusion about his own chances with twelve-year-old girls based on that.

"I think he's super cute," I say. And that's true.

"Then why aren't you with him?"

"Because I'm with Ben. Because Josh and I are just friends. Because I'm singing with the band now, and that would make things awkward. Because— Okay, look. I used to have acne just like yours. It started when I was eleven, and I hate to admit it, but I *hated* looking in the mirror."

"And it just went away?"

"No. My mom took me to a dermatologist, and he gave me some cream. It works most of the time, but I still get the occasional breakout. You just haven't noticed, because when that happens, as it does to just about everyone, I cover it up with makeup. I'm sure Emery does the same thing." In fact, I know she does.

"I don't think makeup is the solution to my problems."

I smile. "That wasn't what I was suggesting. And I don't think you should see a dermatologist to make you more attractive to someone else. You don't want someone who only wants you if you look a certain way." A lesson I wish I could go back and teach thirteen-year-old me, and the middle school assholes she dealt with. "But if acne treatment would make you feel more comfortable in your own skin, then go for it. Ask your mom or dad to take you."

"Eh, maybe." He shrugs again as he unpauses the game. "But I'm not really missing out on anything, as long as I have you and Grammie." Yet he's thinking about it. I can tell. "We tried Clue after lunch, but it was a total disaster. So was Battleship. But checkers . . . Checkers is our game. She can't forget what she's guessed or where she dropped a bomb, and she's *really* good at it. She beat me four times."

"At checkers?"

"Yeah." Cody laughs. "I tried to get her to try this one, but she says she doesn't like scary games. I think I might be able to talk her into *Plants vs. Zombies*, though, on her iPad. I played that one when I was little. The zombies aren't scary, and you shoot them with vegetables, so . . ." Another shrug.

I laugh, and when I look up, I find my father watching us from the kitchen, where he's holding a coffee mug. He looks . . . pensive. Regretful. As if he wishes he were in here with us. Which, of course, he could be.

"Hey." I wave him forward. "Wanna play?"

"No, no, that's not really my thing."

I let my character die, then set my controller back on the

charger. "I gotta bow out," I tell Cody. "I'm practicing with the band in a few minutes." Tomorrow night is Sage's party, and I've agreed to sing not one, but two songs. And maybe to harmonize on the originals.

"Okay. Thanks for playing." Cody loads his solo game, and in seconds, I've lost him to the lure of bullets and melee weapons made of rusty lawnmower blades and broken golf clubs.

I head into the kitchen, because my dad's still standing there, watching Cody. "Okay, out with it," I whisper. "Why are you staring at your son from the adjacent room, instead of going in there and actually spending time with him?"

"Because if I go in there, he'll clam up, like a . . . clam."

I smile, and my dad frowns at me. "What's so funny?" he asks.

"I see now why Emery's metaphors are so bad."

His frown deepens. "How did you get him to talk to you?" He's still staring at Cody, as if his youngest son is some puzzle he can't quite solve.

"I asked him questions."

"That's it?"

"Yeah. I play games with him, and I ask him questions. When my thumbs get tired, we may watch a movie instead. But that's it. That's how people spend time together. You should try it."

My dad gives me a wary look, as if it can't possibly be that easy.

"Pretend it's a game of golf. Only instead of playing on a course with your doctor friends, you're playing in there with your son, and instead of hitting an actual ball with a real golf club, you're pounding an animated zombie's rotting skull with a broken cartoon club you scavenged from the corpse of a golfer who probably looked"—I glance at him up and down—"very much like you."

He scowls at the screen. "That's supposed to be a golf club?"

I squint. "I think it's a wedge. Could be an iron."

My dad laughs out loud, and Cody glances at us from the living room.

Someone knocks on the back door, and when I leave the kitchen to answer it, my dad is still frowning at Cody's video game.

"Hey!" Josh says as I let him in. "Have you seen Gabe? He's not out here." Josh and John Thomas usually head straight to the garage when they come over to practice. Sometimes they're out there when Gabe isn't even home, because John Thomas keeps his drum set in our garage, and Dad and Cynthia don't mind.

"I'll go find him." I close the door behind Josh, and as I head into the hall, I hear leather groan as he sinks onto the couch.

"What'cha playin'?"

"*DeathBite*."

"Oooh, I didn't know that was out already. Mind if I join?"

I smile as I pass Cody's empty room, then Gabe's. In our room, Emery is stretched out on her bed, staring at her phone with her AirPods peeking from her ears, but Gabe isn't with her. She pretends she doesn't see me, and that's fine.

Grammie's door is cracked open. I don't hear the TV or

anything, but movement from inside catches my eye, so I peek in. Gabe is standing next to her bed. For just a second, I get this super-warm feeling, deep in my stomach. Satisfaction. Or maybe relief. I've been trying to get him to come visit her while he still has a chance, but he always seems to have something else to do. But now he's here, and—

Then I realize that Grammie is sound asleep, facing me. Facing *away* from Gabe. And that he's holding one of her pill bottles.

It's open.

He hasn't seen me yet. He slaps his other hand over his mouth and tosses his head back. His throat bobs as he swallows.

I step into the room. "Josh is here."

Gabe's focus jumps over my head, and he stiffens until he realizes there's no one behind me. That he hasn't *really* been caught.

Normally, there's a smile lurking at the edges of his mouth, waiting to pop out at me. There's a joke waiting to fall from his tongue. Not today. Today he looks tense.

"What is that?" I ask as he screws the lid back on the bottle. Senior citizens don't use childproof lids.

"Hydrocodone."

A painkiller. An opiate. I know, from my middle school drug awareness program, that it can be addictive. I know that it's made from a modified codeine molecule—I can even sketch that out for you—because my mom was a registered nurse who thought my school's drug awareness program was insufficient.

I know that hydrocodone makes some people itch. I know that you can get sick from withdrawal if you stop taking it suddenly.

But I know most of that in the same way I know that fire burns. That childbirth hurts. I've never been burned or given birth, so while I can rattle off those facts, I don't really understand them on a personal level.

I don't understand this either.

"Does your leg hurt?" My grandmother always said her hip still ached from a break a decade before, and Gabe broke his leg last year. Maybe that's what the pill's for.

"Sometimes." He hesitates for a second. If this were a scene in a play, the script would call it a *beat*. "Are you going to be weird about this?"

That's what I need. I need a beat. A moment to think.

"No."

"Seriously, it's just one pill." Clearly, he doesn't believe me. "Not a big deal."

"I know." And I *do* know, because when I was fourteen, I broke my arm and the doctor prescribed hydrocodone. I took two of them before my mom switched me over to Tylenol. The hydrocodone didn't make me feel high. It didn't relax me. It made me throw up, which gave me a headache and made the throbbing in my arm worse.

But the pills weren't a big deal.

"You're really not going to say anything?"

"No."

He's frowning. He still doesn't believe me. "Michaela . . ."

For the first time since I met Gabe, he looks angry, and a flut-
tery feeling of panic blossoms in my stomach. Emery hates me,
and Cynthia resents me. My dad loves me, but he's hardly the
confidant my mother was. But Gabe and I have become friends,
since I've been singing with the band.

I don't want to lose that. So I tell him my worst secret to
make us even. To prove he can trust me.

"When I was a freshman, I sold a bottle of hydrocodone to a
guy at school." I shouldn't be telling him that. It's the truth, but
I probably shouldn't tell *anyone*. Ever.

"Seriously?"

"Yeah. I didn't know him. He just came up to me in the hall
and tapped on my cast—I had a broken arm—and asked if the
doctor gave me Oxy. I told him I had hydrocodone." I said
the whole word, just like that, and he laughed. "He said he'd
buy any extras. Two dollars a pill."

The next day, I brought him the bottle. Twenty-eight pills.
He gave me fifty-six dollars in cash, in a corner near the boys'
bathroom, while his friend watched for teachers.

Gabe looks amused. And a little sad. "You got ripped off."

Maybe so. But I felt so guilty about selling drugs that I
couldn't spend the money on myself. So, I bought my mom a
birthday present. I told her I used Christmas money from Dad
and Grandma Louise.

I told her I flushed the pills.

So, I can't be "weird" about Gabe taking one hydrocodone,
without being a total hypocrite. But . . . "Doesn't she need
them?" I nod at Grammie.

"Yeah, but she has plenty, and when she runs low, hospice brings her more. That's how it works." He shrugs, and it's eerie how much he looks like Cody when he does that. "No one counts the pills. Not Mom. Not hospice."

I nod. "Okay. But you're not taking them all the time, right?"

Gabe rolls his eyes. "I couldn't even if I wanted to. Mom's stressed, but she's not stupid." He glances at Grammie, then holds out the bottle. "They just help me relax. You want one?"

I shake my head. "They make me throw up."

"That sucks."

"Yeah."

⸺∞⸺

"Why do they call you John Thomas, anyway?" I ask the drummer, while Gabe and Josh plug in the mics and amps. The garage door is standing open, and it's still cold outside, but I don't have to sit on a bucket by the exit anymore. "Instead of just John."

"Because my brother's John William and my dad's John Michael, and they gotta call me somethin'." He plays a rim shot. *Ba dum tsh.* And he's clearly cracked himself up.

"Seriously, though, those are their names," John Thomas says when no one else laughs.

"Hey, Mick, you ready?" Josh asks, and I turn to see him standing by the new mic stand. The third one, which he hauled all the way here today, just for me.

"Yes." I plug in the extra mic and clip it into the stand.

"Did you have a chance to think about the bridge on 'Hourglass'?"

"Yeah, I spent some time on it last night. I think we need a key change. Half a step up to sort of . . . build. You know? I printed this out, in case you wanted to try it." I take two folded pieces of sheet music from my back pocket and hand one to Gabe and the other to Josh.

Last night, I used a free app to transpose the guitar and bass parts for the bridge and the last chorus. The app is pretty cool. You can play or sing music into the mic on your phone, and it translates that into sheet music, which you can then put in any key you want. Then play it back.

Josh looks at Gabriel. John Thomas shrugs at them both; his part doesn't really change.

Josh flattens the sheet music on top of the big amp and begins to finger the notes on his guitar, trying them out. Gabe does it too, but he's frowning, and I think his eyes are a little glassy. Or do they always look like that?

"Let's try it." Josh pops the new mic out of its stand and hands it to me. Then he turns to the rest of the band. "Let's take it from the second verse, and we'll let Michaela have the bridge. Okay?"

I nod. There's no spotlight here. The garage is dirty and kind of dim, and I can't get my chill bumps to go away with the door open. But this music feels just as good as what we sing onstage at school. This feels . . . real.

John Thomas counts us off, tapping one stick on the rim of his snare, and both guitars come in. Josh starts singing. Gabe and I only have harmony on the verses. It's simple but nice. Haunting. Then comes the bridge.

Josh gestures to his new sheet music to remind everyone of the chord change. I take the vocals up half a step, and I let my volume build. The bridge sounds more intense now. More meaningful. Like an escalation of the tone.

Josh's eyes widen. He looks inspired. He surprises us with a different chord at the end of the bridge, and it's like a revelation. It opens the bridge up into the chorus, where he joins my vocals. Gabe's harmony weaves through the lyrics, echoing. Answering. Underlining the new intensity of the final chorus.

The last notes ring out, and as they echo around us, bouncing off the walls of the garage, we stare at one another in stunned silence.

"That's it," Gabe breathes. "That's what it needed." He's smiling. He looks like himself again.

"New chord?" I ask Josh.

He shrugs. "It just felt right, in the moment."

So we play it again, just like that. And again. Then we go through the entire set list one more time, because they've added me as harmony to several of the songs. I'm not an official band member, but it's starting to feel like I am.

By the time we wrap up, it's nearly 10:00 p.m., and I have half a dozen messages from Ben, as well as a missed call. Georgia's been texting too.

"Okay, that was great," Josh says.

"Better than great," Gabe insists. "The awesome thing about failing so many times—"

"There's an awesome thing about failure?" John Thomas seems dubious.

"—is that when you finally get it right, it feels *amazing!*" Gabe's eyes look brighter. He always lights up when he plays, but tonight he really looks exhilarated.

"I guess that's true." Josh turns an amused smile on us all. "Okay, we're on for an hour and a half tomorrow night; then we're just guests at the party. Sage is paying us fifty bucks, which will hardly cover gas, once we split it, so I suggest we all drive together."

"Can't," John Thomas says. "I'm riding with Tori, and we're leaving as soon as we're done playing. We're not really into parties."

"I'm picking up Violet," Gabe says.

"What!" I smack him on the shoulder. "Why didn't you *say* anything?" He's been trying to get the orchestra's second chair violinist to go out with him for a couple of weeks. She's the only reason he agreed to play upright bass in the pit for *Into the Woods*, and I suspect she's the only reason he's still in the orchestra at all, rather than focusing all of his time on the garage band without a name.

"It's new." He smiles. "I didn't want to jinx it."

"Well, congrats." I turn back to Josh and John Thomas. "Ben's picking me up anyway, so . . ."

"Okay, but we'll all have to help load the equipment," Josh says. "My dad's gonna let us use his van. So can we meet here at five to load up; then we can go our separate ways and regroup at Sage's?"

Everyone agrees.

"And this time, there will be *no* crowd-surfing," Josh adds.

Gabe frowns. "I feel like that's an unfair restriction. Crowd-surfing is *awesome*."

I stare at him. "You've crowd-surfed?"

John Thomas huffs. "No. He jumped off the stage at a talent show back in October, but no one caught him. He dislocated his right shoulder when he hit the ground."

"It was fine," Gabe insists. "That's not even my favorite arm."

Josh rolls his eyes. "Gabriel. You're right-handed."

He grins. "It isn't my favorite arm *anymore*."

I laugh as I follow them out of the garage.

"Good work on that bridge," Josh says to me, while Gabe locks the door. We're standing in the backyard, shivering. My phone buzzes in my pocket with another message. "You should try writing a song of your own. I think you've got an ear for it."

As I head inside to text Georgia and call Ben, I can't quit smiling.

# twenty

N o!"

I sit straight up, startled awake, and for a second, as I stare into the dark, I can't figure out why. Then Grammie starts shouting again.

"No! I don't need your help. Get out! Go get Patricia!"

"Mom, it's me. It's Cynthia." Her voice comes from the hall. "Please let me help you. Patty isn't here."

"Where's Patty?" Grammie asks as I stare through our open bedroom door, blinking at the bright hallway.

"She's in Dallas, Mom. Where she lives. And Ed's in Arizona. I'm the only one who's here. I'm *always* the only one who's here," Cynthia adds, lowering her voice.

"Who . . . ?" Grammie's voice cracks, and I sit up. "Who are *you*?"

"Mom. It's me," Cynthia says again. "It's Cindy."

I throw back my covers, and Emery groans. "This isn't your problem," she says. "Go back to sleep."

"Your grandmother isn't a problem," I snap.

"Yes, she is. I'm sorry if that sounds harsh, but it's true."

"No, it—"

"Yes." Emery sits up, her shadow silhouette staring at me in the dark. "It is. When we were little, she took us to the library for puppet shows and story time. She taught Gabe how to harmonize and me how to paint with watercolors. She's the one I called when I got my period at school for the first time, because I didn't want to deal with my mother. But now she's just . . . gone, most of the time. And there's nothing you can do but get in the way. If she doesn't know who Mom is, she certainly won't know you. And this is hard enough for Mom without you inserting yourself where you don't belong."

That's what Emery thinks about my entire existence. That I've inserted myself where I don't belong. But in this case, she's not wrong.

My dad's shadow passes in the hallway. "What can I do?"

"I don't *know*." Cynthia groans. "I don't know how to deal with her when she's like this, and I *really* need to get her cleaned up. Change the sheets . . ."

"Want me to call hospice? I can see if they'll send someone."

"No, let me give it one more try. Will you come talk to her? Drape your stethoscope over your shoulders, and she might think you're her doctor."

I tap my phone where it sits on the charger, to wake up the screen. It's 2:58 a.m. I climb out of bed.

"Seriously," Emery whispers. "Leave it alone."

"I'm just getting water."

She mumbles something I can't understand as she rolls over to face the wall.

The hallway tile is cold beneath my bare feet. I pass by the bathroom without going in, because the cup in there is Emery's, and I know from experience that it tastes like toothpaste. In the kitchen, I fill a glass with water from the tap, with only moonlight to see by. The hall light goes out, and the living room falls into darkness, familiar shadows formed by moonlight leaking through the curtains.

"It's going to be okay." My dad's voice comes closer with each word, and I don't want to interrupt this private moment—to insert myself—so I drop into a squat behind the peninsula so they won't see me. "I can't promise it's going to be easy, but I can promise it will pass. And that I will be here with you as much as I can. As much as you'll have me."

I scoot to the end of the counter and peek around the corner, and I see Dad and Cynthia framed in the archway that leads into the hall, lit by moonlight shining in through the living room window. His arms are around her back, and her head is on his shoulder. Tears shine on her cheeks.

"I just . . . I don't know how anyone's supposed to do this. Yesterday, she tried to get out of bed. When I got home from my run, she was shouting her head off. 'I'm stuck! I'm stuck!' I ran in there, and she had both legs over the rails, and she was twisted sideways. Her feet were blue, Oscar! I had to massage them for half an hour to get the blood back into them. And she was crying the whole time. Promising she wouldn't try to get up again."

"I'm so sorry, hon."

"This is torture. She's my *mother*. She doesn't want to be seen like this, and I don't want to see her like this, but . . ."

"But there's no other choice."

"Right."

"Cyn . . . Honey . . ." My dad sighs. "I don't think she has very much longer."

"You don't know that. *No one* knows that."

"She's been refusing chemo for months, Cynthia, and it'd be too late now, even if she were to change her mind. The cancer's everywhere, and she seems a little worse every day. I don't think it's going to be long, hon."

She sighs. "I can't stand to think about it."

A sob gets caught in my throat, and when I blink, tears roll down my cheeks. Cynthia doesn't talk like this when she knows we can hear. She doesn't even acknowledge that her mother is actually really sick.

I think about it a lot, but I can't decide which is worse: losing your mother suddenly, while you're both still young, or having your entire life with her, then having to watch her horrifying, at times humiliating, decline.

At least I will always remember my mother as beautiful. As young and strong. At least she always knew who I was.

But she never had this. She never had my dad comforting her in the middle of the night. She didn't get Saturday morning breakfasts or Friday night dates. Not real dates, anyway. She was a secret. *I* was a secret. And as glad as I am that he's here for Cynthia right now, when she really, really needs him, there's a part of me that feels *so bitter* about the injustice of that—of the fact that for years, his presence here has only been possible because of his absence from my life.

His absence from my *mom's* life.

But none of that is Cynthia's fault.

I stay hidden, and neither of them sees me as they head past the kitchen into the main suite.

On my way back to bed, I take the pictures of my mother from the living room and arrange them on top of my new chest of drawers. I never want to forget her. Not her face, or her voice, or her ironic, rapid-fire deployment of every cliché she could think of, just to see me smile. But I don't want to wield her like a weapon against Cynthia.

My stepmother has enough problems without me adding to them.

---

"Hey!" I call as I knock on Grammie's door. She's sitting up in bed, writing in a little leather-bound notebook, with her up-close glasses perched on her nose.

"Come in, Emery!" She smiles, and I see no sign of last night's trauma in her expression. Then she frowns as she squints at me over her glasses. "Michaela. Sorry, dear. You two look so much alike."

"So they tell me." I step into the room and take a seat in the chair by her bed. There's a book of crossword puzzles open on her tray table—Dad says they're good for memory—next to a half-eaten chocolate bar. "How far did you get?" I pick up the book, and I laugh out loud when I see that she's filled in all the little squares with expletives.

"Don't like crosswords, huh?" I ask as I set the book back down.

"Oh, I love them. They're really helping me remember words that have been buried in my brain for decades."

"Such as five across?" I glance at the book again. "I don't think I've ever even heard that one."

"It's most effective as an adjective, but it can also be deployed as a verb, in emergencies."

"I'll keep that in mind. Something smells good." I twist in my chair, and I see that her lunch is sitting on her nightstand. Tomato soup and grilled cheese—provolone and pesto. The soup looks untouched, and it's started to congeal on top. She's had maybe three bites out of the sandwich, despite the neat triangles Cynthia has cut it into.

"Not hungry today?"

"I don't like pesto. Help yourself, if you want some," she says. I'm not going to do that, of course. She needs to eat her lunch. "Would it kill her to make a *normal* grilled cheese? Cheddar, or God forbid a slice of American?"

"Shall I send it back to the kitchen?" I pick up the plate like a waitress, balancing it on one hand.

"I don't care what you do with it. Feed it to the neighborhood dogs. Just get rid of it. Thank you!" she adds as I carry the plate into the hall.

"No," Cynthia snaps as I set it on the counter. "She did *not* send you in here with that."

I can only shrug. "She might like a regular grilled cheese better. Maybe cheddar. Or American."

"You mean like this?" Cynthia spins toward the fridge and pulls out two triangles of grilled cheese—the inside is orange—sealed in a sandwich bag. There's a single bite missing from one corner. "I took this to her an hour ago, and she called it 'unimaginative.'"

I want to laugh, but Cynthia is clearly at the end of her rope. "Don't worry. I'm sure she'll eat when she's hungry."

"You don't get it," Emery says, and I spin to find her sitting at the table with a bowl of yogurt and granola, her phone open to TikTok, one AirPod lying on the table. "She may never be hungry again. A decline in appetite is common, near the end."

"How do you know that?" Cynthia asks. But she doesn't debate the "merit of the argument," as Georgia would say.

Emery only shrugs. But she's clearly been googling. Or talking to Dad.

"Yes, that's my concern," Cynthia admits as she returns the cheddar sandwich to the refrigerator. "So, we're all just going to have to encourage her to eat, and I'll keep making her favorite foods. Several different versions of them, if I have to." She waves one hand at the uneaten soup and the "imaginative" version of grilled cheese. "So, you two are going to a party tonight?" Cynthia looks so hopeful that Emery and I are socializing together voluntarily. "Is this a theater thing?"

"Sort of." Emery shoots me a "keep your mouth shut" look. "Sage Andersen is throwing a party. She's the actress playing Cinderella's Stepmother."

"And she's throwing a Valentine's Day party for the cast?"

I open my mouth, and Emery shoots me that look again. There's clearly something she doesn't want me to say, but I have no idea what that is. "It's not really for Valentine's Day." Which is tomorrow, anyway. "This is just when- -" My mouth snaps shut, before I can say "when her parents are out of town." Because *that's* what Emery doesn't want me to tell her mom. "When she could have the party," I finish.

Which is not only for the cast. But I'm not saying another word, for fear of being murdered by my half sister.

"Well, you guys have fun, but be home by eleven."

Gabe doesn't have to be home until midnight, because he's a senior, and he's almost eighteen.

"Are you riding together?" Cynthia asks as she picks up the untouched half of Grammie's rejected sandwich.

Emery and I glance at each other. "No," we say in unison.

At least we agree about something.

—⟨∞⟩—

"Your dad hates me," Ben says as we turn into Sage's neighborhood. Which, it turns out, is also his neighborhood.

I should have guessed.

I'm supposed to tell him he's wrong. That my dad doesn't hate him. But I can't pretend I haven't seen the way my dad looks at him. And the truth is that I can't really expect him to *like* Emery's ex. Even for me.

"Seriously, that man wouldn't pound my back if I were choking."

"He definitely would. He took the Hippocratic oath." I have no idea if that's true, or if doctors still do that, but it makes Ben laugh, and that makes me smile. He's *so* pretty.

Sage Andersen's house is the second one on the left, after we entered the neighborhood, and it's massive. Not as big as Ben's, or as ornate. But not a place I could have pictured myself attending a party, back in Oak Valley.

So much has changed so fast, and it feels weird to think that my mother would hardly recognize me if she could see me now. I wonder what she would think of my new friends. Of my new boyfriend . . .

Ben parks at the curb, a block past the house, because that's the closest spot we can find. Then he gets out and runs around the hood of the car to open my door. It's cheesy, but, as Georgia would say, I'll allow it.

"You look great," he says as I get out. And according to his lingering gaze, he really means that.

"Thanks." Emery advised me to dress up, because "everyone will go all out." And I rightly assumed that was her attempt to sabotage my first appearance at a West Bradford party. So, after Emery left to get ready with Mara, I asked Lexie for advice. She showed up on my front porch half an hour later, ready to go through all my clothes.

Unfortunately, nothing in my closet met with Lexie's approval for a party. So, we wound up at her house, where she pulled a silky blue crop top from her closet. It laces shut, leaving most of my back exposed.

She swore it will look great while I'm onstage. Not that

there will be an actual stage at a high school party. But she was evidently right about the shirt. Ben keeps finding reasons to touch my back, and since there's nothing there but laced-up spaghetti straps, he's actually touching my shoulder. The indention of my spine. That little dip just above the waist of my jeans. And every single time, my heart leaps into my throat.

I feel a little shaky as we walk down the street, hand in hand, and at first I think that's because this is pretty off-brand for me: a big party in a rich neighborhood. I'm not even wearing my own clothes. I'm a total imposter.

But the closer we get to Sage's house, the clearer it becomes that these heart palpitations are at least a little bit about singing with the band. At a big party in a rich neighborhood.

Sage's house is up on a hill, with a tiered front yard and a million steps, which really makes me wish I'd turned down Lexie's red heels.

There are people standing on the steps, and on every stone-bordered tier of the lawn. There are more people on the front porch, and I can see them through every window on the first floor.

"Holy shit," I whisper.

Ben laughs.

I don't recognize a single face inside. Oh, wait, yes I do. Kat Torrez is holding a bottle of beer, talking to a couple of tall, broad guys who can only be football players. I smile at her, but I can't tell if she sees me.

Ben greets several people on the way to the kitchen, where he grabs two plastic cups and hands me one. It's beer. I can tell from the smell. I'm sure I won't like it, even before I try it. But I try it anyway.

I'm right. It tastes like liquid yeast, so I just hold the cup as he leads me toward the back door.

The entire rear wall of Sage's living room—I haven't seen her yet—is glass. The room is two stories tall, and the windows go all the way up, showing off a huge backyard that was obviously designed for entertaining. Strings of outdoor lights and a winding stone walkway connect half a dozen arrangements of outdoor furniture and a built-in fire pit, where a cart stands stacked with s'mores supplies. There's a pool and a spa, set off from the rest of the yard by a tall wrought iron fence, and it must be locked, because that space is entirely empty. And . . .

I was wrong. There *is* a stage. Sort of.

There's a raised deck on one side of the yard, opposite the pool, and Gabe, Josh, and John Thomas are already out there, setting up the drum set, mics, and amps. Fortunately, the deck isn't tall enough for crowd-surfing.

"I should go get ready," I say, and when Ben offers to help, the warm sensation inside me swells into a full-body flush.

"How the hell did you get all this up that hill?" I ask as I set down my beer and unfold two mic stands.

"There's a delivery entrance on the side," Josh says. "The van's parked over there."

"Where do you want this?" Ben asks, and I turn to see him holding Gabe's amp in both hands. That thing is not light.

"Right there." Gabe points, and Ben sets the amp in place and starts hooking up the wires.

I watch them as we work, but I can't tell how Gabe feels about Ben. I don't know whether he believes Emery, or whether he's even heard her side of their breakup, but he's not being rude or anything.

It's cold out, but there are several tall outdoor heaters already lit up and radiating warmth, and once a crowd forms out here, it will feel warmer. For now, there's just a handful of people watching us get ready. Two of them are Violet and Tori, Gabe's and John Thomas's dates, who're huddled next to the nearest heater, holding plastic cups.

When we've set everything up, I give my beer to Ben, and he chats with Violet and Tori while we warm up. People are starting to come outside now, drawn by the practice chords and harmonic exercises, and several of the faces are familiar. The theater kids know Josh and I are playing tonight, and they've joined Ben, Violet, and Tori. Lexie, Bella, and Jon are among them. Across the yard, Emery, Mara, and Cole Houser are standing with Aaron, the Narrator, and Link, the Wolf, near the fire pit.

"Thanks, you guys!" Sage jogs up onstage, rubbing her hands together for warmth. "I'm so excited to hear you guys play. Who should I . . . ?" She holds out a folded fifty-dollar bill.

Josh takes it and shoves it into his pocket. "Thanks. We're good to go?"

"If you're all set up!" Sage gives us a thumbs-up as she backs off the stage.

As Josh steps up to the mic, I realize the band still has no name. I have no idea how he's going to introduce us, but my heart is racing. I feel like this is a test. A preview of "Michaela Onstage." If I can do this in front of a hundred classmates, most of whom I've never met, then surely I can survive *Into the Woods* in the auditorium, where I won't even be able to see the audience, thanks to the bright lights.

Josh doesn't introduce us.

"Hey!" he calls out, and the theater kids erupt into applause and cheers. "Hope you guys have a great time tonight. Thanks for letting us be a part of that." Then he turns to nod at John Thomas, who counts us off for the first song. And before I can overthink it or get any more nervous than I already am, we're singing. Just like that.

We open with a fast song. It's a cover, as is most of our set, and it's designed to draw people in. To bring them out of the house. And it does exactly that. By the time the final chord fades from Sage's backyard, her huge living room, visible through the wall of windows, is nearly empty. Everyone's out here watching. Dancing. Singing along.

Emery is sitting at the fire pit, roasting a marshmallow, pretending not to watch. Mara is with her, but Cole has joined the rest of the theater kids, and he looks impressed. So does Ben.

I'm tingling. Glowing. Maybe it's the half beer I drank, but I think it's . . . well, everything else, really. The cold, and the music, and the cheers.

We play a couple of more songs, and I'm starting to relax into it. John Thomas is a rock star, twirling his drumsticks, occasionally tossing them in the air, and he gets cheers every time. We sound different outside, and we're hooked into Sage's sound system, which is broadcasting us all over the massive yard. I wonder what her neighbors think. They're probably all out for the night. Maybe that's why we're only playing for the first hour and a half of the party, so the noise will die down before everyone comes home from their Saturday night out.

After the third song, Josh takes his mic from the stand. "Now that we have a bigger crowd, I'd like to introduce the band. I'm Josh Kang, and this is Gabriel Bosch, on the bass. Back there on the drums, we have John Thomas Mitchell." Cheers erupt again. Everyone loves a drummer. "And this lovely lady on my right, for those who haven't met her, is Michaela Rutherford, who's agreed to join us tonight, specifically to sing our two originals, which are both duets. Including this one."

The crowd cheers again, especially the theater kids, and I wave as I take a sip of water from one of the bottles Sage handed out. While Josh returns his mic to its stand, I remove mine so I can hold it.

My nerves feel like a tingling flush, all over my body. Everyone's looking at me.

This song's slower. It starts with Gabe on the bass, and he looks the part of a rock star, with his hair and the intense, thoughtful way he stares mostly at the stage. Then Josh joins in on the guitar, with a preview of the chorus.

I take a deep breath. And I start singing.

No one's dancing now. They're listening, some swaying, as I sing Josh's earnest melody. It's soulful. It's like a river of pain flowing through me, with hope bobbing on the surface, and I *feel* it. I really feel it.

The first verse builds toward a high note, and I hit it, strong and clear. The theater kids burst into hoots and applause. Then we slide into the chorus, and Josh and Gabe are singing with me. That swaying from the audience becomes slow dancing in pairs and the occasional human triangle.

Josh takes his verse, and I harmonize, echoing with lines from my own verse. It's a playful game, with the lyrics. I'm echoing, but I'm also contrasting his half of the story. Correcting his point of view, even as he tells his side. Sowing doubt.

We launch into the chorus together—there's no bridge on this one—and it's a melancholy beauty. It ends on a haunting harmony, a sustained note, and when it fades, our audience explodes in applause, led, of course, by our fellow cast members.

"Thank you!" Josh calls, taking his mic in hand again. "Michaela Rutherford!" He gestures to me with one open palm, and the applause swells again. "We'll be right back!"

I step off the stage, and I'm surrounded by smiling faces. Kind words. The world is made of love, and finally, I feel like a part of it.

Someone hands me a cup, and I take a long, slow drink.

# twenty-one

Holy shit, that was amazing!" Lexie finds me in the crowd. Bella and Jon are right behind her, and I can see Ben making his way after them. His face is radiant, his smile wide and bright. "That was an original?"

"Yeah. Josh wrote it," I tell them.

"Sounds like he wrote it just for you." Ben leans in close and kisses the back of my jaw. His breath is warm in my ear. His hand captures my free one, his fingers winding through mine. "Now *I* want to sing with you."

Bella elbows him. "You sing with her almost every day."

"That's right." Ben grins. "But you can't blame me for being jealous."

A smile sneaks up on me. "You're jealous?" No one's ever liked me enough to be jealous before.

Emery is *so* full of shit. Ben likes me for me.

"What boyfriend wouldn't be? You look *incredible* up there."

Warmth blooms deep inside me, spreading through my

limbs. I sip from my cup again. This isn't beer. It's soda with something in it. Something sweet on the front of my tongue, and sharp on the back. It's better than beer, but I only drink half of it, because I'm not a drinker, and I still have to sing.

"Hey!" Cole Houser joins us, and he's practically hauling Emery with him. "You guys are awesome! I didn't know there was going to be an original."

"We have two, actually," I tell him, while Emery sips from her cup. "We're closing with a brand-new one called 'Hourglass.' We were still making changes to it last night."

Cole elbows Emery, and she glares at him as her drink sloshes over the edge of her cup. "You guys really are good," she tells me.

"Thank you. Really." I can't stop smiling.

"In fact, I think you're way better with the band than in the—"

Cole elbows her again, and her mouth snaps shut. We all know what she was going to say, and I can't tell whether or not she means it. Am I actually better with the band than I am in the musical? How can she possibly know that, when we're only three weeks into rehearsals for *Into the Woods*? We're still using a CD player and duct tape Xs on the floor of the stage to represent unfinished props and set pieces.

The obvious answer is that she wants me to quit so she can have my role. But I'm so high on approval right now that I don't even care that she can't just be happy for me, for once.

I didn't take her spot in the band. She was never in the band. She has no reason to resent me tonight.

"Mick!" Josh pushes his way through the crowd, and our group cheers as our circle opens to include him. "Oh, hey!" he says, when he realizes he's surrounded by cast members. By friends.

"You guys are great up there!" Bella shouts, and Jon laughs, because she's way too loud, even for a party. Her cup is empty. I hope no one refills it.

"Thanks." Josh turns to me. "You ready?"

"Yeah." I take another sip from my cup, and when I can't find anywhere to set it, Lexie takes it from me and finishes it in two swallows.

"Mmm," she says. "Vanilla vodka."

"Really?" I feel like I should have known what I was drinking, but there's no time to dwell on that, because Josh is tugging me across Sage Andersen's backyard, toward the stage, through a crowd that seems bigger than ever. Has the party grown? People shout at us, compliments falling like rain.

Okay, some of them feel more like hail. Some are comments about my shirt, or my heels, or the fit of my pants, and I realize that there's a possibility I might know more people than just the theater crowd at school on Monday.

There's also every possibility that I won't be recognized when I'm wearing my own clothes instead of Lexie's.

People cheer when we take the stage again. We sing four more songs, and I'm worried about closing with "Hourglass" suddenly. Like Josh's other original, it's slow and poignant, rather than fast and dance-worthy. And people don't know it, so they can't sing along. But it's too late to change plans now.

"Okay! You guys have been great!" Josh says, after our last cover song. I gulp from my water bottle, and when I turn, I see that Gabe and John Thomas are doing the same. John Thomas is sweaty, despite the cold; he gets really worked up on the drums. "We have one more for you. It's another original, and it's gonna slow things down. And again, it features my girl Michaela."

He means it in the friend way. Not, like, *my* girl, my girl. Still, it makes me smile. I've never in my life felt more a part of something. More welcomed and . . . acclaimed. Yes, it's just a stupid high school party. But right now, being up onstage feels like *everything*. Like the whole world is watching. But not in the judgy, under-a-microscope, everyone's-looking-for-something-to-criticize kind of way.

This crowd just wants to have fun, and they're looking to us to show them how. To get them there. That feels empowering. If I think about it too much, it might feel overwhelming, but the vodka and all the applause have just made me feel warm.

The music starts, and the applause dies down. People are waiting. They're listening, and—

Oh, shit, we're singing again.

I grab my mic and meet Josh's gaze. "Key change," he mouths as he starts strumming his guitar. I nod. I hadn't *exactly* forgotten, but the reminder is good, because everything is . . . warm. Just *slightly* fuzzy.

We kill it with "Hourglass." The harmonies are smooth and sweet. I do remember the key change, and the build on the bridge is *so* satisfying. I can feel it in my pulse. In the rapt, soft buzz from the crowd. Then Josh hits that new chord. John Thomas's drum fill matches the passion of the changes we've made, and the final chorus is *powerful*. It resonates.

The song ends, and there's a moment of *almost* silence, except for some idiot moaning about dropping a marshmallow in the fire pit. Then someone shouts out approval—I think it's Lexie—and applause breaks out. There's whistling and hooting. People are taking pictures, and I think several of them have been filming.

Maybe I can find a clip to send to Georgia.

"Thank you!" Josh shouts into the mic. "That's it for us. Thanks again!"

And then it's over. Now we're just guests at the party.

Guests everyone knows.

"Michaela!" someone shouts as I step offstage. The guys are packing up equipment, and I'm going to help, but first I need some more water. My throat has had it. "Hey!"

I turn, and it's some guy I've never seen before. He's wearing a *Rick and Morty* T-shirt and a goofy purple scarf. "Hi."

"You were great! Fuckin' hot!"

"Um . . . thanks." He puts his arm around my shoulders and holds his phone up. "Smile."

"What?" I manage to comprehend the selfie an instant before he clicks the button. I get a quick glimpse of my shellshocked smile, my face pressed against a stranger's sweaty cheek, and then I feel a hand at my back. My top suddenly feels different. Looser.

Someone has untied the laces.

"Shit!" I push the selfie-taker away and reach back, trying to find the ends of the laces and draw them back together. The crop top is drooping in front, showing cleavage, but nothing too revealing yet.

"That wasn't me!" the selfie guy shouts as someone pulls him away from me. It's Ben.

"Hands off," he growls. "Have some fucking respect." He turns to me, and his cheeks are flushed. He's pissed, his jaw bulging. "Here. Let me help." He turns me by my shoulders and takes the laces from me. I position the front of the top while he ties me up. "Is that too tight?"

"No, it's fine. Thanks."

"Oh my God!" Lexie appears out of the crowd. "You okay?"

"That asshole!" Bella slurs, and I can't process anything else. The crowd feels different now. Bigger. Packed tighter. Rowdier. Strangers are calling my name. Lexie's heels seem to hate me, and the grass is trying to suck them right off my feet.

"I'm fine," I insist. "What did you guys think of the last song?"

"Beautiful!" Bella declares. "You guys should record it and put it on Spotify."

Lexie shrugs. "It's way better than most of the originals I listen to."

"Really?" I ask, and she nods. "Ben?"

"You were great." He pulls me close, his fingers sliding beneath the laces at my back. "Hypnotic."

"And the song?" I actually contributed to the composition, and his opinion matters. I really want him to like it.

Ben lets me go. "It looked . . . intimate."

"It did?"

"Yeah. Fortunately, I know from experience that stage chemistry isn't real." He leans in for a kiss. "I'll go get you a drink. Right back." Then he's gone. And I'm suddenly freezing.

Sage's party playlist is coming from the speakers now, and Bella and Jon are dancing. Kind of. Really, they're grinding, and it's . . . well, it's hot. But I feel like I shouldn't look.

"I have to help pack up." I start backing toward the stage, and Lexie falls into step with me.

"Really, you guys were great," she says.

"Michaela!" someone shouts, and I turn to see some jerk grabbing his crotch through his jeans. "I got a mic you can sing into!"

"Ignore them. They're drunk."

"Hey!" Another guy falls into step on my other side, and I turn to shout at him to back off, but then I realize it's Cole.

He holds up both hands to show me he's harmless. "Just me. Thought you guys might need some help." He looks and sounds sober. God bless him.

"Yes. Thank you."

He jumps onto the raised deck and claps Josh on the back. "What can I do?"

Lexie pitches in, and we manage to haul everything through a tandem garage that opens into Sage's backyard on one end, and into the delivery entrance on the other, which is where Josh's dad's van is parked. It takes about a dozen trips, but we can't leave the equipment sitting out unless we want to lose it. Or find strangers banging on John Thomas's drum set and breaking Gabe's strings.

"Thanks," Josh says as he locks the van. He shoves the keys into his pocket. "Okay, that's it. I'll have to break the fifty and split it on Monday, but—"

"Keep mine," I say. "You hauled everything here, and you wrote the songs."

"No, I—"

"Yes," I insist. "I won't take it. You guys split it three ways. At least that way it will cover your gas. And I didn't drive."

"Okay, well, thanks." John Thomas pulls me in for a hug. "Tori and I are heading out. I'll come over tomorrow and help unload the van."

"Yeah, thanks," Gabe says. "Good set. Even without the crowd-surfing."

John Thomas rolls his eyes. "Good set." Then he's gone.

Gabe wanders off to find Violet, and the rest of us head into the backyard again, where Josh and Cole help Sage take fireplace pokers and marshmallow skewers away from a bunch of drunk idiots trying to spar with them like fencing swords. For good measure, they turn off the fire pit. It's almost 9:00 p.m., and the ratio of drunk-to-sober party guests has shifted to favor the inebriated.

"There you are!" Ben appears at my side again and hands me a cup. I take a sip. It tastes just like the last one, but stronger. I'll just hold it for a while, then set it down somewhere. He's drinking beer, and his cup's already half empty. "There's karaoke inside. Sing with me!"

"I think my throat's had it for tonight, but you go ahead. It's my turn to applaud."

Ben pouts, but he's ready for some love from an audience, and I'm ready to be supportive. However, when we get to the den where the karaoke machine is hooked up to a giant television and a big speaker, Sage informs us that "I've got the selections sorted to include duets only!"

"Why?" I ask.

"Because tomorrow's Valentine's Day!" she shouts, and everybody cheers. There's a line forming, and someone's passing around a binder with a list of songs. She lowers her voice. "And because duets mean no one can grandstand. And . . . because it's my party, and I said so!"

"Okay then!" Who am I to criticize?

"Sing with me!" Ben begs. "Just wet your whistle, and your throat will feel better." He pushes my cup toward my face.

I take a sip, and he pushes the cup at me again. So I take one more. "Go pick a song!" I say before he can insist I finish the drink.

Ben spins around and snatches the selection booklet, and suddenly Lexie and Bella are in my face. "Cole and Emery are going to sing together!" Lexie says.

"What? How'd that happen?"

"We did it!" Bella's slurring her words. "Em's drunk, so we told her she'd already promised to do it, and she doesn't me-member that's a total lie."

"And we told Cole she wanted us to ask him," Lexie adds. "And of course he said yes. He's not really drunk. Just buzzed enough not to freak out about singing in front of people."

"So we signed them up!" Bella throws her arms into the air, in a ta-da pose. She's very proud of herself.

I'm very worried about her balance.

I set my cup on an end table and grab two bottles of water from a cooler near the door. I give her one of them.

"There are four couples ahead of us," Ben says as he joins us. "One of them is Cole and Em. Not sure how *that* happened."

Bella bursts into laughter.

"Sage! You're up!" someone shouts.

"Oh!" Sage Andersen hauls a football player to the front of the room with her, and he fumbles his way through "Like I'm Gonna Lose You," off-key and slightly off tempo—he's no John Legend—but he has fun, and his football friends love it. I'm sure it'll get a thousand views when he posts it.

Josh surprises me by singing Charlie Puth's part in a duet of "I Hope" with Kat Torrez, and Kat is *super* into it. She feels this song, and I feel her feel it.

Emery sways through the chorus with one hand up, the other clutching her drink, as if Kat and Josh are singing her anthem. Singing it just for her.

Bella and Jon bring the house down with "Señorita," and immediately sign up again for "I Know What You Did Last Summer." They've found their sound.

"Em and Cole!" Sage calls. "You're up!" But Emery's suddenly nowhere to be found, and Cole's freaking out.

"She changed her mind," he whispers to Bella.

"No. No, honey, she's probably just in the bathroom. Lexie will find her. Right, Lex?"

"Yeah." Lexie disappears into the massive house on an Emery hunt.

"Michaela, you and Ben are next, so just go now," Bella says, her hand tight around Cole's to keep him from running. "Cole and Em can go after you."

Ben shrugs and grabs a mic. Grinning, he calls me up, and everyone cheers. I have no idea what he's signed us up for until the title shows up on the screen and the music starts.

"Just Give Me a Reason." Pink and Nate Ruess.

I *love* this one. It's thematically irrelevant—our relationship isn't old enough to have those kinds of problems—but perfect for our vocal ranges. And Ben's a total show-off. His voice is rich and intense.

I hit Pink's high part, right before the final chorus starts to repeat, and the room cheers.

I don't think I've ever had so much fun in my entire life. That second half drink has kept the world warm and fuzzy, and I'm relaxed enough to enjoy the song without nerves.

And I have to say, we *kill* it. People come in from the other rooms, abandoning some football video game, a pool tournament, and the food spread in the kitchen just to watch us. Which means that when our song is over and the applause has died down—when it's Emery and Cole's turn—the room is *packed*.

Cole looks sick. He's not going to do it. As much as he likes Emery—and I can see that, every time he says a single word to her—he's not going to sing in front of this crowd.

He tries to tell her. I can't hear him, because Ben and I are still at the front of the room, but I can see him near the back wall, shaking his head. Emery is practically pleading with him. She may have been buzzed when Bella convinced her that this was her idea, but she looks sober now, and she's just watched Ben and me bring down the house. She sees us surrounded by friends, old and new, accepting praise.

She wants her turn. And it's duets only.

Finally, Cole nods. She loops her arm through his, and by the time Sage has their song loaded—I have no idea who picked it out—she's hauled him up to the front of the room and handed him a mic. "Just watch me," she says, and I'm close enough to hear that. "Look at *me*. No one else. Just sing for me. Okay?"

Cole nods. The music starts and I almost groan. It's Lady A's "Just a Kiss." It's a great duet. A love song. It'll show off Emery's voice perfectly, but if Cole isn't a strong singer . . . If he freaks out . . .

Emery looks at him as she starts singing. Her first verse is soft and pretty. It's sweet. And *I* know she's looking at him to keep him from freaking out. To make him forget about the crowd and focus on the song. To keep him distracted enough to forget he's scared. But that's not what it looks like.

It looks like she's in love. Like she's singing to him for real.

Like this is a fragile, brand-new connection, and that first kiss the song talks about will be just enough . . . for now.

Her first verse is only four lines long, but I hold my breath as I wait them out, terrified for Cole. I know how he feels. But I don't know how he *sounds*.

Then he starts singing, and my mouth literally drops open. I'm staring at him in utter shock. He's *amazing*. His voice is full and smooth, his vibrato subtle and effortless. He's really, really good. He's . . . he's *trained*.

That boy's had lessons.

Emery smiles when she hears him, and she looks beautiful.

They hit the chorus, and it's like they've been singing together their whole lives. Like they were born in the land of harmony and could live there forever. Like their babies would be born in choir robes. I've never seen Cole like this, but I get the feeling that Emery has. I think she knew he could do this. That's why she wanted him to audition for Jack in *Into the Woods*.

Another verse. Another chorus. Then comes the bridge and a change of pace. An endless, sweet melody, and more flawless harmony.

They finish as sweetly as they started, and I am *stunned*. And I'm not alone.

"Holy shit!" Mara cries. She leaps forward and throws her arms around them both. "You two talented bitches have been *holding out*!"

She's obviously drunk, but she's not wrong.

I push past Lexie, Bella, and Jon, and I lean around Mara in the huddle. "That was incredible, you guys. Really. That was great."

Cole beams at me. "Thanks, Michaela."

"Really?" Emery looks a little stunned herself.

"Yes. Absolutely phenomenal. You guys killed it."

"Thanks." Emery looks like she's about to cry, but she blinks rapidly instead and hands over the mic when Lexie reaches for it.

"Bella! Bitch, get up here!" Lexie says. The playful opening notes of "Best Friend" start, and everyone cheers. Bella grabs a mic and takes the opening lines. When she starts dancing, I sneak out to find a bathroom.

When I emerge, relieved but suddenly pretty damn tired—the night has caught up with me—I can't find Ben. I have to be home in half an hour, and he's my ride.

# twenty-two

I'm starting to worry. I have no idea what will happen if I'm late for curfew in my dad's house, but I suspect Cynthia's just waiting for an excuse to ground me from the car she didn't want me to have in the first place, and if I'm late, I can't exactly argue that that's unfair. But I have no idea where Ben's gone.

Lexie, Bella, and Jon are dancing in a drunken triangle in the packed living room, and I haven't seen Gabe in the past hour, since Sage shooed him out of the pool, after someone dared him to climb the fence and cannonball, fully clothed. I think Violet took him somewhere to dry off.

I *really* hope Ben has sobered up. I should have taken that last beer away from him.

Actually, I should have driven myself. We'll file that under "lessons learned."

He isn't in the kitchen, he's not dancing in the living room, karaoke-ing in the den, playing video games or pool in the game room, and he isn't among the dozen people still huddled against the cold outside. Most of whom appear to be vaping. So I start opening closed doors.

That feels like a bad idea, and I don't really expect to find him in any of the bedrooms, but I'm desperate. I now have twenty minutes to get home, and Emery may not care if she gets grounded, but I do.

I have something to lose.

The first bedroom is empty.

In the second, I find a couple I don't recognize making out on the bed, half dressed. They don't see me, so I close the door and back away.

The third room is a repeat of the second—another couple, another bed—only this guest room is done in shades of blue, rather than shades of taupe.

I open a fourth door and find what can only be Sage's bedroom. And there's my sister, making out with Cole Houser on an overstuffed pink bench at the end of Sage's fluffy white bed.

I did not see that coming, but after watching them sing together, I probably should have.

"What the hell?" Emery shouts. Her eyes focus, sort of— she's still drunk—and she groans. "Michaela, go away." Then her gaze lands on Cole, and she groans again. Like she's just realized what she's doing.

Suddenly Emery's eyes widen, and she slaps one hand over her mouth. She pushes herself off the bench and lurches toward Sage's private bathroom. A second later, I hear her retching.

"Should I go in there?" Cole whispers, his brows drawn low, his gaze desperate and helpless.

"Do you still hope to make it to eighteen?" I head into the bathroom and wet a rag from the shelf. I hand it to Emery, who's on her knees in front of the toilet. "Do you need a ride home?"

"No!" She grabs the rag and swipes at her mouth. "Get out! Both of you!"

She doesn't have to tell me twice, but Cole clearly has no idea what to do.

"Save yourself," I mutter on my way out the door. "We have to think of ourselves in times like these." Except my date is MIA, and my curfew is in—I check my phone—twelve minutes. "Seriously. Linger at your own risk."

I leave Cole trying to talk Emery into letting him into the bathroom, and I do another circuit of the house. And finally, I find Ben passed out on one of the living room couches.

Passed out *cold*.

"Shit," I mumble as I sink onto my knees on the floor in front of him. "Ben. Wake up." He obviously can't drive like this, and I'm not sure I can even get him into the car. Not that I have any desire to drive a car that's worth more than my undergraduate degree will cost.

Ben drives a BMW. What if I wreck it?

"Ben!" I shake his shoulder. He snorts in his sleep and rolls over to face the back of the couch. But his eyes don't open.

"*Damn* it." I lean back onto my heels and text Gabe, hoping he can take me home, but he's not answering his phone. Which probably means his date is going *really* well.

Who does that leave? Georgia would totally come for me, but

she's an hour away. Bella and Lexie are drunk. I have no idea how long they're planning to stay, or how they're getting home, but—

"Michaela? You okay?"

I look up to find Josh staring down at me.

"Oh my God, I'm so happy to see you!" I stand and throw my arms around him. "My curfew is in eight minutes, and Ben's passed out. I can't get him to his car by myself, and I've never driven a BMW, and even once I get him home, I don't know how to get *myself*—"

"So you need a ride?"

"Yeah. Thanks. But what about Ben?"

Josh actually laughs. "He'll sleep it off and go home in the morning. As usual."

As usual?

Did he think I was just going to pass out here, with him? Did he forget to tell me I'd need to find a ride home? What kind of date ends with the guy passed out drunk and the girl stranded, *seven* minutes before her curfew?

"Okay. Thanks. You're sure you don't mind?"

Josh shrugs. "You live two blocks from me. Come on."

I follow him as he winds his way through the house, not toward the front door, but toward the kitchen, through a side entrance and into that tandem garage. The front bay door is still open, and by some miracle, no one has parked behind his van.

Only that's not actually a miracle. There are two of those plastic "Slow! Kids at Play!" sandwich boards blocking the end of the driveway. Josh grabs them both and tosses them into the back of the van as I get in the passenger's side.

"Those are yours?"

"Yeah. My little brother and his friend like to ride their bikes in the cul-de-sac, and I grabbed these on the way out tonight. I figured otherwise, we'd never get out of here."

"Good thinking," I say as he backs the bulky van out of the driveway. "Wait!" I shout, and he slams on the brakes.

"What's wrong?"

"I can't leave Emery. She's a pain, but she's my sister."

"Cole just took her home."

"You're sure?"

"Yeah. I saw her get into his car, right before I found you. That's why I was looking. Because you weren't with them, and the last time I saw Ben, he was . . ."

"Drunk?"

"Yeah."

"*You* haven't been drinking, right?"

"I had one beer." He glances at the clock on the dashboard as he shifts into drive. "Four hours ago. I'm not much of a partier."

"Then what are you still doing here?"

Josh shrugs. He keeps his eyes on the road, and I don't push for an answer. "You were really great tonight," he says a minute later.

"So were you."

"Thanks, but I mean—"

"No, seriously. You were awesome. So were Gabe and John

Thomas. I think you guys could really be something, if you manage to name the damn band."

"We need you." Josh blurts it, as if the words have been sitting on his tongue for hours, waiting for a chance to break free.

"What?" There's a pressure building deep in my chest.

"In the band. We need you. I think you should join officially."

"I— Really? You all talked about this?" Gabe didn't say anything to me, and the last thing I want is to intrude anywhere else I'm not wanted.

"No," Josh admits. "I haven't said anything to the guys yet, but I know they'll agree. We were great out there tonight, and you were a part of that."

"That's sweet, Josh, but . . ." I glance at my phone as he turns into our neighborhood, and the sticker on his windshield opens the gate. Ten fifty-eight. Two minutes to grounded.

"I just want to know . . . I mean, if we were to ask you to join, would you say yes?"

"The band?" I feel like we should be really clear about what we're actually talking about, because this feels . . . loaded. He hasn't even asked the other guys yet, which means he's basically speaking for himself. And Ben thinks he wrote that song just for me. And that our "Hourglass" duet sounded intimate. "We're just talking about the band, right? Because—"

"Yes, the band." Josh turns down my street, and my house is up ahead. He's still not looking at me, but I stare at his profile as shadows roll across it, in streetlights shining through the windshield. "Just think about it, okay? And I'll talk to Gabe and John Thomas."

"I will, but if they're not cool with it, don't push, okay? I don't want to introduce any friction."

"I won't." He pulls into my driveway, and the front door opens. My dad sticks his head out. I hold up my phone and show him the time. Eleven o'clock, on the dot. He nods and goes back inside.

"Thanks for the ride. I really do love singing with you guys."

Josh shifts into park. His knee rises as he takes his foot off the brake. "Will you write with me?" he asks as I push the passenger's side door open.

"I— What?"

"A song. Will you write an original with me? For the band."

"Okay." I might be joining the band anyway, so I shrug. "I gotta go for now, though. Thanks again."

Josh nods. I close the door and head inside as he backs out of the driveway.

"Cutting it close," my dad says from the couch. He's sitting sideways, with his back to the arm so he can see the foyer.

"And yet, I made it." I push the front door closed and frown at him from the entry. "Do you always wait up for curfew?" My mom used to do that, but she was much more subtle. She would just pretend she stayed up to watch *Gilmore Girls* reruns, and that it was a total coincidence that she was still awake when I got home.

"No," he admits. Then he takes a sip of something amber from a short glass.

"I can do it!" Grammie shouts from down the hall.

*Oh.* Dad and Cynthia are still up because Grammie's having another bad night.

"Anything I can do?" I ask.

"No, but thanks for asking. Cynthia says you're really good to her."

I shrug. I'm not even sure what that means. I'm just *normal* to Grammie. "'Night," I say as I head down the hall.

"Good night, Michaela."

Emery is lying facedown on her bed, still fully clothed. "How'd you get home?" she mumbles as I close the door. "Because I know damn well Ben didn't bring you."

I grab a T-shirt from my dresser and reach back to unlace Lexie's top. "I thought we agreed not to talk about Ben."

"I never agreed to that." She sits up in bed. Eyeliner is smeared down both of her cheeks, and her lipstick is history. Her eyes are bloodshot and half-open. If Dad saw her come in, I can't figure out how she's not grounded. She looks wasted. "He's an asshole, Michaela."

"No, he's drunk. As are *you*. If I'm supposed to hold that against people at a party, I won't have any friends left."

Except Josh. And Cole.

"That's not what I'm talking about." Emery stands—she's a little unsteady—and pulls her shirt over her head. It lands on the floor, and I suspect it's going to live there for a while. "He's a cheater."

"He's not—"

"You never want to listen when I try to tell you, but—"

"And I'm not going to listen now. You're drunk, and you hate him. You'll say anything to break us up. And the truth is that I understand that impulse. I get why you hate me—"

"I don't *hate* you," she mumbles as she pulls a night shirt over her head.

"—but I'm not going to let your mind games mess things up for me at a brand-new school." I step out of my jeans and pull on a pair of yoga pants. "You have friends to fall back on. Guys waiting in the wings to step into the spotlight."

"I don't—"

"Link drools every time you walk down the hall, and Cole would—"

"Don't," she snaps. "And do *not* tell anyone about . . . what you saw. About Cole."

"He's nice, Emery. He drove you home, and I think he totally wanted to hold your hair back while you were puking. You could do worse."

"Cole's not . . . He's not . . ."

"He's not what? A show-off?"

"He's *too* nice."

"Wait, according to you, Ben's an asshole, so I shouldn't be with him, but you can't give Cole a chance because he's too nice? Explain to me again how you're not a hypocrite?"

"I'm not a hypocrite. I'm just saying . . ." She sighs, and she looks like she might throw up again. "Cole's too good for me, and I'm *way* too good for Ben."

Oddly, I know what she means. Even if I don't agree.

"Fortunately, I'm not too good for Ben." In fact, of the two of us, I'm definitely the one who's dating up.

"Yes, you are. You're way too good for Ben McGrath."

"Okay, look. How 'bout this? I won't lecture you about Cole, and you don't lecture me about Ben, okay? We'll just stay out of each other's personal lives."

"Michaela. Please just listen to me." Emery sits up on her knees in bed. "I'm telling you he's an asshole, and you have a chance to dump him *before* he cheats. Before you have to decide whether to be me in this scenario, or my mom."

The woman who left and feels tortured, or the woman who stayed and feels tortured.

Only I would be acting on questionable information, at best. Considering Emery's flair for drama, it's entirely possible that Ben's "cheating" was just running lines with someone else. Maybe he looked at some other girl or spoke to a female friend in the hall. It's not like Emery is good at keeping things in perspective or placing blame where it belongs.

"You want me to dump my boyfriend *before* he makes a mistake? You want me to break up with him for literally no reason. That makes no sense."

"I'm giving you a chance to learn from my mistakes. But if you want to make them all yourself, that's fine with me."

It isn't, really. She's made that much crystal clear. But I have no reason to believe Ben has lied to me, yet I've personally seen Emery exaggerate to try to get her way. Why would I blow up my life based on her word, when I know the real problem is that she's jealous?

"Yeah." I turn off my lamp, and the room goes dark. "I'm gonna make my own mistakes." That's what being sixteen is all about, right?

---

"Pass." Cody draws a domino from the "bone pile," as Grammie calls it. The chicken our dominoes have built has several legs, but Cody has nothing in his hand that will play.

Grammie lays down a double six, and I groan. She's been holding onto that, and there's nothing left that can be played on it.

She laughs, and I can't resist a smile, even though I'm losing my millionth game of Chickenfoot. She's having a good morning, which is a relief after last night.

Cynthia's so thankful that she woke us up an hour ago to a Sunday brunch feast. Sausage *and* bacon. Hash browns *and* pancakes with homemade whipped cream. And eggs, for those who like them.

I do not.

"Come on," Grammie says when I have to pass. "Someone still has a six left. There's one missing—" Her mouth snaps shut as she looks at her own hand. "Oh. Never mind." But I'm not buying that. She knew she was the only one who could play on her double.

She's having a *really* good day.

My phone buzzes, and I pull it from my pocket. A text from Ben shows up on the lock screen.

please tell me you got home ok

I type "yes" in reply and go back to the game. A second later, I pull my phone out and add, "Josh gave me a ride."

I can't decide if I added that because I want to be honest, since Ben was jealous of us onstage together, or because he *deserves* to be a little jealous, considering that he left me without a ride home.

I don't believe he actually cheated on Emery, but I *am* pissed about being stranded.

"Good," Ben replies, and though I read the message on my lock screen, I don't actually open it. Which he'll know, from the read receipts.

We finish our game, and I start some homework in the kitchen with a bowl of Cheez-Its while Cody plays checkers with Grammie. I'm halfway through my French vocab when Ben calls.

I run my fingers through my hair, then prop the phone against the saltshaker and answer. His face appears on the screen. He's walking, and I recognize the hand-plastered walls behind his head as his hallway. He's at home.

"Hey," he says. "I'm *so* sorry."

It's a good start, so I shrug. "It's fine. I found a ride."

"I promise that'll never happen again. It was just rough,

watching my girlfriend sing a love song with some other guy in front of two hundred people, and I had too much, and . . ."

I glance around the room to make sure no one's listening. Fortunately, I'm alone. I pull my AirPods from my pocket and sync them so no one will hear him.

"It was rough, how?"

"You know. To people who don't understand that stage chemistry isn't real, it totally looked like my girl was up there pouring her heart out to someone else, so—"

"It was just a song, Ben. A paying gig." Sort of paying, anyway.

"I know. I totally overreacted. It's just that I really like you, and this is still new, between us, and I don't want people to mistake you and Josh as a couple."

Which was why Ben wanted to do the karaoke duet.

"You're right. You overreacted." Yet a pleased flush creeps over me. I'd almost rather he overreact than underreact—at least that tells me he cares.

"Guilty. Let me make it up to you?"

"How?"

"Was that your doorbell?" he asks, both brows arched.

"No, I didn't hear any—"

"I definitely heard the doorbell. You better go check."

"Okaaay . . ." I cross through the kitchen into the living room and look out the transom window to the left of the door. "There's no one there."

"Open it," Ben insists, and I feel a smile sneaking up on me as he grins at me from his bed, leaning against his leather-padded headboard. I've been in his room twice. He keeps it very clean.

"What did you do?"

Instead of answering, he whistles a nonchalant, innocent tune.

I open the door and find a vase with a dozen red roses on the porch. "Oh my God." I've never gotten roses before, but I know they're expensive. Especially on Valentine's Day.

"Too cliché?" he asks.

"They're perfectly cliché," I assure him. "And *gorgeous*. But I gotta put you in my pocket so I can lift the vase."

"That's fine," he says, and I slide my phone into my back pocket while I pick up the flowers and push the front door shut with my foot. "Check the card," Ben says into my ear, through my AirPods.

I set the roses on the island and pluck the card from the plastic. It reads, "5 p.m. Wear something else of Lexie's."

"Did you read it?" Ben asks as I pull my phone from my pocket.

"Yeah." And it's his handwriting. Which means he bought and delivered the flowers himself. "But it's Sunday—"

"It's Valentine's Day."

"I know, but it's a school night."

"I promise to have you home by nine," he says. "That's your weekday curfew, right?"

"It's creepy that you went out with my sister."

He laughs. "You have no idea. So, see you at five?"

"Maybe. What are we doing?"

"Another cliché. Dinner and a movie."

"What's playing?"

"Anything you want to see. I'm not sure if you've heard, but I have my own theater."

"Okay." Why on earth would I say no to that? "I'll see you at five."

Ben grins and hangs up.

Lexie takes pity on me and brings over some clothes. Emery glares at us from her bed while I try them on.

Cole has texted her twice today—I saw the messages on her lock screen—but I don't think she's replied. She's totally freaked out about making out with him last night, and as bad as I feel for him, I'm going to stick to what I said. That we should stay out of each other's personal lives.

I settle on a cowl neck minidress with spaghetti straps—pink, since our theme for the night is unironic romance clichés.

I'm *way* more into this than I want to admit.

While I do my makeup, Lexie talks Emery into a Gal-entine extravaganza at our house, involving pizza, ice cream, and horror movies, which I'm pretty sure Emery only agrees to because Mara is grounded for coming home drunk.

Ben rings the bell at five on the dot, and when I answer the door, he whistles. He's holding a single long-stem rose, and I know before we even get to his car that I forgive him. He really is sorry for stranding me at the party. And I am ready for my Valentine's Day cliché.

I kinda feel like I deserve it.

# twenty-three

On the way back from the bathroom, I stop in Grammie's room to check on her, holding my flat iron in its heat-proof sleeve. Gabe is standing by her bed. Grammie's asleep and snoring, her skin drawn tight over her cheekbones because she hasn't been eating well—not a single full meal, most days—and she's lost weight pretty quickly. There are dark circles under her eyes.

"How's she doing?" I whisper.

"I don't know. I don't know how to tell," he amends as he stares at her, his expression a blend of frustration and helplessness. "I don't know what's normal for . . . this stage."

"Me neither." Emery knows, because she googles it, but she never comes in here, and I think those two things are related. If knowing what comes next will make me not want to visit, I think I'll just maintain my ignorance. More and more often, Grammie doesn't know who any of us are. Sometimes she doesn't know where she is, or what year it is. But when she's truly with us, I feel like she deserves to have company.

There are tubes coming out of her now, snaking from beneath the covers, draining fluid into bags hooked onto the bars of her bed. I haven't asked where they're coming from or why she needs them. All I know is that she's sicker by the day, and she's declining all treatment except pain management. Which usually just makes her sleep.

She looks like a ghost, lying there.

Gabe lingers, staring down at his grandmother. He seems to be waiting for me to go, but I'm not leaving him in here alone. If he wants one of her pills, he's going to have to take it with me watching.

I think he's right that they don't count the pills, especially now that the doctor said she can basically have them whenever she needs them. The hospice nurse brought two more bottles yesterday.

When I don't budge, he sighs, "See you after school." Then he leaves. Without a pill.

I head across the hall and set the flat iron on top of my chest of drawers.

"Will you please throw those out?" Emery snaps, the second she steps into our room. Her makeup and hair are perfect, and she's holding her Friday morning smoothie. Which is different from her Monday through Thursday morning smoothie, because it has a handful of mini-chocolate chips in it. "It's been two weeks, Michaela."

I glance at the vase standing on my chest of drawers. "They're still alive." Kind of. "And it's only been twelve days."

"They're making me sick."

"My roses are making you sick?" I shove my chemistry text into my bag.

"I'm allergic."

"To roses, or to human affection?"

"To cheesy, clichéd gestures. Also, to pollen."

I'm guessing Ben never gave her roses. Which suddenly makes me feel guilty about keeping them here, where she has to see them every day. But I have nowhere else to put them, and throwing them out while they're still alive feels like an insult to Ben.

"I'm going to press them," I tell her as I toss my backpack over my shoulder. "This weekend. I promise. Do you want a ride to school?" Mara is still grounded from her car for coming home drunk the night of the party. Two weeks down, two more to go.

Emery is also grounded—turns out Dad *did* notice she'd been drinking—but she doesn't have a car, so her grounding is a lot less consequential.

"Yeah. Thanks. Gabe's started picking Violet up in the mornings, and I hate sitting in the back seat."

Or . . . she hates watching them together. I think she actually *is* allergic to human affection.

"Speaking of Gabriel, have you noticed anything kinda weird going on with him lately?"

"Yes, now that you mention it." She gives me a dramatic tilt of her head. "I don't think he's jumped off of or crawled out of anything interesting in *weeks*."

"Emery, he seems . . . different." I need to know if I'm imagining a problem, or if I should be worried. But I promised Gabe I wouldn't say anything about the pills.

"Different, how?"

"You know how nothing ever seems to bother him?" I do my best Gabriel impersonation. "'Yeah, it's fine that I just cut my finger off chopping onions—I have nine to spare!'"

"That's just who he is." She shrugs. "That's also why Dad pays for super-good medical insurance."

"I know. And I love it that nothing seems to bother him. Except that now things seem to be bothering him. A lot. I'm not sure he's . . . okay."

Emery bristles. She looks like I just called her puppy ugly. "You have no idea what you're talking about. You've known him for, like, five minutes."

"So tell me, then. What am I missing?"

"Nothing. Everybody gets sad, and Gabe's really good at shaking it off. He'll psych himself up. Play some loud music, or take a road trip to Kansas for some famous barbecue sandwich, or—"

"Jump off the garage roof . . ."

"Yeah. So, he might seem down every now and then, but give it a minute, and the wind will change. Next thing you know, he'll be organizing a one-man flash mob in the park or talking you into a hot dog eating contest."

"A *one*-man flash mob?"

"It was just him dancing alone near the carousel. But it was funny."

Of course it was.

"My point is that he's fine, and you're sticking your nose in where it doesn't belong."

"Okay. Sorry." Message received, loud and clear. "I'll be ready in five," I tell her.

"Whatever." She disappears out the door, drinking from her reusable metal straw.

———— ∞ ————

"That was awesome!" I squeal as the pounding of the judge's gavel echoes in my head.

Everyone in the "courtroom" turns to look at me, and I flinch, suddenly worried that I'm not supposed to be speaking yet. That maybe there's a grace period between the final gavel bang and the speak-freely portion of the day.

Georgia laughs as she turns to face me from the defense's side at the front of the room. "Thank you!" she shouts across the small crowd.

The prosecution's lead attorney scowls at her, but the mock trial judge smiles, so I think it's fine. Though shouting in the courtroom may be slightly unprofessional. Even for mock trial.

"Seriously," I say as she picks her way up the steps toward me in her lawyer heels. "You were amazing."

"Really? You weren't bored?"

I was a little bored. I just spent three hours sitting silently in a chair, watching people argue about a fictional murder.

But . . . "Really. So . . ." I shrug, watching as spectators gather their things and attorneys pack up their props. "How do you know who won?" I expected a mock jury to read a mock verdict. I came for that drama.

"We'll get the ballots back in an hour or so, with comments from the judges." She leans in closer to whisper. "We won, though. Hands down."

I follow her as she says goodbye to her teammates, congratulating each of them by name, and I wind up sitting in her passenger's seat in the parking lot, while Georgia changes out of her lawyer clothes in the back seat.

"You didn't have to drive all the way out here," she says as I twist around to unzip her dress.

"Of course I did. Ms. Bond gave us a Saturday off, and I haven't seen you in a month. And I've never seen a mock trial." I frown as she shimmies out of the dress. "There was a lot less mocking than I expected."

"And a lot less mocking than I'd like to engage in. But I don't make the rules. So . . ." She leaves the dress wadded up on the floorboard and tugs a T-shirt over her head. "How are rehearsals going?"

"Fine. We're four weeks in. Deep into 'scene work.'"

"Emery's still playing the evil stepsister?"

"She excels at the role, even offstage. I feel bad for her, though."

"Why would you feel bad for her?"

"Because she feels like Ben got the entire theater department in the divorce—"

"You mean the breakup?"

"Yeah."

"So," Georgia says. "I got curious this morning, while we were waiting for the judges to arrive, and I looked up last year's West Bradford musical. The local paper mentioned Emery in the review."

"Seriously?"

"Yeah. Just a sec." Georgia stands, hunched over, to pull up her jeans, then crawls between the two front seats and drops into place behind the wheel. She grabs her phone from the center console and opens the browser, then hands it to me. The article is still loaded on her screen.

"This calls her a 'comedic delight.'" She played Grandma Addams, and now that I've seen her as a wicked stepsister—also a funny role—I can totally picture her nailing her part in *The Addams Family*. "Shit. This also says they expect to see her in larger roles, in future productions."

"Yeah. And I'm guessing she's read this, and this year she was expecting bigger things for herself."

"Yeah. Cinderella is a dramatic role. A lead. I think she was really trying to prove that Ben wasn't, like, carrying her. That she can stand on her own two feet onstage. But every time I turn around, I'm *stepping* on her feet. So . . ."

"You're just living your life," Georgia insists. "If that puts you in her way, maybe she's the one who needs to move over."

"I love you," I tell her.

"I know," she replies with a wink.

---

"Hey! Where is everyone?" Cynthia calls from the kitchen. "It's a big day, right? You're all going to need a big breakfast!"

"It's just a regular day for me," Cody mumbles as he passes me in the hallway.

It isn't that big a day for the rest of us either. Though I will admit, I'm a little nervous. We're seven weeks into rehearsal, and while the first six weeks seemed to drag on, suddenly everything feels like it's moving very quickly. We went through the entire production yesterday for the first time—no pausing to adjust or correct things—and today is crew view. We'll be performing in front of an audience for the first time, and that's kind of terrifying, even if that audience is just the backstage crew, sitting in-house so they can see how it goes and start visualizing their jobs. Opening and closing curtains. Bringing in the heavy props. Lighting and sound. We've been practicing without all that so far.

And since it's a live music production, the orchestra will be in-house too this afternoon. Watching and listening. Mentally running through their own parts, along with the soundtrack we use for practice.

It'll be kind of cool to see Gabriel and Cole in the audience.

On my way to the kitchen, I pass Gabe's door and I can hear him snoring, so I knock, because he's supposed to be up by now. In fact, if he's going to drop Cody off at school, he needs to be in the car in fifteen minutes.

When he doesn't answer, I open the door. He's asleep on his bed, on top of the covers. Fully clothed, with shoes and everything. But they're yesterday's clothes.

"Hey." I sink onto the edge of the mattress. "It's seven fifteen. Time to get up." I nudge his knee. "Past time, actually."

Gabe mumbles something unintelligible as his eyes flutter open. "Michaela." My name is the first word I recognize, but it sounds a little slurred.

"Yeah. You okay?"

"I saw you, you know." His eyes are glazed, his words mushy. Shit. I glance around for his vape pen as I get up to close the door, but I don't see it. But . . .

I pry an orangish plastic cylinder from his right fist. It's one of Grammie's prescription bottles. For hydrocodone.

"Hey." I'm whispering now, afraid that someone will hear. "How many of these did you take? Should I go get someone?" I start to stand, but he grabs my arm, and when I sink onto the mattress again, he looks more awake. He looks . . . scared.

"No," he says. "I'm fine. I only took one. Just need to wake up." He pushes himself upright, blinking rapidly.

"You sure?" It's hard to believe that one pill did this, especially if he took it last night.

"Yeah. Just give me a minute."

"Okay." But I'm not leaving him until I'm sure he's awake. "What were you saying a minute ago? Something about seeing me?"

"Nothing," he mumbles. "I was half asleep."

"I know. But what did you mean?" It wasn't a dream. It felt more like something he'd just *remembered*, when he woke up and saw my face. "Gabriel. Tell me."

"I saw you," he says again. "Last year."

I shake my head. "I've been here for less than two months," I remind him. Maybe he *was* dreaming.

"Not here." He sits up, and he looks more awake now. He also looks like he regrets what he's saying. But he's committed. "Dad was hiding texts, so I took his phone one night when he went to the bathroom. He doesn't know I know his code. And I saw—"

"My messages." I'm starting to understand.

"Yeah." His nod is exaggerated, but he seems more alert by the minute. "I scrolled up and read a bunch of them. I didn't understand who you were, at first. But then I read a text where you called him 'Dad,' and . . ." He shrugs. "I figured it out. Some of it, anyway. But I got some of it really wrong. I didn't know that Mom already knew. I didn't know that it had been over with your mother for years. I thought . . ." He shrugs again.

"You thought he was still cheating."

"Yeah. And that he was hiding a secret kid." He snorts. "That's the part I got right. So I found you."

"You found me? When? Where? *How?*"

"In his checkbook, of all places. The only man in the world who still writes paper checks is our dad. And he wrote ninety percent of them to your mom."

Child support. She always deposited them electronically, with her phone.

"You saw the duplicates?"

He nods. "Still in the checkbook, in his top desk drawer. Once I had her name, you were easy to find online. Then, when we played Oak Valley, back in August, I asked around about you, and someone pointed you out. You were in the bleachers, just sitting there, cheering for your football team. Looking *just* enough like Emery that I couldn't deny it." He's awake now, but he doesn't sound like himself. "You were real. You were *his*. And I thought my mom had no idea."

"Did you tell her?" Surely I would have heard about this if he had.

"No! I didn't want to be the one to break up their marriage." Gabe runs one hand through his hair. "So I just . . ." He shrugs. "Lived with it. With his secret."

"You thought Dad was cheating—you knew about his hidden kid—and you felt like you had to keep that quiet?"

"I didn't want to hurt my mom."

I feel weirdly guilty. "I can't imagine the pressure that must have been." Feeling like his whole world would fall apart if he opened his mouth. The weight of that secret must have been enormous. Crushing.

"It was stressful," he admits. Then he forces a smile. "But it's fine, because stress builds character, right?"

"It must. You are definitely a character."

Gabe laughs as he pulls his shirt off. "No time to shower. I'll just run through the sprinkler in the front yard."

I smile—he sounds more like himself now—but I'm starting to understand that there's a reason Gabe tries so hard to see the bright side of everything.

"Is this crew view thing really going to take three and a half hours?" He's on his feet now, digging through his dresser.

"I have no idea. This is my first time. But I'd be prepared for a long day."

"Well then, we're in luck. I am *always* prepared!" Gabe disappears into the bathroom he shares with Cody, and I head across the hall.

Grammie's head is lying at a weird angle, so I try to fluff her pillow without waking her, but her eyes fly open. She blinks up at me, her milky blue irises glazed with confusion. She mumbles something incoherent, and I think it may be a name, but it isn't mine. It's not Emery's either. Or Cynthia's.

"Morning, Grammie," I say. "Sorry to wake you up. I was just trying to make you more comfortable."

"Morning," she mumbles as she tries to push herself upright. I grab the bed remote and lift the head end of her bed until she's sitting.

"I have to go to school, but I'm glad I got to see you first. Try to eat something today, okay?"

She nods, but I'm not sure she really understands what I'm saying, or who I am. That breaks my heart. I can't imagine how hard this is for Cynthia.

Cody sits at the breakfast bar in the kitchen, waiting for Dad to take him to school, since Gabe's running late. He's eating toast and scrambled eggs, and although I smell bacon, I've evidently shown up too late to snag any.

"How is she?" Cynthia asks as I take a triangle of buttered toast from the plate sitting on the counter.

"Confused."

"Yeah, there's been more and more of that." She sighs. "Eggs?"

"No, thanks."

"She doesn't like eggs," Cody says.

"That's right. Sorry." Cynthia looks frazzled. She sounds exhausted. Most mornings, she seems to channel her grief into frantic overreactions aimed at the grime in the shower or the spot of oil in the driveway. But I guess there's only so long a person can maintain that level of energy.

"No worries," I tell her.

"We'll be late tonight, remember?" Emery breezes through the living room into the kitchen and sets her empty smoothie cup in the sink.

"Of course! Today's dress rehearsal, right? I made a big breakfast."

Emery rolls her eyes at her mother. "That's in two weeks. Today's crew view. And tomorrow afternoon, we run it with the crew doing their jobs for the first time. It'll be a long day."

"Basically, she's saying we'll all be extra cranky all weekend," I translate for Cynthia. "Though in some cases"—I toss a glance at Emery—"I'm not sure you'll be able to tell any difference."

"Whatever. Let's go." Emery heads out the kitchen door.

I dig my keys from my bag and scruff Cody's hair on my way out. "See you tonight."

# twenty-four

Stretches!" Ms. Bond calls from the apron, and the cast forms a large circle in the center of the stage. "Let's go, guys! We have an audience today, and I don't want to waste their time."

It feels weird to see people sitting in the house seats. This has been a friendly space for so long, during so many rehearsals, that I've felt like it was *ours*, kind of, for almost two months now. The cast has climbed over those chairs and napped stretching out across them. We've done homework there and practiced harmonies. Now it suddenly feels like we've lost ownership of the theater, with an audience seated out there.

The space feels foreign now, as if I never *really* knew it. It feels intimidating.

Emery and Mara, our warm-up captains, stand back-to-back in the center of the circle and lead us through a series of stretches. Emery loves that job, because all eyes are on her. That's one of the things we don't have in common. When I'm singing, I can forget that people are staring at me. I can assume they're just listening. But when I'm not, all I can think about is what everyone else is thinking while they look at me.

I stare into the audience as we sit on the stage and stretch, touching our toes and extending our arms over our heads. Grabbing our own elbows. The house lights are on, so I can see the faces. The orchestra kids are clustered on the right, and I see Violet sitting with her friends, holding a folder with musical notes and clefs printed on it. But I don't see Gabe.

"Vocal warm-ups!" Ms. Bond calls, when we're all limber. She's backstage now, standing in front of the soundboard with Tate, the stage-right ASM—assistant stage manager—showing her something with the controls. Behind Tate, the costume mistress—a junior from my English class—is waiting to show them something that's gone wrong with one of the costumes. I think it's Jack's mother's dress.

Today, Ms. Bond's T-shirt reads, "All Drama Must Remain on the Stage." I wish I had a shirt just like it to wear at home.

Kat Torrez and Jon Escobedo, our vocal captains, step into the center of the circle to demonstrate a series of alliterative nonsense syllables sung in various pitches and harmonies. While we sing the warm-ups, the audience fidgets. They whisper and laugh, and I find it distracting.

Are they laughing at us? At *me*? I feel like I'm on display. Which, of course, I am.

Mr. Oliver, the orchestra conductor, walks across the front of the house, right in front of the stage, holding a clipboard and his thick musical score. He keeps glancing at his clipboard, then at his orchestra students, silently taking attendance. As we finish the warm-ups, he sets his music on the apron. "Has anyone seen Gabriel Bosch?"

No one speaks. Violet stares at the folder on her lap.

Uh-oh.

"Okay!" Ms. Bond appears onstage again, and we open our circle to form an arc facing her. "Today, we're just going to run the whole thing so the crew and pit can get a feel for the show, and for what they'll be doing."

Mr. Oliver knoels backward on a chair in the front row, quietly talking to the orchestra kids. Probably asking about Gabriel. I can't hear what he's saying, but I can tell that they don't have an answer for him.

"Please remember all the notes Sarah and I gave you yesterday and do your best to implement them. Tate, you're on music, right?" Ms. Bond calls toward stage right.

"Right!" Tate calls. She's standing in front of the soundboard again, where she'll be during the actual performance, though right now she's still working with a school-issued Chromebook loaded with special theater audio software and hooked up to speakers at the front of the stage.

"And Fitz"—Owen Fitzhugh, our stage-left ASM—"will be on book, but that's to double-check your lines, *not* to give them to you. The first person who asks for a line will stay late and sweep up backstage. It's important that you say your lines accurately, because from this point on, they are not just lines of dialogue; they're also cues for the crew, who will be bringing your props and set pieces onstage."

I catch Emery's gaze across the circle and mouth, "Gabe?"

She shrugs. I want to text him, but I know better than to pull my phone out onstage.

"And one last thing," Ms. Bond says as she backs toward the steps leading down from the stage and into the house. "Yesterday's run-through was *not* a dumpster fire!" The cast cheers as we all stand. "I know today's will be even better! Okay, opening positions!"

*Into the Woods* opens with three mini-sets lined up onstage. In the stage-left set, I, as Cinderella, am scrubbing the hearth in front of a stone fireplace. We haven't actually finished the fireplace yet, so I'm on my knees in front of a tall frame made of two-by-fours.

In the center set, Ben and Lexie are minding their bakery, which also doesn't exist yet, and stage right, Jon, as Jack, is brushing Milky White with a prop horse brush. Though, since we haven't finished the papier-mâché cow yet, he's only brushing the wooden bovine skeleton.

Ms. Bond cues the music. Tate presses a button, and the first notes rise from the speakers positioned on the apron.

Mr. Oliver stands in front of the stage with his score and a pencil, ready to take notes. He's scowling, though. He still hasn't found Gabe.

I'm onstage for the first couple of scenes, but as soon as I get backstage, I pull my phone from my pocket. It takes a second for my eyes to adjust to the darkened wings, even with the blue lens lights that are supposed to help with the transition, and when they do, I track Gabe's cell.

House rule: we all have to keep tracking enabled, in case of an emergency or a kidnapping. Seriously. Cynthia has a whole speech prepared on the topic.

Gabe is at school. There's some fudge factor with the little location dot, but he appears to be not far from my dot and Emery's.

Emery is standing with Mara in the second wing, even though she doesn't go on for ages. I tug her onto the tarp beneath one of the tall papier-mâché trees, which is waiting for a round of accent paint on the leaves. "Gabe's here somewhere," I whisper. "You need to go find him."

"I can't leave." She gestures at the stage, where Jack is talking to the Mysterious Man now. "This is crew view," she hisses.

"I know, but—"

"And this is Michaela and Emery," Cole whispers as he leads a tall, skinny freshman toward us from the storage area. "They're superstars! They're also two of the people we'll be miking. Guys, this is Zack, our audio two. And since I'm graduating, he'll be next year's A-1."

"Hey, Zack," I say.

"Hey." Emery frowns. "Aren't you guys supposed to be watching from the house?"

Cole's smile fades. "I just wanted to give him a tour."

Things have been weird between them in the three weeks since Sage's party, and I feel bad for Cole. But I kind of feel bad for Emery too.

Cole takes Zack toward the backstage stairs leading into the house, and Emery turns to me. "*You* go find Gabe, if you want. But I'm not leaving."

"Em, I think something's wrong."

She shrugs. "Violet dumped him last night."

"What? Why?"

"I don't know. But that's life, and as you might have heard, the show must go on. And Gabe's not even *in* the show."

"Yeah. But—"

"Michaela. He's a big boy. He'll be fine."

But she doesn't know that roof jumping and road trips aren't the only way Gabe copes with stress, and *I* don't know what he did with Grammie's pill bottle. "I'm going to find him. If I'm not back in time, you can go on for me."

Her brows rise, and I realize that the hard part won't be getting her onstage as Cinderella. It'll be taking my part back afterward. "You sure?"

"Yeah. But *only* if I'm not back in time."

"Jon, we need you and Milky White to come in about a *second* earlier, after Cinderella exits," Tate whispers from my right as Jon/Jack comes offstage. "You're still getting there just a *beat* too late."

"Okay. I'll be right back," I whisper to Emery. Then, as Little Red Riding Hood and the Wolf launch into "Hello, Little Girl," I take off running down the yellow-and-black walkway, through the set storage area and the makeup lab. I burst into the arts wing and peek into every classroom I pass, but they're all locked, except for the band room, where some kind of ensemble is rehearsing.

As I'm passing the boys' bathroom, I hear water running, so I suck in a deep breath and push the door open. "Gabe?" I call from the doorway.

The water stops. "What?"

"Are you alone?"

"Yeah. Michaela?"

I step into the boys' room and let the door close behind me. Gabe's standing at the sink. He swipes water from his chin with his forearm as he turns to face me. "Mr. Oliver's looking for you. What are you doing in here?"

He glances at the urinals. "I'll give you two guesses."

"For half an hour? In the middle of rehearsal?" I shake my head. "You're hiding."

"Fortunately, you're very good at hide-and-seek." Gabe frowns as he leans against the last stall. "Aren't you supposed to be onstage?"

"Not until the end of scene two." When Cinderella runs into the Baker's Wife, after fleeing the festival. "Emery will go on in my place, if I'm not back."

He snorts. "If you let her go on, you're gonna have to pull her offstage with a cane."

"She told me Violet broke up with you," I say.

"Yeah, but now I can sing out loud in the car, or eat onions at lunch, or . . . book a singles cruise." He sounds like himself, but he doesn't *look* like himself.

"Okay, then." I push the door open and hold it for him. "If you're all good, let's go to rehearsal."

"Not a chance." Gabe huffs. "I was only doing the musical because of Violet. The last thing I want now is to spend hours vamping chords and staring at her across the pit."

I blink up at him. "But we need you." Gabe's the only bass

player who signed up for the pit. The two people who could replace him would have to be talked into taking the part, and they'd be weeks behind in rehearsals.

"How am I supposed to spend most of the next three weeks with her, Michaela?" Something changes in his eyes. The jokes are gone now, and what's left is viscerally real. It's like staring into an open wound. "She was *using* me to make her ex jealous."

Violet's ex is Bella's brother. "She told you that?"

"No. She just said she was sorry, but she'd made a mistake when she broke up with him. So, there's no reason for me to play in the pit, or to go back in the auditorium."

"So, this morning? The pills? That was about Violet?"

He rolls his eyes, and for a second, he looks exactly like Emery. "Seriously?"

"I just want to understand."

"Well, that's exactly what I *don't* want." He paces to the end of the row of sinks, then turns back to face me. "Sometimes I don't want to think, but my mind won't stop turning things over and over. Looking at all the angles. Sometimes I can't sleep because I can't stop trying to make sense out of things that aren't ever going to make sense. I just need everything to *slow down*. Every now and then, I just need to *feel okay*." His expression is fierce, and bitter, and intense. His eyes seem to be begging me to understand. "Don't you?"

"Yeah." Yeah, I do. But there's no shortcut for me, because pills don't work. "I'm worried about you," I admit, and it costs me a lot to say that. I'm scared he'll shut me out now.

"Don't be. I'm fine. I'm just not going to play in the pit."

"So then, why are you here, Gabriel?"

He frowns. "What do you mean?"

"Rehoarsal started half an hour ago, but you didn't go home. You're still standing in the closest bathroom to the auditorium. Why is that, if you don't want to be here?"

Gabe shrugs.

"Okay, come on. You made a commitment to the orchestra— to the entire production—and you can't just quit on us. Violet isn't the one you'll be letting down."

"I can't—"

"Just go sit down and watch the damn musical. Cheer for your sisters," I add before he can argue again. "Unless you want Violet to know she ran you off."

"Damn it," Gabe swears. "Singles cruise . . . singles cruise . . . ," he mumbles as he follows me back down the hall and through the brightly lit storage area, piled high with old set pieces and furniture. But he goes through a side door into the auditorium when I veer backstage.

In the spotlight, Jack's mother sends him to bed without supper, and Aaron, the Narrator, delivers his line. Then Loxie enters from upstage, pulling an imaginary cow behind her. The soundtrack plays music from the festival Cinderella has just fled, which is my cue. I start to rush onstage, my lines already queued up in my head, but Emery steps in front of me. We make eye contact, and for just a second, she hesitates, and I think she's going to do the right thing. I'm back in time. It's my role.

Then she dashes out of the wing and into the light.

She's onstage, playing *my* part!

# twenty-five

Onstage, Emery looks over her shoulder, checking to make sure she hasn't been followed from the festival. Lexie, the Baker's Wife, turns, expecting to find me, and her eyes widen when she sees Emery instead. But then she recovers and delivers her line.

Fuming, I stare at them as they play out the scene. My face is *burning*. I can feel everyone backstage staring at me.

"What the hell is she doing?" Ben hisses, appearing at my side in the dark. He's onstage for most of the play, so he never wanders very far from the wings.

"Taking her shot," I whisper.

"You can't let her—"

"I know."

"She's going to sing your song." He sounds as pissed as I am.

"I *know*." But there's nothing I can do about that, until she comes offstage. Which won't be until after my duet with Lexie.

I try to keep it in perspective. "A Very Nice Prince" is only *one* of my songs.

"Ms. Bond's going to kill you both."

"I know."

I move forward and peek past the wing one curtain. The short sections of curtain are called wings, and the spaces between them are legs, so when you break a leg, you're really just taking the stage. Which, in this case, Em has done instead of me.

I feel like breaking her *actual* leg.

Ms. Bond is watching from the house left aisle, standing next to Mr. Oliver, her arms crossed over her shirt, and I realize that despite what her shirt says, we have not left the drama on the stage. But I can't tell what she's thinking as she watches Emery. She has the best poker face in the world.

"What the hell is Em doing?" Ben whispers fiercely, and I turn to see that he's cornered Mara near the unfinished frame of Rapunzel's tower.

"Get out of my face," she hisses, pushing him back.

"Hey. It's fine," I whisper, tugging on his arm. "I asked her to go on for me if I wasn't back in time."

"You were back," he says. "I saw you."

I can't argue with that, so I just watch Emery and Lexie sing "A Very Nice Prince." I don't think Emery sings it as well as I do, but her acting is good, and she clearly knows the part. She's the best-case scenario, as an understudy.

But it's *my* role.

Finally, Lexie and Emery exit the stage. Em doesn't look at me, but I don't have time to dwell on that, or on how pissed I am, because both the stepsisters *and* Cinderella are in "First Midnight," along with most of the cast, wandering through the woods alone and in pairs, singing individual lines that sum up our characters' failures in the second scene.

We sing our bit in unison; then the blackout plunges the entire stage into darkness, and Ben takes his next position: the Baker is lying asleep on the floor of the forest, under a tree. Only really, he's sleeping next to the bright pink X on the floor, marking the spot where that tree will go, once it's finished.

Suddenly Ms. Bond is at my side in the dark. "Michaela? Emery?" she whispers. "May I see you in the girls' dressing room, please?" Then she marches toward the room at the back, and we follow in silence.

I wonder if Emery can feel the anger radiating from my body, because I certainly can.

Ms. Bond leaves the dressing room door cracked open so we can hear the music and keep up with the progress onstage. She sits on the edge of a long table against one wall, where two old sewing machines stand next to folded bits of costumes in progress.

This room is shaped like a drastically lopsided rectangle, with one really short side. The three long walls are lined with closet rods and stuffed with old costumes. The costumes for this production—most of which we're still working on—hang on a rolling rack next to the door.

The only chairs in the room are the bench seat pulled out of an old car, which has clearly been in here since the dawn of time. Generations of old cast members have signed it in every color that Sharpie has ever put in stores. Fortunately, there are no mirrors in here either. I don't think I could stand to see myself right now.

"What happened?" Ms. Bond doesn't look mad exactly, but she isn't happy either. "Michaela does not look sick or injured, and she's clearly not absent. So why was Emery onstage?"

"Michaela left after her scene at the grave," Emery says, referring to Cinderella's mother's grave, "and she asked me to go on for her."

"I asked her to go on if I didn't make it back." I take a beat and unclench my fists. "But I *did* make it back, and she went on anyway."

"She walked in right as her cue played, and she wasn't in the right headspace," Emery snaps. "Anyone could see that. She would have just been going through the motions, if she even made it out there on time. So, I made a judgment call."

My temper flares, a burst of white-hot flames engulfing me. "Your judgment sucks!"

"You left in the middle of rehearsal!" Emery fires back, and now we're straight-up arguing in front of the woman who could have us both removed from this production in a heartbeat.

"Why did you leave?" Ms. Bond asks me.

"It was a personal matter." I'm not going to rat out Gabe, but . . . "A family issue."

Ms. Bond frowns at me, and then her gaze slips toward Emery. "Aren't you two sisters?"

"*Half* sisters," Emery says.

Ms. Bond exhales slowly. "Sarah told me that about a week after I posted the cast list. I admit that if I'd known about your relationship when I cast the parts, we wouldn't be in this situation."

"What does that mean?" Emery demands. Then she seems to think better of her tone, and she takes a step back. Her elbow hits the mannequin currently wearing a weird, shimmery, clingy gown that's too big to fit any girl in the cast. Which we know, because we've all tried it on.

The mannequin wobbles, and the dress shimmers in the bright overhead lights, but it doesn't fall.

Ms. Bond sighs. A mannequin crashing to the floor would have been audible from the house.

"It means I wouldn't have cast one sister as the other's understudy under the best of circumstances. If I'd known. That inevitably leads to the wrong kind of drama. And my understanding of the situation is that this"—she gestures to the space between Emery and me—"is not the best of circumstances. So, what are we going to do about it?"

Emery glares at me, but beneath her anger, there's something else. It feels like panic. Like she's about to hyperventilate, right in front of me.

And suddenly I'm a little less angry.

*Why* can't I stay mad at her?

"Are you kicking one of us out of the show?" I say. Because that's clearly what Emery is afraid to ask.

"No." Ms. Bond leans back a little and crosses her arms over her T-shirt. "As far as I'm concerned, this theater program gets both of you or neither of you. And I'll leave that up to you two. Can you work together? Or do I need to shuffle some cast members and make some calls?"

Emery shrugs. I roll my eyes at her. She wants this just as badly as I do, and she isn't a good enough actor to pretend that she doesn't.

"We want to stay in the play," I say. "Right?"

Emery nods. "I'm sorry. I just . . . Michaela left, and I wanted to show you what I could do. Understudies are supposed to get a chance to go on, aren't they? For practice?"

"Yes, and they will," Ms. Bond says. "If you'd read your production schedule, you'd know that the understudy rehearsal is next week."

Emery knows that. I've heard her and Mara talking about it.

"Is everything okay with this family situation?" Ms. Bond asks, and it takes me a second to realize she's not talking about Emery as my understudy. She's talking about whatever made me leave rehearsal.

"I think so."

"Okay, then." She takes a breath. "Emery, what you did was a betrayal not only of your sister and fellow cast member, but of the entire cast and crew of this show. This is not musical chairs. Parts are not interchangeable. We have to be able to count on each other to know lines and cues. To hit marks onstage. We have to be able to count on the flymen not to drop curtains on us all and the orchestra to vamp musical sections long enough for us to set scenery and find marks. We have to be able to count on Mr. Lacey to time the lights properly so you can be seen onstage. On Cole and Zack to mic everyone so you can be heard. On the costume mistress to keep up with quick change sheets and the crew to move set pieces. And when any one of us messes up, everyone is affected."

"I know," Emery says. "I'm sorry."

"A mistake is one thing, but what you did was intentional, and it betrayed the trust of everyone involved in this production. You intentionally introduced chaos into a production, which could have thrown the entire cast off of their game. And if it happens again, you're out. Even if that means I have to go on as Lucinda to fill your role. Am I clear?"

"Yes." Emery looks mortified, and I find myself embarrassed too. For her. For us both.

"Will this happen again?"

"No. I swear. And I'm so sorry."

"Thank you. Let's move on then." Ms. Bond gestures at the door. "Go watch for your cue."

Emery glances at her, then at me. Then she leaves, though she obviously wants to hear whatever she's about to be left out of.

Ms. Bond pushes the door almost closed after Emery. "I should have called you in way before this. As you've no doubt noticed, theater kids are a tight-knit group, both cast and crew, and they can start to feel like family. Which means that even as a teacher, I hear things. More than most teachers might, since I spend so much more time with my students."

I nod, because I'm not sure where she's going with this.

"What I'm trying to say is that I shouldn't have relied on

rumors. I should have just asked you if you're okay. If you need to talk."

"About . . . what?"

"About your mom? Your new family? Unless those rumors weren't accurate . . . ?"

"They probably were." I exhale. I still hate telling this story. "Emery and I have the same dad, but neither of us knew that until my mom died almost two months ago. Now I live with her, and she's not really thrilled about that. Or about the fact that I got the role she wanted."

Ms. Bond nods slowly. "Yeah, I can imagine that's a lot of tension."

And that's just the beginning. I can't tell whether she doesn't know about Ben or doesn't consider his part in this to be any of her business. But I'm not going to bring him up.

"So, how are you doing?"

I shrug. "Fine."

Ms. Bond's brows rise: skepticism on display.

"Really. I only auditioned as a kind of tribute to my mom. She loved musicals, and this was one of her favorites. But then I got really into it, so . . ."

"I'm glad to hear that. And if you ever need to talk . . ."

"Thanks," I say, and she stands to reach for the doorknob. "Wait, there is one thing I wanted to ask. About the programs. Will the cast get to write anything in them? Because if we do, I wanted to dedicate my performance to my mom."

Her exhalation is a little shaky, and I wonder if she's lost someone. "Yes, of course. You each get a paragraph next to your headshot in the program. And I think that sounds perfect. I'll make sure you get an early copy."

"Thank you," I say as she pulls the door open.

Onstage, the opening notes from "Agony" begin, and I stand in the wings to watch Josh, as Cinderella's Prince, sing the duet with Wyatt Borden, who's playing Rapunzel's Prince. Josh is great, whining dramatically—and melodically—as he tries to figure out why Cinderella has run from him.

Everyone backstage seems to be staring at me, and probably at Emery. I'm sure they all wonder what Ms. Bond said to us. Except for Cole. He's standing in the shadows, singing Wyatt's part beneath his breath, and he doesn't seem to have noticed that we're back.

He's better than Wyatt. I wish he had auditioned.

Someone grabs me, spinning me away from the curtain with one arm around my waist, and I start to scream. Then a hand clamps over my mouth. "Quiet backstage!" Link whispers, grinning down at me. He's wearing wolf ears on a headband, as he has since the second week of rehearsal. "My, what big eyes you have. I've got somethin' big for you, princess, and I'm not talkin' about my teeth."

He smells like pot.

"Fuck off." Ben pulls me free and shoves Link back. "Show up to rehearsal high again, and you're going to need those ears surgically removed from someplace uncomfortable," he growls.

Link chuckles as he wanders into the darkest backstage area.

"I'm *sick* of half the cast treating this production like some kind of joke." Ben stares down at me in the light bleeding from the stage. His gaze softens. "You good?"

"Yeah. Link's an asshole, but he's harmless." I'm pretty sure. What I *know* is that he's great as the Wolf, even if he's worthless once the spotlight fades.

I go on for my duet with Lexie, then again at the end of scene three for "Second Midnight," with most of the cast. Including Emery. After the blackout, as we rush through the wings, Aaron, the Narrator, steps between Emery and me, one arm around each of our shoulders. "Our heroines, thrust together not just onstage, but in real life as well, must decide whether or not they're willing to push past their personal grievances for the good of—"

"Oh my God, get off me!" Emery shoves him away, and Aaron laughs. Until he sees Kat Torrez glaring at him from her ready position in the wings.

I have no idea what consequence she threatened him with for narrating people's real lives, but I'm more than ready to find out.

———⊂∞⊃———

I'm surprised when Emery rides home with me, instead of with Gabe, but I'm glad. She keeps looking at me, but every time I turn, she looks out the window.

Ben keeps texting me, asking why she went on in my part and what Ms. Bond said to us. He thinks she shouldn't be in the show anymore. That she's too unpredictable. That the rest of the cast can't trust her now. And, honestly, he has a point.

Everyone was staring at her backstage during the whole show. Whispering. They could all see that I was there, watching her perform in my role, which means I clearly could have gone onstage. They don't know what happened, and neither of us has said anything. No one is very happy with her.

But Ms. Bond made her decision, and I don't want Emery kicked off the show. I just want her to stay out of my personal life. And I want Emery and Ben to get over whatever happened between them and stop putting me in the middle.

"What?" I finally say when I see Emery staring at me again out of the corner of my eye. I think she's trying to apologize but keeps losing her nerve.

"Nothing."

"Just spit it out," I snap as I turn into our neighborhood. The gate is up ahead, but there are two cars in front of us, including Gabe's.

"Why? You're not going to believe me."

She's definitely trying to apologize. "Try me."

Emery sighs. "Mara went to rehearsal early to work on her costume, and she saw Ben and Sage Andersen come out of the boys' dressing room."

"So?"

"*So*, they were in there *alone*."

"So what? They're friends."

"They're not friends, Michaela."

"Yes, they are. Sage invited him to her party."

"Sage invited *everyone* to her party." The first car goes

through the gate, and Gabe drives through after it, but I miss my chance, because I'm talking to Emery. "She probably didn't even know half the people there."

I pull forward and type in the code. "She knows Ben."

Emery rolls her eyes. "Oh, I know. She knows him so well that they were alone together in the boys' dressing room, with the door closed. Which is against the rules. And there's only one reason for that."

"There are literally dozens of reasons for that, Emery. If it's even true." And you know what's *really* against the rules? Going onstage in someone else's role, for no reason.

She crosses her arms over her shirt. "I told you you wouldn't believe me."

"I thought you were going to say you were sorry. For going on in my place."

Emery huffs as I pull through the gate.

"You owe me an apology. You knew I was there. You looked right at me, and you went onstage anyway."

"I know. And I *am* sorry, okay? It was not my finest moment. I just . . . I saw my shot, and I took it. Suddenly it just— It felt like if I didn't go on then, I might never get another chance. It sounds stupid now, but in that moment . . ."

"Yeah, I get that," I admit. "That's exactly how I felt when I auditioned. Like if I didn't take that opportunity to say goodbye to my mom—to sing for her—I might never get another one."

"You were serious about that?" I can feel Emery staring at me. "That's *really* why you auditioned?"

"Of course I was serious. Why wouldn't I be?" I glance at her as I turn onto our street. "You still think I was playing the dead mom card."

"Okay, look. I'll forgive you for that, if you forgive me for this."

"That's—" I don't even have words for how messed up that is. "I had every right to audition, but you had *no* right to go on in my place!"

"Fine."

"Em—"

"No, you're right. You're a saint, and I'm a bitch, and I'm sorry I said anything. About anything. I'm not lying, though," she says as I pull into the driveway. "Mara said she saw them, and I believe her. And I know what Ben's doing to you, because he did it to me. And he knows you won't believe a thing I say about him, so he can basically do whatever he wants. Even if he's making you look like a fool. Just like he did to me. Just like Dad did to Mom."

But that's the thing. Finding out what her dad did is killing Emery. It's changed the way she sees everything. She's viewing the whole world through a cheater filter, and she can't let it go.

Which means she is the least reliable source of information on Ben McGrath in the entire world.

# twenty-six

I'm not saying Emery lied to you." Ben reaches down for the button at the bottom of the driver's seat, and it hums as it slides back, putting enough room between him and the BMW steering wheel that he can turn and face me. He could tell I was upset— Emery's words kept haunting me, even though I don't really believe them—so he came over. But there's no privacy in a house full of people, so we're sitting in the driveway.

In the rain.

"I'm saying that Mara misunderstood what she saw."

My chest feels tight. "What did she see?"

"After school, Link and I were in the dressing room, and Sage came in to bring his costume boots. She'd been gluing fur to them, to look like wolf paws. While she was there, he closed the door so he could smoke. She and I didn't want to smell like pot, so we left. Mara saw us come out of the dressing room together, and I guess she didn't know Link was still in there."

"Okay." I could ask Sage, but if she is hooking up with my

boyfriend, she won't admit it. And Link is hardly a reliable source of anything but secondhand smoke. Or whatever. "You sure you're not . . . into her?"

Ben arches one brow at me. "No, I'm not into Sage Andersen. And even if I were, she wouldn't be into me. Sage isn't really a theater kid; she's just padding her college résumé. But at the end of the day, her heart belongs to cheerleading, and she only dates athletes."

"You play baseball and soccer."

He laughs. "Football and basketball are the only sports that matter."

He's not wrong about that. At least in Oklahoma.

"Is this . . . ?" His gaze narrows on me in concern. "Is this about your dad? I mean, it can't be easy to find out about him like you did, and I understand how that could make you see cheaters everywhere, but . . ."

"No." That's part of Emery's problem, I think. But I'm not projecting my personal trauma—my dad's sins—onto Ben. At least, I don't think I am.

That wouldn't be fair to him.

He smiles, and a little fire ignites deep in my chest. "I like that you're jealous, though. That means you like me, right?"

I roll my eyes. "You know I like you."

"Good." Ben leans toward me, his gaze caught on my lips, and heat pools in my stomach. Rain hits the roof of the car like missiles exploding upon impact.

I meet him in the middle, and we kiss over the gearshift. "I don't want to lose you over some stupid rumor," he murmurs against my lips as his fingers slide into the hair at the back of my head. "It's hard enough for me to think about you out there in the garage at night, alone with those other guys."

"One of those guys is my brother," I remind him.

"The other two are not. But I trust you," he adds, whispering into my ear, and the warmth of his breath sends shivers down my spine.

"I trust you too." In the seven weeks we've been together, he's given me no reason not to. And though he isn't my first boyfriend, he's the first one who's ever made me feel all tingly inside. As if my organs have been replaced with firecrackers and someone's lit a fuse.

Light flashes through the window, and I jerk away from Ben, because that wasn't lightning. My dad's car pulls around us and parks beneath the port cochere. "That's dinner," I say. "I gotta go. But thanks for coming over."

"I'm at your beck and call. Especially with rewards like these." Ben leans in for one more long kiss, and I'm smiling as I get out of the car. I race down the driveway to meet my dad under the covered section of driveway, but I'm soaked before I've gone four steps.

"Ben?" he asks, watching as the BMW backs out of the driveway.

"Yeah. There was drama today."

"Drama, as opposed to theater?"

"Exactly."

My dad's gaze narrows on the closed kitchen door as rain pounds on the roof over our heads. "What am I about to walk into, exactly?"

"Nothing. Em and I are fine, I swear." She and Ben aren't, but my Switzerland routine seems to be keeping me out of the line of fire. Mostly.

"Need some help?" I ask as he ducks into his passenger's side to grab two large white paper sacks, their tops folded over. There's a long receipt from his favorite Mexican place taped to one of them.

"Yeah. Will you grab the drinks?"

I lean in through the open passenger's side door and pick up two cardboard drink carriers from the floorboard. They each hold three sodas, every paper cup dripping with condensation.

The car smells like nachos. My stomach rumbles.

I follow him inside and close the door as my dad sets the bags on the table.

"Oh my God, I'm starving." Emery pops up from the couch and descends upon the food like a ravenous hyena. She rips open the first one and starts setting Styrofoam containers on the table. "There are no straws. Dad, you forgot the straws!"

"I didn't forget them. I chose not to take any." He pulls the lid from one of the cups and hands it to her. "Look, the cup is perfectly functional without lids or straws. Just like the ones in the cabinet."

"Cody!" Emery growls as he slams his Algebra book shut at the breakfast bar. "This is your fault."

Cody shrugs. "Just doing my part for the planet. That's why we bought the metal straws."

"They're fine for smoothies, but sodas taste weird coming out of metal," Emery insists.

"Then just drink from the cup." I grab a Dr Pepper and set it at my place.

"Enchiladas, double rice." My dad sets a take-out container on my empty placemat, and I resist pointing out that these food containers are probably doing more harm than the straws would have. Instead, I find Cynthia's fajita chicken salad among the containers. "Want me to take this to her?"

My dad plucks it from my hands "I got it. You guys go ahead. I'll be right back."

While we all sit with our food, he grabs a Diet Coke from one of the drink carriers and takes Cynthia's food through the living room, into the hall.

"How long has she been in there?" I ask Cody.

He dunks a corn chip into a plastic container of salsa. "Since before I got home from school. She came out to use the bathroom once, but that's it, so far. She hasn't even told me to do my homework."

Yet that's exactly what he was doing when the rest of us got home from rehearsal.

"Any change?" I ask, and Cody shrugs.

"No," Dad answers for him as he steps back into the living room, empty-handed. He sighs as he crosses the kitchen and sinks into his chair at the table. "Guys . . ." He shakes his head and reaches for his cup, which Gabe hands him.

We chew in silence while he takes his time. Sipping from his soda.

I feel sick. I don't want to hear this, and I don't really need to. I know what he's going to say. The gist of it, anyway.

"This morning, Grammie fell asleep, and she wouldn't wake up for breakfast. Or lunch."

"Why?" Cody asks. "She's just tired?"

"Yes, basically." Dad flips open his container and stares at a huge chimichanga. Usually, he orders fajitas and limits himself to one tortilla, then eats the rest with his fork. But today, he's basically ordered a giant deep-fried burrito, and I feel like that says a lot about his current state of mind.

Cody has nachos, and I think he's adorable.

"Basically?" Emery dips one wedge of her quesadilla in salsa and lets it drip onto the rest of her food. "What do you mean by 'basically'?"

"She isn't sleepy," Dad explains. "Well, she's not *just* sleepy. She's tired on a larger scale than that. Her body literally doesn't have enough energy to keep her awake."

"Because she's not eating?"

"Yes." Dad picks up his plastic fork, but when he tries to cut the chimichanga, two of the tines break off. "Damn it." He drops the broken fork into the trash on his way into the kitchen, where he grabs a metal fork. "Anyway, it's because she isn't eating, but it's also because her body has been fighting for so long. Fighting dementia *and* cancer. And she's just plain tired. Too tired."

"Too tired for what?" Cody asks. He hasn't touched his nachos yet.

"For anything," Emery tells him. "For everything."

"That's right," Dad says.

Cody picks a cube of tomato from one of his chips and sets it on a paper napkin. "So, how long will she sleep?"

"Well, that's the thing," Dad tells him. "It isn't just that she slept through breakfast and lunch. It's that we couldn't wake her up. She's what we call 'nonresponsive.'"

"But she woke up for dinner," Cody says. "I saw her. She didn't know who I was, but she ate some grapes and drank some water."

"Yes. Your mother got her to take a few bites of fruit, but that's the first food she's eaten in about eighteen hours, and it's nowhere near enough. Bud, we don't expect her to wake up again."

"What does that mean?" Cody glances around the table, and I can only give him a sad smile.

"She's dying." Gabe picks up a flour-tortilla-bound concoction and bites into it. According to the writing on his container, he's ordered something called an Atomic Chicken Wrap. I have no idea what that is, but I can see the jalapeño slices from here.

"Is that true?" Cody asks.

"You know it is," Emery insists. "That's why she came here. You've always known that."

"But, I mean, is that true *right now*?" Cody's seconds away from tears, and I don't know how to help. Maybe I shouldn't have pushed him to spend time with her. Maybe this would be easier if he'd kept his distance. "Is she dying right now?"

"Okay. I need to explain how this works." Dad sets his fork down. "Yes, Grammie is dying. I'm really sorry to have to say that, but it's true. But no, she's not dying right this second. She may even wake up again, though if she does, it probably won't be for very long. And she probably won't be coherent. What's probably going to happen is that she'll stay asleep until her body just gives out. And your mom—"

Dad's voice breaks, and Cody starts crying. I take his hand under the table, and he squeezes it until I can feel my bones grind together.

"This is going to be very, very hard on your mom. The hospice nurse was here today, and she said to call her if anything changes. Your mom doesn't want to leave Grammie's room, even to sleep, so she's going to stay on the—"

"Why?" Cody asks. Gabe stares at his food.

"Because she doesn't want to miss it," Emery explains. "She wants to be there when Grammie goes."

"That's right." Dad sighs. "She doesn't want Grammie to be alone. Or to need anything that she doesn't have."

"So, what are we supposed to do?" Cody asks.

My dad exhales slowly. We all look at him, because that's the million-dollar question. "Nothing," he finally says. "There's nothing anyone can do. They put her on liquid morphine yesterday, instead of the pills, because it's easier to swallow and she can have more of it, and that's probably why she's so sleepy. But it also suppresses her appetite, and—"

"Then stop giving it to her!" Cody cries.

"This was her choice," Emery tells him. "It would be cruel to keep her in pain, when they can make her comfortable, and she chose comfort. She's earned that, Cody."

I feel lost in this conversation. She's not my grandmother. I don't really have any place here, and my grief can't really compare with theirs. Yet my enchiladas look blurry beneath the tears standing in my eyes.

"Yeah." Cody nods. "Okay."

"So, how long?" Gabe asks. "Until it's over?"

My dad shrugs. "There's really no way to tell. It could be tonight, but I've seen cases like this last as long as ten days."

"*Ten days?*" I turn to Emery, and I see my horror reflected on her face. Ten days, when she can't eat or drink? When she doesn't wake up, and she's not hooked up to any tubes or machines, except the tubes I now know are draining her kidneys?

Ten days in that bed will mean that Cynthia is just watching her mother slowly starve to death. Or dehydrate to death. Or however that happens. She'll just sit there and watch her mother waste away.

"What about Ed and Patty? Her other kids?" I ask, and Gabe gives me a strange look. I'm asking about people I've never even met. Gabe, Emery, and Cody's aunt and uncle.

"We're going to have to call them," my dad says. "And at some point, they'll come up here. But it's difficult to say when that should be, since there's nothing they can do for her, and we don't know when . . ."

Cody sniffles.

"So, basically, we're just all going to be here for your mom as much as we can, in any way we can. And we're going to wait. Because that's all we can do."

No one eats much. Most of our Mexican takeout goes straight into the fridge.

———∞∞∞———

"Ten days was lowballing it." Emery's lying on her bed, on her stomach, in front of her history textbook, but she's not reading.

I'm not either. "What does that mean?"

"According to the internet—"

"A reputable source of information, if one ever existed."

"—a person can live more than twenty days without water."

"Yeah, but that's probably a best-case scenario," I speculate. "For young, healthy people in their prime." Grammie is none of those things.

"I'm just saying, Dad could be wrong. This could last a lot longer."

"Not that it matters to you."

Emery sits up on her bed. "What the hell does that mean?"

"Nothing." I shouldn't have said it. It's none of my business.

"Bullshit. Out with it, Michaela."

"Fine." I sit up too, and we're facing each other now, across the wide strip of carpet between our matching beds. "You never go see her. I didn't get a chance to say goodbye to my mom or my grandmother, and you're wasting an opportunity you're never going to get back. And I know you care. If you didn't, you wouldn't be googling morbid shit like that."

"Of course I care. She's my grandmother. But she's also *not* my grandmother. Not anymore. And it's weird, seeing her like that. It's *hard*, in a way you're never gonna understand, because your grandma was still herself when she died, right? So you might not have gotten to say goodbye, but the other way to look at that is that you didn't *have* to say goodbye for weeks at a time. Over and over. You didn't have to watch her die."

"You're not doing that either." It's a low blow, and again, I shouldn't have said it. But Emery doesn't deny it.

"What good would that do?" she demands, and there are tears standing in her eyes now. "I can't help her. How is it going to benefit anyone for me to sit in there and make myself miserably sad?"

"It won't." Though her mother might appreciate the company. "But this is the only chance you're ever going to get to say goodbye. Or tell her anything at all. That you're going to miss her. That you wish she could be there to dance at your wedding. To meet your kids. Whatever. She's going to be gone soon, and you're never going to get to say that." I swallow the huge lump in my throat and wipe my eyes. "Trust me, Emery. That's a *horrible* feeling. And from what I can tell so far, it doesn't go away."

She sniffles and swipes at her eyes. "Yeah. Okay, I'll go say goodbye." Then she heaves a teary laugh. "She *does* think I've been visiting her, by the way. Because half the time, she thinks you're me."

I laugh with her, because it's either that or I'm going to cry.

⸻ ◦◦◦ ⸻

I wake up to the scent of bacon frying. Emery is still asleep. She didn't set her alarm because this morning is the "dry tech" rehearsal, when the crew runs through the show on their own, practicing transitions without the cast onstage. We don't have to be there until two this afternoon.

And if there's bacon, that means Cynthia is cooking Saturday morning breakfast. Which means Grammie must have woken up. Maybe she *requested* bacon.

I get up and head straight to the kitchen, where I'm surprised to find my dad at the stove, with his back to me. "Damn it," I mumble, and he turns.

"Well, I wasn't going to force-feed you." He takes a dramatic bite of a strip of bacon from the platter on the counter.

"I just . . . I thought you were Cynthia, which would mean . . ."

"No change, I'm afraid," Dad says. "So I'm picking up the slack. How do you like your eggs?"

"She doesn't like eggs," Emery says as she comes in from the hallway, her hair standing up at odd angles.

Dad frowns at the skillet. "Well, that's inconvenient."

"You'd already have known that, if you were ever here for breakfast," she adds.

He gives her a grave nod. "Tough but fair." Then he turns to me. "What's your stance on hash browns?"

"Pro," I say. "But Cody doesn't like the kind with 'things' in them." Things are, of course, the red peppers and onions that come in one brand of shredded hash browns.

"Duly noted. Breakfast in ten."

I brush my teeth and use the restroom, then knock on Grammie's door. It's ajar, but I don't want to barge in.

"Come in," Cynthia says.

Grammie's room feels different this morning. She's hardly been awake in a day and a half now, and not at all in more than fifteen hours. But her glass of water is standing on the tray waiting for her, and it must be fresh, because the ice hasn't melted yet.

Cynthia is cradling a steaming mug of coffee, which I'm guessing my dad brought her. There are dark circles under her eyes, and she's still in her pajamas. Despite the fact that Grammie's recliner holds a pillow and a folded blanket, I don't think my stepmother has slept at all in the past twenty-four hours.

"How is she?"

"No change," Cynthia says.

Grammie's head rests on her favorite pillow, and her hair's been neatly brushed. She's breathing slowly and evenly, and it really does look like she's just sleeping. That's not what this is, though. Her arms are out straight, the covers folded back and neatly tucked beneath them.

She doesn't sleep like that. No one sleeps like that, except maybe vampires.

I start to take Grammie's hand, but then I think maybe I shouldn't. Since she's not *really* sleeping.

"It's okay," Cynthia says. "You can touch her. You can talk to her." She shrugs. "Her hospice nurse says she thinks Grammie can hear us."

Emery should be here.

I take Grammie's hand. It's soft, and smooth, and warm. It feels normal. "Hey, Grammie."

"Do you mind if I run to the bathroom while you're here?" Cynthia asks.

"Go ahead. You can shower and change, too, if you want."

She hesitates. "You sure?"

"Of course. I don't have to be anywhere until after lunch."

"Thank you." Cynthia lays her hand on my shoulder on her way out. She tries to disguise a soft sob as a hiccup, but I know what crying sounds like.

She pulls the door mostly shut on her way out, and I sit in the chair she was in. I take Grammie's other hand, and I tell her about the play. About how funny Emery is as Lucinda. About how well Gabe plays the upright bass, perched on his tall stool, and how great he is at the bass guitar.

"Hey," Emery says, and when I look up, I see her in the doorway.

"Hey. Come in."

She comes in, but she hangs back from the bed. She stares at Grammie's midsection for a second. Then she takes a deep breath and drags her gaze up to her grandmother's face. And bursts into tears.

I get up and pull her into a hug, and she lets me. She cries on my shoulder, her tears soaking through my shirt, and she holds me so tight that for a second I can't breathe. And I'm crying too now. I can't help it. I'm crying for Grammie, but I'm not *only* crying for her.

*God*, I miss my mom. She'd know what to say right now. She'd know how to make Emery feel better about this. She'd know how to make Emery see how lucky she is to have this chance, even if it hurts. My mom did that all the time. She helped brand-new mothers say goodbye to sick babies.

She could handle Emery without even blinking.

But I'm not my mom. I don't know how to do this.

"What were you saying to her?" Emery sniffles as she finally lets me go.

I grab the tissues from the nightstand, and she plucks one from the box and blots her eyes with it. "I was just telling her about the musical. About your comedic chops. About Gabe in the pit."

Emery wipes her nose and drops the tissue into the trash, then grabs another one. "I don't think I even told her that I'd auditioned."

"She knew." Because I told her.

"So, I can just . . . talk to her? You think she can hear?"

"I think so," Cynthia says as she steps into the room. Her hair is wet and she's wearing clean clothes. And she's crying, so I think she's been standing out there for a minute. I think she's been listening. "I think she'd love to hear anything you want to tell her."

# twenty-seven

In the afternoon, I drive Emery to school for the first tech run. The crew ran through everything on their own this morning at the dry tech, but it's rough, going through the entire musical with both cast and crew for the first time. With all the props. We start with just the scene transitions, singing the ends and beginnings of every song, so the crew can practice putting everything in place. Then we do a complete run-through. It's fun but exhausting. And in a way, it feels like we're starting over from scratch. But it's cool to have more props and set pieces. The trees look *fantastic*. Creepy and dark.

During breaks, I see Josh scribbling in the little notebook he carries in his back pocket. When he catches me watching, he smiles.

The band is on a break, because this close to opening night, the musical is taking up all our time. And because things are really sad and intense at home right now, which would make band practice in the backyard super awkward. But I know Josh is writing songs.

We have Sunday off, so I do my homework in Grammie's room in the morning. She hasn't woken up at all. We're taking turns relieving Cynthia for showers and short naps, but she's terrified that she'll miss something—I'm not sure whether she thinks her mother will wake up or die—so my dad brought home a baby monitor last night. Cynthia aimed the camera at her mother's bed, and she keeps the receiver—an LCD screen with a speaker— with her at all times.

She's living her life on pause, working jigsaw puzzles and watching home-and-garden shows on Grammie's TV. She eats and drinks what we bring her, but I'm not sure she's even tasting it. Nothing matters except being in her mother's room. Watching the slow, steady rise and fall of Grammie's chest. Waiting for a change.

Any change.

I spend the afternoon at Ben's, because my dad insists that we all do a little self-care. Ben and I watch movies and make out on a couch in his den, because we can sit closer without the theater chair arm between us.

He's very sweet about the whole thing. About how sad I am. He understands that I need a distraction, and he's more than happy to be that distraction. The only time I feel good right now is when I'm onstage or with Ben.

Emery was right about one thing: he does make me feel special. Pretty. Loved. We've been together for almost two months, and my hands still reach for him like magnets drawn to metal. My gaze finds him every time he walks into a room.

He does for me what Gabe's pills don't. He makes me feel good.

Ben's parents are home, but they don't bother us. His mother is preparing for some charity event she's on the board of, and his dad . . . Well, I seem to be the only part of Ben's life that his dad actually approves of. As if Ben and me groping each other on the couch somehow makes up for Ben appearing onstage, possibly in tights. As if I balance some heteronormative scale in his head.

In his ego.

That's *really* messed up, but it's led to Ben's dad leaving him alone. Which is why I pretend I don't see Mr. McGrath watching us, hovering in the den doorway with a short glass half-full of something amber. He only stays for a couple of minutes.

Famous lawyer or not, Ben's dad's a total creep. In fact, there are moments when I think it's harder for Ben to be stuck at his house without me than it is for me to be at home, watching Cynthia slowly come unglued.

When I get home from Ben's on Sunday night, my dad is on the couch with Cody, holding a PlayStation remote. "So, what's the difference between a blade and a knife?"

I laugh as I drop my keys in the bowl on the breakfast bar.

"Well, a knife is just a knife." Cody clicks a button, and a notebook opens on the screen. "You mostly find butcher knives in abandoned kitchens or sticking out of corpses." He flips through several pages, going through weapons too fast for me to focus on them, until he stops on a page that has a picture of a machete taped to it, with stats handwritten beneath. "But a blade could be a hatchet, or a machete, or even a sword, if you manage to find one."

"They're really rare, though," I tell him, leaning over the back of the couch. "If you find one, do whatever you have to do to get it. Trade anything you have."

"Why?" Dad asks as Cody flips through more notebook pages.

"Because a sword lets you swing from a distance, and when you're hunting zombies, you want to be as far away as you can," Cody says. "Which is why ranged weapons are really the way to go. But guns are risky, because of the noise . . ."

I smile as I head down the hall.

———⁂———

Monday's rehearsal is intense. After warm-ups, we sit in a semicircle onstage with the crew lined up behind us. Cole is whispering to Zack, his freshman A-2, showing him something about the microphone pack he's holding.

"Okay, opening night is in ten days! This is crunch time, and I'm going to need everybody's very best from now on," Ms. Bond shouts. She's at the front of the stage, but there's no apron today, because the panels over the pit have been removed, even though it's still empty.

Gabe's rehearsing with the rest of the pit orchestra in their classroom.

"Oh, *now* she wants our best," Link mumbles. "I'm so glad

she said that, because I was all set to give her my most average."

Kat elbows him from her position across the semicircle from me.

Ms. Bond frowns at them both. "We're going to do two complete run-throughs this afternoon. The second will just be a normal rehearsal, now with costumes! But the first will be our understudy pass. Which means that at any point in the play, I can call for an understudy substitution. Michaela, if I call for Emery as Cinderella in a scene that also calls for the stepsisters, you'll go on as Lucinda." Because Emery is the only understudy who also has a role of her own. Maybe she really *would* have been Cinderella if I weren't here. "You can just read the part. You have your book?"

I hold up my script.

"Great. Any questions?"

"Yes. Are we doing costumes in the understudy pass, or just the second one?" Lexie asks.

"Just the second one. Anything else?" Today Ms. Bond's shirt reads, "Theater: It's a stage I'm going through."

No hands rise, but I know from experience that there will be questions. Probably in the middle of a scene.

"All right, the understudy pass is always a laugh, and I want you guys to have fun with it. Okay?"

There's a chorus of okays, and a couple of actual cheers as we stand.

"Starting positions!" Ms. Bond calls. "And let's put Emery in for Cinderella, and Stacy for Baker's Wife."

Stacy is one of the crew members, but she's been at all the rehearsals, since she's also an understudy. Mostly, she's been painting trees backstage. But today, she looks excited.

Emery's smile takes up her entire face.

"Where's Jon?" Julie Upton asks as she takes her position as Jack's mother.

"Dentist!" Bella calls from backstage. "He'll be here at four forty-five."

"Oh, that's right." Ms. Bond frowns. Jack doesn't have an understudy. "Cole?"

Cole freezes. Then he turns slowly. "Yeah?"

"Can you grab a book and take Jon's part for now?"

"I . . . um . . ."

Ms. Bond takes him aside, and since I'm standing in the stage-left wings, ready to go on as Lucinda, I can hear her whispering as Emery kneels onstage in front of a newly finished fireplace set piece.

"What about Scott?" Cole asks. Scott is our male swing. He doesn't have his own role, but he knows every part. He's not awesome at any of them, but he can literally step into every role, should we need him.

"I can put him in," Ms. Bond whispers. "But I'd rather have you out there. It's a low-pressure situation, Cole. There's no one in the house"—she gestures to all the empty seats out front— "and we've got several stand-ins today. People will make mistakes, and we'll all have fun. You don't have to do this, but I think you should. I think you've got something to show people, and your theater family is the friendliest audience you're ever going to find." She shrugs. "You can take your book and read Jack's lines."

"I know the part," Cole whispers. "But . . ."

"Just give it a shot, okay? Who knows. You might actually like it."

"You were great at karaoke," I remind him softly. "And there were lots of people watching."

"Okay," he says finally.

Emery gives him a supportive smile as he walks across the stage and takes Jack's starting position, in front of Milky White. Which is just a wooden frame mounted on wheels and unpainted papier-mâché, so far. Cole's holding his book, but it isn't open.

Aaron takes his position up front. The music begins, and he starts narrating. Emery scrubs the floor while I wait in the wings, just feet from her, with Mara and Sage, who're playing Florinda and Cinderella's Stepmother.

I can't see Cole very well from where I'm standing, but I can hear him, and if I didn't already know that he was terrified of being onstage, I'd say he was born there. It's like a switch has been flipped. Like he isn't Cole anymore at all.

Which, of course, is the goal.

The prologue goes well. Kat nails the Witch's tongue-twisting lettuce rant, and no one's surprised. She's amazing. Jon arrives in the middle of the prologue, and I smile as I watch him watching Cole play his part. For a second, he looks jealous. But then Cole hits the tone just right on his piggy joke, and Jon laughs. He crosses his arms and settles in to watch. And when

Cole comes offstage, Jon fades into the shadows, going unseen, so that Cole will continue in the role.

At the end of scene one, Ms. Bond claps as she walks onstage. Everyone's smiling. It wasn't a flawless performance—I suck at Lucinda's high-pitched cackle—but it was fun to see friends in different roles. To relax, a little.

"That was great!" Ms. Bond calls. "And Cole! *My God*, man! Where have you been hiding that?"

The entire cast applauds, and Cole's face flushes. He takes a dramatic stage bow. Then he makes a show of handing off the role to Jon.

"Okay!" Ms. Bond backs off the stage, toward the stairs. "Let's put Michaela back as Cinderella, and sub Trey in for Ben, in the Baker role."

---

"So, how was the understudy . . . thing?" Dad asks without looking up from the TV screen. He took today off, so he's wearing Saturday clothes, clutching the PlayStation remote like it might save his life.

Cody sits next to him, in front of a half-empty Dr Pepper bottle and a plate scattered with crumbs. I think my dad's been eating pizza rolls.

On the screen, their characters are surrounded by a horde of zombies, some swollen, their radiation-bloated bellies clearly about to burst. Which means that he won't hear my answer, even though he remembered to ask.

"The understudy run-through," I correct him. "It was fun!

Emery was great as Cinderella, and Cole stole the show." I drop my keys in the bowl and set my backpack next to the coffee table.

"Cole Houser?" my dad asks, swinging his remote dramatically as, on-screen, his character swings a machete. "He's in the play?"

"He's the lead audio tech, but he stepped in as Jack for the first scene."

"Okay, pizza or pho?" Cynthia says as she comes into the kitchen from the main suite. Her hair is wet, and she's holding two takeout menus. "Or ramen? What's the difference between pho and ramen?"

"Rice noodles, as opposed to wheat," Dad tells her.

"Vietnamese, as opposed to Japanese," Gabe adds as he comes in from the hall, holding his phone. "And I vote ramen."

"Pizza!" Cody shouts.

I grab my bag and leave them to sort out dinner, because it's already nearly eight, and I have homework. But I stop on my way to my room when I hear Emery's voice coming from Grammie's room.

". . . and I think I was just as good as Michaela in the role," she says.

I press my back against the wall, just out of sight.

"I mean, she *is* pretty good. But so am I. I wish you could have seen it, Grammie. I love being up there. I love the lights and the music. I love being *seen*. Even when I'm pretending to be someone else. Maybe someone took video from backstage. I'll ask around and see if I can find something to play for you."

Emery sniffles, and my eyes water. I can't see her, but I know she's sitting in the chair next to Grammie's bed. And I know Grammie hasn't moved. They're not bathing her or changing her clothes anymore, because the hospice nurse said that her state is so fragile now that just rolling her over could be . . . traumatic.

"Anyway, I just wanted to tell you that before . . . I mean . . . I just wanted to say that I love you. In case you can hear. And I'm so sorry I didn't come sooner." Emery's voice breaks on a sob, and my tears fall. "I just . . . I couldn't do it before. But I'm here now, and I really hope it's not too late. I hope you can hear me. I hope you know how much we love you, and how much fun it was when you first moved in, listening to you cuss at Mom. No one else really does that. And—"

I go into my room to give her privacy. But instead of doing my homework, I lie on my bed and cry into my pillow.

God, I miss my mother.

— ◦◦◦ —

"If Sage doesn't quit missing her line, right after 'Witch's Lament,' I swear I'm going to choke her," Emery says as I turn my car into the driveway, after Tuesday's rehearsal. "And I think her shoes are too small. She's taking these tiny steps. Or maybe that's her interpretation of walking through the woods in stilettos." Emery slams my car door and slings her backpack over her shoulder. "Either way, the buckles keep falling off."

"I hadn't noticed that, but you're right. She takes *absurdly* small steps onstage."

I follow her through the front door. Or, I try to, but Emery stops in the doorway, like she's suddenly frozen there.

"Emery, what—" But then I hear it. Cody is crying.

"Hey, girls, come in and close the door," my dad says. He went to work this morning, but he's in weekend clothes again, and it's only 7:15. Rehearsal got out early.

Finally, Emery moves, and I push past her to drop my keys in the bowl. Dad has his back to us, sitting on the couch. His arm is around Cody.

Gabe's not home yet. Orchestra rehearsal ran long.

Cody twists on the couch to look at us. His face is red and wet. "She's gone," he says. "Grammie died. She just stopped breathing."

"Oh God," I whisper. "I'm so sorry."

Emery drops her bag in the entry and sinks onto the couch next to Cody. She wraps her arm around him, relieving Dad, who stands and guides me into the kitchen. "It *just* happened," he whispers. "Cynthia's in there with her, and I need to call hospice so they can send someone out. Can you . . . ?" He gestures toward Emery and Cody.

I'm not sure what he wants from me, but I nod. "Go do what you've got to do," I whisper.

Dad thanks me by squeezing my arm. He pulls his phone out of his back pocket on his way to his room, and I hear the door close softly as I sink onto the couch on Cody's other side. His English textbook is still open on the coffee table. I put my arm around him, and we sit like that while Dad makes his phone call. We're still sitting like that, listening to Cynthia sob softly from down the hall, when Gabe comes into the house through the kitchen.

He takes one look at Emery and Cody, and he knows. I stand up and hug him, and he squeezes me really hard, for a long time, his chin digging into my shoulder. But that's it. After a minute, he lets me go and disappears into his room with his backpack.

I sit on the couch again, and I try not to think about anything. Distantly, I hear the doorbell ring, and I see Dad let the hospice nurse in. It's a man today. He follows Dad into Grammie's room, and Cynthia's sobs get louder.

Emery is crying silently, and Cody's just staring at the coffee table now. I ask him if he's hungry, but he shakes his head. He mumbles something about having a sandwich later, and I tell him that I'd be happy to make it for him, whenever he's ready.

She wasn't my grandmother. I should be able to hold myself together for them.

Only that isn't what happens.

Half an hour later, the doorbell rings, and Dad and Cynthia are still in Grammie's room with the nurse, so I answer it. There are two women and a man on the porch. They're all wearing slacks and nice shirts, with nametags that say they work at one of the local funeral homes.

I burst into tears.

"I'm sorry," I mumble as I step back to let them in.

"It's okay. Take all the time you need," one of the women says.

The man is pushing a gurney. There's a dark cloth folded on top of it.

"Cody, come with me." Emery leads her brother down the hall and into his room. I can tell it's his room and not ours, from the creak of the hinges.

"Dad!" I call, because I can't make myself go back there. I can't see Grammie like this. I can't watch them load her on the gurney. Because so far, I've managed not to imagine any of those things happening to my mother, but if I see them now . . .

If I see them . . .

I grab my keys and race out the door. It takes me ten minutes to get to Ben's house. I text him from his driveway, and seconds later, the front door flies open. "I'm *so sorry*," he says as he folds me into his arms.

"It's okay," I tell him, because that's what you say. Even when it's not even close to true. "I'm fine" is the only lie you're actually supposed to tell, and some of us get really good at selling it.

"Are your parents home?" I ask, shivering despite his embrace. It's mid-March now, and still cold, but this chill seems to be leaking from deep inside me. I couldn't get warm, even blasting the heat in my car. Not even now, burrowing into Ben's hug.

"No, they're at dinner with a client."

"Good." I tug him into the house and close the door behind us. "I . . . um . . . I need to think about something else, or I'm going to lose my shit." My eyes are watering again. There's an uncomfortable feeling just beneath my skin, as if my flesh no longer fits over my bones. I feel like I don't fit, in the most fundamental sense.

"Michaela?" Ben's staring at me. He looks worried.

"The nurse came, and then the funeral people came, and they had a gurney, and I started thinking about my mom. I had to get out of there, and I need to be somewhere else." I'm not making sense. I feel like I'm out of step with reality, and at any second, the universe is going to figure that out and suck me out into the void. Leave me spinning in the dark. "I need to feel something real. Something good."

"You want a drink?" He turns toward the den and the bar, but I grab his hand.

"No, that's not how I want to feel." I slide my hand beneath his shirt and splay it across the warm expanse of his stomach. I curl my fingers against his flesh. He feels real. Soft and hard, at the same time. Grounded and solid.

I go up on my toes and kiss him. "I want to," I whisper in his ear. "Now. Please."

Ben takes a step back, frowning at me. Searching my eyes. "You sure? This may not be the right time—"

"It is." I blink away my tears.

We haven't done this before. I've *never* done this. And I know it won't fix anything. I'm not stupid, and I'm not naive. I just need to be very, very not alone. In a tactile sense. I need to be physically present. To be sure I'm here, but not so *here* that I'm thinking about anything. Anything at all.

I need to *feel*.

"I'm sure," I say before he can ask again. "Do you have a condom?"

He quirks one brow at me. And he starts to smile, which turns my insides into liquid warmth. "Was that a serious question?"

Ben takes my hand, and I follow him to his room.

My heart is racing.

———∞———

On the way home, I hit a long stoplight, and I text Georgia.

Grammie died and I did it with Ben

She texts me back immediately, but I can't read the message until I pull into my driveway and shift into park. The hearse is gone, thank goodness. All the windows are lit up, but I'm not ready to go inside.

God, that's a lot for one text

Then . . .

How are you?

"Sore and sad," I reply. Then I add, "Confused. More later." I'm still processing. She's right; it's a lot.

Sex wasn't what I expected, but my expectations were nebulous at best, and I have no regrets. Ben was sweet, and that was the only meaningful decision I've made for myself in months. The only thing I've had any control over.

No regrets.

Inside, there are two pizza boxes on the counter. There's a slice of pepperoni left in one, and the other is untouched, though normally the Bosches would pretty much devour both pies.

The living room and kitchen lights are all on, but both rooms are empty. I can hear Cynthia crying softly from their room. Dad's comforting her. I'm not sure either of them noticed that I left.

I snag a slice of pizza and carry it on a napkin to my room.

Emery's on her bed. She pulls her AirPods from her ears as I shut the door. "Where'd you go?"

Instead of answering, I kick off my shoes and curl up on my bed with my pizza.

"Michaela. It's pretty shitty of you to ignore me the day my grandmother dies." She drops the AirPods into their case and sets it on her charger.

"I'm not ignoring you. I just . . . I went to Ben's. We . . ." I shrug and chew more pizza.

Emery stares at me, and I can see her processing. Interpreting. "Oh . . . *my* God." She says it just like that. Inflected with drama.

"Don't," I snap. "*I* get to decide who I sleep with. And when. And why."

"No arguments." She shrugs. "You're free to make your own mistakes. We've already established that. But you should know this doesn't mean the same thing to him that it means to you."

"You don't know what it means to me."

"Bullshit. I know." She stands and crosses our room toward her chest of drawers, where she pulls a pair of socks from the top drawer. "I've *been* you."

I don't even try to stop my eyes from rolling. "Being his ex doesn't make you, like, *me* from a former life, Emery."

"It kinda does, though." She sits on the end of her bed to pull the socks on. "At least now you'll *really* get to know him."

I throw the rest of my pizza away. It tastes sour now.

# twenty-eight

"Two funerals in two months." Georgia whistles softly as she grabs a hanger from my closet and drapes the shoulders of her dress over it. "Do you have any idea how tragic that is?"

I give her a look as I flop down on my bed, on my stomach, with my arms folded at the end of the mattress. "I am not unaware."

She hangs her dress over the closet door and sits on the floor at the foot of my bed. She's not staying the night, but she brought some casual clothes to change into, which means I can change too. Thank God. I hope I never have to wear another black dress.

"Are you also aware that your brother was high at the funeral? Like, totally stoned."

"Yes. He doesn't make it look like very much fun." When Gabe is high, he looks sleepy and sounds slow. Unfocused.

She huffs. "I think he's doing it wrong. I mean, what's the point of taking . . . whatever he's on, if it doesn't make you feel good?"

"It's hydrocodone. Do you think my dad noticed?"

"No. And I *know* your stepmother didn't."

She's right about that. Cynthia hasn't seen *anything* in three days. She's running on fumes. And caffeine. She's everywhere all at once, cooking and cleaning for company as if this were a party, rather than a funeral reception. Because every time she stops moving, she starts crying.

And crying is contagious.

Cynthia's brother and sister came in for the funeral, with their families, and they're in the living room right now, as they've been for most of the past two days. I'm glad they've been sleeping at a hotel. I'm also glad they're about to leave. Cynthia and her brother, Ed, don't get along, and I feel like that's saying a lot, considering that she welcomed her husband's love child into her house at a moment's notice. How horrible must that man be if *Cynthia* doesn't like him?

Fortunately, both of his kids are in college, and though they drove in for the funeral together, they haven't been hanging out. I'm not sure they like their dad either.

The buzz of conversation rises from the front of the house, and I get up to close the door. The living room is still full of family and friends, but they aren't *my* family and friends. They're strangers eating from cold-cut trays, on clear plastic plates. And since I don't know them, I get to escape into my room with Georgia. At least until she leaves.

Gabe, Emery, and Cody are stuck out there, accepting awkward condolences in their dress clothes. Pretending these people with their kind words and short visits have any idea what

Cynthia's been through over the past few months. The past few days, in particular.

These strangers didn't hear her whisper to my dad, late at night, that it would be better if this were all just *over*. They didn't hear her ask why her mother had to *linger*. Why we all have to watch her slowly waste away, when this isn't what she would have wanted. When this isn't what anyone would ever want for her.

They didn't have to hear her cry from guilt after she said those things, worrying that only a horrible person would want to rush her mother out of this world, because watching her die is hard.

They just get to drink wine and eat mini-quiches; then they get to leave and forget about all this. About the closed door and the unworn clothing. The medicine that will never be taken and the reading glasses that will never again perch on the end of a long, slightly upturned nose.

I shake my head and I try not to think about those things either.

"So . . . what did you think of Ben?" He looked great at the funeral, all dressed up. Though I felt guilty for noticing, under the circumstances.

Georgia's brows both rise. "That boy's not real."

"What do you mean?"

"He's too pretty for the real world."

I make a grand gesture with one extended arm. "That's why he lives on the stage."

She rolls her eyes. "Seriously, though, he's really hot. And he seems like he's really into you."

"Yeah. He's been super supportive."

"He's Emery's ex?" Georgia doesn't like Emery, and I can't tell if that's because she's heard my stories, from when I first got here, or because Emery personally offended her somehow. Either way, she's been nothing but nice to *all* of my family. And not just because we buried Grammie this afternoon.

Georgia's been nice because that's who she is. Unless you meet her in a mock trial courtroom, where she *will* object you to death. And possibly impeach you.

"Yes, he's her ex," I say. "They were together for more than ten months."

"And he's your leading man onstage?"

"Not exactly. The script hints that the Baker and Cinderella wind up together, raising Little Red Riding Hood and Jack, but it's not explicit that they're *together*, together."

"But in real life, you two are . . . explicit?"

"Once," I tell her. "Just once, so far." I've hardly seen him since that night. Emery and I missed rehearsal the day after Grammie died, and the cast limped along with one of the swings in my role, and one of the ASMs reading for Lucinda. But we both went yesterday, because they were practicing costume changes, and we just couldn't miss that. And because we were no use here at home.

Ben came to the funeral, of course, and he even brought a little pack of tissues in his pocket, in case I needed them. Which I did. But he left right afterward for rehearsal. Which Emery and I are missing again.

Today is Friday. Opening night is next Thursday.

I feel bad for Ms. Bond. She's missing one of her lead cast members *and* the understudy, six days before opening night. The swings can step in to rehearse with everyone, but that's not the same, and it's not supposed to happen this often. And if anyone else has an appointment or an injury, there's no one to fill in for them.

"So, are you going to get your own room now?" Georgia whispers.

"I don't know. We haven't talked about that. And I'm not going to ask." The truth is that I don't really care anymore. Emery and I get along okay, most of the time. And I remember how awful it was, having to go through my mom's things. Having to get rid of her stuff. I don't want to rush Cynthia into that.

Also, I'm not sure I want to sleep in the room where Grammie died. Not that I believe she would, like, haunt me or anything. But that's *her* room. Not mine. Taking it over would feel weird.

"I get that. But a little privacy would come in handy now, with you and Ben . . ."

"Yeah, we're not going to be hanging out here much, with or without my own room."

"Because of Emery?"

"Yeah. And because my dad doesn't really like Ben."

Georgia huffs. "I repeat: because of Emery?"

"Yeah. I think he thinks that only an asshole would date sisters. But he doesn't really have the moral latitude to sermonize about asshole moves, so he mostly just grunts a lot when Ben's here. Tries to make him uncomfortable so he'll leave."

"It's weird to see your dad here," Georgia says. "With his other kids. And his wife."

"Yeah. Sometimes that still feels weird to me too." Even though I've been here for two full months now. If I squint my eyes just right, I can see into the past and still picture my father as the bachelor weekend dad I thought he was. But now it's *that* version of him that feels weird and made-up.

Georgia leaves around nine as Cynthia's saying goodbye to her brother and sister. As I walk Georgia to her car, parked out front, I hear Patty promise to drive back up from Dallas next week to help go through her mother's things. But I'll believe that when I see it.

"So, I'll be back next week for opening night," Georgia says as I hug her goodbye in the orangish glow of the streetlight outside our house.

"But that's Thursday." A school night. "And it's an hour-long drive."

"Yeah. I've already cleared it with my mom." Georgia opens her back door and hangs her dress inside the car. "She'll probably track my phone all the way home, but she gets it. I'm not missing your first performance."

"It might be easier for you to just come to dress rehearsal. That's practically the same thing."

She closes the door and gives me a look. "No, it isn't."

She's right. It isn't. I haven't actually performed yet, but Ben assures me that there's nothing like the energy of an honest-to-God crowd. Someone to perform *for*, especially your first time. He says that really turns the lights on in every actor.

That's when you become addicted to the theater.

"Okay, then, I'll see you on Thursday. Drive carefully and text me when you get home." This will only be the second time Georgia has driven on the highway. Her first was on her way here.

"I will," she promises as she gets into the driver's seat. Then she closes the door, and her car pulls away from the curb. Cynthia's brother's sedan pulls out of the driveway seconds later.

"Thank God they're gone," Emery says, dropping into an armchair as I close the living room door behind me. "If I have to hear how sorry someone is for my loss one more time . . ."

I totally get that. Georgia's right: two funerals in two months is two too many.

"Can I take this off now?" Cody plucks at his dress shirt. I suspect his jacket is wadded up on his bedroom floor.

"Yes." My dad shrugs out of his own jacket, folds it in half, and drapes it over the back of one of the kitchen barstools. "Cyn, why don't you lie down? The girls and I will start putting up all these leftovers. I don't think we'll have to cook for a month."

"We have to deal with the food because we're girls?" Emery groans. "Being burdened with ovaries sucks."

I agree with her, but I'd rather put up the quiches and cold cuts than put that exhausted look back on Cynthia's face.

"No, you're helping because you're the only ones still in here," Dad says. "When the guys get back, they'll help too. Despite being burdened by testes."

Emery stares at him. "I cannot believe you just said that."

"You started it," he fires back, half grinning.

Emery exhales. "Can I change first? The last thing I need is to drop some Lit'l Smokies on my dress. The barbecue sauce will never come out."

"Of course," my dad says, and Emery disappears into the hall. But we both know she won't come back until she's run both of her brothers out of their rooms.

"How're you holding up?" Dad asks me as he starts pulling containers from a drawer.

I cover a glass dish of some kind of weird gelatin salad with plastic wrap. "That's right up there with 'I'm so sorry for your loss.'"

He flinches. "Yeah, I guess it is. Sorry."

"But to actually answer the question, I'm fine."

"Really? I know you and Grammie had gotten close."

"Yeah." And I knew she was dying when I got to know her, so I feel like I should have been better prepared for this. But there is no way to prepare for death. It's awful, whether you see it coming or it blindsides you. "I'm just glad this can at least start to be over for Cynthia now."

Dad sighs as he pulls open the fridge. "Me too. I'm going to try to get her to take a—"

"Dad!" Emery shouts. "Dad! Mom! Somebody help!"

Dad blinks at me, then takes off around the kitchen peninsula and across the living room. I drop the weird salad on the counter with a heavy *thunk* and follow him, leaving the fridge standing open.

By the time we get to Gabe's room, Cody's standing in the doorway with his pants still unbuttoned, a T-shirt clutched in one fist. He's staring into his brother's room in utter terror.

Dad pushes past him, and I follow him inside, where I see Emery kneeling on the floor next to Gabe, tears pouring down her face.

"He won't wake up," she says.

Gabe is breathing, but just barely. His chest is hardly moving.

"Gabe!" Dad sinks onto the floor on his other side and puts one hand on his forehead, then his cheek. "He's cool. Gabriel!" He pulls back Gabe's right eyelid, then his left. "Pinpoint pupils and depressed respiration. Did he take something?"

"I don't know!" Emery cries.

Cody watches it all from the doorway, his knuckles white around a handful of his shirt. His jaw clenched.

"Em, go get your mom," Dad orders. "And keep Cody in the living room." He pulls out his phone and dials 911.

I pace back and forth, feeling helpless. Worthless. Terrified.

I knew. I knew what he was doing, and I didn't say anything.

"Nine-One-One, what is your emergency?" the voice on the other end of the line says.

"This is Dr. Oscar Bosch, and I need an ambulance at my home. Do you have my address?"

The 911 operator reads our address back to him, from whatever display she's looking at.

"Yes, that's it. My son is on the floor, unresponsive. He's seventeen. Depressed respiration. Pinpoint pupils. I've palpated for a head injury, and there's nothing. I suspect he's had an overdose, but I don't know what he took. I don't see any pills or—"

My pulse racing, I spin around and start opening his drawers. Pawing through his underwear and shirts. The hospice nurse took away all of Grammie's unused narcotics after he pronounced her death, but what if Gabe had already taken something while she was unresponsive? When she no longer needed the pills?

There's nothing in his dresser, so I go through his desk drawers while my dad talks to the 911 operator, who's telling him to stay on the line. To roll Gabe over in case he vomits. To lock up any pets and clear a path from the front door to prepare for the ambulance's arrival.

Gabe's desk is clean too, so I grab his backpack and dump the contents onto his bed.

Oh my God.

"Dad!" I hand him the small glass vial and the plastic, needle-less syringe. "It was in his bag."

"Damn it, Gabe!" my dad whispers as he takes the vial. "It's oral morphine," he says into the phone. "I have no idea how much he took, but my daughter just found it in his bag. Please hurry."

For the first time in my entire life, my dad sounds scared. His hands are shaking, clutching the bottle of morphine.

"They're on the way, sir. Stay on the line. You should hear the sirens in just a couple of minutes."

"Oscar?" Cynthia calls as her footsteps thump softly from the hall. "Gabe? What—?" She falls silent as she appears in the doorway, with Emery looking over her shoulder. "What happened? Is he okay?"

Dad shows her the bottle.

"Oh my God. How much did he take?"

"I have no idea, but small doses of this can—"

"I know!" she moans. "The nurse told me, when she brought it. I should have locked it up. I just didn't think . . ." She stares down at Gabe. And finally, I hear the sirens.

"They're here," Dad says into the phone. "Thank you." Then he hangs up and turns to me. "Michaela, go open the front door. Everyone, stay out of the hall and give them space to maneuver."

I race past Cody in the living room—he's staring at nothing, tears standing in his eyes—and throw open the front door.

There are two men running up the sidewalk from an ambulance parked in the driveway, and one of them is carrying a bulky red medical bag with a white plus sign on the front. The ambulance lights are flashing, painting our living room with a red strobe shining through gaps in the curtains. Through the open front door. "Back there." I point them toward the hallway as they rush past me into the house.

"He's gonna be fine," I tell Cody. And I really, really hope I'm not lying to him.

⌾⌾⌾

"What the hell was he thinking?" Emery paces angrily back and forth in front of our row of four molded plastic chairs. At first, she looked as scared as Cody still does, but over the past hour, her fear evolved into irritation, and now she's just plain pissed off. "This was an *entirely preventable* catastrophe. He didn't trip and fall into the orchestra pit. He didn't step on a nail. He took a controlled substance that didn't belong to him, and now we're all spending Friday night in the hospital." She shoots me a pointed look. "Why do people insist on making mistakes that are entirely preventable?"

I refrain from reminding her that alcohol is also a controlled substance—at least for teenagers—and too much of that can also put you in the hospital. Or make you late for curfew. Under entirely preventable circumstances. Because I figure you're allowed to be a bit of a hypocrite when your brother ODs on the day of your grandmother's funeral.

The emergency room waiting area is way too bright for 11:00 p.m. It's cold and it smells like sterile cleaning chemicals. And they won't let us go into the back, where the ambulance took Gabe. Where Dad and Cynthia are.

"I think the concept that Gabe has thought anything through at all in the past month is flawed at best," I tell her.

"What does that mean?" She turns to glare at me when I don't answer, and I nod at Cody, who's sitting in the chair on my right. He has a giant set of headphones on and he's playing a game on his iPad, but that doesn't mean he can't hear us. Or that he's not listening.

"Cody." Emery leans forward to lift one of the headphones from his ears. "Go get us some snacks from the machine over there. Okay? Anything you want." She hands him her debit card.

He frowns at each of us. Then he sets his iPad on the seat of his chair and heads for the vending machine in an alcove on the other side of the empty lobby.

"Get me some Doritos!" Emery calls after him as she sinks into the chair on my left. "Okay, what do you know?"

"Gabe's been taking Grammie's hydrocodone since before I moved in. Just the pills. He swore it was only occasionally, but . . ." I shrug.

She blinks at me. "And you didn't say anything?"

"What was I supposed to say? Hey, Dad, your son's stealing pills, and also I'm a giant tattletale? That would have helped me feel extra welcome, in a house where I already didn't belong." And Emery would have told everyone at school that I could not be trusted.

"Okay, you couldn't tell him. But you could have told *me*."

"Oh, really?" My eyes narrow as I glare at her. "When you were yelling at me for stealing your whole life? For stealing your room, and your boyfriend, and your role? For breathing the air in your general vicinity?"

"I didn't—"

"Yeah, you did." Cody tosses a bag of Doritos into her lap. They're Cool Ranch, when we all know she's a nacho girl, and that's probably on purpose. "And I'm twelve, not stupid," he adds. "I know what you're talking about. And I knew Gabe was getting high."

"You . . . ?" Emery gapes at him as he picks up his iPad and sinks into his chair again. "How am I the only one who didn't know?"

"You aren't." He wakes up the tablet but leaves his headphones hanging over the arm of the chair. "People who only look at themselves can't see anyone else's problems."

*Whoa.* Twelve going on wise old man.

"Ouch," Emery says. But she doesn't debate the merit. "Still, though, is it any better to see what's going on, if you're not going to do anything about it?"

"I didn't know it was this bad," I tell her. "I'm not sure it *was*, before Violet dumped him. Before he got ahold of the liquid morphine. Did you hear what the nurse told your mom about that?"

"No. You?"

I shake my head.

"I heard," Cody says. "I was playing chess with Grammie when the nurse brought it. She said it's not like the pills. It's a lot stronger, and they only prescribe it to people who're already used to high doses of painkillers."

"Shit," Emery breathes. "*Shit.*" She starts picking at a hangnail on her thumb.

"But I didn't know he was taking the pills." Cody looks scared again. "I thought he was, like, vaping. If I'd known he was taking Grammie's meds, I would have—"

"I know," I tell him. "I would have, too, if I'd known it was this bad. But he swore he was fine." And I felt like any more of a reaction from me would be an overreaction. More of me inserting myself where I didn't belong.

But the view from a hospital waiting room chair looks very different. It changes my perspective.

If Gabe doesn't recover, I'll never, ever forgive myself.

# twenty-nine

He's awake." Dad's smiling from ear to ear, but he looks exhausted. I swear, he's ten years older than he was when he got in his car to follow the ambulance.

I glance at my phone. It's just after midnight. It's Saturday morning now, and I'm down to 30 percent power on my phone.

"Gabe's okay?" Cody's suddenly wide awake, though he's been dozing on my shoulder for nearly an hour.

"Well, he's *awake*," my dad hedges. "They still have to run some tests, and they want him to see a counselor, so they're going to admit him at least for tonight."

"Then he can come home?"

"Maybe." Dad sinks into the chair on Cody's other side. "But there's also a possibility that he'll spend some time in an inpatient program."

"What's that?"

"Rehab," Emery tells Cody. "It's like summer camp for addicts."

"Not exactly." Dad gives her a look. "But we're still working all that out. It's possible he can do outpatient meetings and counseling. But he needs to see someone. Regularly. And we're all going to have to watch him."

Cody fidgets with the corner of his iPad case, opening it over and over, and letting the magnet pull it closed again. "What do you mean? Like, spy on him?"

"No. Bud, Gabe has a problem—"

"Capital P," Emery interjects.

"—and we're all going to have to be there for him. Even if that means watching for the signs we missed this time. And it's not your fault, if you didn't see it," Dad hurries to add. "Your mom and I didn't see it either, and seeing these things is part of our job. But from now on, if you think that Gabe is acting weird—sad, or extra sleepy—you need to tell one of us."

He's talking to all three of us now.

"No buts. Not wanting to tattle is one thing, but your brother nearly died tonight. He didn't do it on purpose. He didn't understand that oral morphine is an entirely different beast than the pills the doctor gave him when he broke his leg. But that doesn't mean we won't need to watch him."

Dad's phone buzzes, and he pulls it from his pocket to glance at the text. "They've put him in a room. You can come see him for a few minutes, if you want, before Michaela takes you all home."

Fortunately, I drove separately.

We follow Dad out of the waiting area to a bank of elevators. Gabe's on the third floor, and when the elevator door slides open, we step out into a sterile white hallway that feels very quiet. Very still. I can hear soft voices and computer keys clacking from the nurse's station on my right, but other than that, it feels like the whole hospital is sleeping.

"This way." Dad turns left, following a small sign on the wall that lists room numbers, pointing visitors in either direction. Gabe's door is ajar. Dad pushes it open to let us all in, and we stand around the bed in awkward silence.

"Hey," Gabe finally says. There's a tube in his arm, and he looks pale. His eyes are ringed in dark circles.

"Hey." I lean over the bed to hug him, and I'm relieved that he still feels solid, despite his bruised appearance. I think he's actually okay. Physically, anyway.

"Thank you. Both of you." Gabe glances from Emery to me, then back.

"I just found you," she insists, her arms crossed over her T-shirt. She doesn't look mad now, though. She looks tired and uncomfortable. Like she's not sure how she should be acting. "Michaela is the one who found the morphine."

"I'm sorry," Gabe says, and I'm not sure whether or not he's talking to me. "I swear, this wasn't my goal." He lifts his left arm, and the IV line taped to his hand comes with it. "I wasn't trying to . . ."

"We know," Cynthia tells him. There are fresh tears in her eyes. She's been through enough. I wish she would come home with the rest of us, but I already know she won't. "We know it was an accident."

"Not sure I believe that," I tease Gabe. "Only you would try to upstage the deceased at her own funeral."

Gabe snorts, and the tension in the room shatters. "I couldn't upstage Grammie if I tried."

"Well, then, stop trying," Cynthia says.

"Sorry. But hey!" Gabe's eyebrows rise halfway up his forehead. "That was my second ambulance ride. I'm pretty sure the next one's free."

Emery laughs, and even Cynthia smiles.

My dad pulls me aside while Gabe promises not to ever scare us like that again, and he wraps me into a hug that swallows me whole. "Thank you," he whispers into my hair. "If you hadn't found that bottle . . ."

I hug him back, and my eyes burn as they water. I don't feel like I deserve his thanks. "I'm sorry," I say, my face buried in his shoulder. "I'm so sorry."

"For what?"

I lead him into the hall. "I knew he was taking pills. I should have said something."

"Yeah, that would have helped," he admits. Then he pulls me into another hug. "But that doesn't make this your fault. Gabe made his own decisions, and if you hadn't found that bottle of morphine . . . If we didn't know what he'd taken, or how to treat it the moment the EMTs got there, this could have gone very, very differently. We could be planning another funeral right now. And I'm not sure any of us could have handled that." Dad lets me go and looks down at me, meeting my teary gaze with one of his own. "You saved his life, Michaela. And you might have saved Cynthia's too. Thank you."

I hug him again, because I don't know what to say. I still feel guilty.

But when we go back into Gabe's room, Cynthia shifts to stand next to me, and she wraps one arm around my waist. She clutches me against her, clinging to me, her hand tight around my hip, and this is the strangest feeling of acceptance. Of gratitude. This hug feels loaded with everything she can't say right now. Everything she may never be able to say.

I sniffle, and I hug her back.

—❧—

"Do I have to brush my teeth?" Cody asks as we plod through the front door. "It's nearly one in the morning."

"Not tonight," Emery says as she locks the door behind us. "Michaela and I are just going to crash. You should do the same thing."

I have my doubts, though, as I drape my jeans over the end of my bed and crawl beneath the covers. I'm not sure sleep is even going to be possible, after the day we've had. But it turns out that I'm exhausted. We all are. It's all just been . . . a lot.

I sleep until ten thirty in the morning, and when I finally wake up, Emery is still snoring, drooling on her pillow.

—❧—

"Okay, cast and crew, welcome to your first dress rehearsal!" Ms. Bond calls out from down right. Today, her shirt reads, "I'm not talking to myself. It's called a MONOLOGUE!" and I think that one may be my favorite.

We face her from our warm-up semicircle, spanning the entire stage. "It's been a long road—a lot of set-building, prop-painting, costume-sewing, line-learning hard work, but I hope it's been fun!"

We cheer, in part because we're supposed to, but in part because it *has* been fun. If we didn't love theater, we wouldn't still be here.

"And because we're all sleep-deprived and disoriented, here's a reminder: today is Monday. Opening night is Thursday. Between now and then, we will run *four* full dress rehearsals as if they are real performances. No noise backstage. No stopping to adjust transitions or quick changes. No walking through the rough parts. Full. Dress. Rehearsal." She punctuates all three words by tapping one fist into the open palm of her opposite hand. "I'm going to dismiss you in a second, and you're going to spend the next twenty minutes making sure your costumes are all lined up, that your change sheet is accurate and taped up in your section of the dressing room. Then you're going to quickly get into costumes and makeup. Lizzy"—the junior who's our head of hair and makeup—"is waiting in the makeup lab to help those of you who have more elaborate needs."

Mostly, that's Link as the Wolf, and Kat as the Witch.

"Crew, you're going to make—well, first, you're going to sweep the stage." She gestures to Mr. Lacey, the school's tech director, who's in charge of the entire theater space. He holds up two large push brooms. "Then you're going to make sure that all of the props are in their designated, taped-off locations backstage. Clear the backstage area of all food and drink, except for Red Riding Hood's pastries, of course." Which are plastic. "And the flymen?" Ms. Bond turns to look up at the fly rail, a narrow backstage loft where a complicated series of counterweighted ropes keep the curtains and muslin drops, painted as background scenery, suspended above the stage until they're needed. "Who's on the fly rail?"

"Kellen!" a deep voice calls out, and I look up to see Kellen Pierce waving from overhead, stage left.

"Hey, Kellen, how are we coming with the stage-right second wing? It's still not quite in the right position."

"We're on it!" Mr. Lacey calls out. "We'll have it in place by the time they take the stage today."

"Great, thanks. Cole, I need you to run a quick sound check; then you and Zack get everyone miked. And, girls, you'll have to be miked backstage, because Cole is not allowed in the girls' dressing room. Any questions? Comments? Concerns?" Ms. Bond looks around the circle at us. No hands rise. "Great! Go! Be back here in twenty minutes, ready to perform as if this were opening night!"

The dressing room is a flurry of hurried movements and excited chatter as we change into our costumes for the opening number. For the stepsisters, that's a matching set of lacy, old-fashioned petticoats and thick tights that cover more than my regular school clothes do. They're intentionally overdone, and with the elaborate wigs and makeup, Mara and Emery look perfect as Florinda and Lucinda, only half-ready for the festival.

Their favorite schtick is to pretend they're each other's mirror images, in the middle of the dressing room, and mimic each other's stupid dance moves.

Honestly, it looks like fun, and it makes me miss Georgia, who would totally do slow-motion, mirror-image dance moves with me.

Cinderella's costume for act 1, scene 1 is a dowdy gray dress and an apron smudged with "fireplace ashes." Which are really just streaks made with black eye shadow. Once I have it on, I head into the makeup lab, a room lined with unbroken lengths of mirrors and countertops, with a chair at each station. The girls' side is cluttered with curling irons and eye shadow, the boys' side with stage foundation and wigs.

"Where's Sage?" Mara asks as I'm applying eyeliner and false lashes. "She said she'd do my eye shadow."

"She went to the bathroom," Josh says from across the room, where he's fitting a curly, colonial men's wig over his hair. He's also wearing a ruffled shirt and black leather boots that lace up to his knees, over black pants. He really does look like an old-fashioned prince.

"Here. I'll do it." Emery picks up Mara's makeup palette and her brush bag. "Sit down."

I finish my makeup and head backstage, humming vocal warm-ups under my breath. Nerves buzz beneath my skin. I take a series of deep breaths, trying to calm myself down. It's just dress rehearsal. There's no audience.

"Moving the stage-right wing three curtain!" Kellen shouts, and I look up to see him pulling one of the big, thick ropes in the fly loft, hand over hand.

"Wrong curtain!" Mr. Lacey shouts. "Put that one back and move the one to your left."

Everyone backstage is looking up to make sure we're not about to be flattened by a curtain moved in error—those things weigh a *ton*—while the stage-right ASM speaks into her headset, keeping Ms. Bond apprised.

Kellen moves to his right and starts pulling on another rope.

"Left!" Mr. Lacey shouts as the large back curtain begins to rise. That curtain, along with the rear wall of the stage, forms the crossover, a two-foot-wide walkway used by cast and crew to move, unseen, between stage left and stage right during the production. "The one to your *left!*"

Kellen stops, and beneath the curtain, I notice light reflecting off something shiny in the dark crossover. It's a decorative chrome buckle from one of Sage's shoes. I squat to reach for it, and I realize it's still attached to her shoe. Which she's wearing. Sage Andersen is standing in the deep shadows of the crossover.

Like the rest of the backstage area, that space is supposed to be lit by blue light, which is difficult for the audience to distinguish past the brightly lit stage. But someone has turned off the crossover lights. And when I squint into the shadows, I see that Sage's shoes are in the company of a pair of brown loafers I'd know anywhere.

For one stunning moment, I wallow in disbelief as nausea twists my stomach into knots.

*No.* There's a rational explanation.

But they're not moving. If there were some good reason for Sage and Ben to be alone in the dark crossover, which no one will use until the play begins, then why are they standing there, still as statues, evidently hoping that no one has seen their feet?

I stand quietly and march to the end of the crossover, digging my phone from a pocket hidden in Cinderella's skirt while Kellen finally properly positions the out-of-place wing curtain. I turn on the flashlight app as I round the end of the long curtain, and Sage gasps as the bright light hits her eyes.

To their credit, they're not currently . . . doing anything. But unless they're planning some kind of super-secret surprise party for me, in the world's tightest venue, I can't think of a single innocent reason for them to be alone back there, in the dark.

"Michaela," Sage says. "Hey. We were, um . . ."

I ignore her as Ben heads toward me.

"Can we talk?" His voice is low. Soft. It's a tone I've found soothing before, but now I want to stab him in the gut with Josh's plastic sword. I want to keep stabbing, and stabbing, until he hurts like I'm hurting right now.

"What the hell would I possibly have to say to you?" People are staring now, but they don't understand until Ben steps out from behind the backdrop. Until Sage slinks out from behind the other end, stage left.

Everyone's whispering. Staring. Tate, the stage-right ASM, is speaking to Ms. Bond again over her headset. I hear my name and Ben's. And Sage's. But I can't hear Ms. Bond's reply.

"Michaela . . . ," Ben says.

I shove my phone back into my pocket and spin, intending to run out into the hall. I just need a minute to process without everyone staring at me. I have to get out of here before tears ruin my makeup. But Emery is standing in the storage area doorway, watching. Blocking my escape.

"Go ahead," I snap as I push past her. "Say I told you so."

"I wasn't—" she starts, but I'm not listening. I can't. Not yet. I race through the storage area into the makeup lab, where I drop into my chair and grab a tissue. Sniffling, I press the tissue beneath both of my eyes to catch tears before they fall.

"*Mo-ther-fucker!*" Emery's voice echoes from behind me. "You can't control yourself, can you? You're like a toddler in a roomful of toys, trying to play with them all at once. But we're not toys, and we're not here for your amusement."

I get up and toss my tissue into the trash on my way out of the makeup lab. Kat Torrez is standing in the storage area doorway, and she makes room for me there too, at the back of a silent, loosely gathered crowd. There's a small smile on her face and a quiet tension in her frame. She looks like a cat who can't decide if it's going to pounce on its wounded prey or just watch it struggle.

Emery is backstage, next to Rapunzel's stone tower, and she looks half-mad in her curly blond wig and fancy underwear. But people aren't just looking at her. They're looking at Ben too, and someone has turned the blue lights back on, so we can see him perfectly well.

"Do you have any idea what it's been like, watching you walk around here like God's gift to theater?" Emery demands. "Spitting out pretty poison with every word you speak? Knowing that no one would believe me, if I said it out loud?"

Ben exhales. "Em—"

"Don't . . . fucking . . . *'Em'* me. *You're* the problem here."

Ben starts to walk past her. To escape with the tatters of his dignity. But she steps into his path. "Nuh-uh. You're not going anywhere. You're gonna stand right there and listen."

I suck in a breath. Emery is on *fire*. She's practically glowing. And no one's stopping her. Not Sarah, the stage manager. Not either of the ASMs. I have no idea where Ms. Bond and Mr. Lacey are, but they have to know what's going on. Since the headsets were issued, Sarah's *always* talking in Ms. Bond's ear, coordinating things and keeping her apprised of what costumes don't fit and who keeps dropping a line in act 2. But there are no teachers here right now. I think they've decided to let this play out.

I have no idea where Sage went.

"I'm not—" Ben starts, and Emery cuts him off.

"You are a *horrible* person. You lie. You cheat. You *twist* things, and then you wave your hands around like a magician doing a trick, and you tell us that nothing we saw or heard was real. That we just imagined the whole thing. And we believe you, because you don't *seem* like a bad guy."

"I don't . . . Emery, this is—"

"Save it. Everyone knows who you really are now, and that's not gonna go away. But *you* are. You're going to go onstage and sing your songs, because this is theater, and the show must go on. But after that, you're going to disappear. You're going to graduate and go spin your fairy tale at some Ivy League theater program, where they may or may not buy your act. But all that really matters around here is that you'll be *someone else's problem.*"

Emery spins around and marches toward me. "I only have one thing to say to you, Michaela," she says as Kat moves out of her way. "Fuck. Ben. McGrath." Then she heads through the storage area into the makeup lab, where I hear her chair squeal against the floor.

Aaron opens his mouth, one arm raised in his Narrator pose, ready to comment on Emery's *utter* takedown of the theater It boy—or maybe on the awkward silence we're now mired in—and Kat steps forward to grab his arm before he can speak. "Not one word," she growls. Then she lets him go.

"Okay!" Ms. Bond appears from behind the wing one curtain. She looks somehow both tense and relieved. "Now that we've cleared the air . . . Emery is right. This show *will* go on. Opening positions in five minutes, please. And you *will* all leave the drama offstage . . ."

Finally, the spell is broken. People shuffle off to check props and sets, adjust costumes, or put the finishing touches on their makeup. One of the crew members kneels to unjam one of the wheels on Rapunzel's tower. Somewhere backstage, Link practices his wolf howl.

"Well, that was fun." Kat leans against the frame of the door leading to the storage area, her arms crossed over the front of her costume. "Definitely worth the wait."

"You've—" I frown. "You've been waiting for that?"

"For a year and a half. Ben and I were together for half of our sophomore year. He was my first boyfriend. My first . . . lots of things."

"He cheated on you?"

"With my best friend."

"And you couldn't have *told* me that?" I don't mean to sound angry, but . . . I'm a little angry.

Kat's brows rise. "Would you have believed me?"

Two months ago? Right after my mom died? I honestly don't know. I really, really, really wanted Ben to be real. To be as nice as he is beautiful. As kind as he is talented.

Kat shrugs. "Maybe he learned something. And if not, maybe the next girl will be smarter than we were."

But that's not it. It's not that we weren't smart. It's that we were vulnerable. We needed Ben to be something that he isn't: a good guy.

Kat heads into the makeup lab to adjust her crazy witch hair, and Josh finds me in the wings. "Hey, Mick. You okay?"

"Yeah. Well, no," I admit. "I just caught my boyfriend cheating on me with a fellow cast member, in case you missed that whole drama." Though he definitely did not. "And the worst part is that I'm going to have to admit that Emery was right."

"*That's* the worst part?"

I laugh. "You obviously don't have a sister."

"Nope. Just the one brother."

Evan, who's nine and likes to ride his bike in the cul-de-sac. I remember.

"You sure you're good?" Josh asks as Ms. Bond rushes past us, carrying a wig that's been singed with a curling iron.

"I'll be fine." Thanks to Emery, Ben can't paint me as the guilty party. Everyone knows who he is now.

"I, um . . . I wrote a new song," Josh whispers. "I know you probably aren't in the right headspace for that, at the moment, but when you are . . . I mean, if you *ever* are . . . I think it's pretty good. And I'd love to hear you sing it."

"Another duet?"

"Yeah." He rocks backward onto his heels, and his sword smacks against his boots.

"Okay. Yeah, I'll take a look at it. And I think I *am* going to write one of my own. A solo." I'm suddenly feeling super inspired. Like I have something important to get off my chest. And if I set it to music, it isn't just ranting—it's art.

Link brushes by us, smelling like pot, and Josh grins at me. "I can't wait to hear it."

"Cinderella," Tate Snyder hisses from the stage-right ASM stand, where her book is open to act 1, scene 1. "Onstage!"

I turn to find that everyone else is in place, Ben standing awkwardly next to Lexie, in front of the bakery background. I walk onstage and kneel in front of the painted fireplace with my hand broom and dustpan. Josh smiles at me from the wings.

The music starts.

And the show goes on.

# thirty

They say that something goes wrong on every opening night, and if I had to guess, I would have blamed Ben for whatever would inevitably go wrong. Since he got caught with Sage, all of the drama has been about him. But when I walk into the makeup lab two hours before showtime, his isn't the name being whispered from every makeup station.

"What's going on?" I ask Lexie as I settle into the chair to her right.

"Link got suspended," Bella whispers from the station on my right. "He got caught vaping at school, and now he's totally ineligible."

"Shit. So, Scott's going on?"

"Normally, that would be the plan. That's what the swings are for." Lexie applies more blush than she would normally wear, since it has to be seen from the audience. "But Scott's at home with the flu. He's out for the whole show."

"Well, that explains why Sarah's in the hall, having a total breakdown." Our stage manager is out there sucking down an iced latte like it's antivenom that can save her from show business itself. "So, Haley, then?" Our female swing won't be obviously female, in the Wolf's costume.

"Not exactly . . ." Bella turns to look pointedly at something behind me, and I follow her gaze in the mirror.

On the other side of the makeup lab, Ms. Bond is huddled with Cole Houser. She's holding the Wolf's furry headpiece. He's holding mic tape and a handful of wires, and he looks terrified. But he knows the part. We all know he does. And the Wolf is only in two scenes.

"This isn't a rehearsal," Cole says. At least, that's what it looks and sounds like, from across the room. "I can't—"

Emery sets down her eyeliner and marches across the makeup lab. She does that a lot now. She marches. Walking with purpose. And people look at her differently since Monday's outburst. "Cole." She puts one hand on his shoulder. I can't hear what she says next, but I can see the effect she has on him. And I happen to know they've been texting a lot over the past couple of days. Late at night, after she's supposed to be asleep.

I watch in the mirror as I start my makeup. They talk for a couple of minutes. Then Cole takes a deep breath and hands his tape and wires to Zack, the freshman A-2. Ms. Bond gives Cole the Wolf headpiece, and he fits it over his head. And the entire room cheers.

Evidently we were all watching. Waiting.

"You're going to be great," Emery tells him, and we all echo her.

An hour later, I'm made up and in costume. I pass Ben backstage, and for a second, a familiar panicky feeling flutters in my stomach. I fight a ridiculous urge to hide behind a curtain, just to avoid him.

But then he looks away, and I remember that *he's* the one with a reason to hide.

The hardest part of the breakup was that I couldn't go home and tell my mom about it. Cynthia probably would have offered some advice, if I'd asked for it. My dad would have too. Fortunately, though she never even met him, my mother had already prepared me for dealing with a guy like Ben.

When I was in the ninth grade, this girl at school was really, really mean to me, and my mom told me not to let her live rent free in my head. What she meant by that was that I shouldn't waste so much of my time and attention on someone undeserving of them.

And there is no one in my life less deserving of my time and attention than Ben McGrath.

He and I haven't spoken anything but lines from the script since Monday, and I'm not sure we ever will. Before I blocked his number, he called me twice, trying to "explain." But I don't want to hear that he made a mistake and deserves a second chance. Or that having a side chick somehow makes him feel like the "real" man his dad wants him to be. The truth is that it doesn't matter why he cheated.

It matters that he *did*.

But Sage actually apologized.

I forgave her, but I'm not ready to forget. We girls shouldn't do that to each other. We should be supportive, even when we aren't actually friends. And we should believe each other. Which is why I apologized to Emery.

I should have believed her.

I should have at least listened.

The cast warms up in Ms. Bond's classroom, far enough away from the theater that the audience milling in the lobby can't hear us. My nerves are a living thing crawling around inside me, trying to chew its way out. My heart is beating too fast. Every now and then I remember that several hundred sets of eyes are about to be on me—we're sold out!—and I lose my shit, just a little bit.

But every time that happens, there's someone there to put a hand on my shoulder or shoot a smile at me from across the room. To tell me I'm going to be great. To remind me about the cast party on Saturday, after the final performance.

"Michaela," Ms. Bond calls after the warm-ups. Cole is in one corner, softly practicing the Wolf's solo, "Hello, Little Girl," while Anna, our Little Red Riding Hood, play-prances around him for ambiance.

"Yeah?" I turn to find Ms. Bond holding up one of the programs. "Fresh off the presses," she says as she hands it to me. "Page twelve."

I flip through to page twelve, and there's my headshot, fifth one down. Next to that is the paragraph of text I submitted.

I would like to dedicate my performance to my mother, Jessica Dawn Rutherford, who died unexpectedly in

January. *Into the Woods* was her favorite musical, and though I can only wish she were with the rest of my family in the audience, I will be singing tonight for her. Love you, Mom. Miss you more than anything.

"Thank you." I tuck the program into my backpack with my change of clothes, fighting back tears. "And thank you for giving me this opportunity," I say, brushing my hands over Cinderella's dress.

"Oh, honey, you earned that. Now, go find your place. We're on in fifteen minutes."

I give Cole a supportive smile, then head across the hall, through the makeup lab and the storage area, into the wings.

I can hear the audience, but I can't see them. I have no idea where my family is sitting, but I know Georgia is with them. She's been texting me all night. She says she's next to Cody, playing phone app games while they wait for the curtain to rise.

She says that Gabe is standing down front, staring into the pit, talking to his friends. Threatening to climb over the rail and sit with them, instead of in the house. He's doing well since he got out of the hospital. His parents decided he could do outpatient counseling, and he's already back at school, though he won't be playing in the pit, because Dad thought that would be too much stress, too soon. The orchestra assistant conductor is going to fill in for him on the upright bass.

I wonder if Ben's parents are out there in the audience. I wonder if his dad's watching. I wonder if that would make this easier for him, or harder.

I wonder why I even care.

Ms. Bond rushes through the wings, waving us all onstage. My heart leaps into my throat as I kneel again, with my broom and dustpan. I've done this a million times, yet somehow it feels different now.

Aaron waits in wing one, ready to go on. To start the show. The curtain rises. The lights go on, and I feel seen as I have never been seen before. Utterly, terrifyingly exposed.

Then the music starts . . .

—— ∞ ——

I sing tonight for my mom. The music and lyrics aren't new, but my emotion is. My passion is. I hear her harmony, instead of Ben's. I see her face at random in the crowd. I *feel* her, as if she were onstage with me, and I'm worried this might be the last time I ever feel her.

My tears spill over at the end of "No One Is Alone," and I break character a little so that I don't have to look at Ben. So that he can't have this moment in my memory.

This was never truly about singing with him, and I wish I'd never forgotten that. It's always been my mother's song.

—— ∞ ——

"Oh my God, you were great!" I can't tell who's saying it. Whose hand brushes my shoulder on the way past. But I return the sentiment for the dozenth time since the final curtain closed. We're all saying it. And it's true, every time.

We really were great. We're all high on how great we were.

Backstage, the endorphins flow like river rapids, and we ride a euphoric current. I'll probably hear the applause in my sleep.

Em and Mara made everyone laugh, as did Josh and Wyatt as the princes. Lexie was sympathetic and tragic as the doomed Baker's Wife. And Ben somehow excels under pressure. He gave the best performance of his life, I think, just to spite us all.

But Cole stole the show. Again. His Wolf was a pitch-perfect blend of hungry and lustful. Slightly inappropriate and entirely entertaining. And his howl put Link's to shame.

He got his own curtain call. As did Kat.

They're both backstage right now, soaking up well-deserved praise.

"Michaela!" Emery grabs my shoulders. Her eyes are wide, and they're full of happy tears. "I think we killed it!"

"We definitely did. It is dead. Whatever *it* is."

"And it'll be even better tomorrow night!"

"Yes, it will." I hand her Cinderella's gray dress. "Because you're going on as Cinderella."

"What? No, I —"

"I'm done." I drape the gray shawl I wore for most of the second act over her arm. "I got what I wanted." A tribute to my mom. A moment in the light. I sang, and I loved it. Once. But . . . "Theater isn't my thing. I'm a nervous wreck, and I'm not that great an actor," I tell her. "I like to sing, but I think I prefer a different kind of stage."

I catch Josh's eye from across the room, and he smiles. We've been working on my song together, late at night. My solo. And I think it's really, really good. The band's going to record it. We're going to upload it to Spotify, where it'll probably die of neglect. But at least it'll be out there. And we can perform it live, with the rest of our set.

"I've already told Ms. Bond, and Haley's ready to go on as Lucinda. If you come in an hour early tomorrow, Lexie, Ms. Bond, and I will walk through some of the tricky parts with you, before anyone gets here."

"Oh my God. You're serious?"

"Yeah. You're Cinderella. And I'll be here watching." Though I haven't decided whether I want to sit in the audience or abuse my privilege and hang out backstage and help the crew.

"Thank you." Emery's tears fall, and she pulls me into a hug so tight I can't breathe. Then she clutches the costume and runs off through the storage area, calling for Mara.

"That was the nicest thing I've ever seen," Josh says.

"Oh, pshaw." I wave off his compliment. "It was selfish. Now I'll have more time to write originals and sing with the band."

"Yeah. Because those last three performances would really have stood in your way."

"I got what I wanted," I tell him. We're standing just a little too close, but neither of us moves back. We can still feel the magic of the stage. The heat of the lights. The glow from the applause. It's made me a little bold. "Most of what I want, anyway." I smile up at him. "And there's time for the rest. But it's Emery's turn to shine."

---

Josh and I hang out after the show, talking about our performance. And our new song. Dad extended our curfew, because
he has no idea how long it actually takes to close down after a
show, and Emery's not going to tell him the truth. She, Cole,
and Mara went out for ice cream.

By the time I get home, all the lights are off, and the living
room is empty. Everyone's in bed. I drop my keys in the bowl
and head through the living room, but something catches my
eye on an end table. Moonlight shining off—

A picture of my mother. One of the ones that should be on
top of my chest of drawers.

I pick it up.

A light comes on in the kitchen, and I turn to see Cynthia
holding a mug with a tea tag dangling from one side. "I put it
there," she says.

"Why?" I blink tears away as I set the picture down again.

"Because Jessica was your mother, and mothers deserve to
be truly remembered. Not hidden away in a back room." She
shrugs and sips from her mug. "And any member of your family
is a member of mine."

I sob as I cross the living room. Cynthia puts her tea down
just in time to catch me as I throw my arms around her. I cry on
her shoulder, and it takes me a minute to realize that she's crying too.

After a minute, we stand up straight and wipe away our
tears. She reclaims her tea, and I straighten my shirt. "Okay,
then. Good night," I say.

"'Night, Michaela," she answers. And as she heads down the

short hall toward the main suite, she turns one more time. "I hope you know how happy we are that you wound up with us."

I nod. Finally, I really, truly believe that.

In our room, Emery is already out cold. Her phone is on its dock, and it'll probably wake me up absurdly early, even as she sleeps through it. She's smiling in her sleep, and I wonder if she's dreaming about Cole. I hope so.

She is definitely, certainly *not* dreaming about Ben McGrath.

I heard somewhere that girls either harbor a secret love for their first sexual partner or hate them forever. I'm not sure which way this one's going to go for me. I mean, I definitely don't love Ben, but I'm not sure I hate him either. It's not that simple; there are more possibilities than just love and hate.

Ben's not a movie villain any more than I'm a real princess. He's just a boy who turned out to be an asshole. He's probably more than that, in his own head. He's probably the star of his own show. God knows I'm the star of mine. And he may even outgrow being an asshole. Maybe he'll learn from his mistakes while he's still young, unlike my father.

I've been thinking about it—a lot—and I don't think Cynthia was wrong to keep my dad around, even though he was, without a doubt, a huge asshole, once upon a time.

But Em and I aren't wrong to steer clear of Ben either. His life isn't as easy as most people think, but that doesn't excuse what he did. And it doesn't mean we should try to fix him.

Most days, it's hard enough to keep myself together. Especially on days when I really, really miss my mom.

But if she were here, she'd probably laugh at me when I start feeling sorry for myself, and then she'd throw a bunch of clichés at me with a grin. She'd say, "Chin up, Michaela! Life's not fair, but time heals all wounds."

I see her face as I turn off the light and close my eyes. "'Night, Mom," I tell her. "All's well that ends well."

# acknowledgments

This was a book entirely conceived of, written, edited, and produced during the days of covid-19. I got the idea two months after I (mostly) recovered from covid myself and I was working on the proposal as my father-in-law died in our home of covid and cancer. Much of this book was influenced by my experience with his end of life and with the care he got from the home hospice staff. So I must first of all thank them and all the healthcare workers who put their lives on the line day after day to care for those in need.

Several months later, as I was writing the last half of the book, I had the opportunity to interview and shadow the drama/theater/makeup arts teacher at my kids' high school alma mater. An *enormous* thank you must go to the real Emily Bond and her students, for letting me observe the high school musical theater process. For letting me poke around backstage for weeks, for answering all my questions, and for generally making me feel welcome in a world I haven't stepped foot in since I was seventeen and on stage in my own high school theater.

Thank you, also, to my fantastic literary agent, Ginger Clark, and to the entire Bloomsbury team, for making this book happen during one of the most challenging periods in the publishing industry. Specifically, thanks must go to Oona Patrick, Jeff Curry, Jill Amack, Laura Phillips, Rebecca McGlynn, and Nicholas Church in Production/Managing Editorial. To John Candell and Donna Mark in Design. To editors Allison Moore, Camille Kellogg, and Sarah Shumway. And to Faye Bi, Erica Barmash, Valentina Rice, and Alona Fryman in Marketing and Publicity. Michaela's story would still just be words on my screen without you all.